ZIGZAG

ALSO BY NOEL HYND

Novels

REVENGE

THE SANDLER INQUIRY

FALSE FLAGS

FLOWERS FROM BERLIN

THE KHRUSHCHEV OBJECTIVE

(with Christopher Creighton)

TRUMAN'S SPY

Nonfiction

THE COP AND THE KID

(with William Fox)

THE GIANTS OF THE POLO GROUNDS

Screenplay

AGENCY

Noel Hynd

ZIG ZAG

ZEBRA BOOKS
KENSINGTON PUBLISHING CORP.

ZEBRA BOOKS

are published by

Kensington Publishing Corp.
475 Park Avenue South
New York, NY 10016

Library of Congress Catalog Card Number: 92-070443

ISBN 0-8217-3485-7

First printing: June, 1992

Printed in the United States of America

for
Shelley and Bill Swift
my hosts of the highways
with appreciation

"There ain't a dime's worth of difference between the two major parties in this country."

—George C. Wallace

Governor of Alabama and third-party Presidential candidate, 1968

PROLOGUE

AT a few minutes past three A.M. on an icy Thursday morning in February, an off-duty Baltimore County police detective named Al Lakaitis turned off Taylor Road onto a deserted Route 1 just south of the city limits.

Less than a second later, through the light mist of sleet that was falling out of a dark winter sky, Detective Lakaitis saw the high beams of an oncoming car in the wrong lane rise over the crest of a hill. Then, with horror, the tired police officer realized that the vehicle was speeding head-on toward him in excess of eighty miles per hour.

Lakaitis later remembered swearing aloud and saving his own life by turning his steering wheel with a violent jerk. With a resounding crack, the other car caught a piece of his as it passed. But Lakaitis managed to swerve wildly, banking his own car onto a sidewalk and into a mass of commercial garbage. His heart pounded, his temper blazed, and he turned to watch what had nearly been the instrument of his death.

For years afterward, Lakaitis would recall the next few seconds as if they had happened in slow motion. He sat transfixed in his seat, his heart racing, and watched as the car careened, veered, spectacularly took out a standing traffic light, and then crossed lanes again. The car left the road, ran up and down a slope, went sidelong into a parked truck, turned over onto its right side and skidded sixty-some feet down the roadway to a halt, leaving a trail of sparks and gasoline behind it. Surprisingly, there was no fire and no explosion. The sleet had prevented it.

Lakaitis, a forty-four-year-old bachelor who had been on his way home after an eight-to-midnight shift that ran late, was suddenly faced with a change of plans. He backed his own car onto the road, illuminated a flashing red emergency light on his dashboard, and turned in the direction of the accident. As he drove, he radioed the 911 dispatcher, who recognized his voice.

"We have a ten-thirty-five at Route One near Garland Boulevard!" he said. "I need any available sector car, an ambulance, and a fire truck!"

Lakaitis reached the overturned vehicle within ninety seconds of the moment of final impact. He parked his own car across the nearest traffic lane, remaining more than fifty feet from the overturned vehicle. In the piercing, damp cold, he moved his crimson emergency light to the roof of his car and left his four-way flashers on. He had the presence of mind to take with him a heavy flashlight as he moved quickly but cautiously to the wrecked car.

When he reached it, its engine was still roaring. The car, which was a black Ford Tempo, was propped up flush on its right side, braced against a mangled blue mailbox. The rear wheels of the car were free of the ground. They were racing furiously.

As Lakaitis shined his flashlight into the car, he saw the slumped body of a man—motionless, bloodied, and battered, particularly around the head. The body was leaning downward, partially tangled in a seat belt, but not restrained by it. At the same time, Lakaitis was aware of the sound of air brakes somewhere nearby. He realized that a truck coming the other way up Route 1 had seen the aftermath of the accident and had stopped.

But Lakaitis did not immediately look up. Instead, hoisting himself against the side of the car, he managed to lean in. He carefully avoided the driver's blood and the shards of glass that seemed to be everywhere. Lakaitis turned off the ignition, arresting the car's engine. Then he put a hand on the man in the front seat.

He felt for a pulse at the man's left wrist. He couldn't find one, but his own fingers were numb. He was conscious of the heavy smell of alcohol within the car, as if a whiskey bottle had been shattered.

"Damn," he muttered to himself. Then he was aware of a truck driver breathlessly joining him.

"What happened? Need help?"

"Give me a hand," Lakaitis barked. He didn't have to explain what needed to be done. The truck driver was a former marine who knew how to move an injured body. Fearing that an explosion might still not be out of the question, the two men extricated the body from the car. Another police unit arrived with blankets. A fire engine was there within five minutes, an ambulance within six. An attempt was made to revive the badly injured driver, who appeared to be a white male in his late fifties or early sixties. The attempt failed. The paramedics pronounced the man dead at the scene. The police concurred. There was little other traffic on so vile an evening, but what there was began to back up.

Lakaitis, who otherwise would have been home by this time gaining some much needed sleep, spent the next few hours at the hospital and back at his station house, filling out forms, identifying the body from the licenses and credit cards in the dead man's wallet, and attempting to notify relatives. When no relatives were immediately located—the man apparently had lived alone—the job passed to a younger member of the force: Police Officer Christine Nevell. Officer Nevell, twenty-four, and a graduate of the University of Maryland, was in her second year on the job. She was also scheduled for the following day shift.

Lakaitis, meanwhile, involuntarily racked up seven hours of overtime, while missing an entire night of sleep. Thus his commander, Capt. Robert Mooney, the chief of detectives for Baltimore, excused him from work the next day. Lakaitis went home around eleven o'clock in the morning, immediately following the accident. This time he arrived uneventfully. Unaccustomed to the day off, he slept for a dozen hours, rose for four, and then took three sleeping pills and a beer to put him back to sleep and back on schedule. The home remedy worked.

The next day was a Friday. The detective was scheduled to work from four P.M. to midnight again. But he dressed early for his shift. There were a few things on his mind.

Lakaitis was no genius. He was a conservative, somewhat unimaginative man, loyal to his department, serious about carefully following orders, and blessed with a very firm sense of responsibility. He was something of a plodder in his chosen vocation, but he was also innately curious. And during his four sleepless hours the previous night, he kept replaying the accident scene in his mind.

From start to finish. Several things disturbed him. He wasn't at all sure that he'd seen everything properly. Lakaitis had worked in homicide for the past four years, long enough to develop a sense of smell, and, well . . .

He made his first stop at the police garage the next morning at eleven o'clock. There he located the dead man's Tempo. It was untouched from the time it had been towed in.

At first, Lakaitis had been wondering why the car's engine had continued to race after the accident. The man's foot had no longer been on the accelerator.

He found his answer. There were several small stones on the floor of the car. One of them had been firmly imbedded between the sideboard by the driver's foot and the accelerator.

Accidentally? he wondered.

The stones explained why the car had been speeding out of control, and why its wheels wouldn't stop, though nothing explained where they had come from.

But why hadn't the driver sought to stop the car by hitting the brake? Or pulling out the key? Or throwing it into reverse?

Had the driver been filthy drunk, as the whiskey smell suggested? There was indeed a broken bottle of Jack Daniel's in the front of the car. Had the driver had a stroke? Or a heart attack? Or a drug overdose? Was that why the driver had been unable to control or brake the vehicle?

Then Lakaitis reconfirmed something that chilled him. It was a detail that he'd noticed subliminally at the scene of the accident and wanted to look at again. It was something that had since bothered him in his waking hours.

There was a great deal of blood on the rear of the driver's seat. It had obviously come from the driver's head wounds. And it had flowed straight down the back of the seat.

Lakaitis closed the car door and slowly walked away. What he had seen he knew to be an impossibility.

One hour later he sat before Captain Mooney.

Mooney was—on the surface, at least—a quiet, even-tempered, white-haired man. He was an old-fashioned former chain smoker who had already had one heart attack and didn't much care for the prospects of a second. He was three months short of voluntary retirement after twenty-five years on the force and hoped to live to see it.

"Did anyone find relatives for the man who died in that car wreck?" Lakaitis asked.

"Officer Nevell is still making phone calls," Mooney answered. "Ask her."

"The whole thing is queer, Cap," Lakaitis said. "The little details tell me that."

"Why's that?"

"Blood fresh out of a body runs like water. But then it coagulates in about three minutes. It hits a surface like a car seat and it doesn't run anymore. You know that."

"Yeah? So?"

There had been plenty of blood to run like water on the driver's seat of the Tempo, Lakaitis explained. But it had flowed only one way—downward.

"The car turned over at the time that the driver should have sustained his fatal head injuries," Lakaitis explained. "Some of the blood, you know, most of the blood, should have run *crosswise* on that seat when the body was thrown to the right. But none of it did. The dead guy had his fatal head injuries while he was sitting upright in his seat. That was *before* the car crashed and turned over, Cap."

The chief of detectives scratched his right ear, grimaced slightly, and thought about it. "All right," he said softly. "I hear you."

Mooney looked back to Lakaitis. "What are you telling me, Al? You want it as an open case? Is that it?"

Lakaitis hunched his shoulders and smiled. "It kind of came my way once already." That was one of the wittiest things Lakaitis had ever said.

"Don't you have a pretty heavy caseload right now?"

"Come on, Cap. Let me work on it. What's one more?"

Mooney grimaced again. "Okay. Might as well. You got it."

Lakaitis smiled. "Thanks." He rose to leave. "Is anyone doing a P.M.?"

"No. Want me to order one?"

"Definitely."

Mooney glanced at something on his desk. "This one will go to . . . Dr. Michael Bauerman," he answered. "Know him?"

"That twerp? Does it have to?"

"I know you guys don't like him. But Mike's not a bad fellow. It's his draw."

"He's a smartass."

"In the end, he always cooperates."

Had Al Lakaitis not made his presentation to Captain Mooney, the death on Route 1 might never have drawn any further scrutiny. Instead, an autopsy was done late that Friday afternoon.

Mike Bauerman was something of an anomaly in the medical examiner's office: he was young and aggressively bright. He'd interned at nearby Johns Hopkins and had been headed for a profitable but predictable ear, nose, and throat practice in the suburbs. Then he'd become fascinated with forensic medicine. Thus he'd landed—for the time being, anyway—as an assistant medical examiner among police, courts, defense lawyers, accident victims, claims adjusters, murderers, and prosecutors on Baltimore's seamy underside. If he had a fault, it was a mild arrogance. He also had a propensity to impose his conclusions on others, and nose his way into what was actually police work.

Dr. Bauerman wasn't surprised when Al Lakaitis turned up unannounced at the medical examiner's office shortly before five o'clock that same afternoon. The doctor had expected someone sooner. He had just finished the autopsy on the man in the Tempo and had already turned up enough inconsistent material to entertain even the most jaded student of near-perfect crimes.

"It's a homicide," Bauerman said when Lakaitis found him scrubbing his hands in the men's room.

"Why?"

"Got an hour?"

"I got half an hour, Mike. Talk to me."

"The deceased's heart was perfectly healthy," Bauerman explained. "And there was no alcohol in his blood. So no cardiac arrest, no driving while intoxicated."

Bauerman toweled off his hands while Lakaitis waited. "The individual died from a pair of deep gashes to the skull, resulting in massive cerebral hemorrhaging," said the AME. "Beyond that, there were only three minor contusions to the body. How does a driver get thrown around violently enough to suffer head injuries like that, yet only pick up a couple more mild bruises?"

Lakaitis suggested that the doctor come over to the police garage and look at the car. "I want to know if there's anything in the car that could have made head wounds like that."

"I have other work and I don't need to go see a wrecked car," Dr. Bauerman said, tossing away a wad of paper towels and then leaning against the towel dispenser. He looked up at Lakaitis, who stood about four inches taller than he. "I won't find anything in the car that made those wounds and you won't, either," Bauerman said. "Don't waste your time looking. I already know it's a murder."

"Why's that?"

"I read your account. The car careened, spun, tumbled, and crashed?"

"Yeah. It did."

"No seat belt. Your report said, 'Entangled by the belt but not restrained by it.' Right?" Bauerman's faculties of recall were immense. He could quote at random from almost anything he'd read.

"Right," said Lakaitis after a moment.

"So the individual's got to be bouncing all over the car, no?" Bauerman asked.

"Yeah."

"From all that bouncing," Bauerman continued, "two fatal head wounds, but only three minor bruises, right?"

Lakaitis nodded.

"No way," the doctor said. "He'd have contusions and lacerations all over. But moreover, dead bodies don't bruise, Lakaitis. This individual was deceased before the car came down Route One."

Lakaitis stood blankly before the doctor for several seconds, having heard his own suspicions confirmed. "Thanks," he finally said. "Good work."

"Look for someone with a tire iron," concluded Dr. Bauerman.

Over the years in his duties as a policeman, Lakaitis had effected numerous forcible arrests. He'd been punched, slashed, kicked, and stabbed. He'd been shot at. Twice, drunk drivers had attempted to run him down. This was a first, however. Never before had someone already dead nearly killed him.

He opened a file on the case. Officer Nevell provided him with the deceased individual's wallet and identification. There were no other items recovered from the car. Nor had Officer Nevell been successful in locating any next of kin. So through the weekend, Al Lakaitis had a fresh mystery on his hands. He had already informally named it. The Route One Case.

A man had died in a car, but the crash hadn't killed him. Who or what did?

Well, Lakaitis told himself, he'd asked for this one. Mentally, he dug in. Nothing, however, could have prepared him for what happened when he came in on Sunday morning to work some overtime.

The new file and its contents were gone from his desk. He asked around.

"Captain Mooney has it," one of the sergeants told him. "The Moon and some jerkoff in a suit."

Jerkoffs in suits, especially when described as such, were always trouble.

"Where are they?"

The sergeant motioned his head toward the chief's office. Lakaitis went to Mooney's door and knocked.

"Yeah?" Captain Mooney's voice called from behind the door.

Lakaitis entered. "Morning, Captain," he said tentatively.

"Ah, Detective Albert Lakaitis," Mooney said with uncharacteristic formality, his eyes opening wider than usual. "Might as well come in. This concerns you."

As advertised, there was another man present. He wore a dark gray suit, white shirt, and regimental tie. He said nothing. The chief of detectives offered no introduction. Lakaitis had lived his life close enough to Washington to know a Fed when he saw one. The only question was, what sort of Fed? Lakaitis wasn't entirely sure he wanted to know. Instinct again: he didn't like anything about this stranger.

"Sit down," Mooney said.

Lakaitis sat.

"Detective Lakaitis is one of our best men," Mooney said to the man in the suit. The visitor gave a slight nod. Still no introduction. And Lakaitis knew that when his commander gave character references to strangers, he was warding off trouble.

"Detective Lakaitis filed the initial accident report in The Route One Case," Mooney continued, choosing his words with considerable caution. "He was preparing to investigate." There was a pause. Mooney raised his eyes to Lakaitis. "Apparently, Al, no further work will be required. The case is wrapped."

Lakaitis was shocked. "Wrapped how?"

Neither Mooney nor his visitor spoke for a moment. Then Mooney found a few words as the visitor stared at the floor.

"Federal court order, Al," he said, holding up a folded piece of paper and glancing at it. "United States Superior Court, District of Columbia. This case is both solved and sealed." He paused and set down the paper. "I think that's all I'm really permitted to tell you."

A long silence gripped the room.

"Solved how?" Lakaitis pressed.

The man in the gray suit looked at him, folding his legs at the same time. "Solved means solved, Officer. Period."

Lakaitis looked back to his captain.

"Sorry, Al. That's all. The good news is you get credit for a wrapped-up case since it was on your desk. If there are any notes that weren't in your file please bring them in here right away."

"There aren't."

Mooney looked mildly angry. "I'm obliged to tell you this: We're also under a federal gag order. You're not to discuss the case with anyone, including me or other members of this department. Officer Nevell has been similarly informed, as has Dr. Bauerman. I think that's everyone involved."

Lakaitis looked from one man to the other, searching unsuccessfully for something to say.

"I told our guest that this is a very professional department," Mooney said. "No one will have any problem obeying a federal court order."

Both men looked at the detective for a response.

"No problem at all," Lakaitis said without emotion.

"Thank you, Al," Mooney concluded. The detective took his cue to leave. Not another syllable from the other man, who stayed behind with the chief of detectives.

The precise date of the stranger's visit to Baltimore had been Sunday, February 10, 1985, less than one month after President Ronald Reagan had taken the oath of office a second time. The death on Route

1, or more accurately, the wreck on Route 1, had occurred in the early morning of February 7. Ever after, as these dates—the seventh and the tenth of February—passed annually on the calendar, Lakaitis would note them.

Captain Mooney left the department later in the year as scheduled. Dr. Bauerman left the medical examiner's office in 1989 to join a lucrative private practice out of state. Christine Nevell married, stayed on the force, took maternity leave twice, then retired while still comparatively young at thirty-one.

Albert Lakaitis eventually made lieutenant. He put in his full twenty years on the Baltimore police force, took his pension, and went into private security work. He never again sought to discuss the Route One Case with another living soul.

Nor, in his wildest flights of imagination, did he suspect that anyone would ever again mention it to him.

<<<< *1* >>>>

*B*EFORE 62,000 people at a football field in northern New Jersey, Senator John Roosevelt Lord—known simply as John Lord to the millions of Americans who were prepared to vote for him—stood calmly at the center of a stage. He was framed by lights and flags and shielded from the American public by bulletproof Plexiglass. As he spoke, he smoothly warped the truth.

No, he had never sold Ku Klux Klan literature while a senior at the University of Texas back in the early 1960s, he said, and he had never been a member of the American Nazi party. Nor had he ever stood in a backwoods redneck Methodist church hall on a hot night in northern Arkansas in 1961 and given a speech entitled "The Myth of the So-called Holocaust." The only myths he knew about, he explained, were those perpetuated by the liberal eastern media. Those "self-proclaimed experts," as he called them, those men and women who put their own spin on the news, well, they reckoned that they knew what was better for America than the average American did himself. These folks in New York and Washington and Los Angeles had a vested stake in seeing that a "little guy," as he termed himself, a self-professed outsider, "a man who stands up for America and American values," couldn't gain entry to the White House.

"Those people in the press," he told the assembled multitude, "those knights of the keyboard, those overpaid pretty faces you see on your TV screen, those people who don't get upset at muggers in your neighborhood or foreign gas in your car or your tax dollars being wasted, they say John Lord shouldn't get in the back door of the White House." He folded his arms and surveyed the twenty acres of presumptive voters before him, wall-to-wall audience packed across the synthetic turf of the stadium and far into the structure's uppermost tier. "Well, guess what! We're going in the *front* door of the White House and *you,* the American people, are going to make it happen!"

Notice, observed a few of the media members present, *how smoothly John Lord had shifted from a defensive statement to one of counterattack. Who exactly was going to stop this man?*

It was an otherwise beautiful spring night in May 1996. The only thing polluting it—in the opinion of many who were not among the adoring throng at the stadium—was John Lord, United States senator from Texas, running for the Presidency of the United States. Him and the mountainous groundswell of approval that shook before him as if to prepare him his path.

Lord was tall and handsome, sandy haired and blue-eyed, a genuine American Aryan. He made one think that God may have bestowed the gifts of saviorhood on an ill-chosen man. As Lord spoke, 62,000 true believers hung on his every word. And he had no shortage of words. He bellowed and he whispered. He stabbed the air with a finger and slashed it with a hand to punctuate his own sentences. He retreated momentarily and came very still, like a Texas copperhead dozing in the scorching sun of the Big Bend. Only marginally did he maintain the decorum of the others who'd aspired to the Presidency in the decades before him.

Lord was an American original, something mean and angry that reared up one night from the darkest underside of the American psyche. Lord punched the country's political establishment in its porcine face, touched every imaginable nerve or fear of the average voter and—like most successful demagogues of his century—brought millions of people to their feet.

He was, much of the mainstream press insisted, the wrong man at a dreadful time. The cyclical political pendulum of the twentieth century was swinging again in America. The mid-1990s were a time—much like the thirties and the sixties—of revolt and civil disobedience, of anarchy in art and revolution in music, of disruptions on college campuses, of turbulence in the drug-plagued financially starved cities, of disenchantment among the young, frustration and fury among the poor, and reaction from the working and middle classes.

The wealthy, as usual, were well equipped to ride out the storm. But for the rest of the country, various plagues were upon the American population. Rampant bank failures, unending through the nineties. Incurable recession and unemployment, this time touching millions of white collars. Corruption. Cynicism. Racial, ethnic, and religious intolerance. All the traditional elements, in other words, of twentieth century fascism.

Lord presided from a podium surging with American flags. He wore a dark suit and a red and white-striped tie. There was something simultaneously high tech and low cornball about his delivery—something calculated from the sandy barren hills of west Texas where he'd been born fifty-some years earlier. But, oh, how John Lord could work an audience.

Any audience.

He could work a supermarket aisle of eleven Iowa voters during the February caucuses and he could mesmerize a coffee klatch of twenty-six middle-aged middle-class New Hampshire women during the snowdrifts of January. Similarly, he could pack Joe Louis Arena in Michigan or, as he'd done here, Giants Stadium in north Jersey. And television? Pontificating, whispering, fire in his gorgeously intractable blue eyes, sweat on his brow, passion in his tones—how silkily he could work a television audience of 50,000,000. Those whom he didn't thrill, he terrified.

Lord finished his litany of denials. Then he switched gears. He didn't like the Russians. Never did, and never would. Then he blew holes in some of the easiest targets—the Democrats and the Republicans, "the guys in Washington who are so anxious to cut deals with our old enemy."

Lord asked why drug gangs flourished so freely during the last sixteen years if Republican administrations were tough on crime. Why were huge sections of cities controlled by armed bandits and why were even the suburbs now unsafe? He asked why "the little guy" was still paying billions to bail out Republican bankers who'd retired at taxpayers' expense "with French art on their walls and French wine in their bellies." He wanted to know why Democrats still wanted to give out welfare handouts to America's "underclass." Then he went on to bash Asians in general and Japanese and Koreans in particular for attempting a "yellow economic subjugation of the United States of America."

"What failed at Pearl Harbor has succeeded in corporate boardrooms and family budgets," Lord said, "and your Republican and Democratic leaders let it happen." When the wave of applause welled down, he added, "Of course, maybe they didn't see anything *wrong* with it." More howling. "Or maybe," he said, "they just don't care!"

Slightly less howling. "But I'll tell you one thing!" Another wave was building. He went for the punch line. "During the first days of my Presidency, there's going to be one sudden stop to it!"

There was a roar that shook the northern part of the state. And it gave him a breather. He took a hard shot at Israel and, with no elaboration, "Zionist spy rings in the United States." Then he blasted mainland China and its rulers, the last remaining major Marxist government on the planet. He bashed the Republicans for not sticking up for the pro-democracy elements in China way back in 1989 and ripped Congress and the President for allowing American troops to be drawn into costly, bloody guerrilla wars and "firefights" with drug gangs in South America and "oil sheiks" in the Middle East.

"I'd like to see this country return to what it used to be," he said. "A country with predominantly white Christian values, not a black yellow red and white third world country like Cuba." That brought part of the crowd to its feet.

Lord stepped back and basked in the enthusiasm of his audience. "People are afraid to say what's on their minds today. So I say it for them," he said. Lord liked this line. It was one of his favorites. He used it selectively, suggesting that he was reflecting views held by millions. "You know where I stand," he said. "And that's why you know I'll never double-cross you."

John Lord was as straightforward as a punch in the nose, as subtle as a belch. His campaign was a strange Southwestern gumbo of Uncle Sam, Billy Graham, and Huey Long, all bowlderized, sanitized, and made video-friendly for the mid-1990s. Another thing about it: it worked. So what that some political observers called him a modern George Wallace, and didn't mean it as a compliment? Who cared that historians with long memories or a keen sense of American political systems recalled how, when an earlier brand of totalitarianism was on the rise in the 1930s, Franklin Roosevelt had called Huey Long "the most dangerous man in America"—and that Lord resembled Long?

And so what that well into the 1980s Lord had belonged to a Louisiana organization called the Freedom Lobby, recognized for years as one of the most anti-Semitic organizations in North America? Much of the electorate didn't want to reflect. They wanted to react. And Lord's message was bringing angry white voters to the polls. Some said that he was even *creating* millions of new angry white voters with the vehemence of his message.

This, Lord denied. "I don't make people angry," he said. "The state of our republic makes people angry," he reasoned. "If they vote for me, it's a free country." He had a point. It was, though his critics said that it wouldn't be for long if John Lord were ever elected President.

Lord touched all the familiar remaining bases. Crime and drugs. Religion. Morals. The Russians. He spent plenty of time on the Russians. Who could have foreseen the deposition of Boris Yeltsin in February 1995? Who could have predicted that a group of Russian Nationalists from the Red Army could have toppled a winner of a Nobel Peace Prize? Certainly not the United States government, which was now stuck with empty alliances and new but antiquated nonaggression treaties.

It was close to nine forty-five when John Lord concluded his rally for the evening. He stepped away from the podium, still protected by glass, and he held up two hands as if in triumph. This evening Lord had been, Texans would have said, at his tobacco-chewin', turkey-shootin' best.

Then he did what other politicians had rarely dared to do in the last thirty years. He stood and took questions from people who'd stood in line for an hour. He took them all, friendly and hostile. Lord was the master of the public forum. He answered every question with great verve and apparent sincerity. When the questions turned hostile, he'd grin and say calmly, "I don't agree with you, sir." Or, with utmost irony, "We seem to think differently, ma'am."

He was blessed with an utterly confident temperament. He could say everything and nothing, whether he meant it or not. He could, if he had to, filibuster a question to death or dodge it with the dexterity of a linguistic acrobat. But tonight he didn't need to. The image he projected under the springtime skies of the Northeast was one of great candor. When he left the stage, his legion of admirers stood almost as one. They thundered an ovation upon him that shook the concrete and steel stadium more than any football victory had. From the top row of the farthest grandstand, Lord was a small figure making his way through a crowd. From the middle distance on the field, he was like a Caesar in retreat from his forum. Upon the giant video screens that were high up against the walls of the arena, his image swayed through the night like a beacon. And with the help of a recording on the speaker system, the crowd stood and joined in an impromptu singing of "God Bless America." Senator Lord's rallies always closed with such spontaneity.

Afterward, thousands of people stood in line to shake hands with him. He did not rush through the crowd to make the eleven or eleven thirty P.M. news shows. Rather, he stayed and pressed the flesh with as many of the fervent throng as was possible. Later a helicopter lifted him back into Manhattan where he would stay the night, meet a few media people, and make television appearances geared for West Coast consumption. Lord loved to work the media almost as much as he loved to trash it. The more hostile the press grew, the more difficult or accusing their questions, the more belligerent their tone, the better Senator Lord looked.

Yet, anyone who saw the performance at the football field that night, if he'd been unconvinced already, had to know that this year the two major parties in the United States, which had shared power since the great civil war a century and a half earlier, would have their hands full.

The official party primaries, for example, were mere flexings of Lord's political muscle. The U.S. senator from Texas was vying for neither party's nomination, having founded the Party of the United States of America, his own vehicle for national office. The USA party, as it was called, had been regarded as a backwoods joke two years earlier when Lord founded it. Detractors were not laughing anymore. An articulate but controversial black candidate was leading the Democratic field. A lightly regarded incumbent Vice President led the Republicans. The time was right. John Roosevelt Lord was not about to go away.

He was running for President, all right, and he was running like the wind. He was running with enthusiasm, verve, tenacity, money, smarts, and insolence. And the professional politicians and analysts, who had discounted him as recently as late 1995, were about to entertain the unthinkable. Within one year, in a three-way race and with a little more help from the tide of world events, there was an actual chance that John Lord, with his backwoods, quasiracist, America First "Old Time" low-key high-tech candidacy, just could—if all worked out—capture the Presidency of the United States as the first overtly fascist candidate in the nation's history.

It was a free country, after all, and John Lord had figured out exactly how to get himself elected.

<<<< **2** >>>>

VLADIMIR LITVINOV is ensconced as President of the Russian Republic and we're about to elect John Lord President," said newspaperman Harry Dubrow, glancing with disapproval at the front page of the rival *New York Times*. "God Almighty. After fifty years we're finally friendly with the damned Russians again, and this Lord guy wants to screw it up!" Harry shook his head. "And you tell me the world is not in trouble?"

"I didn't say the world wasn't in trouble," Paul Townsend answered patiently from behind the desk in his fourth-floor office. "I just said that I personally have stopped trying to save it."

"So has everyone else," Dubrow grumbled. He stood before Townsend, both men in white shirtsleeves. "That's the problem."

"Not Lord," countered Townsend with mock reproach. "Now there's a man with an agenda."

"Yeah. The Rise and Fall of the Fourth Reich. Or maybe it'll just be Cold War: Part Two. I can't wait."

Dubrow flipped through the newspaper to the competitor's sports section. "At least the Yankees are out of last place," he grumbled. "Here it is, end of May, and they're not even in the cellar yet."

"Just wait for June," said Townsend with qualified optimism. "Once the pitching hits midseason form, once the batting averages level off at .220, the team will dive like a submarine."

"Did you hear about these two old Jewish guys who went hunting in the North woods?" Harry asked after an appropriate pause. "They're out there in the forest when this huge beast crashes out of the trees and comes after them. They both run. 'Cy!' screams one of them. 'What is it? A bear?' "

Townsend waited. "Come on, Harry," he said.

Harry finished. " 'Don't ask me!' Cy screams back. 'I'm in textiles! *You're* in furs!"

Townsend grinned in spite of himself. "Go to work for once, would you?" he said. "Earn an honest dollar."

Harry smiled and folded the *New York Times.* With an aggressive slap that made loose papers flutter on Townsend's desktop, he returned the newspaper and departed.

Harry was graying, affable, and puffy-cheeked. He was Brooklyn-born and had never in his life left New York City for any length of time. He worked in the next office, and on the surface should have had nothing at all simpatico with a Scottish–Irish–German–English mongrel of a reporter from Ohio. Yet the professional arrangement between Harry Dubrow and Paul Townsend made life considerably more bearable for both.

"This is *my* goddamned office!" Townsend called after him, his voice rising. "I didn't summon you in here, you know, you dickhead!"

Townsend waited for an answer, but the corridor outside responded with silence. Harry was already gone—or at least not answering until later in the day. Their friendship was frequently measured by the vehemence of the affectionate insults they could lob back and forth—little verbal hand grenades between kindred souls. Presumably, Harry would be back with something else in the near future.

It was an early morning in May 1996. The editorial offices of the *New York Sun*—a sprawling new concrete fortress on West 116th Street in what was now known as "gentrified Harlem"—were still quiet. It was a perfect moment for Townsend to begin what he referred to as his "daily deathwatch." Like every other working day of late, Townsend, laboring in a small room in a quiet corner of the *Sun* Building, would have the last word on the lives of several fellow human beings.

Townsend was forty-nine years old. He was sturdy, dark-haired, and rugged-looking. Despite the fact that he considered himself smack in the center of a surly middle age, his deep brown eyes remained as sharp as his wits. His body was likewise strong, both from physical exercise and years of journalistic combat. Yet, he was also many things he never dreamed he would become. Among them: Townsend was the main obituary writer for a thick, young, technicolor, half-serious, half-trashy, seminewsy, semigossipy, computerized, editorially conservative sixty-cent tabloid. "Fast format," was the polite term for it in newspaper circles. Dull, gray and respectable it was not. But whatever else it was, the *Sun* was New York's newest daily. And it had a circulation of—as Townsend indelicately put it—"1.3 million mouth-breathing morons every morning."

The dreadful truth was, there was nothing in the world that Paul Townsend could do so skillfully as put into perspective the life of someone no longer living. It was a bizarre talent, being a first-string Death Page Man. But it was a talent, nonetheless. And sometimes—as might be imagined—it led him in some very strange directions.

The *New York Sun* had come into existence a year earlier after the *New York Daily News* and the *New York Post* had gone belly-up following ruinously uninspired ownership and lengthy job actions by printers and delivery drivers. The *Sun.* Even the paper's name struck Townsend as a curiosity. Seventy years ago a similarly named paper had been one of New York's best. Now, in an era of ozone depletion and global warming, the name had been revivified. Townsend wondered whether someone had intended some double-edge irony to the name. Or had some marketing school wizard bumbled onto the name because it was short and hot?

Who knew? Who cared? Having set up shop after the other two tabloids had ceased publication, the *Sun* had picked the carcasses. The *Sun* now maintained a "clippings" morgue that comprised an underused room full of withered file clippings and microfilm references from the two defunct papers. Underused, because it was in an isolated corner of the basement. And underused, because back upstairs on the second floor across from Internal Administration there was a mainframe IBM WLE-2000—"Big Wally" the *Sun* staffers called it—that could summon up the most extensive newspaper file in the United States on almost any human being living or dead within a few minutes.

Problem was, Townsend hated computers both personally and philosophically. Remorselessly, he remained the only *Sun* writer who had successfully resisted even learning how to use Big Wally. So instead, opting for the less fashionable and more tactile way of doing things, Townsend took his daily prowl through the basement clippings morgue with a list of names that he'd plucked from the day's death notices, looking for previous occasions when any of the names had appeared in print. In more ways than one, he proudly considered himself a basement sort of guy.

Once again, he had on his agenda a handful of men and women who had passed from this earth within the last twenty-four hours. Townsend was already formulating the final listings, hoping—perversely ironic as it sounded—to add some life to a few stories on death.

Townsend did not write normal obituaries. Tomb-cold dead is what most obits were, complete with the deceased's accolades, titles, club memberships, marriages, and surviving family members—the print version of a tasteful embalming. Each day Townsend left the morgue rattling bunches of photocopies. From here he would find warts and sin, loves and hates, and flesh and blood until he had a portrait as vibrant as a Copley or a Wyeth. If the deceased had been a womanizer, he printed it. If the departed had been roundly disliked in his community, Townsend ran it. If the dead guy had been a slumlord, Townsend used that term to describe him. After all, why not?

This had all started one memorable evening, soon after his hiring at the *Sun.* An unbanishable urge had been upon Townsend and he had run a particular obit for an old pal:

JERRY LOHRMAN, 51
SKIRTCHASER AND DEADBEAT

July 1. Jerry Lohrman of Yonkers, described by friends and foes alike as a world-class profligate, expired today of a heart attack at the Maui Inn, a mock-Hawaiian bar on Route 1 in Westchester. When the end came, he had a blonde on one arm and a glass in the other hand. Both, it was observed, had had help from a bottle. . . .

As it happened, Lohrman's friends and family were amused by the write-up. A "Leave 'em Laughing" death-page style for the mid-nineties had been midwifed into existence. Paul Townsend was off and running.

Yet, if the departed had been a solid citizen, Townsend printed that as well. Poets, plumbers, loan sharks, bank vice presidents, mechanics, pimps, and arbitrage traders: they all received the same candid treatment from Paul Townsend. The *New York Sun*'s obit pages coursed with humanity, giving Townsend a bizarre sort of daily following. It was a thing to behold.

Originally, a few of Townsend's senior editors at the *Sun* had hated his approach and would have liked to have seen Townsend dismembered. The rest of the editors felt, why be lenient? Yet now his write-ups were widely imitated and Townsend had even picked off an occasional prize for daily newspaper writing. In this way, each year he had the last word on approximately two thousand lives—as well as a certain grudging autonomy around his own publication. And all agreed that Paul Townsend had a knack of really capturing the deceased. That, and the fact that this clearly was no ordinary Death Page scribbler.

* * *

Townsend walked to the fourth-floor men's room, where he bantered with some of the sportswriters who worked down the corridor. He washed his hands. Townsend was one of the few writers remaining on any New York paper with ink stains on his hands. Townsend was forty-nine years old and Harry Dubrow was positively ancient at sixty. Most of the rest of the staff on the *Sun* were these disgusting young guys. The term "guys" encompassed women as well, and "young" was disparagingly tossed toward anyone under thirty-five with a six-figure income. Strangely enough, despite being a "young" paper, the *Sun* was already a place of considerable generational antagonisms.

"The Brat Crew," Townsend called the younger staffers. "Nintendo wizards." When he thought about them, he seethed with resentment. Inevitably they were "J-schoolers"—journalism school graduates—who were expert at the computer part of the work and hopeless at the heart and soul of it. They were fast and proficient at video display terminals. They knew how to access and define macros. They could merge, do a hard hyphen and explain ProDOS. They were computer literate but literature illiterate. They had never studied anything but software magazines, comic books, and the liner notes on laser music cassettes. They had never studied foreign languages, history or geography. And they didn't write or edit stories, they "processed" them.

"A heavy read for these brats is the ass-end of a parking ticket," Townsend had once fumed to Harry in one of his more ornery moods. "They don't know squat!"

"Ah, come on, Paul," Harry soothed. "They're not bad kids. Not all of them. Everyone has some lessons to learn when he's young."

Harry's apologia only set Townsend off. "Know who I really hold responsible?" he ranted. "The public! The great unwashed masses out there know no distinction between solid old-fashioned pavement-pounding journalism and this flash-and-splash new stuff. And our schools and universities are responsible, too. They deep-sixed those old-fashioned curriculums for computers and film study."

"Ah, Paulie, lighten up. You'll live longer."

And so it would go. Day after day.

Poor old Harry Dubrow, Townsend thought to himself as he dried his hands. Harry may have been less critical of the Nintendo wizards, but he had also turned into the office dinosaur. Similarly, Harry suffered one of the anachronistic fixations of New Yorkers his age: he still lived and died with the Yankees. Not only did Harry's baseball team play in New Jersey now, but they hadn't won a championship since Harry was a man in his forties back in 1978. Townsend would use this to edge Harry away from the kids.

"Tell me, Harry," he once asked. "When was the last time you saw anyone under thirty listening to a ball game on the radio? Answer me that."

"Los Angeles. Dodger Stadium. 1988," Harry finally retorted. "A beautiful blond girl about twenty-five. She was wearing a blue skirt and peach blouse." Townsend never asked again.

Townsend shook his head a final time for Poor Old Harry. He didn't like to think about Harry with too much perspective. Once Harry retired in six months, Townsend would be the house fossil. And he would hate every second of it.

The trouble was, he loved Harry as much as he didn't love the younger newspeople. Townsend longed for an age that he was just old enough to remember, when newswriters wore baggy-assed suits and were pleased to be recognized as an ungentrified, cynical, foulmouthed, nosy, and ill-mannered bunch. They subsisted on booze, coffee, poisonous amounts of nicotine, rumors, old shoes, and hard work. They proudly caused no end of trouble and held no joy greater than poking holes in an official story. For all of those reasons many of them had been relatively young when they burned out, retired, or died.

Townsend left the washroom and allowed his thoughts to shift into gear for the day. Who were these people in the day's death notices? Why had they died? How had they lived? Whose lives had been touched by theirs? Whose lives were now diminished?

There was a plumber from Queens. There was an editor of books from New York and Nantucket. A restauranteur who'd found fame in the 1970s and ruin in the 1990s had committed suicide. An old Cuban wrestler—once the "Champion of the Free World"—had died in a car crash. A young endocrinologist had lost a bout with cancer. A woman who'd taught Italian renaissance studies at New York University had dropped dead after thirty-two years of teaching.

Like any other daily, the *Sun* had prewritten obituaries on the famous, the wealthy, and the noteworthy. Townsend would tinker with anything that was already on file. But with notices like today's, he had a free hand completely.

Townsend returned to his quiet corner of the fourth floor and settled in at his desk. For a moment he was distracted by a note from Harry, a telephone message taken in the few minutes he had been away.

A woman had called. She'd left her name—if Townsend was accurately reading Harry's scrawl—as Sarah Stuart.

"Know her, don't you?" Harry asked, sticking his head back in the door a moment later. "She said she knows you."

"Yeah, I know her," he said.

Harry waited. He knew the answer anyway. He had taken calls from the same woman before. Now he was snooping, and Townsend knew it.

"One of your legion of college-aged groupies?" Harry teased gently.

Townsend raised his eyes. "Divorced, late thirties. She has a teenage son away at boarding school."

Harry shrugged. "Sounds perfect to me," he said. "She asked if you would call her back."

Townsend ran his hand through his hair, studying more urgent matters that were on his desk.

"I will," he said. "Eventually."

"Sure," Harry said. " 'Eventually,' " he echoed reproachfully as he rolled his eyes and departed. "A beautiful woman and you'll call back 'eventually.' "

On most days Townsend's telephone would ring with a different sort of call, usually from bereaved family members or from funeral homes. Today it didn't. He sifted through his material and estimated the layout of his page. Today nothing unusual leaped out of the clippings, though a couple of the previously unknown names were starting to come into focus as human beings. Arbitrarily, he decided to go for a class act this morning. He'd try to write up the university professor first. Her name was Barbara Rizzo Moore.

Townsend picked up the telephone. He called the deceased's family. He talked to Mrs. Moore's daughter as he pecked out notes on a battered manual typewriter. He confirmed how old the woman had been and of what she had died. He asked questions based on a single clipping he'd found in the *Sun*'s morgue. He inquired about her approach to her teaching course. On a lark, he asked if the deceased had believed in God or what wine—if any—she might have preferred or how often she might have visited Italy. Townsend liked to ask questions that were none of a traditional obituary writer's business. In that fashion, he provoked people into chatting.

"Why," a younger peer once asked, "do people talk to you?"

"It's like any other reporting," Paul Townsend explained. "People tell you things. Why *shouldn't* they talk to me? Try it sometime, dickhead."

Dickhead. Here was Paul Townsend's favorite cheek-to-jowl epithet for those he held in contempt. It was a linguistic holdover from his days in the military, a quarter century earlier. And it used to cost him an occasional trip to the dentist when he used it out on the street. Nowadays, in the newsroom, it cost him $10 each time he was reported to have used it, that being the fine levied under the *Sun*'s Abusive Language

Regulation of July 30, 1995. No profanity. Better to purify the air throughout the offices.

There was an abrasive little twenty-six-year-old named Lou DiCarlo in Internal Administration across from Big Wally, the research computer. Lou habitually spoke in a loud Bronx honk and gleefully administered the fines. He was also the Computer Room Steward, charged with watching over Big Wally, all the software books, and the video display screens. "What you are, Lou," Townsend had told him on several occasions, "is a high-tech janitor. A custodian of profanity and microchips. But a janitor, nonetheless."

Because everyone other than Townsend knew how to use the computer, and Townsend continued to resist it, Lou didn't seem—at $55,000 per annum—to have much else to do. So Lou also made about six phone calls a day for no real reason to an older sister named Caryn—pronounced Karen—who was a sports staffer in Harry Dubrow's department.

Harry, of course, got along with everyone. He had wild fantasies about getting along even better with Caryn DiCarlo. Caryn was thirty-one years old, a J-schooler via Northwestern University. She had short dark hair, a shape that took Harry's breath away, and wore her skirts midthigh. A rustle of her stockings—which the sports editor claimed he could hear an office away—could drive Harry into a private frenzy. So far, Townsend was impartial to her.

Her brother Lou was another story. Lou evoked strong feelings from Paul Townsend, and not just because they had locked horns on a handful of occasions. It was a matter of table manners. Lou had closely cropped black hair and nose jewelry that changed from day to day. Townsend not only disliked Lou, but loathed the idea of working with people who attached precious metals to their nostrils.

In constructing an obituary, Townsend preferred the telephone for some lines of questioning while he liked to appear in person for others. He felt more at home asking the clinical questions over the phone. For stories where there needed to be an extra bit of trust—an extra bond to develop between a reporter and the subject for a major write-up—he would prefer to go talk to friends and family in person. There he'd ask questions that really started people talking.

When Dr. Moore's daughter was talked out, Townsend thanked her. Then he put in calls to the professor's associates at the university. He learned she was a scholar who specialized in the works of Pallaiuolo, Castagno, and Da Vinci. She liked to paint, herself. She was well liked by her peers. Townsend talked to one of her students. By noon he had a full portrait of the woman. He began his lead:

BARBARA RIZZO MOORE, 62
PROFESSOR AND SCHOLAR
OF ITALIAN ART, CULTURE

May 16. Barbara Rizzo Moore, for many years a much loved and much appreciated expert on Italian life and culture, died of a stroke today at age 62. She had visited Italy as recently as last month. A bottle of Antelliore, her favorite Tuscan wine, and a copy of *The Divine Comedy,* her favorite book, were at her bedside, along with her family, when she passed away. On the wall of her bedroom, the room where she died, were prints of Donatello. It was said that Dr. Moore was surrounded to the end by the things and people she loved. . . .

Eventually, Townsend had enough to fill six column inches. He called back Dr. Moore's daughter and read what he had. The Moore family was pleased.

Townsend repeated the procedure with the other five names. The plumber proved the most obtuse, as he left no relatives. A call to his church, however, yielded a young priest who had known the man. Townsend held two column inches open on his page and manufactured two accurate paragraphs. It was 6:20 P.M. The telephone rang on his desk.

"Townsend," he answered.

"Hello, Paul." It was a woman's voice. He recognized it.

After a moment's pause, he replied. "Hello, Sarah," he said in return.

She answered his pause with one of her own. "I'm not calling for any of the predictable reasons," she said, already sounding ill at ease with the conversation. "It's actually to ask a favor. May I?"

"Of course."

He heard her draw a breath. "I want to talk to you about a man's obituary," she said.

"Whose?"

"His name is Leonard Wolik. Former State Department official from late in the Eisenhower administration until the Reagan administration."

Townsend paused, frowning and glancing among the papers before him. He had an excellent memory for the names that had passed across his desk, but he was drawing a blank on this one.

"I don't remember it." He reached for a notepad. "When did Wolik die?"

"He hasn't yet."

Slowly, almost irritably, Townsend let the pencil slip from his hands. It clacked onto his desk. "Am I missing something?" he asked. "I'm not following you."

"He's my father, Paul," she said. "He's terminally ill."

The words arrested Townsend's attention. "Oh, Lord, Sarah," he answered. "I'm sorry. I never knew your family name, so I didn't recognize it."

She forged ahead with words that were obviously difficult. "Here's the favor, Paul. He has maybe as little as a day or two to live. He wants to talk to you. No one else. *You."*

"Why me?"

"He has a story to tell," she said. "Right now. He'd like you to hear it from his own lips before he dies. Then I won't bother you again. You can decide for yourself whether or not you want to write it."

"Yeah, but why *me?"*

She blew out a breath. "You write the notices for the *Sun,"* she said, as if it were self-evident. "He likes the way you do them. He wants—" Her voice broke off.

"All right," he said. His voice wavered between sympathy and impatience. "We don't normally do auditions for my page," he continued. He pondered it for a moment as the line was silent. She waited. "I guess one exception isn't going to hurt anyone."

"Oh, God." She started to cry. "Thank you, Paul. It will mean a lot, and—"

"Does it have to be tonight?"

"Could it be?"

"How about eight o'clock?"

Eight o'clock would be fine, she said. Her father lived outside the city, she explained. But it wasn't far. She would meet Townsend at his apartment building with her car. She thanked him again.

Harry Dubrow passed into the room as he put down the telephone. He placed a final proof of that day's *Sun* on Townsend's desk and looked at a second copy of his own.

For a moment Townsend stared at the telephone. Harry watched him and must have read his expression.

"Bad news?" Harry asked.

"Her father's dying," Townsend said. "I never even knew he was ill."

"You haven't seen her lately, have you?"

Townsend shook his head. Harry waited for a moment and concluded that his friend needed some cheering.

"Paul?" he asked softly. "Why don't Episcopalians have cockroaches?"

"Why, Harry?"

"There's no food in the house."

Townsend managed a smile. Townsend sat back down in the chair at his desk and reached for the paper which he had helped create.

He studied the front page of the proof. His eyes were assaulted by the lead stories.

Local: New Asian heroin gangs had now seized entire blocks on and around Avenue D. They executed their rivals by firing squad and set up "horse corrals" for newly addicted hemp-heads to enjoy their product, which could now be freebased and smoked.

Local: A priest had been violently mugged outside his church on East 73rd Street in Manhattan the previous afternoon. Townsend sighed. Here was Townsend's lead obit sometime in the next few days.

State: Car insurance rates, which had risen 12 percent in 1996, would rise another 18 percent in 1997, despite record profits by the insurance companies.

State *and* national: The New York Presidential primary, starring Senator John Lord, was being held that day.

National: Polls showed that Senator Lord could carry Ohio in a three-way race. His eyes focused for a moment. It disgusted Townsend thoroughly that his own paper treated Lord more than kindly.

International: Widespread student and worker discontent was sweeping mainland China again, a spillover of the rebellious mood worldwide among the young. Even the old Maoists were now having trouble fighting off the flow of history.

"Some screwed-up world we live in, Harry," he said, almost by way of summation. He left the proof on his desk. He'd seen enough of the next morning's *Sun*. From Harry, he knew what was in the sports pages. He didn't own any stocks, didn't read the comics, didn't care about show business, and he'd done the deaths, himself. What else was there in his benighted rag? "Some world."

Harry grunted in response, then went along his way. "See you tomorrow," he said in leaving.

Townsend proofread his own page, then closed for the day. A few minutes later, he reached for the jacket that hung on the back on his chair. He pulled it on. It was almost seven o'clock. Paul Townsend had once again minted the final words on a handful of people he had never known. It was a strange accomplishment and he did it every day.

He was reaching for the light switch on the wall when his phone rang a final time. Against his better judgment, he took it.

"Townsend," he answered.

It was Mr. Velez, the superintendent at his building. Mr. Velez had everyone's work number and only called in case of an emergency. Mr. Velez on the telephone, at any hour of the day or night, was never welcome news.

"Yes, Pablo. What's the problem?"

Pablo explained. There were two police officers at Townsend's building looking for him. The police officers had found Townsend's name on the registration of his car. On his end of the line, the superintendent handed the telephone to one of the men in blue.

A male officer who identified himself as Wixted came on the line. He explained that he was holding in his hand the registration of Townsend's car. "Where did you leave the vehicle, sir?" Wixted asked.

"On the street. Ninety-fourth between Columbus and Amsterdam, halfway down the block on the south side. Why? Where the hell is it now?"

The car was pretty much where he had left it, the officer said. Or at least most of the chassis was. Part of the hood, however, had landed halfway down the block and a section of front fender bearing the license plates had landed clear across Amsterdam. The doors were gone, the roof had a hole in it and so did the floor. But that was as much as anyone could tell since currently the vehicle was inverted.

"What the hell do you mean, 'inverted'?" Townsend demanded.

"Upside down," Officer Wixted said.

It was highly recommended, the officer continued, that Townsend leave work right away on this otherwise pleasant evening in late spring, and come take a look.

< < < < **3** > > > >

*W*HO would want to blow him up? Who would plant a homemade fragmentation bomb beneath the dashboard of Townsend's car? Who, at this late date, wanted him dead quite that badly?

These were the questions Paul Townsend turned over mentally as he surveyed the twisted metal on West 94th Street in Upper Manhattan. There wasn't much mistake in the motivation of the bomber. The only mistake was the means of delivery and the time that it went off.

Inevitably, there was a crowd. Several dozen of the curious were kept behind police lines as Townsend stood with a New York Police Department bomb squad sergeant named Vincent Foliari. Townsend answered the predictable questions.

"Somebody have something against you?" Foliari asked, leading Townsend to the wreckage.

"A lot of people, I suppose."

"What do you do for a living, Mr. Townsend?"

"I'm a reporter. For the *New York Sun.*"

"Oh," he pulled up next to the chassis. A few wisps of steam and smoke were still rising from it. "That explains it. What do you write?"

"Obituaries."

"Is that a fact?," he answered, mildly amused by a perceived irony. "You nearly became one, yourself."

Foliari was a classically handsome man with dark eyes and very black hair. He wore a stylish navy blue suit with his gold detective's shield prominently folded onto the breast pocket of his jacket. He had the face of a Roman centurion and, best of all, knew what he was talking about.

The bomb was equivalent to about a pound of dynamite, Foliari explained. It had been packed in a long lead pipe and attached to the undercarriage of the car. It probably had been strapped or taped, but not bolted. Bolting takes more time and is trickier.

"My guess is that it had a balance- or vibration-type fuse," Foliari said.

"What the hell is that?" Townsend asked.

"It's electronic and very sensitive to motion. Almost anything will set it off. You get in and slam the door. Pow! She blows. Or you turn on the ignition. The car vibrates. She blows. Too sensitive for this job, though. That's why she blew prematurely."

"Something else set it off?"

"You bet."

Witnesses, said Foliari, had various explanations. A car parked in front of Townsend's had been trying to edge its way out of a tight parking slot at the time the bomb blew. Townsend looked at the car in front of his. It was a new silver-gray BMW. Its rear section was wrecked.

"The driver's in the emergency room at Roosevelt right now," Foliari said.

Also, a heavy truck—a moving van—had been rumbling across 94th Street at the same time. Speculation was that a bump from the neighboring vehicle combined with the rumble of the truck had triggered the fuse.

Foliari motioned with his head to the roof of the building nearest the car. The windows were blown out on the three lowest floors. But Foliari motioned to the roof.

"How high do you think that building is?" he asked.

"Ten floors," said Townsend. "Maybe a hundred twenty feet."

Foliari agreed. "If you'd been sitting in your car," the bomb squad detective said, "your legs would be up on the roof right now. The rest of you would be in a rubber bag." He paused.

"You think this was random, Mr. Townsend? Or you think someone wanted you in particular?"

Townsend was still gazing at the rooftop. He returned his eyes to Sergeant Foliari. "My line of work is a little similar to yours," he said. "I don't believe in coincidence."

"You want to come over to the Two-Four Precinct tonight or tomorrow?" the detective asked. "We can talk about who might have done this."

"How's Friday morning?"

"Not perfect."

"That's the best I can do."

"I can't force you to come at all." Foliari thought about it for a moment, then shrugged. "I guess Friday's okay," he finally said. A team of bomb squad detectives with a video camera was taking a detailed scan of the crime scene. "You got a family?" Foliari asked Townsend.

"Yes." Townsend offered no details.

"You got insurance?"

"No."

"You should get some."

"You know how much it costs," Townsend answered with a tired, annoyed tone, "to insure a car in this neighborhood?"

Foliari stared at him for a moment, then caught the misunderstanding. "I meant *life* insurance," he said. "Somebody hates you that much, they're going to try again."

"Thanks for the tip."

"My pleasure." Folinari took a pack of Camels out of his pocket and lit one. "I got to call a police department wrecker," he explained. "They'll take your car to a garage in Astoria. I'll give you the address. It'll be there a few days. Then disposal of the property is on you."

"Thanks," Townsend said sourly.

Foliari gave him a long gaze as he tried to assess him. "This type of thing happen to you often?" he asked.

"Not for a while."

Foliari gave him another long look. "We'll talk Friday," he said in conclusion.

Townsend agreed that, yes, that would be a good idea.

For many years earlier, and not so long into his unlovely past, Paul Townsend had practiced exactly the type of investigative journalism that provoked many such incidents as the bombing of his car. He had maintained the life-style that had him legally carrying a Smith & Wesson, even if he was home brushing his teeth.

Paul Townsend had been born and raised in Ohio, gone to university there, then done military service just in time to be in Viet Nam for the Tet offensive of 1968. In some ways, official and unofficial, he'd been seeing hostile fire ever since.

He had fooled around with a few other careers in the early 1970s. He had been an insurance investigator in Illinois for a while, then moved east and went into the low-paying, unrewarding field of writing for major American magazines. In his first year, he grossed thirty-seven hundred dollars and survived only by working part-time as a bartender.

Nonetheless, the few articles he wrote were excellent. He parlayed them into interviews with various news agencies, then edged his way into newswriting when he latched on at the city desk of the *Philadelphia*

Bulletin in the early part of the same decade. There he worked his way up, becoming an excellent reporter. When he left the *Bulletin* in 1977, Townsend did some magazine work on a steadier basis, then caught on with the *New York Daily News* in 1981 where he first made the acquaintance of Harry Dubrow.

Two years later, Townsend met a cute flight attendant named Nora from Minnesota. He married her in 1984 and gave a hint of settling down. Their only child, a daughter named Emily, was born four years later.

Yet, as a news writer, Paul Townsend had specialized at investigating subjects who didn't particularly care to be investigated. He had been a down-the-middle, hard-news type of guy who had sharp elbows when he went after the big stories. In doing so, he had made enemies of everyone from the Mayor of New York to the Roman Catholic Archdiocese of Brooklyn to the State of Israel. The British government hated him, as did—among other formal parties—his landlord, the Trustees of Columbia University, the Philadelphia City Council, the parking enforcement bureaus in six different cities, three gas companies, the Peloponnesian Society of Queens, fifteen banks, seven labor unions, one major film studio, the animal rights people, the antiabortion lobby, five congressmen, and three senators.

He had also antagonized many *in*formal groups. There were, for example, the politicians who controlled the gambling dens downtown in Manhattan and the White Warlocks Motorcycle Club who hung out at their clubhouse in Bensonhurst. The Sons of Calabria hated him, so did the Peruvian ambassador to the United Nations and all the major crime families in New York, Philadelphia, and Atlantic City. It was an exciting way to live: there were hundreds of people who would have appreciated seeing Paul Townsend's face on the side of a milk carton under the word MISSING, or, even better, peering beatifically out from his own obit page. Several took action to nudge that possibility forward.

Once, Townsend had moved his wife and daughter to a brother-in-law's house in Rhode Island when the Brooklyn district attorney tipped him that the White Warlocks planned to firebomb his house, preferably with him in it. Another time, someone named Carmine down on Mulberry Street was bragging that a $25,000 price had been put on Townsend's head. There was no way to know how many other threats he didn't even know about.

On another occasion he ran a story exposing labor racketeering in one of the restaurant workers' unions. One night a week later, all four of the tires on his car were slashed. Two months later, when he continued to investigate the same topic, he went to his car one morning and found bullet holes in its rear window. He decided that the holes made excellent ventilation and kept them there. One night the following week, someone broke into his car with a chain saw, cut out the seats, and cut the wheel off the steering column. Townsend bought a new car—a Made in Singapore junker. The chain saw man—or men—came back and cut it in half one night. His wife Nora, was hysterical. Yet on the surface, Townsend took things calmly. His vehicle, he attempted to explain, was an excellent barometer of reader reaction.

In truth, Paul Townsend's insides were churning while he remained too stubborn to take a hint. Then came April 16th, 1993. His five-year-old daughter, Emily, returned home from school in tears, soaking wet. Two men had stepped out of a car, taken her schoolbooks, handed her a note, and then thrown water in the girl's face.

Emily came home with the note. "This could have been acid," it read. "Next time it will be."

Two days later, Townsend's wife took their daughter to California. "When you quit that job," Nora said to him, "you can come join us." Meanwhile, she took a job in a bank. She didn't even want his money.

But he didn't quit his job. He thought of himself as an urban kamikaze. He held fast to the quaint notion that one man with access to a printing press could make a difference in the lives of ordinary people. He was convinced he was a mix between King Kong and the Lone Ranger. He was not yet mature enough to understand true wisdom: the knowledge of how much he didn't know—or couldn't do.

And King Kong? The Lone Ranger? In reality, he sat alone in the living room of his Upper West Side apartment, shades pulled, gun on his hip, watching the street. He became paranoid as hell, especially after the death threats. When driving, he constantly studied headlights in his rearview mirror.

Some nights he bolted upright in bed, but could never recall what he'd been dreaming. On other nights, sleepless, he'd arise from bed at a random moment and move sideways to the window. He'd peer out past a drawn curtain. If he saw a stationary figure, his heart would kick in his chest. He wondered and worried. He lived for the day when out of one of the unresolved jigsaw puzzles of his past would step an old adversary who, for reasons which defied ready comprehension or explanation, would demand a moment of reckoning—most likely, Townsend reasoned, silencer-equipped and with a bullet in the back.

And what riches, what great moral triumph, had he received in return? He was convinced that there were probably not two dozen people in the city of eight million who were personally grateful to him.

Eventually, he became like the people he investigated: always searching for an angle or looking over his shoulder. His glands stopped working right. He suffered brain-splitting migraines. He was eternally tense. He was after bad guys so much and so hard that even the many people who liked him were skittish about being around him.

Paul Townsend didn't like the situation. Neither did anyone else. He snapped at friends. He was quarrelsome. His editors called it being "burned out." He had been doing it for seven years. They said he needed a rest.

The "rest" constituted a stint on rewrite in the sports department. From putting people in jail, he went to two paragraphs on football games he'd never seen, rewriting dumb-assed illiterate stuff sent in by twenty-year-old stringers with purple-tinted spiked hair:

SLIPPERY ROCK BEATS GETTYSBURG, 17-10.

Findlay, Pa.—Slippery Rock beat Gettysburg today 17—10 in a game played before a homecoming crowd of 2,356.

Halfback Duane Taylor scored two touchdowns for Slippery Rock and kicked two extra points.

And so on. It was a humiliating move. All over the city, even back in Philadelphia where Townsend had made himself unpopular before New York, his old enemies were having a big laugh. At this point in his life, all of his gods were dead and Paul Townsend became a deeply bitter man.

One night he started home but ended up instead in the Old Dublin Bar on West 86th Street. Three or four beers made him feel better. The fifth one went down with consummate ease. The sixth one was the last he would remember, though he would eventually entertain a faint recollection of starting breakfast the next day with an $8 bottle of cold duck.

Three days later, he found himself in Beth Israel Hospital, drying out from a world-class drinking binge coupled with a nervous breakdown. He had a black eye that he couldn't account for, his wallet was missing, and he couldn't be sure whether he'd been wearing a watch when the drinking began. If so, it had now vanished. At this point, when word filtered around the city of Townsend's condition and whereabouts, much of the world, with great appreciation, figured that Paul Townsend would never be heard from again. Or at least not in print. So the threats against his life and property stopped.

He spent three months drying out. He made two trips to California, attempting a reconciliation with his family, piecing back together his shattered nerves. His wife said he could stay with her if he slept downstairs on the sofa. She slept upstairs in a big bed. He didn't have to ask to know that she was already involved with someone else. Sometimes he wished his instincts as a reporter would desert him so that he could lead a normal life like anyone else.

But they wouldn't, Goddamn them.

He returned to New York. The *News* folded. He collected severance pay. There was talk of a new nonunion paper starting up to challenge the one Long Island-based tabloid that remained. But plans were embryonic, financing was questionable, and Townsend didn't pay much attention. No one in the city seemed capable of reading—much less writing—in the English language, and there were hundreds of former newspeople on the street, anyway. Few were better, but almost all were younger, and none carried as much personal and professional baggage. In fact, he noted with dismay, some of the best of his peers were running inns in Vermont or motels in Arizona, though the very shrewdest and most aggressive of them had graduated to writing million-dollar books.

So while a decision on his future hung in a distant balance, Townsend took a cue from Harry Dubrow, an incorrigible horseplayer. Townsend spent a few days at Aqueduct, recklessly attempting to solve the mysteries of two-year-old maiden races and six-furlong claimers.

As if by magic, he turned a $400 bankroll into $1,650 in five days. He reckoned that he was onto a new career. But the wizardry inexplicably vanished and he found the $1,650 just as easily back down to $280 the following Tuesday. So much for the ponies. Besides, he was starting to spot some of his old adversaries, a bunch of overweight white guys with bad haircuts, milling around the $100-Win windows and muttering ominously to each other as they squinted narrowly at him.

Nora announced that she was buying a house in California. He talked to her on the phone. The schools were good, she'd found a home in the sunshine of Pasadena, and in her new life-style there were no guns stashed in various drawers around the house, no door frames cemented to the floor, no strange, threatening telephone messages at two in the morning, and no sudden trips to hide in Rhode Island. She wasn't even afraid to start the car each day.

Townsend flew out to California to visit, liked some of what he saw, stayed in a hotel, and thought things might improve between him and his family. He embraced the idea of moving west and reporting on sewer construction for a sleepy suburban weekly. But when he asked his wife to sleep with him again, she told him that she wanted a divorce. Enraged, depressed, and shattered for the second time within six months, he returned to New York wondering if maybe he'd had it wrong all along. Maybe the world could be a better place if he just shot himself. Well, okay, he reasoned. He already had the gun.

One night he pulled out the Smith & Wesson, loaded it with two bullets, and neatly laid it on the desk in front of him. Then he drafted a suicide note. It was a fine bit of writing. He pinned the note to his shirt. He cocked the gun and laid it back on the desk in front of him. He began to draw deep even breaths in an attempt to summon up the courage to pull a trigger.

Through the mouth, he wondered, or through the side of the head? Always tough decisions. He picked up the gun. He held it calmly. It was heavy and the palm of his hand was wet. He touched the nose of the pistol to his temple. Directly through the brain, he concluded, was definitely the classy way to go.

After an hour of agonizing, putting the gun down, picking it up again, and repeating the procedure so many times that he lost count, he decided to hell with that, too. He threw away the note and went to bed. It was a good career move. The next day, in what had to be the supreme irony of his life, an irony that only he, having sat poised with his instrument of suicide the previous evening, could appreciate, his telephone rang.

It was Harry Dubrow, who had been one of Townsend's best friends when the *News* finally folded. Harry had covered City Hall and the City Council as a daily beat. A close look at the inner workings of both each day, Harry used to say, was almost indistinguishable from taking ipecac each morning.

A new paper would start up by September 1994, Dubrow explained. Harry had already climbed aboard. "They're calling it the *New York Sun*. It's going to be one of those unreadable four-color rags with too many pictures of movie stars."

Silence, then suspiciously, Townsend asked, "Who's publishing it?"

"I dunno," Dubrow said.

"Harry, you answer too quickly when you're lying."

Dubrow confessed. Max Kohlheimer would be the publisher. Kohlheimer was a billionaire from Arizona, famous for glitzy helium-headed scandal sheets and contributions to disreputable conservative causes. It was Kohlheimer's contention that most newspapers were not tasteless enough. And among many newspeople, Kohlheimer was known as a particularly cold-blooded bastard. "The world's only living heart donor," some called him.

Townsend snarled. "Another one of *his* rags? So who the hell cares? I'm not working for that asshole."

Harry was undeterred. "They probably won't be doing very much investigative stuff," said Harry. "Might not do any at all. And Christ knows there'll only be a handful of openings."

"Sounds reprehensible," said Townsend. His spirit was exhausted. His tone of voice matched. "Tell you what, Harry. If you see a dummy issue, kill it with a stick. And if you see my pal Max Kohlheimer, kill him with a butter knife."

"Knock it off, Townsend. Look, I'll bet you fifty bucks that after two weeks you'll love it."

"Harry, you're an optimist and a sick gambler. I'm surprised you don't bet over-under each day on the temperature."

"I never thought of that, Paul," Harry said in amazement. But then Harry forged ahead. "What I have to know today, however, is whether you're at least interested. I mean, can we put your name on the list?"

"What goddamned list?"

"For staff writing positions when they get filled."

"I said the paper sounds awful," Townsend repeated. "Aren't you listening? Why the hell would I—?"

"I heard you the first time. I'm sure it *is* awful. I promise you it *will be* awful. They're making entry-level people into copy editors and paying them sixty grand a year."

This time, Paul Townsend groaned. "The copy editor is a paper's last line of defense against libel and error," he said, "factual and grammatical. And they're making it an entry-level position for a bunch of dickheads a year out of J-School?"

"There are better newsmen than me currently holding down positions on the ass-end of city sanitation trucks," Harry said, suddenly quite somber. "I'm climbing aboard while I have the chance. What about you?"

Loud and clear, Townsend barked an inspired string of profanities into his end of the telephone.

"Come on, Paul," Harry coaxed. "You were one of the best investigative writers in this country for a decade."

"The best, goddamn it!"

"Then at least get back on a paper."

"Don't bother me," Townsend insisted. "What you described won't be a newspaper."

"That's the spirit," sang Dubrow. "Thank you. I'll put down your name."

"Don't you *dare,* Harry, you dickhead!"

"It's already done."

Townsend hung up. A month later, the nascent *Sun* offered Harry the editorship of the sports page, plus a column and—just to show that there was some justice in the world—the best salary of his life. Curiously, Townsend was offered the unwanted job in obits—editor of the page and main writer, with two younger assistants as needed, the latter positions to rotate through the *Sun*'s staff and cover Townsend's duties on his days off.

To everyone's surprise—perhaps just to show that he was an ornery, crusty, unpredictable old goat to the end—Townsend swallowed hard and accepted it. And perhaps because, since he had decided to live, he would someway need to make money. The cramped one-bedroom apartment that he now rented in a brick walk-up on West 98th Street cost $2,144 a month, and would have cost even more if the landlord properly maintained the building. A man had to do something if he'd decided to stay alive. And by this time in his life, print journalism was the only thing Townsend knew. Plus, the dead were the only people who conversed to him with any clarity.

Writing obituaries was, even in the mid-1990s, considered the worst job on almost any newspaper. An investigative reporter wasn't so much transferred to it as he was sentenced to it. A death sentence, as it were. Yet to his own surprise, eventually Paul Townsend decided that he actually *liked* writing obituaries. Daily he found human drama in the way ordinary people had lived the last years or last months of their lives. Better, he met mostly good people and—for once in his life—made no enemies. In a small way, it renewed his faith in the nobility and courage of mankind.

It was a strange way to live, waking up each day wondering eagerly if anyone interesting had slipped into the next dimension overnight. But there he was, anyway. Resurrected as a chronicler of the dead. A poor man's Plutarche. A fast format Boswell. A study in contradictions and complexities.

It would not have been stretching the point to suggest that Paul Townsend was the best writer on any bad American newspaper who had the worst job that paper had to offer. Nor would it have been stretching a further point to suggest that it was a situation just waiting for something major to happen. Something like the evening of May 19, when his car was attacked on West 94th Street.

Then at 8:30 he arrived back at his building and saw a familiar woman standing in the otherwise empty lobby, arms folded and impatient. She was a very pretty woman with dark brown hair, a good figure, and high cheekbones. The truth was, she was in her late thirties, but didn't look it. She was agile, trim, and nicely attired.

"I'm sorry, Sarah," he said. "I forgot."

"I nearly gave up on you, Paul. We talked less than two hours ago."

"I've been with the police. Remember the car I used to drive? It just got hit on Ninety-fourth Street."

" 'Hit'? What do you mean? A collision?"

"Vandalized."

"Badly?"

"Totaled."

"Oh, God," she said. "What's this city coming to? I'm sorry." She leaned to him. He kissed her.

"Bad week for both of us, I guess."

She agreed that it was.

"Where's your car?" he asked.

It was around the corner, she said, parked in a free parking meter. She would go retrieve the auto while he stopped in his apartment for a moment.

She departed. Townsend walked upstairs.

He barely had time to turn around. He knew that she would be back around the corner practically before he was downstairs. And Heaven knew, the way the evening was going, it was already nearing nine. What time could he possibly expect to get home? Half past midnight? One? Two?

He glanced at his mail. Mostly bills, a few ads. He abandoned it in his living room, strewn casually across an end table next to the folio from his office. The more important stop he had to make was near his bed. There was a solid bedside table to the right of where he slept. The lower part of it gave the appearance of a bookcase. But this particular piece of furniture was not what it appeared. First, it weighed three hundred pounds. Second, it was bolted to the floor.

Townsend lifted a catch hidden on the side of the table and heard a click. A row of shelves unlatched and swung loose like a gate. Townsend opened it completely, then knelt. On the steel safe hidden within, he worked a quick combination. The safe opened.

In a yellow chamois cloth there was the snub-nosed six-cylinder Smith & Wesson revolver. It was held in a small clip-on holster. Townsend pulled it out of the safe. He released the safety catch and checked the weapon. The first two chambers were empty. The next two contained rounds. The final two were empty as well.

There was an array of bullets in the chamois cloth as well. He picked them up. He threaded three of them into the revolver, leaving the chamber above the pistol's hammer empty. No use blowing off your hip accidentally. The remaining bullets he returned to the safe, which he closed again and locked.

From somewhere in the indecipherable jumble of his past, there apparently remained someone who didn't forget. Someone who lay in wait and someone who wanted to see Townsend's picture prominently displayed on the very page he edited.

Whoever it was, he reasoned, he had been keeping his own counsel for a long time. Townsend's enemy had lain in wait and had finally struck with the bomb on West 94th Street. Townsend could barely imagine who still might be grinding an ax. Years had passed since he'd printed an expose on anyone. He was clearly in no position to harm anyone, he figured further. But old grudges, died hard—especially the type held against him.

His pistol permit was already in his wallet. Friends in the police department had helped him procure it during the first round of attempts on his life back in the 1980s. He had always carried it. This evening and over the next days, he decided, he would carry the permit's companion piece. Just for good measure. He clipped the loaded pistol to his belt on the left side. It was hidden beneath his suit jacket.

He heard the distinctive honk of Sarah's horn on the street below. He flicked out his light. Moments later, he was down the steps. When he hit the street again, he took precautions anew, stopping and looking both ways as he stepped out of his building.

He was amazed how quickly the old fears and instincts came back to him. He stepped into the car with her.

Sarah turned a few corners and was onto an access ramp of the new West Side Expressway. She drove assertively but with caution, gliding in and out of traffic, and moving northward to the calmer, greener counties beyond the limits of New York City.

Through it all, an eerie sense of quietude was upon Townsend, a sense that he recognized. It was roughly equivalent to the drop in barometric pressure that any human being can feel and which inevitably portends a storm.

S*ARAH STUART* eased her car from the highway onto a two-lane road north of Chappaqua. In the little that remained of the evening light, she drove through a stretch of orchards and old houses.

She had fallen silent over the past few minutes, but the dashboard radio softly played a piano concerto from New York's single remaining classical music station. As Sarah drove, Townsend instinctively attempted to memorize the directions:

Route 120 for twelve minutes at forty miles per hour. A right turn past a picket fence. Seven and a half minutes on an unmarked two-lane road. No houses. No signs indicating a town. Memorization proved difficult as the daylight died. He felt thirsty and supposed it was anxiety creeping upon him.

From the corner of his eye, he looked at her. He and Sarah spent many enjoyable hours together, though both would have admitted that theirs was a relationship more of convenience than passion.

He liked her and felt comfortable with her. He guessed she felt the same way, though he had never asked her. They had met a few years earlier at a press gathering at the Waldorf-Astoria. She had first told him that she was a stringer for a European press service based in London. Then later, when he tried to get her to be more specific, she revealed that her reports were features on art, books, theater, and films in the United States. Further, she had once written soft news and features in those fields for the *Washington Star*. Out of curiosity, he asked a friend who had worked on the *Star* whether he recognized her name. The friend confirmed that her byline had appeared there many times. Further snooping revealed that it still turned up with regularity in various European papers, frequently above stories that were translated.

To Townsend, it had barely mattered that she was on the cozy fringes of his own profession. Sarah had divorced a man named Stuart a few years earlier. Her former husband was an orthopedic surgeon who had dumped her for a graduate student from the University of Massacusetts. Sarah had a son by him named Andrew.

Andy was the one individual she liked to talk about. Andy went to one of the $17,000-a-year prep schools in Connecticut. "Sounds like your boy's old man is paying through the teeth for this one," Townsend said in good humor.

"My former husband is paying several times," Sarah said confidently.

Andy rowed on Lake Quinnipiac in the fall, played tennis in the spring, and maintained a B average, Sarah said. She had shown Townsend many photographs. During the most recent Christmas and spring vacations, he had even met Andy face to face. Understandably, if Sarah Stuart discussed anything personal at all, she was more intent on discussing her son than ever mentioning her ex-husband and his current twenty-five-year-old wife.

Sarah Stuart was, he observed quickly, financially very comfortable. She maintained an apartment in New York and had one in southern California as well. She divided her time between the two and spent it as she damned well saw fit. No one set a schedule for her, least of all any man. She only had one anchor: she made a point of being in the East, she said, when her son had his school vacations.

All of which fascinated Townsend. In her own way, she was her own person. She came and went from New York when she wished, did the same in California, and he knew that she would jet off to Europe for short visits with friends when that urge was upon her, too. And when she went to Europe, her news bureau paid and usually put her up in one of the better hotels. Townsend could tell by the matchbooks that were in evidence in her apartment upon her returns.

It was relatively recently—about eight months earlier—that they had become lovers, and it had been a chance sort of encounter. A few weeks after first introductions at the Waldorf, they had run into each other at a book party for a mutual friend who wrote a political column for the other Washington paper. They had been surprised to see each other there. They left after drinks. Townsend asked if she would join him for dinner. She did. He decided to splurge a little. They went to a trendy new Italian place in Chelsea.

The evening went well. He accompanied her home by taxi—she

maintained her apartment in the East Fifties—and was not surprised when she invited him up. She poured cognac liberally for both of them. Their interest in each other grew over the course of the evening. They soon found themselves commiserating about everything—newspaper publishing, crime in New York, national politics, and their former marriages. When the hour grew late, she asked if he wished to stay a little longer. He answered that he'd be pleased to stay, but he would be even more pleased to become her lover.

Perhaps it was the way he said it or because on that evening she was more receptive than she might have been on some other night. But the moment was right and her answer was yes, even if their affair began as a Well-why-not? sort of thing.

In the ensuing months, they did not behave like a pair of graduate students who had suddenly discovered sex and each other. Their relationship was both discreet and convenient. She might disappear for a week or two to any of her other venues. He might not call for several days. Then a telephone would ring. An unwritten, unspoken rule emerged between them, a recognition that they were both adults with many private facets of their lives—past, present, and future. Therefore, they would ask no questions that probed other relationships or where one or the other might have been recently. Townsend had no reason to think that she did not have other lovers in other places, or perhaps even another occasional man or two in New York. Nor, despite an occasional twinge of jealousy, did he have any grounds to object. But he never asked. He trained himself not to let it trouble him, and he made certain that he sought no significance or explanation from her undiscussed absences.

Sometimes he would get a post card by surprise, bearing cancellation marks from anywhere from Palm Beach to Rio de Janeiro to Paris. Sometimes she would call him upon her return. She would say, "I'm back," then not tell from where. He didn't inquire. What good would it do to know? What difference would it make to ask? In their time together, they guided their conversation to what they felt like telling each other.

"I'm back. *And* I've been thinking about you," she might say next. That generally meant that she'd been away, didn't feel like being home alone, and was building up some enthusiasm for an intimate dinner for two, then a night of good adult sex, no questions asked. After chronicling the dead all day, such a call always aroused him and came as a pleasant surprise.

Since the first night they had made love, they had seen each other maybe fifteen to twenty times. They would go to a movie or a play or out to dinner if one wanted an evening of companionship. They would call each other if either had an extra ticket to an event. The evenings were never planned far in advance, yet were always pleasant, in part due to their spontaneity. Most times the evening would end with sex. Sometimes it didn't, but there were never any hard feelings.

Sometimes Paul would initiate the physical part. Other times Sarah would. In a weird kind of way, he felt that they understood each other perfectly. He once found himself paraphrasing Robert Frost: "Good fences make good lovers." At other times, with only mild facetiousness, he thought of theirs as a perfect "nineties" relationship: convenient, limited, comfortable, and nonimpassioned, an economical blend of time, risk, and emotion.

Bizarre stuff, he thought further, compared to what he might have hoped for one day when he was twenty-five. His shattered marriage to Nora—and the fact that his daughter Emily was growing up in a single parent home—was, after all, the one deep and sincere regret of his life. But Paul Townsend had long since given up most things that were on the dream sheets of his youth. Besides, their relationship worked. And it was a nice part of his life, as he hoped it also was for her, even if she remained a bit of a cipher. With so much of any adult's life mired in failure, compromise, or disappointment, who was to say there was anything imperfect about what Sarah Stuart and Paul Townsend meant to each other?

After many minutes of silence, as her car continued through Westchester County, he spoke again. "Tell me," he asked, "are we close to our destination?"

"We're almost there," she said.

"Then how would you feel like giving me a little background? I don't know the first thing about your family."

"My father has had cancer for the last two years," she said after what seemed like several seconds. "He has other problems, too. Gout. Phlebitis. A deteriorating back."

"Where are we going? Is it a hospital?"

"He's come home to die," she said.

"Whose home?"

"His own. That's where we're going."

"Who takes care of him? Your mother?"

"She's deceased also. I'm his only family."

"Presumably a dying man is not waiting alone."

"We have nurses," Sarah answered. "Around the clock." She paused. "It won't be too much longer."

Too much longer. For a moment, Townsend thought she was talking about travel time. Then he realized she was talking about her father, and how long he had to live. Headlights appeared on the road behind them and threw light into their car. Townsend was instantly on edge. He felt his hand drifting to the firearm on his left hip. Sarah knew he carried a weapon occasionally. He wondered if Sarah had any idea he was carrying it now.

"My father is in his sixties and giving up," she continued. Her gaze was intent upon her rearview mirror. "Deteriorating eyesight. Horrible back pain. Feels sick all the time. How long do you think a man can go on like that?"

"It depends on what he might care to live for," Townsend said, distracted for a moment. Then his attention lapsed a second time as the bright beams from behind them swept away and disappeared. The vehicle must have turned off, he told himself, and no, they were not being followed.

"Obviously, your father has something important on his mind," Townsend said. "Do you have any idea what it is?"

"I know exactly what it is."

He gazed at her. The unwritten rule about asking questions edged before him. He lowered his window slightly and waited. She turned onto a wet winding two-lane road. A shower had come through and the smells of a late spring curled through the car window. They were within sight of houses again. Townsend sensed they were near their destination.

Then she looked squarely at him. "How's your memory these days, Paul?" she asked. "Do the names Igor Popov or Michal Goleniewski mean anything to you?"

"Oh, God," he answered. He felt confusion mingling with anger. "The names strike a distant chord."

"My father said they'd strike more than that," she answered.

Silently, Townsend folded his arms across his chest.

"How would you describe them?" she asked.

"The enigmas of another generation," he said, recalling, and as if that were the approproate starting point. "Popov and Goleniewski were Soviet intelligence officers. Each defected to the United States thirty-some years ago. Early 1960s, I think."

"My father wants to talk about it."

"Why?" he asked. "Who could give much of a damn in 1996 about a bunch of spooks from the Kennedy administration?"

"My father said you once wrote a long investigative report on the CIA. You covered a pair of Soviet defectors named Nosenko and Golitsin."

"Yeah. It was 1977, 1978. Thereabouts. Early in Jimmy Carter's administration. Back when a lot of new stuff was declassified under Stansfield Turner.

"Your article was published January 1977," she said. "I read it yesterday. My father showed me a clipping. You worked for the *Philadelphia Bulletin* back then." As she spoke, she made a sharp turn with the wheel of the car.

"I'm a little surprised by all this," he said.

"Why's that?"

"You and I have never talked much about my 'previous lifetime.' I thought you knew me only as an obit writer."

She laughed very softly.

"What's funny?" he inquired.

"Don't you think I might have heard of you?" she asked. "I mean, come on, Paul. Okay, so I wrote soft news. Might I not have heard of one of the better investigative reporters in New York? Don't you think someone might have read some of your stories?"

"Well," he answered with all honesty, "it's nice to know someone read them."

She laughed again, slightly less this time. "Remember much about the case?" she then asked after a suitable pause. "Popov and Goleniewski, I mean."

"It was a long, involved case and no one understood it," he said. "Nosenko and Golitsin were a pair of Soviet intelligence officers. About the same time as the two you just mentioned. Golitsin was a legitimate defection and Nosenko was a fake. Or maybe it was the other way around. I don't remember."

"Still have your notes?"

"I made a point of throwing them away. Many years ago."

"What a shame. Why'd you do that?"

"Most reporters working hard news destroy their notes," he said, surprised she didn't know. "That way they can't be subpoenaed."

"Oh," she said.

By now it was dark inside the car, aside from the dim green glow of the instrument panel. Sarah turned off the road and was on gravel. High trees ominously overhung a driveway. Dark hedges rose on each side of the car. Somewhere close by a major-league dog began barking furiously. Lights appeared, then the rear of a building. Next Townsend saw more lights and the outline of a large, rambling house.

The car stopped. Sarah Stuart cut the engine and the world suddenly was very quiet. She stepped out of the vehicle. Townsend did, also. In the fresh air he was conscious of wet young leaves ticking together. He glanced behind them to see if any other cars were following. He saw no one. They were alone. A breeze came up and a large hedge by the driveway murmured as if it were alive.

They entered the house through a sparsely furnished kitchen. Somewhere in the distance a television made its low, monotonous rumble. Sarah led him to a drawing room and he seated himself. Townsend noted the familiar surroundings: A desk in a corner with an unmatching wooden chair. An anonymous portrait on the wall and a pair of settees—one a deep green, the other a bluish print. No books. No photographs. No reading material. There was a fireplace which was remarkably clean. The room conveyed the sense of having been hastily assembled—no piece had any connection with any other. Then again, Townsend reasoned as he remained standing, it might have been that way for twenty years.

Sarah vanished for several minutes. Distantly, Townsend heard Sarah discussing something with the nurse. Then there was the sound of a door shutting. Townsend was still remarking on what to make of this when he heard voices again—that of Sarah and an older man. The voices approached until a door flew open.

Sarah wheeled an older, obviously ill man into the room. He wore pajamas and a heavy robe. His hands were bony and tremulous. His thin ankles disappeared into a heavy pair of slippers. He looked at Townsend with steady but anxious eyes.

"Ah." Townsend's host gave him a nod. "You've come." She had said that he was in his sixties. He looked a decade worse off than that, but Townsend assumed it was the disease.

"I've come," Townsend said politely.

"I'm grateful."

The man motioned to the settee with the print pattern, indicating that the reporter should sit. Townsend did.

"I read your stuff all the time," the man said in a voice that rasped. "I think you're a fine writer."

"I'm flattered."

"I liked the old investigative stuff, too," the man said. "Liked it even more, in fact."

"It seems to have gone out of style," Townsend answered.

"That, or you grew tired of being on the entire world's hit list," the old man said. He forced a laugh. "Tell me honestly. Which was it?"

"A bit of both."

"Tell the ugly truth and everyone hates you for it, right? Particularly the people you're trying to help," the man said.

Townsend gave him a grudging smile. "Let's just say that part of my career is over."

"We'll see," the man said. "Do you know me?" he asked.

Townsend looked at him carefully. "I don't recall ever seeing you before in my life."

"Did my daughter tell you anything about me? My name perhaps?"

"No more than that," Townsend answered.

"Well, that's good. That means we can start from the top." He glanced to her approvingly, but kept talking. "My name is Leonard Wolik," he began, "and I—"

"Dad . . . ?" Sarah said abruptly.

He turned sharply on her. "Now you hush, young lady!" he said with surprising vehemence. "We've had our discussion, you and I. I'm telling my story. All of it! Exactly how it happened!" He settled back. "You're not going to deny me my last wish, are you?" he asked.

Something strangely ominous hung between father and daughter. Then Sarah, looking exasperated, settled into a Queen Anne chair. She folded her arms and watched the conversation. "Good. That's my girl," her father said, calm again.

Townsend had no interpretation for the moment whatsoever.

"I worked in the State Department from 1959 until 1984," the dying man continued. "Started under an ornamental old general, ended under a senile second-lead movie star. And I've got a story to tell you. I hope you'll print it after I'm dead. But that will be your decision."

"Why are you telling it to me?" Townsend asked.

"I liked your investigative work," the man said. "Now I like your obituaries. Perfect blend." A flicker of another smile crossed the old man's face. "Plus, no one else in God's creation would print what really happened. I've got some of the inside dope on the *biggest goddamned secret of the 1960s!* Maybe the biggest security scandal of the cold war. A spy story and a political story. Of course, *you*'ll have to prove it. And fill in the missing pieces. So far, no one in my lifetime has the brass *cajones* to touch the story."

"Maybe I don't, either," Townsend said.

"Ha!" Townsend's host snorted. "Of course you will. You're a professional troublemaker."

"I'm a *retired* troublemaker. There's a difference."

"Oh, yes?" the old man snorted. "Then why print all those smart-assed obituaries if you don't like stirring things up a bit?"

"That's the style that's currently in vogue."

"Well, I'm currently terminally ill," the man shot back. "And I'm giving out a death-page notice that's going to stir things up quite a bit after I'm gone. So we're just made for each other, aren't we?"

For a moment, the sick man's gaze was frozen upon Townsend's. Townsend moved first, reaching into his jacket and withdrawing a small notebook of lined pages. Then he readied a felt-tipped pen.

Simultaneously, the man reached for a glass of water. Sarah's hand rested on her father's shoulder for a moment. He sipped with thin unsteady fingers and set the glass down again. From force of habit, Townsend studied him carefully.

"Let's not waste time," Townsend said at length. "I'm listening. Give me whatever you want. I'll use it as I see fit."

"That's all I'm asking," said the dying man.

Townsend settled his body backward into the settee and looked at the man before him. He felt his instincts as a reporter shift into an advanced gear.

Almost involuntarily, he sat back to listen.

<<<< **5** >>>>

*H*AD it begun thirty years ago? Forty? It was not Townsend's night for understanding guideposts in time. The man introduced as Leonard Wolik threw around names and dates as if they were last season's confetti. Within minutes, he'd made time spiral. They were back many springtimes ago when the world may have been more miserable but both were younger and presumably happier.

"I graduated from Columbia University with a degree in modern political systems, Mr. Townsend," Sarah's father explained. "May 1954. Cum laude. Got on a train to Washington, and got a job working for peanuts in Senator Pastore's office. Senator Pastore was a good man. He came from Rhode Island."

Townsend nodded, wondering where things were heading.

"I stayed with Senator Pastore's office for two years. Then I went back to Columbia to teach and earn a master of science in government. I took some time out in 1958 to volunteer for John F. Kennedy's final Senate campaign in Massachusetts. I loved Kennedy," he said with a pause. "I liked the man and I loved the fresh attitude he brought to government. I don't know if you'll ever see anything like that again," he said. "I know I won't."

Townsend muttered a few sympathetic words and nudged the dying man back on track.

Wolik had been fluent in German and French by the time he picked up a master's degree on Morningside Heights. He looked for another job in the federal government, aced the civil service test, and won an appointment as a junior foreign service officer.

"Naturally," the shaky voice continued, "since I knew two other languages well, the State Department sent me to school in Washington to learn a third: Spanish. Then I drew my first tour in Central America. They knew I could speak in all these languages. Now I had to prove that I could think in them."

Professing to see himself with a vantage point of many years, the old man described himself as a young Foreign Service officer with unlimited potential in a day when the cold war was as icy as ever. It was heady stuff. This was the era before equality in hiring had unlocked the white upper-middle-class male enclaves of the State Department to those who brought to the table none of those three impeccable attributes for advancement. If a sharp young diplomat had a touch of Camelot-era idealism sprinkled in, so much the better. Then the newspapers could call it "new style" or "Kennedy Era." They needed to call it something.

"So what dates are we now talking about?" Townsend asked. "Can you tell me exactly?"

"December 1960," came a very quick answer. "December third. That was the first day I went to work for Uncle Sam. I was one month shy of my twenty-ninth birthday. I remember it well."

Townsend busied himself with his pen.

"I got sent to Panama. Not exactly the beacon of enlightenment in the Western world. Spent most of my time listening to radio broadcasts from Cuba. Nineteen fifty-nine was the year Castro took over."

Townsend, remembering also, was nodding, but keeping quiet and not looking up.

"The whole Caribbean was reeling. All the islands were flooded with Cuban refugees. I was sitting in the embassy in Panama City, twenty-one months into my tour when the American navy was blockading Cuba."

Wolik did his two years in Panama City posted at a visa desk, stamping passports and deciding which Panamanians deserved to visit relatives in the United States and which did not.

"Washington was next," Sarah's father said. "Back then it was pretty much unavoidable: one of every three tours had to be stateside. So I drew Washington on my second two-year tour, which seemed okay at the time."

The higher-ups moved him into the political division, he said, and for the first half of his tour, he translated French into English for the upper reaches of the senior staff, coupled with snippets of advice. This was not glamour stuff. Then he spent twelve months as part of one of the new projects early in Lyndon Johnson's only elected term. He wrote theoretical papers concerning European policy toward Africa and Central America. They called it Post-Colonial Era Policy Studies, a name thought up by some of the Think Tank people serving during the J.F.K. years. Even those writing papers on it weren't sure such an era existed.

"I was dutifully at my desk in Washington in November 1963," he said hesitantly, "when I heard that President Kennedy had been murdered." The old man gave Townsend a look that suggested that he might take a diversion and go off for many hours on that topic alone. But then he maintained the course that he had obviously charted for the evening.

All in all, young Wolik had found it disheartening, the direction of his career as well as the permutations of history. Or so said the man before Townsend, in explaining the move.

"I figured I was wasting my time in the Foreign Service. So I tried for one of the better appointments next. Vienna, Paris, Rome, or London. If I didn't get what I wanted, I'd find a real job and stay in the States." He shrugged. "But I still had this hankering for some excitement."

Again, Townsend found himself nodding.

In August 1964, Wolik's posting assignment came back. He was on his way to Paris, effective October 1.

"Worse things could have happened to you," Townsend offered.

"Worse things did," came a quick response.

The mid-sixties were not an easy time in France, he recalled. Discontent with America was rampant. The *Parti Communiste Français* was the second largest Marxist party in Western Europe. The French had entertained an affinity for John F. Kennedy on account of his Catholicism and his captivating wife. But following the events of Dallas, anti-American graffiti had again become as common as *pissoires* throughout the city—and almost as fragrant. The old French people were silent. The young didn't remember the war and didn't want to hear about it.

"Hell!" Sarah's father raged. "Lyndon Johnson and Charles de Gaulle were no one's ideal dancing partners! Beyond blue jeans, Marlboros, le rock, and Coca-Cola, the French didn't care squat about anything American!"

Worse, the old man in the Elysée palace, *le grand Charles* himself, was making ominous noises about developing France's own *force de frappe* and withdrawing France from NATO. All in all, on some days for American businesspeople and diplomats, it bordered on hostile fire in a so-called friendly country.

Kennedy's ambassador to France, Kenneth Merriman, had served since J.F.K.'s inauguration in 1961. He was Harvard-educated and from a monied northeastern family. He was an intellectual, a former governor, and had experience in international diplomacy dating back to World War II. Even de Gaulle, who didn't like anyone, liked Ken Merriman. The ambassador was, in short, a man whom Democratic administrations always called on, and with both reason and success. Yet he was sixty-one years old in March 1964 and had stated privately that he wanted a few years of peace before he was too old to enjoy them.

Thus, Kennedy had received Merriman's resignation in September 1963, effective as soon as a successor could be found. The Secretary of State, Dean Rusk, had come up with a few names but had never settled on an actual successor with the President. Then, following the events of Dallas, Lyndon Johnson talked Merriman into remaining at his post until Johnson could find his own candidate. As an interim measure, and out of apparent loyalty to his country during a crisis, Merriman agreed to remain.

But by February 1965, Merriman was insistent. His sixty-third birthday was on the horizon. Then when his daughter became engaged Merriman shuttled back and forth between Paris and Washington. He was overseeing the wedding plans, some said. Others took a more cynical view, claiming that Merriman couldn't tolerate his future son-in-law, a brash young Texan, and was trying to torpedo the nuptials. In any event, the marriage went on.

Privately, he also told Dean Rusk he was not returning to France. Enough was enough. In the American diplomatic structure in France, this left an obvious space at the top.

"L.B.J. filled the void with a void of his own," the old man said. "When Ambassador Merriman went home in February 1965, his place was taken by an acting ambassador, a buffoon known to all of us as Colbert Davies. Davies was from Houston. Johnson followed a blue-blood like Kenneth Merriman with a loud, obnoxious cowboy in a ten-gallon hat."

Townsend grinned. Yes, that sounded like Johnson. Off to the side, Sarah rolled her eyes in displeasure over something.

In Paris, the story went, ten-gallon chapeau or not, Colbert Davies appeared deeply in over his *tête*.

"Johnson might have done him a larger favor," the retired diplomat remarked, "by confiscating his passport. He might have done all of us that favor."

On the day he arrived, Colbert Davies seemed to know four words of French—*oui, non, jamais,* and something which didn't seem to be any of the other three. Nonetheless, Davies threw around all four interchangably. He liked to attend diplomatic functions and ogle the wives of the other European diplomats, paying particular attention to their breasts, which he always seemed to be appraising when he spoke to them.

But aside from that, Davies hated the food, found the French people rude and disagreeable, and generally found dealing with foreigners to be the worst part of the Foreign Service. Within the embassy walls, things weren't much better. Davies fought daily with the career State Department people on his own staff.

"We called him 'Lyndon's Man,'" Townsend's host said. "The perfect, one hundred percent uncouth appointment by an uncouth American President."

Townsend was now writing extensive notes.

"Davies had no vision and was monumentally untalented at following instructions from Washington," the man said. "What kind of diplomat does that sound like to you? No instinct of his own and unable to act on anyone else's initiative. Davies only had two qualifications for his post. First, he was Johnson's friend. Well, hell. Most Texans in the government had had the foresight to contribute heavily to L.B.J.'s reelection in 1964—even if they were politically more tuned in to Goldwater. But second, Davies was said to have been promised Paris only briefly: a year or two. He wanted enough time to transact some business and then go home. That seemed to be satisfactory to everyone."

The "business," according to Sarah's father, was petroleum wholesaling. Davies told people that he had been a wildcatter in Texas in his youth and now presided over HOCO, the Houston Oil Co., a small independent oil drilling and producing outfit.

Paris in the mid-sixties was perfect to strike up friendships with Arab interests from Benghazi and Tripoli. Several Libyan producers kept expensive flats and mistresses along the Avenue Foch. Davies was courting the Libyans, who were pro-West at the time, and was angling for joint ventures in North Africa.

But as the tale rambled forward, Townsend edged toward another conclusion about Colbert Davies. Lurking beneath the narrative was the suggestion that there was more to Colbert Davies than met the eye. Davies, for example, must have been a deceptively shrewd judge of character and ability, particularly among the younger Foreign Service employees assigned to the embassy. Over the ensuing weeks, Davies fell into many lengthy political and philosophical conversations with the young Wolik.

"Come in here, young man!" Colbert Davies liked to roar. "Come in and bounce some ideas off me." Usually, Davies would close an office door with a deft swipe of a boot.

"I figured he was trying to keep away from a major diplomatic gaffe between the time he arrived and the time he could be confirmed. 'Bounce some ideas,' " the old man said, heavy with sarcasm. He seemed to mock Davies's memory with a suggestion of Davies's booming Lone Star speech patterns.

"The trouble was," he continued with a grimace, "one might just as soon have written the ideas on an orange, set Davies's head at the center of a target, clown-in-the-amusement-arcade style, and thrown it at his nose. It would have been an altogether better way to bounce ideas off him."

"You were that impressed with his intellectual baggage," Townsend said.

"That impressed! Davies didn't care about diplomacy. No aptitude. No insight. Why not just court his Libyan friends directly? Was the prestige of the ambassador's office that valuable? *Why was Colbert Davies there?"*

Townsend shrugged. "You said Davies was Johnson's friend," Townsend offered. "Maybe he was there partially as a favor."

"That was the spin I had on it for a long time, also," the old man said thoughtfully. He paused to consume another half glass of water. Sarah, who had been very still, rose, refilled her father's glass, and quietly sat down again.

"Maybe Davies harbored the fantasy that if he sat astride of some great diplomatic triumph he would gain in his own career," the old man suggested. "Yet the politics of the embassy overwhelmed him. How is he going to preside over an *entente cordiale* for postwar Europe when he can't even talk the per diem secretaries from the political section into taking shorthand for the USIA people?"

All that seemed true, that is, until a day in April of the same year,

1965, when Davies enticed the young Wolik even deeper into diplomatic quicksand.

Wolik was not a bad compliment to the acting ambassador. Wolik was young and bright. The ambassador struck no one as either. Wolik had no inside pull. Davies had the right amount and seemed in a position to develop more. When Davies felt in the mood to talk ideas with Wolik, the younger man would do it on the Q.T. No one else in the embassy ever knew what was discussed. Wolik never repeated anything.

"It was a time," the former Foreign Service officer said, "in which strings could blatantly be pulled. Do favors for the right mentor, be circumspect, and the next thing you know you've shot up three grades in the Foreign Service virtually overnight."

Townsend nodded. He continued to fill the notepad on his lap.

"What you're saying," Townsend said, gently chiding his host, "was that you were a co-conspirator. Davies was in over his head, but you were helping him get on with his job."

"Exactly! But Colbert Davies was my boss, after all. And I wasn't out to sabotage my superior, my employer, or my country. I wouldn't do something like that." He drew a breath. "Ever hear of a man named Alexi Zarudni?"

Townsend said he hadn't.

"I'd never heard the name, either, up until April 15, 1965," he said. "I remember the date clearly. We had a flood of Americans coming into the embassy to apply for extensions to their American tax returns. Every time you looked up there was someone with a polyester necktie asking directions to the IRS office." And that was precisely the day when Colbert Davies set Leonard Wolik on a course that would change his life.

Davies turned up in the younger man's office toward ten in the morning. That was unusual in itself. Normally the acting ambassador summoned a lesser employee to his own suite of offices. But this day would be very different.

The acting ambassador arrived in Wolik's office in shirtsleeves, looking as if he'd been up a good part of the night. He pushed the door half shut before he said a word.

"I wonder if you'd come with me at noon today," Davies asked. "I've got something I want you to see and hear. You can't tell anyone about it. When it's finished, it's very possible that it will never have had happened. Roger, son?"

Wolik blinked twice and admitted that, no, it wasn't Roger, at least not completely. So Davies knocked the door shut with one of those boots and expanded on the day's agenda.

Davies asked Wolik to leave work at a quarter hour before noon that day and proceed to the Métro stop at Place de la Concorde. He was to take a train in the direction of Neuilly, but get out after two stops and wait on the platform. Let a train or two go by. Make damn well sure no one was trailing him, Davies instructed, and then reverse his direction, return to Place de la Concorde and take the Mairie d'Issy line to Sèvres-Babylone. Wolik was to come up the steps, walk to the corner where the Boulevard Raspail intersected with St. Germain and wait. A car would pick him up.

"It all seemed awfully melodramatic," Sarah's father said as she kept a watchful eye upon him. "I asked who'd be in the car. Where would it take me? Davies told me not to worry. He was acting officially. But I demanded to know what this was about."

"So what did he say?" Townsend asked.

"He said he had a Ruskie—that was the term he used—who wanted to defect to the West. But before he brought in the CIA station in Paris, he wanted my opinion. He wanted to see if I thought his pigeon was telling the truth." He paused. "He also told me that I didn't have to get involved, if I didn't want to. If the defection blew up in his face I might want to be clean of it."

"But I assume you went?" Townsend said.

"Naturally, I went! It's as if you were happily married and in love with your wife. But what if you could go to bed with Brigitte Bardot? Wouldn't most men sneak off for an overnight?"

"I suppose most would," Townsend said. For a moment, he felt Sarah Stuart's eyes assessing him.

The old man grinned and seemed charged up again.

A few minutes before noon that same April 15, Wolik did exactly as instructed. He left the embassy and boarded the Métro. He went to the stop at the Avenue Franklin D. Roosevelt, waited for two trains and reversed himself. He kept watch of the time. It was twenty-two minutes after noon when he stood at the corner of Raspail and St. Germain. He waited seven more minutes. A white Peugeot 303 with an Avis sticker on its rear bumper came by, stopped abruptly, and jerked slightly to the curb. The man at the wheel leaned over and rolled down a window.

"Thanks, son!" Colbert Davies yelled. "You alone?"

Through his years in the Foreign Service, Wolik had never before seen an ambassador personally drive anything anywhere, much less serve as a chauffeur, much less drive a shaky stick shift. So for a moment Wolik stared in disbelief.

"I'm alone," Wolik finally answered.

"Then get in, son!" Davies said in a deafening bellow that was barely audible above the rumble of traffic. "Let's move!"

Very tentatively, Wolik stepped into the car. The Peugeot's tires squealed even as Wolik was closing his door.

Davies was an atrocious driver, unable to master the standard shift, not fast enough to navigate the busy boulevards, and not daring enough to slip through the tight Parisian side streets. At least once Davies appeared lost, but Wolik knew better than to ask.

"Back home in Texas," Davies proclaimed, "we don't use eyeglasses to drive. We have our windshields ground to our prescription."

Davies grinned. Wolik was young and impressionable and wasn't sure for several seconds whether Davies was joking.

Somehow fifty minutes later, they had found their way into a warren of back streets just north of Père-Lachaise cemetery. Davies was a man with a mission now, ditching the car onto a sidewalk and hurrying Wolik to follow in his wake.

Davies barged into a small café on the rue de la Réunion. A waiter asked them something in French which Davies didn't acknowledge. Wolik began to answer, but the Texan surged directly toward a table within a booth at the rear of the room.

A single man was seated alone at the booth. He had an excellent view of the door, as well as quick access to a service exit. He had been watching the two Americans since they had entered. Even now, he seemed to be simultaneously looking at them and staring past them, waiting to see who might follow.

The man was massive, barrel-chested, large-armed, and ominous. He had a huge, battered, frowning face and a high forehead with two large scars. He sat in an ugly bluish-gray cloud of his own cigarette smoke, occupying the entire side of a banquette intended for two. There was a large empty coffee cup in front of him and an untouched glass of water. A half-smoked pack of Gitanes lay near the water. A crumpled empty pack was near a full ashtray. Across his lap, Wolik noticed with a sudden kick in his own chest, was a pistol. Wolik assumed it was loaded.

Davies eased Wolik into a seat across from the Russian. Davies followed, sitting next to the younger man. "It's all right," Davies whispered, "I know he's armed. He has to be."

Young Wolik, his cheeks flush at the café table, gave a dumb nod.

"It was the first time in my life," the speaker recalled to Townsend, "that I ever felt ill at ease sitting with my back to a door. Then again, I was facing a gun for the first time, too."

Townsend openly empathized with the feeling.

"This is Alexi Zarudni," Davies said routinely, initiating the conversation. "Alexi says he would like to live in America."

"How nice," Wolik managed feebly.

"I felt this Russian's eyes boring into me the whole time," the sick man said. "I was so damned nervous that I broke a sweat. I remember that I offered my hand. You know, for a handshake. As if I were at a Kiwanas meeting. The Russian stared at my right hand for two minutes before he accepted it with his left."

"So who was he?" Townsend asked. "And what did he want?"

This part, too, was embedded in memory, complete with past history.

Zarudni had been known to the CIA since April 1957 when he had made an attempt to defect to the British in Helsinki. Zarudni had been listed as a minor consular official. But in reality he had been the second ranking Soviet KGB official in Scandinavia. In return for £20,000 (negotiable) and lifetime asylum (nonnegotiable), Zarudni had been prepared to deliver to NATO an index of rocket sites across northern Russia, as well as a complete up-to-date classified directory of Soviet air defenses ringing the Arctic Circle. Since the defenses had been carefully hidden under the snowy landscape of the tundra, there were those in the West who were ready to talk deal.

When Zarudni had first contacted the British, he had taken precautions. He had not revealed his actual identity, merely dangling the bait in a message to a British political officer. He had asked that any affirmative response be signaled by an inquiry for a tourist visa directed to a Comrade Suslov in the Soviet Embassy in Helsinki. Predictably, there was no Suslov in Helsinki, but correspondence to the fictitious comrade would eventually cross Zarudni's desk. Moreover, he insisted that any internal British communication about the offer travel back to London by diplomatic pouch. The Soviets—Zarudni insisted—had deciphered much of the British microwave traffic throughout Scandinavia.

Zarudni went back to his post in the Soviet consulate, walked on eggs, and waited. A day went by. Then another. The British dithered for forty-eight hours, tried to assess the value of the intelligence to be received vis-à-vis its cost, and then alerted Washington through their SIS liaison with the CIA. Only then was an inquiry made to Comrade Suslov on the availability of a visa for a visiting English scholar. But by this time the offer in Helsinki had disappeared completely.

At first, conventional wisdom dictated that the defector must have been shot, then entombed in concrete in the embassy cellar. But no staffers had vanished from the Helsinki complex. Clearly, whoever had been set to jump had developed cold feet.

There were unanswerable questions posed both in London and Washington. Why would such a promising source go cold? Similarly, Langley analysts asked why the British had taken two days to alert the Americans. At the time, the Americans and the British blamed each other, politely in person, then bitterly behind each other's back. Years later, the botched Helsinki defection remained an official mystery. But in Paris with Davies and Wolik, Zarudni had explained how it had looked from his end.

"Three days after I make the offer, extra state security people arrive from Moscow and question everyone," the Russian had snarled to the two Americans. "Routine, they say. Nothing routine! Obvious leak through British government!"

Zarudni remained quite incensed. He had ducked the bullet—literally—only by being in charge of on-sight security in Helsinki. The Soviet presence had been a large one there—by western estimates, almost a hundred apparatchiks. There were perplexing questions in Moscow, in other words, just as in London and Washington: intelligence analysts in all three places kept scanning the list of names at the USSR's Finnish outpost.

Nonetheless, Zarudni was aided by the large number of suspects as well as by personally inaugurating a mini-reign of terror among Soviet embassy personnel. Eventually, he produced as scapegoats a couple of informers from the Finnish underworld. He had concluded business with them and would sleep easier knowing that they would be completely silent in the future. So, once he received a green light from Dzerzhynski Square, he sent local housekeeping to remove them from the active list.

But Zarudni had learned his lessons. He would lay low for a few years, never trust the British again, and never deal with the poor whites of any embassy staff. This time in 1965 he was defecting directly to the United States ambassador. Or, as he'd discovered the previous Thursday, when he'd made his initial pitch to Davis at an art gallery opening on the Avenue Bosquet, the *acting* ambassador, Mr. Colbert Davies.

Zarudni sounded like a man anxious to deal. He ran through his life's history: parents, schooling in Minsk, a Red Army armored division on the German front in World War II, postwar recruitment by the NKVD, training, a lousy marriage, promotion within Soviet intelligence, and access to classified files. Zarudni revealed his work names and cover names with which he'd traveled. He'd spent time in a KGB travel bureau around 1956 and could pinpoint where fake passports were made abroad. He had lists from many cities, from Cairo to Jakarta to Chicago and Montreal. Elaborating, he rambled through a discussion of letter boxes, safe houses, legmen, dead drops, and fronts around Paris.

Then he emptied his pockets and showed off his overnight travel kit. There were two recessed fountain pens. One was a mini-transmitter. The other fired a twenty-two-caliber bullet. He also had a tape recorder built inside a cigarette box and—Wolik's personal favorite—a camera concealed inside a Zenith pocket radio, Made in USA.

"Wait till Ambassador Merriman hears about all this!" Davies kept saying, shaking his head like a real yokel. Zarudni remained in the midst of a carcinogenic cloud of tobacco smoke during this entire time, continually lighting a new cigarette with the glowing butt of a dying one.

"In retrospect," the old man told Townsend, "I've learned a little about the state of the espionage arts in 1965. None of this stuff was custom built. But it was the newest stuff on the line. I was going crazy just looking at it."

"But the Russian wasn't there to present a hardware exposition, I assume," Townsend said.

"Not at all. And Zarudni wasn't fooling around with small potatoes like air defense sites, either. He told the ambassador that all the 1957 information had somehow been compromised to the West, anyway. But this time he said he had something big. Really *big:* the inside scoop on something that could rock U.S.–Soviet relations well into the next century."

He hadn't just spent the last few years in Paris trimming his toenails and contemplating the nudes at the art galleries, Zarudni had boasted. In 1962, he had been promoted to one of KGB Chief Yuri Andropov's top assistants abroad. For this task he had been assigned the work name of Voltaire, a surprisingly whimsical allusion to his geographical placement.

He remained a cultural attaché. By day, he coordinated visits by Soviet artists—musicians, dancers, writers, and painters—to France, and organized lectures at the French universities on Marxist theory or Soviet culture. By night, he sat by a receiver at a safe house in Clichy and captured the high-speed high-frequency squirts that came by microwave from the United States. Zarudni would decipher, write an opinion, and ship a transcript to Moscow by the next day's diplomatic pouch on Aeroflot. This way the microwave traffic was never subject to an intercept because the Americans were looking for it in the skies above Moscow. The CIA didn't know it was stopping in Paris on the way back to Mother Russia.

All this time, Zarudni said, he was assisting Andropov, and helping perpetrate the greatest operation against the West that had ever taken place. But he was also taking notes and keeping a separate diary of everything that had happened. This book was half of his ticket to the west. The other half was a pamphlet which he'd put together on his trips back to the Soviet Union. But he had it complete and he was ready to deal.

The pamphlet was an internal memorandum of the KGB, he said, a thirty-six-page pamphlet which he'd smuggled out of the Soviet Union page by page. It was directly above the signature of Yuri Andropov, later to be chairman of the Communist party and Soviet leader in the final spasm of Marxist excess in the pre-glasnost "evil empire" days of the early 1980s.

There were five of these pamphlets in existence, Zarudni had claimed, and he had constructed a sixth to bargain his way to the west. The pamphlet was nothing less than a report to Chairman Khrushchev on the highest penetration of Western intelligence since Kim Philby. There had been several major defections to the West between 1958 and 1965, Zarudni reminded his audience, starting with Igor Popov, a Russian, in 1953, and continuing with Michal Goleniewski, a Pole in 1959. Most of these were actual defections. But at least one was a Soviet provocation—a KGB trick designed to lead western intelligence into a wilderness of disinformation. The problem was, much of Western analysis of Soviet policy through the 1960s and 1970s had stemmed from the existing analysis of these defectors.

"He claimed that the previous defections all fit into one overall pattern, and that Western intelligence had missed the biggest point. It was staring the CIA in the face," the old man said. "Yet for all their computers, for all their Ivy-educated 'experts' on the Soviet bloc, they still weren't on to the biggest intelligence scam of their time. And yet it was within their possession and Zarudni could lead them to it."

"Maybe someone was sitting on it," Townsend suggested.

"Zarudni indicated that the subject was too explosive. If it were known, there was no way anyone could keep a lid on it."

"Then how could it have been missed?" Townsend asked.

"Zarudni said the west missed it because the *key* to the whole picture hadn't been located. And that's what he had. His information would prove which defectors were credible. His defection would put the previous four defectors in perspective."

"What would make you believe him?" Townsend asked.

Sarah was using a linen handkerchief to remove sweat from her father's hairline. He gamely stayed with his story.

"I was skeptical at the time, too," he said. "But Zarudni must have had something, considering what happened next."

"Which was what?"

"I never saw his material," the dying man explained. "And I never saw the Russian again, either. And for that matter, Colbert Davies was recalled in another ninety-six hours as well."

"What?"

Davies and Wolik concluded that Zarudni needed to be passed on to higher authorities. Zarudni was yammering for money and a decision, but it wasn't Davies's function to come up with either. Thus circumstances forced Davies to expand the audience.

They had a direct phone circuit in the embassy in Paris called the Red Line, open to the State Department twenty-four hours a day. It was fabulously expensive, and the unwitting American taxpayers were footing the bill without a squawk.

"The Red Line was thought to be secure, but you never knew," the old man said. "Colbert Davies wanted to call in to Washington. I urged him to put everything in writing, instead. We finally constructed it predawn on the morning of April 16, 1965 and it went out before one P.M., Paris time."

" 'Constructed?' You mean, wrote?" Townsend asked, glancing up.

"Colbert Davies couldn't write an effective extortion note, much less an accurately detailed memo," Sarah's father said. "So who do you think actually wrote the letter? *I* did. What do you think young State Department people did in those days, other than keep the higher-ups from shooting themselves in the foot?"

Wolik wrote a ten-page memorandum of what he had seen and heard. Its contents were kept from the rest of the Paris staff. "Davies had a sense of the dramatic," the story continued. "So he directed our memo all the way to the top."

"To the Secretary of State?" Townsend said.

The man nodded. "The memo was confirmed 'RECEIVED—ADVICE TO FOLLOW IN 24 HOURS.' " He paused. "Next, silence. Two solid days of the most damnable silence I'd ever experienced."

Then Davies was in his office when all hell broke loose. Someone way up high in the nosebleed section of the State Department was on the Red Line. Davies was fired. He was to get his act out to Orly, get on a Pan Am jet at one o'clock that day, and get back to Washington. He was to discuss nothing.

"They even had assigned a couple of our own security people to watch him," said Sarah Stuart's father.

"What are you talking about?"

"Marine guards. I've never seen anything like it. They were acting directly on Johnson's orders as Commander-in-Chief. Davies was to get out to the airport and onto that airplane *without communicating with anyone.* And the marines were ordered to enforce the command."

The sick man had a distant look in his eyes for a moment, then flashed back to his story. "There was this one kid marine. Billy Hamilton. He was a lance corporal. He was totally in awe of what he was doing. Here he was, twenty-two years old, and he was baby-sitting a U.S. ambassador on the orders of the President."

Townsend furiously made notes through this part.

"But here's the best kicker," the man said. "Who came through the main embassy gates just as Davies was on his way out? Kenneth Merriman, looking fit and refreshed, even though his daughter had married some ambitious jerk. Merriman was back in the saddle by evening that same day. He'd been in the air over the Atlantic just as the lynch mob was forming for Davies."

"But Merriman had been trying to retire for months," Townsend protested. "That's what you just told me."

"Something brought him back in one hell of a hurry. Just as fast as Davies was being scuttled."

Townsend thought about it, looking up and ceasing to write. "Was an explanation offered?" he asked.

"They said President Johnson had again prevailed upon Ambassador Merriman to return. *'L'homme indispensable,'* we were to think. Lyndon's *real* man. Johnson had claimed that there was pressing business in the embassy. That's poppycock, of course. The only business was routine. No reason to make such a dramatic shift. So there must have been some very nonroutine business that none of us knew about."

"Were embassy staffers suspicious?" Townsend asked.

"Suspicious? Well, sure. But, there must have been a hundred forty of us in that station, plus the CIA people and the USIA people. And one isn't supposed to gossip." The old man paused for a moment. "But, understand this: I may have been the *only one* aside from Colbert Davies who knew about Zarudni. And obviously, Colbert Davies never told. A man of honor, in a way, particularly for a big, crude guy." Townsend caught Sarah rolling her eyes as her father spoke. "He warned me I didn't want to be part of whatever was going on. Then he kept me out of it."

"Your name wasn't on the memo that went to Washington?"

"Colbert Davies signed it."

"Didn't it look like someone else's work back in Washington? They thought Davies was capable of drafting that memo himself?" Townsend was amused.

"I guess so," the man said. "No one ever came by to ask me the time of day."

Townsend thought for a moment. "And you never communicated with Davies again?"

"Never dared while I worked for the State Department. I figured it could damage my career."

"It very well might have," Townsend allowed.

"I stayed in government for a full twenty-five years," he said proudly. "Made a career of it and took my pension. Served all over the world. Did my last tour in Spain twelve years ago in 1984."

"So? The big question?" Townsend asked at length. "Zarudni? The defector. Or should I say, the would-be defector?"

"Well, that's the rest of it. Comrade Zarudni. Never saw him again, or any of his material."

"At all?"

"At all," the old man confirmed. He scratched a scaly patch of skin on his cheek. "I do know that a week later, curiosity was upon me. So I went to a kiosk and called the Soviet consulate. Asked for Comrade Zarudni. Just wanted to hear his voice."

"And?"

"The first time I called there was a long pause. Then a voice wanted to know who was calling. I claimed I was a promoter who wanted to know about a Soviet violinist. There was another long pause—an *eternity.* Six, seven minutes. The unidentified voice came back. Said Comrade Zarudni was indisposed. So I called back a day later. The same voice asked sharper questions and wouldn't put me through. Said to call back in two days. I did. Some security hood came on the phone and told me there was no Alexi Zarudni. Never had been. Then they put me through to a Comrade Yarmitov. Yarmitov claimed he'd been the chief cultural attaché for several years."

"But he hadn't been. Obviously," Townsend said.

"Sure as I'm sitting here." He paused, fatigue wearing him down. He skipped a beat. "I even ran a little test on Yarmitov. I asked if we'd be seeing *Boris Godunov* in Western Europe that spring. Yarmitov said he would check to see if Comrade Godunov was making concert appearances. Some cultural attaché."

Townsend glanced to Sarah. She lowered her gaze.

"I never saw either of them again," her father continued. "Davies or Zarudni. Disappeared off the face of this earth, that's what they did." He concluded hesitantly. "I did hear things through the grapevine, though." He paused again, this time for several seconds. "See, I had a close friend who was in the CIA station at the embassy. His name was

Bruce McMorris. You know, we'd get together for drinks . . . I'd hear things."

Townsend had a long list of names. He added this one. Sarah watched him write.

"Was McMorris a young man?" Townsend asked. "Old?"

"Younger than I was. In his twenties at the time."

"And what did he tell you?"

He hesitated for a moment, then delivered. "The same day as Davies was recalled to the U.S., an unscheduled Soviet plane left Orly," he said. "Crew of six. But only three passengers. The centerpiece was a man on a stretcher. 'Returning to the USSR for medical treatment,' they said. 'Heart attack.' Rubbish! They sent their sick to western hospitals and everyone knew it. And the two 'doctors' who 'escorted' him? CIA recognized them. They were a couple of the tough boys in leather jackets whom you used to see standing near doors at diplomatic functions."

There was a long silence as Townsend's host stared straight at him. "But that," he said, "wasn't the strangest part. The Russians used to do that to their own people all the time," he said. "What was stranger still was Colbert Davies."

"How?"

"I tried to get in touch with him many years later—around 1985 or '86, after I'd retired from the State Department. I felt things had been left unfinished. If nothing else, I wanted to thank him for keeping me clean. I suspected that I'd had a successful career as a diplomat primarily thanks to his keeping my name off the official accounts of what happened in Paris in 1965. Trouble was, there *was* no Colbert Davies."

"What?" Townsend asked. Sarah, sitting to one side, appeared particularly uncomfortable with what followed.

"Went through the State Department and their records," the man said. "Sued under the Freedom of Information Act. Went through every telephone book in Texas. Contacted everyone anyone had ever heard of in the oil business. Phoned people in the Foreign Service whom I hadn't spoken to in years. No Colbert Davies. No one existed under that name. Never had. His whole cover. The oil business, the friendship with Johnson, the whole story was a fabrication. And God knows what sort! Lyndon's Man, huh? I do know I never figured it out."

Sarah's father took a long final pause, drew a breath, and went for his conclusion.

"Anyone can be traced," Townsend said. "Dead or alive."

"Think so?" It was said as a challenge.

"I do it for a living all the time," Townsend said.

"I'm a dying man, Mr. Townsend," the host said. "I've always liked your work. If this is of any interest to you, it's my gift. If not, thank you for coming. You've eased things for a dying man, just being able to tell my story."

The old man looked to his daughter. He offered Townsend a hand in trust and friendship as well as in parting. Mildly stunned, Townsend rose to take it. Moments later Sarah summoned the nurse and they removed the dying man from the room.

It was two A.M. and the sky was dark. In Sarah's car, where she and Townsend rode otherwise in silence, the music on the radio yielded to the morning news. Senator John Roosevelt Lord had won 22 percent of New York delegates in the Democratic primary. He also finished second in the Republican primary. In certain districts of Kings and Queens counties in New York City, in the suburbs of Rockland and Orange, and—incredibly—in Erie, Cayuga, St. Lawrence, Renssalaer, Chenago, and Warren counties upstate John Lord had takan a majority of votes cast. He had done all this on write-in votes. And he had done all this as a show of strength since he was running with his own USA party, anyway.

"Racist dickhead," Townsend mumbled in fatigue and irritation. The announcer on the radio continued with a fatal stabbing outside a nightclub on East 53rd Street.

"What?" Sarah asked, not hearing Townsend clearly.

"Senator Lord," Townsend repeated.

"Your newspaper treats him very kindly," she said.

"On the *Sun,* all I do is bury the dead. I don't write the editorials and I sure don't formulate official newspaper policy."

"You're a little testy about it, aren't you?"

"I'm tired," he said. It sounded like an apology, but it wasn't.

Sarah didn't answer, but he let the subject drop—too tired to dwell too long on Lord and all those who sailed with him. He had been awake now, he calculated idly, for twenty hours. Through a wall of exhaustion, he could feel how slowly his own mind was working. Four-fifths of an entire day, he reasoned slowly. Awake for twenty hours straight.

He thought back to times as a teenager when he'd done such things as a matter of course. He thought of times in the infantry in Viet Nam when he'd been awake for three days straight, with a little help from some speedballs in his backpack. He'd even thought of times as a young reporter when he'd done doorstep duty for a full day or two at a time, looking for a quote or a comment from someone barricaded inside his home.

He closed his eyes and later realized he must have slept for several minutes, because the next thing he knew, Sarah Stuart had pulled to the curb before his building on West 98th Street. He blinked awake.

"You're home," she said.

"Yeah," he said. "Home." He fought hard to become alert.

He looked at his building and he looked back at Sarah. There was—miraculously—an open parking space in front of his building. "What do you think?" he asked. "Want to come up?"

"For the night?"

"For the night."

"Not this time," she said. "Okay?"

"Okay."

He leaned to her and kissed her.

"Let me know if I can do anything else," he said. "For you or your family."

"Thank you. I appreciate it."

He stepped out of the car to the curb. He glanced across the empty fluorescent-lit sidewalks that flanked him, ever alert for urban danger. He glanced to the dark face of his building, then leaned down to talk before closing the door.

"It's your decision what to use," she said. "I'll stay in touch."

"Do that," he said. He gave her a final nod and closed the car door. Then he watched her car pull away before he entered his building.

In his apartment several minutes later, Townsend stood at his living-room window, staring down at the street, sipping from a bottle of cold beer. He tried mightily to put the events of the day in order.

Someone had blown up his car. Someone had done a sloppy job, because Townsend hadn't been in the car at the time. The "someone" was presumably a malicious echo from the past—an incompetent with a long, simmering grudge.

Simultaneously, his occasional lover had come forth with her father, who had provided text for his own death notice. The old man had provided a story that would be difficult to confirm and which also was, at best, a smaller detail of a larger canvas.

Townsend sipped again and thought.

Down below on the street a panel truck pulled to the curb and turned its light off. But no one stepped out. Events such as this troubled Townsend. What was the occupant or occupants of the truck embarked upon? A mugging? A murder? A tryst with a prostitute in the vehicle's cargo area?

After fifteen minutes, the driver of the truck rolled down his window and threw a brown bag, a sandwich wrapper and two soda cans, onto the sidewalk. Then he rolled up the window, put his lights on again, and sped away.

For some reason that he couldn't define, Townsend was relieved when the truck departed. Then he stood very still, listened hard, and could hear absolutely nothing other than a distant, occasional rumble of traffic on the nearby avenues.

Townsend finished his beer and drew his shades. He began turning off lights in his apartment. He removed from his belt the pistol that he had carried and returned it to the safe.

But, reverting to an old habit, he left the safe's doors open by the bed. It would be a quick reach to the loaded pistol if he needed it. He had practiced the move in the dark many times.

Then Townsend showered and settled into bed. He read a book for a few minutes, then turned out his light. He lay very quietly, listening to the pace of his own heartbeat as his eyes grew accustomed to the dark. Then he closed them.

Already, by force of habit, he was wondering who might have died overnight.

< < < < **6** > > > >

*I*T was barely past nine the next morning and Townsend was alone. He sat in his office at the *Sun*. Understandably, he was more tired than usual. But, as was his habit, he was once again attempting to find perspective—or at least order—in several lives other than his own.

Each day scores of men and women die in any American city. In New York, there are hundreds. A small percentage are considered important enough to be noted in the newspapers. On this morning, locally in New York, Townsend had a music teacher, a labor lawyer, a former air traffic controller, and a former Top 40 AM-radio personality who'd been popular in the seventies. The latter had been known by the name of Jim Arnold. Arnold, forty-eight, had committed suicide by hanging in a motel room. Interesting angle, but grim.

Then, from farther afield, off the international wire services, Townsend pulled a poorly written account of a former East German Communist leader who had died in prison. He marked it for a more thorough rewrite. His morgue files could give him some more background, one of the *Sun*'s international reporters could give him some perspective, and maybe he could scare up a quote from a senator or congressman. Townsend penciled in seven inches on the left side of the page. The corrupt old Red was finally good for something.

Additionally, an acrobat from the Barnum & Bailey Circus had died of head injuries after being hit by a car in Boston ten days earlier. Good for two columns wide and four inches long on the right side of the page. The acrobat had played in New York many times. To those who followed the circus, he was well-known. The wife of a noted Rolls Royce dealer had succumbed after a long battle with leukemia. Townsend sighed. He knew the woman's brother. He made a note in his personal datebook to send a letter of condolence. But—in a macabre sort of way—he longed for a clipping on a snake handler who'd died of a snake bite. Or a cleric who would be missed by his parishioners. Something he could build the page around. But like most days, he could only work with what fate had presented him.

Worse, he was overtired and his thoughts were wandering. On most days, he wondered idly how the terminated lives before him had intersected with other lives in ways no one could ever hope to trace. He pondered this today. But today Leonard Wolik also was in his mind, as was Wolik's daughter, as were Popov and Goleniewski. The whole interrelated bunch of them.

Townsend visited the clippings morgue downstairs for an hour. Then, back in his office he made phone calls for forty minutes, making notes and drafting a format for his page. The German's space expanded. So did the wife of the car dealer. It seemed she had wanted to be an actress when she was young. Her parents had been in the theater. Townsend had never known. Thus were the inner truths of lives revealed only in death. And thus did Townsend's page take shape for the next morning, which would be the edition of May 21, 1996.

His concentration was lousy today, though. Leonard Wolik kept returning, at least in spirit.

Finally, Townsend saw a stretch of available time shortly before noon. He disappeared back downstairs into the tomby silence of the clippings morgue, this time with no hand-held notes. He had only two names in mind. Popov and Goleniewski. He returned three-quarters of an hour later, the light on his phone flashing with seven messages, and very little from the morgue on his two names.

He sat down at his desk and began to return his calls. After the fifth, he set down the receiver.

"Good morning." The voice was male, friendly, and instantly recognizable. It came from his doorway. Townsend looked up and saw Harry Dubrow. "Anything big today?" Harry asked.

"Only if you're immediate family," Townsend said. He leaned back in his chair.

Harry came in and sat down, gripping a sheet of his own pages. Harry's column appeared three times a week. Today was one of those days.

"Nothing the world at large will take any great notice of," Townsend said. "What have *you* got, Harry?"

"Last night's baseball. The Yankees lost to Cleveland. The Mets beat Colorado, but only by one run. So it cost me five bucks. Nothing much else. The Knicks are still in the playoffs. So are the Islanders. The Rangers are one game from out." Harry paused. "That's the good news." A copy of the day's *Sun* lay on a side table. Harry glanced at the front page. "The bad news is this crypto-Nazi Lord all over our paper."

Harry motioned to the story and made a distasteful expression. Townsend nodded.

"Has it occurred to you, Harry," Townsend said, "that by doing our jobs faithfully, we're perpetuating the Lord candidacy?"

"How do you figure that?"

"We put out an interesting newspaper, the *Sun* sells more issues. The *Sun* sells more issues and Max Kohlheimer—our odious master from Phoenix—rakes in more money. Max makes more money, Max plugs Lord all the harder. Not to mention the increased circulation of friendly editorial coverage. Ergo, we work our butts off with the net result of enhancing the Presidential ambitions of one Senator John Lord."

Harry looked uneasy and became very quiet. "What are you suggesting?" he asked.

"Nothing. This is just a nasty thought that keeps coming back to me. One of many that I entertain each day."

"Oh." Harry looked relieved, but only slightly. "Obviously," Townsend continued with evident sarcasm, "it is our particularly loathesome fate to work for the only big city daily in the East that actually applauds Lord's disreputable candidacy."

Townsend picked up a plastic container that had held his morning coffee. He found it empty. Thoughtfully, he chewed the lip of it for a second, then changed the subject. "You should have seen this queer old bird I spent last night with," Townsend said.

"A woman?" Harry asked, intentionally misunderstanding.

"No, not a woman. This wasn't sex, Harry, although a woman led me into this."

"Uh, oh. The female who called you yesterday?"

"Yeah. One and the same," Townsend said. He crumpled the plastic cup and shot it toward the corner recycling bin. It missed.

"She took me to see her father," Townsend continued. "A guy in his sixties, but he seemed much older. Poor unlucky bastard. Looked like he was dying of six different diseases at the same time."

"You mean you *went to see* someone like that? You never do that. You used to call that 'campaigning for a good obit.' "

"I know."

"You used to tell me," Harry protested, "how looking death, real death, in the eye gave you the creeps."

"It does."

"Well, then . . . ?"

"Ah, come on, Harry. Sarah's a friend. A *close* friend. Know what I mean?"

Harry said he knew.

"Anyway," Townsend said, pressing ahead, "I got curious and I felt like getting into a car with Sarah. My own car blew up last night. Did I tell you?"

"What? No!"

"Just a slice of life in the Big Apple, Harry. I'll get to it later."

"Jesus . . ." Harry looked perplexed.

"This old guy," Townsend said. "He gave me his name as Leonard Wolik. Filthy sick. Doubt it he'll last another month. He was mixed up in some spy intrigue back in the sixties."

"Mixed up how?" Harry barely knew which of Townsend's story lines to follow.

Townsend shrugged. "Innocent bystander, maybe. I don't know. Wolik didn't even seem to know, himself."

"What did he tell you?"

"A lot of stuff in general. Very little in specifics."

"Was there anything in it you could believe?"

"They don't usually lie when they're looking the Grim Reaper in the eyeball, Harry. You know that."

Harry allowed that was the case. "Okay," he concluded. "So what?"

"So," Townsend said with another shrug, "this Wolik wanted to tell me a story. Must have been the most exciting thing that ever happened to him, even though he doesn't know what it was."

"So he wants it mentioned in his obit, huh?"

"Guess so." Townsend shrugged.

Outside in the corridor there was the sound of conversation. A messenger with a package was looking for the financial page editor. He was two floors off course. Townsend, out of long habit, instinctively fell silent when there were strangers in the hallway. When the sound of the messenger's footsteps diminished down the hall, Townsend continued.

"I suppose that's the handle in itself, isn't it?" Townsend asked, almost rhetorically. "My headline: 'Career diplomat dies with unanswered questions. Perplexed by sixties' spy intrigue.' "

"Maybe," said Dubrow.

Townsend took a long pause. "Harry, let me ask you something? What do you think was the biggest secret of the 1960s?"

Harry pursed his lips. "In what field?"

"Pick any."

Harry thought some more. "In my field it was how to pitch to Hank Aaron. Even Seaver and Koufax couldn't figure it out."

"Be a pal, Harry. Answer me seriously."

"How the American people could elect as their President a piece of bile like Richard Nixon."

"No secret there, Harry. They did it two times in three opportunities. But the second time was in the 1970s. Plus again, we're flirting with something even worse in John Lord. People get the government they deserve. And you didn't answer my question. What was the biggest secret of the 1960s?"

"This is why I don't usually venture out of sports, Paul," Dubrow said. "Not only is it too depressing, but I don't have any answers. Ask me instead who I believe to be the best pitcher in the National League."

Townsend rolled his eyes and looked heavenward.

Seeing his friend's displeasure, Dubrow took another run at the topic. "Okay. What kind of spy intrigue?" Dubrow asked.

"Damned if I know. It seems this Leonard Wolik was face to face with some would-be Soviet defector back in 1965 in Paris. That's what he claims. The Russian was promising to put the other defectors in their proper perspective. Popov and Goleniewski. Ever heard those names?"

"No."

"Wolik alleges that the Paris operation blew up," said Townsend. "Claimed there was something vital that never got to the west."

"Why didn't this guy just come out and tell you?"

"Because he didn't know what it was, either. His Russian never got around to talking, at least not for his benefit." Townsend then ran through a shortened version of the dying man's tale, from the diplomat's early postings to the story he told of Paris.

"Paul, my friend?" asked Harry at his avuncular best. "Could I ask you a side question?"

"Harry, for you I'll even allow *two* questions."

"Since the old U.S.S.R. no longer exists, could anyone possibly care anymore?"

"That was my reaction, too," Townsend said. "But as you see . . ." He motioned to the papers before him. "That's what I do for a living. I put lives in perspective. So . . ."

"So you're intrigued?"

Townsend's telephone began to ring.

"Well, I'm not bored."

He answered the telephone.

The caller was a man named William Arnetti. He identified himself as the brother of the Jim Arnold, the radio personality who had hanged himself. Harry left the room. Townsend began to talk and type at the same time. With two follow-up calls, he had the deceased in focus. Eight inches. One column. Right-hand side. If today's page had a lead, this was it—the obit with most interest to the greatest number of readers. A man whose star had shown very brightly for six years, but never at any other time in his life. He had been unable to live with obscurity. Twice divorced, he left no children.

Townsend ate lunch at his desk. The German Communist was in place by three in the afternoon. The write-ups on the music teacher, the labor lawyer, and the air traffic controller practically wrote themselves. Three to five inches each. He farmed the writing of the latter to a staffer from the city desk. A long talk with the daughter of the car dealer's wife added dimension to that notice: three inches by two columns on the lower right of the page. Someone from the family would send a photo over. It had to be in Townsend's hands by four. It was. Quiet dignified death notices for quiet dignified men and women. A respectable exit.

By five thirty, the obituary page was complete. Townsend read it and reread it, looking for errors, wondering what he might have missed or what he could improve. It was at this point each day, that he became maniacal for details and accuracy.

He was still reading at a few minutes after six P.M. when Harry appeared again. "Hey, Paul," Harry said. "I've been thinking about it all day. I mean, thinking about it seriously, like you asked me to."

Looking up, "Thinking about what?" Townsend asked.

"The biggest secret of the sixties? Remember?"

"Yeah?" Townsend cocked his head skeptically and waited. "What?"

"It's just my own opinion and all. But you know, you mentioned all the elements: Mid-sixties. CIA. Cuba. Russians. Lyndon Johnson. Texas."

"So?"

"Well," Harry said, explaining himself away. "It's just a wild guess by a daffy soon-to-retire old newsman from the sports pages."

"Forget the disclaimer, Harry. What have you got?"

"Biggest secret of the decade? Maybe the biggest secret of the half century. Here goes: Who really killed John F. Kennedy? And why?"

Townsend looked at his friend for several seconds. Then he ran a hand through his hair and across his chin. "Goddamn it," said Townsend.

"What's wrong?"

"That's the biggest damned secret to me, too, Harry," Townsend said. "That's what's been bothering me all day."

Harry took a moment to conjure up the nerve for what followed. "You know," Dubrow said, rambling forward, "I always had this funny theory about the Kennedy assassination. I always wondered whether Lyndon Johnson had something to do with it."

"Oh, come on. Harry. . . ?"

"Well," Dubrow shrugged defensively, "it happened in Texas. Johnson gained the most. And Johnson appointed the Warren Commission, which didn't incriminate anyone who was still alive." He shrugged again, having outlined his case.

The monstrosity of all this, reaching Townsend through the numbing fatigue of the previous night, left him temporarily speechless.

"Hell, look," Harry continued, picking up momentum now, "it's not as crazy as it sounds. Johnson always wanted to be President. Did *anything* to get elected to Congress and the Senate. While he was alive he stole money, sold influence, fixed elections . . . Just suppose—"

"Harry?" Townsend finally interrupted.

"What?"

"Stick to sports."

Harry shrugged defensively. "Well," he mused, "you asked."

Townsend grinned. But Harry waited. There was more, much more, on his mind. A moment later he gave voice to part of it.

"Paul?" Harry said.

Townsend asked what.

"Make me a promise, would you? If you ever come off that death page and get yourself involved in some good investigative stuff again, let me have a piece of it."

Townsend was surprised. "What do you mean?" he asked.

"Well, you know," Harry said sheepishly, "I've always been a little in awe of what the hard news guys do. I'm looking at retirement in a matter of months and I've never gotten my hands dirty beyond sports. Know what I mean? I'd like to. Just let me back you up sometime, do some footwork. Something so that I can taste it for myself just once."

"I'm not getting back into anything like that," Townsend said, genuinely surprised at the request. "But if I do, Harry, you'll be the guy I holler for."

Townsend extended his hand. The two men shook, sealing the agreement. And still Harry wouldn't move. Townsend stared at him.

"What's going on?" Townsend finally asked.

"You know."

"No, I don't."

"You're holding out on me. The good stuff."

"Harry," Townsend protested, spreading his hands. "What are you talking about? There's nothing—"

"The really good slice of life in the Big Apple stuff," said Harry softly.

Finally, as if a revelation, it dawned on Townsend. So he took a few minutes and told his friend how his car had spontaneously combusted on the Upper West Side the previous afternoon.

Three-quarters of an hour later, Townsend stood in the second-floor computer room, thinking himself alone.

"No! I do *not* believe it!" The voice was adenoidal and harsh— Belmont Avenue all the way.

Townsend looked to his left and saw Lou DiCarlo, he of the nose jewelry and the position in Internal Administration. DiCarlo had a jacket on and was obviously on his way home.

"Hello, Lou," Townsend said pleasantly. "Having a nice day?"

"Paul Townsend in the computer room!" DiCarlo honked. "The *Sun*'s last holdout against technology. I never thought I'd see this day." Lou grinned like a gargoyle. "Are you sick? Or desperate? Or don't you work here anymore?"

"Don't get smart. It's not what you think. I like new experiences."

"You don't know how to use Big Wally. But you'd like to, right?" This evening Lou had a small ersatz ruby in dainty gold filigree clasped to his left nostril.

"Let's suppose I did," Townsend said slowly. He cautiously eyed the screen of the IBM WLE-2000 terminal. On the dark blue background were a set of different instructions or questions, ready to lead a user deep into the combined files of all Kohlheimer newspapers. "Do you know how to run an Open Search?"

"Of course I know," said DiCarlo. "You're the only one on this paper who *doesn't* know."

"Then show me."

DiCarlo considered it, grinned, and motioned to a shelf of software manuals. "There's an instruction book over there," he said. "Study the first two chapters on the PowerSearch program."

"I asked you to show me, Lou."

"I know you did, Townsend. But I don't like you, remember? You're nothing but trouble. I have to adjudicate more fines for you than any other three employees combined. I live for the day when either you retire or the elevator plunges ten flights with you in it. Preferably both." He grinned again. "If you can't run Big Wally, you can stew in your own juice."

DiCarlo turned to leave.

"Lou?" Townsend called after him with utmost civility.

"Yeah?" DiCarlo was outside the computer room.

"You know there are a few people around this paper who do favors for me."

"Yeah, there's a few old goats," he said, returning to the doorway. "So what?"

"That's your sister working for my friend Harry Dubrow, isn't it? Caryn DiCarlo? Sports? Fourth floor?"

"What if it is?"

"Well, see, Harry's one of those 'old goats' you just mentioned," Townsend explained. "But Harry's also got a big budget in sports. He was even asking me about sending someone to cover one of those Trans–Yukon dog-sled races. You know, from Yellow Knife to Whitehorse? Harry owes me favors."

Lou stared for a moment.

"Your sister ever seen Whitehorse in the late spring, Lou? Or should I ask her directly?"

"You're not that low," DiCarlo said.

"Lou," Townsend announced calmly, "anyone who knows me would tell you that I'm every bit that low."

Quietly, Lou squirmed a little. Townsend walked to the shelf, pulled down the software package for PowerSearch, and belligerently opened the instruction manual to the first page. He began to read as he felt DiCarlo's eyes upon him. By the second paragraph Townsend was lost.

"Lou, I'm getting lower by the minute," he warned. "Why don't you do everyone a favor?"

Townsend felt DiCarlo materialize wordlessly beside him. Lou's hand reached foward and flipped shut the PowerSearch book. The younger man pulled off his coat, sat down, and turned on a video display screen.

"What do you want?" Lou asked angrily.

"A few names. Show me how to get complete biographical references," Townsend said. "I also want to cross-reference names: listings of when one name might have appeared in relation to another. Can we do that?"

"You finally got an hour to learn?"

"I have all night."

"I don't, Townsend."

"I'm sure you don't, but the Yukon is damned cold even in May."

"Prick."

"That'll cost you ten bucks, Lou. Abusive Language Regulation."

DiCarlo hesitated for a moment, then blew out a long breath. He grudgingly motioned to a second chair. Townsend pulled it over and sat down next to his captive tutor.

"What you have to remember, Townsend," DiCarlo began, "is that Big Wally is smarter then you are. *Anybody* named Wally is probably smarter than you are. But he's also your friend. You come and ask him questions. If you ask nicely, he gives you the answer."

DiCarlo was positively reverential toward his computer. "Uh huh," Townsend said.

"It's as if," DiCarlo said, laboring for an image, "he's your big, educated, helpful rabbi who can intercede on your behalf. Are you Jewish, Townsend?"

"No."

"He's your rabbi, anyway."

"Could you get to the point, Lou?"

"How many names you got?"

"Two to start. Then maybe two more."

"Give me the first one," DiCarlo said. "I'll access a complete periodical reference and show you your options for cross-references and print. There's also a condensation option. You tell Big Wally you want a condensed printout of the subject and approximately how many words, by increments of twenty-five hundred. Is that the type of thing you want?"

"Sure."

"I'll do the first one," DiCarlo said. "Then I'll guide you through while you do the second. After that, you're on your own. Is that enough?"

Townsend said it was.

"Who do you want? Give me a name."

"Popov." He spelled it out. "First name, Igor." DiCarlo proceeded, starting an access with an open question.

"Living or dead?" DiCarlo asked.

"I don't know. Try both."

"Use 'Unknown' when Big Wally asks you," he said, almost to himself. Four minutes later, DiCarlo had accessed Popov from among the many millions of names in the WLE-2000 storage bank. There were scores of listings and references. Maybe fifty pages' worth.

"So what do you want on Popov? Condensed bio?" Lou prepared to punch a key.

"Give me a ten-thousand-word condensed biography," Townsend asked pensively. "Then give me everything else in the memory bank as well."

"You mean a list of all the other references?"

"No. I mean *everything.*"

"Ah, come on, Townsend!"

"I want a complete printout. And I'm going to want the same for a man named Michal Goleniewski immediately after Popov. *Then* the two others."

"We could be here all night! Do you know what you're asking for?"

"I know exactly, Lou. I like to read."

DiCarlo isolated the first reference and ordered a deferred print. "Fucking Jesus!" he muttered angrily.

"That's ten bucks, Lou. More abusive language. Just teach me how to do it and you can leave."

DiCarlo did, grudgingly but efficiently over the next forty-five minutes. Townsend became a surprisingly quick study of Big Wally's research capacity. As other *Sun* staffers came and went from other display screens. Townsend made notes in a reporter's pad as they proceeded so that he'd be able to repeat the search for other names. Townsend launched an inquiry of Goleniewski second. When he was finished, it was quarter to eight. DiCarlo pushed his chair back from the computer screen.

"Can you handle the rest?" Lou asked.

"I can. Thanks, Lou."

He offered his hand. DiCarlo refused it. Lou picked up his coat, draped it over his shoulder, and retreated toward the door.

"And Lou?" Townsend said.

"What?"

"There's no mutt-sled race till next March. Harry tells me that Caryn's going to be covering tennis."

DiCarlo just stared. "Prick!" he finally said.

Townsend punched a RETURN key on Big Wally's keyboard. Across the room, on Printer Three, a laser hummed to life and began to swiftly put onto white paper the fruits of Townsend's initial inquiries.

"I guess that's another ten bucks, Lou," Townsend said without looking up.

"This doesn't cost me anything. In fact, I make money on it."

"Why's that, Lou?"

"I got a standing bet with your pal Dubrow," Lou said. "I bet Harry that someday *even you* would show up down here wanting to learn Big Wally." DiCarlo grinned. "You go crashing along through life and never care who else you hurt, Townsend. You just cost your pal two hundred bucks."

DiCarlo vanished, leaving Townsend staring at an empty doorway, alone with the sense of having compromised a friend. It was a feeling he was unable to shake. In the background, the menacing hum of the laser printer filled the room as, with maddening equanimity, Big Wally brought forth the official memory of another generation's triumphs and betrayals.

Several minutes later, Townsend gathered together eighty-six pages of printed-out biography, complete with suggested cross-references and sources. He slid them into a manila envelope, wrote his name on the front of it, and sealed it. He was prepared to leave the hateful computer chamber.

Or was he?

In truth, as the day died, he was mentally unable to disengage from the subject before him. He stood at the door for a moment, ready to go home. Then he returned to a keyboard and sat down.

The greatest secret of the sixties.

Why, oh why, couldn't the fates leave him alone? Okay, what the hell, he thought to himself. Everyone else had been banging away at computers for decades. Now prehistoric old Paul Townsend would give it a hack.

Having mastered the biographical access of Big Wally, Townsend sent two other inquiries burrowing deeply into the sterile electronic darkness of the computer's memory:

Colbert Davies, the phantom acting ambassador.

Leonard Wolik, late of a quarter century's servitude to the United States Department of State.

Both inquiries came up not just cold, but frozen. "Nada. Zip. Nothing," Townsend muttered to the empty room. "Suspicious in and of itself."

From his past few years of experience he knew. Plumbers from Jersey City and smoke eaters from Bayside leave more of a written record of their existences than that. How could a pair of diplomats fly through life like Peter Pan and Tinkerbell, never leaving a discernible footprint on anything?

What in hell, he began to wonder, was this all about?

Paul Townsend returned to his fifth-floor office to use the telephone. He dialed the main switchboard in Virginia of the Central Intelligence Agency. He asked if a message could be routed to a Bruce McMorris.

The operator took the message—Townsend's name, current journalistic affiliation, and return telephone number—without confirming whether or not any Bruce McMorris was employed by the agency.

Townsend set down the telephone, leaving his hand upon it for a moment, pondering the day. Another funny thing, he thought to himself: Normally his professional task was to put the lives of the dead in order within a few hours, as thoroughly as possible, and then move on to others the following day. As for Messrs. Popov and Goleniewski, Davies and Wolik, McMorris and all those others who sailed with them? Well, these might take a bit longer. *If* he pursued it, he told himself.

Then he stood. He picked up the envelope bearing the biographical profiles on Popov and Goleniewski and tucked it under his arm. Satisfied with the day, he finally went home.

<< << **7** >> >>

*I*T was barely past two in the afternoon when Tina Hubbell locked the front door to her home in Fort Myers, Florida, and walked to the pale blue 1991 Chevrolet Corsica in her driveway. She was accompanied by one of the important people in her life, her four-year-old daughter, Mindy. Mother and daughter arrived at the car at the same moment. Tina opened the rear door on the driver's side and watched her daughter climb in.

It was only May, but already the heat of the Florida sun, so welcome in the winter, gave an unmistakable indication how relentless it would be during the summer of 1996. Well, that was the trade-off in living in her adopted state. No snow in the winter, no icy sidewalks, and no astronomical oil bills. But a scorching heat in the summer was always possible.

Well, she told herself, summer would again be fine to travel back up north. Her husband, Jim Hubbell, operated a profitable string of three hardware stores in Lee County—two in Fort Myers and one in Cape Coral. Jim had good managers in each store and could probably afford three weeks of vacation this year. Maybe, she mused, as she buckled Mindy into her car seat, the family could take two weeks in July and maybe a third in mid-August. Tina had parents in Maryland. Jim had relatives in Ohio. The family would escape the brutalizing heat of a Florida summer and visit relatives back up north. Both sets of grandparents always welcomed visits.

She smiled to her daughter. It was always fun to plan trips and look forward to them. But today she had errands to do. There was shopping at the supermarket. Then she would need to pick up her older daughter, Laurie, who was seven, after school.

The garage of her ranch-style house was still open. Tina climbed into the driver's seat of her five-year-old automobile and turned on the ignition. The car's air conditioning rumbled to life. With a remote button in her car, she closed the garage door. She adjusted the volume on the car radio. She was tuned, as usual, to a soft rock station from Miami. Then she backed her car out of her driveway. She pulled onto the street, drove forward several feet, then stopped at the mailbox in front of her house.

Tina reached in and pulled out what she expected to be bills, a couple of circulars, and a pair of magazines. She was about to put everything on the seat next to her and not bother with it until that evening.

Then her hand stayed for a moment when she saw the unexpected postmark: New Castle, Delaware.

She knew—she just knew—this was somehow trouble.

Her daughter amused herself with some toys in the car seat. Tina Hubbell looked at the envelope for a second time. It was plain white, business size, and Tina's name and address were typed. But she knew who it was from.

Why did he have to bother her again? Couldn't a former lover stay out of her life? Wasn't their affair long over? Couldn't he do the decent thing and . . . ?

She cursed Allan in particular and all men in general. Then a thousand other thoughts coursed through her mind, most of them angry. Whatever he wanted, she told herself, she wouldn't give him. That part of her life was finished. She held the letter in her hand and entertained the impulse to tear it up unread.

But she didn't. She might be better off, she reasoned, at least *knowing* what he wanted this time.

She looked in the rearview mirror. There was no traffic coming. The street was quiet in the sunshine of midafternoon. Her husband was at work. She switched on her four-way flashers.

Yes, she decided. She would be better off knowing what he wanted, and better off knowing it *now* while Jim, her husband, was at work. So she would open this unwelcome missive immediately. That way she could read it, digest it, then tear it into tiny pieces and scatter it into several different trash cans across Fort Myers. Some pieces she would discard in the supermarket. More in the parking lot. Perhaps some at the car wash.

She opened and read it. The letter was typed. She grew angrier with each second that passed.

As she suspected. Allan wanted to see her again. He insisted that it wasn't an attempt to rekindle their romantic past. Of course, he had insisted the same thing at least twice before, both times subsequent to her marriage. Men were such damnable liars.

She continued to read.

He assumed she was happily married, he wrote, and of this he maintained that he was glad. "You have your life, I have mine," he wrote magnanimously. "But there is something we have to talk about. Something very important. I cannot put it in a letter. You used to be a professional person, same as me. Surely you understand."

No, she didn't. It was signed simply, Al. No salutation. Unquestionably, his handwriting.

She wondered how she had ever seen anything in him, let alone enough to go to bed with him over the course of many months. Of course, people change. Their affair had been . . . How long ago? Eleven years?

She carefully folded the letter back into its envelope. Tina had made her decision on this man long ago, on his approach to life, on everything in which he had been involved. She wanted no part of it. And surely she wanted no part of the possibility of having to explain the past to her husband.

She felt her cheeks flush. Her anger fused into resentment.

Impetuously, she pulled the letter out and read it again. Her reaction hardened. This letter didn't even merit a response, she decided. She crumpled it.

"Mommy?" Mindy asked from the back seat. "Do we go now?"

"Yes, honey," she answered. "We go now."

She switched off her flashers and pulled onto the road. For a moment there was a screeching noise, then a loud horn, then a voice.

A passing car had almost crashed into hers! Tina had pulled out without even looking. The other driver, a male, had skidded to a complete stop. Now he rolled down his window and unleashed a torrent of obscenities at the woman and her child.

She stared at him, first coldly, then flustered. Her heart pounded at the near miss. All she could do was meekly wave back in apology. Had they collided, it would have been her fault.

The other driver held her in a withering stare for several seconds. Then he cooled down and slowly went on his way.

"Bastard," she muttered. "Nearly got us maimed!"

"Who, Mommy?"

"No one," she said, cautiously pulling out now.

"What's 'maimed'?" Mindy asked next.

"Nothing!" she snapped. "And don't tell Daddy that our car nearly got hit."

"Why?"

"Just don't!"

She drove a block. She glanced in her mirror. Mindy was starting to cry. Tina pulled into a safe parking place, got out of the car, and went to her child's door on the sidewalk side. She opened the door, made a funny face at her daughter, and caused the little girl to smile.

Then Tina embraced her daughter. Mrs. Hubbell faced away from her child for several seconds and she stifled what otherwise might have been sobs.

Why, oh why, she asked herself, did the past always have a way of following her? Why couldn't it remain dead? Why couldn't she be left alone? What was done was done. She didn't care about what might have transpired several years ago, and as far as what governments did, she wished to not be included.

But the crumpled letter, she realized, was still in her hand. There seemed no way of letting go of the events of the past, just as the events had no way of letting go of her.

In Ohio, Senator John Lord parlayed his success in New York and New Jersey into a more finely honed strategy for winning the Presidency. At a shopping mall in Steubenville, a young workingman in blue jeans and a heavy shirt had asked Lord a curious question. He asked who the candidate thought his constituency was.

Lord, in response, used the phrase "The Forgotten American." Franklin Roosevelt had used a similar phrase sixty years earlier. Lord was well read, particularly in American political biographies, and the phrase had always appealed to him. He was test marketing it here, perhaps spontaneously, though the concept had been in the back of his mind for many weeks. But now Lord dusted it off and gave it new meaning. His constituency, he elaborated, was The Forgotten American—the voter who has been ignored or betrayed by the major parties for a generation.

Lord was much too sophisticated to use such a phrase without proper attribution. "Franklin Roosevelt used the term many years ago," he told the voter. "Roosevelt spoke for the average American, the man and woman who had been betrayed by the economic interests that caused the Great Depression. In a similar way today I'm speaking for the forgotten man and woman, the people whose financial security has been done in by Republican bankers, crooked big city Democrats, and Asian imports."

It was a low-key, seemingly extemporaneous moment. It played nicely to the attendant crowd. It appeared well on television throughout Ohio and, within another twenty-four hours, before approximately twenty million people across the United States. A lot of Americans, in 1996, apparently felt forgotten.

As for the workingman who'd posed the question, some of the media people attempted to pounce on him after the rally. They wanted to know if—and they were hoping to learn that—he was a shill. But he vanished into the crowd very quickly.

The Forgotten American. John Lord had great political instincts. And he knew how to turn a phrase at just the right time.

Lord had about eighty reporters steadily following him in Ohio. "Laptoppers," he called them, so designated for the inevitable little laptop computers which seemed as much a part of their bodies as their heads. But he called them that with a smile, and the press corps took it as a not at all derogatory comment. It suggested that they were always working, after all, something that would keep their editors happy.

"One of the great dangers of John Lord," wrote Murray Green in *The New Republic,* "is his unending geniality. Even when you hate him you like him. And vice versa." Lord laughed when he read that one. Lord loved political wisdom that contradicted itself. Green's comment seemed like a classic case.

About half of the laptoppers had electronic broadcast equipment or sound crews. Most were from the South. Many were from Texas. Several were what the Lord camp openly referred to as "Hostiles." Mostly, the Hostiles were the credentialed representatives of what was perceived to be the liberal media—mostly wire services, big city journals with liberal editorial policies, and the four major news networks. They were not to be confused with the "Friendlies," whose label was self-explanatory.

Running herd on the press corps was Jerry Huddleston, Lord's media supervisor. Huddleston was a big, lumbering, overweight, fifty-five-year-old Alabaman. He had a bushy mustache and twenty different size fifty-two brown suits. Huddleston helped John Lord navigate through the mine fields that the media set for him.

Jerry Huddleston was an old Lord friend. He was an attorney who had begun his career in Mobile, moved to Texas during the boom of the seventies, and opened his own law firm in Houston. He practiced criminal law and contract law relating to the gas industry. Sometimes the two overlapped. Gradually, Huddleston had been drawn into direct-mail fund-raising for the far fringes of Texas Republican politics, with direct ties to what remained of the old far-right John Birch-styled segment of the Texas Republican party.

"The blessed God-fearing, flag-waving, brew-guzzling, one hundred percent American yahoo wing of the party," he affectionately called it. He did this with a big self-effacing grin, as if to suggest, as he had verbally on other occasions, "Aw, shucks, fellas. These old John Birch boys are good people just like you and me." Huddleston had a cozy manner of speech that could be likened to warm fudge. Similar to his candidate, he was a likable, affable man, hulking and gregarious even to those who disdained his political roots. The press corps used to call him The Big Brown Bear. Now it was just The Bear. The yahoos even knew he called them yahoos, but they liked him, too.

It was in Ohio, as crowds grew from shopping mall to legion hall, that John Lord and Jerry Huddleston advanced some electoral strategy that seemed promising.

They would run a shadow campaign for Lord's candidacy across the primary states of the North. To them, it was axiomatic that in a three-way race in November, Lord could win, with a minimum of 34 percent of the votes cast, a hard core of states from the old Confederacy—Alabama, South Carolina, Mississippi, Louisiana, Georgia, and probably Florida and Arkansas. They felt he could also carry his home bailiwick of Texas. That would give him a base bloc of ninety-two votes in the electoral college. A good start, but far from the two hundred seventy needed to win the election.

Conventional wisdom had it that Lord's next best chances for state-wide victories were in conservative border states. Maryland, Missouri, Oklahoma, for example. But there was nothing conventional about Lord's approach. He and Jerry Huddleston had now made a decision to travel an unorthodox path.

John Lord now planned to prove that his two likely November opponents were vulnerable even in big industrial states and on their home turf in the northern Midwest. Then he would continue the brawl through the Upper Midwest and into California.

To that end, he would run a shadow campaign against them: When the Democrats and Republicans were having their primaries, Lord would have his own. Where possible, he would enter the major party primaries. He would attempt to wound his opponents' credibility by scoring a fifth of the vote in each. In states like Ohio, where he could enter only one party's primary, he asked his supporters in the other party to mark "phantom" ballots for him. That is, they were to vote for him by leaving the ballot blank.

Using this strategy, Senator Lord had plenty of opportunity to shoot himself in the foot. Poor showings would indicate that he was in fact a *weak* national candidate. But strong showings, Lord and Huddleston theorized, would demonstrate to the country that his opponents were vulnerable and that Lord could win in November. His opponents, for example, didn't dare take *him* on in Texas.

"We'll bloody them up them in the spring and finish them off in November," Lord said to his staff.

"Senator, would a poor showing be akin to a loss?" asked Freida Carruthers of CBS News. "And would a bad loss make you reassess your candidacy?" Freida was a big, strapping, square-shouldered woman who, had she been born two generations earlier, might have been a war correspondent for one of Henry Luce's publications.

"I do not plan on losing, Freida," the candidate for President said for perhaps the one-thousandth time. "But why don't you ask my opponents the same question?"

There were a few other things Lord wanted to finish off beside his opponents. But these he wanted to spike right away. Questions about the Ku Klux Klan, for example. And implications about anti-Semitism.

"Ask anything you want up until the end of the Ohio primary voting," Lord politely said to the press corps. "After that, with all due respect, I'm not answering any more questions on either subject."

"Why not?" reporter Roger Caudill of UPI asked.

Lord shrugged. "Come on, Roger. Those issues are dead. I've answered them all. The past doesn't change and the answers don't change. We're wasting time. Yours and mine."

Then Lord explained again, for what he hoped might be a final time. He'd been a member of the Klan when he was very young and he was sorry. And no, he had never distributed anti-Semitic literature. Nor, he added, was his frequent criticism of Israeli policy and a call for a "neutral" position in the Middle East in any way anti-Semitic.

"But in some quarters," pressed Rita Flood of the *Boston Globe,* "it will be interpreted that way."

"No," the candidate replied cordially, "it will be *mis*interpreted that way. And for that, I'm saddened. But I'm not for Arab interests in the Middle East or Israeli interests. I stand for American interests and an equitable policy in the Middle East."

"But that could be construed among Jewish voters as a sellout and an abandonment of Israel," Flood pressed.

"Jewish voters should support me on that issue above all," Lord said. "An equitable policy is the only one that will promote a lasting peace. It's my Holy Land, too, don't forget." Almost always, there was a good, concise quote.

After Ohio, Lord was also planning to unveil a new commodity in the campaign. "Something that proves I'm not a political demon," was the way Lord described it to his permanent staff of sixteen. "And something that proves," he concluded, mocking his own patterns of speech, "that I ain't all that corn pone and 'Southrin'."

His staff knew all along what the "something" was. Her name was Eugenia and she was his wife.

So far, Eugenia Lord, the candidate's wife of thirty-one years, hadn't made an appearance yet on his northern campaign swing. Maybe it was because she was from a starchy old Washington-via-New England family to start with and had enough of politics through her parents. Heaven knew she'd shocked enough people when she had married a rough diamond like Lord back when he was a first-term congressman way, way back in the mid-1960s.

As for the campaign in Ohio, well, above and beyond the discovery of a new theme—The Forgotten American—it was going just fine. Lightning kept striking it in many strange and wonderful ways.

One of Lord's true believers, a man named Dee Roland, who lived in the metropolis of Chillicothe, had a great idea. At the kitchen table one night he started a John Lord for President Club, the only one in Chillicothe. Roland was an unemployed sheet metal worker. Since football season was over, he had nothing to do except watch network television and the Presidential primaries. So Dee Roland made up some campaign buttons that said, GET A FRIEND TO VOTE FOR JOHN LORD.

Roland's rationale was simple.

A poll published in the *Cincinnati Enquirer* concluded that if the November election were held in the current political climate, the three expected candidates would split the vote in Ohio almost evenly. One-third each. Ohio, in other words, was an electoral toss-up.

Applying optimism and a somewhat tentative grasp of statistics, Mr. Roland reasoned that if each potential Lord voter talked one friend into voting for Lord, the scales would be tipped. As indeed, they would be. Hence, Mr. Roland began circulating his old-fashioned red, white, and blue buttons.

GET A FRIEND TO VOTE FOR JOHN LORD.

Very quickly, the Lord regional organizers in Ross County spotted Mr. Roland and the opportunity he presented. Thus the unemployed worker appeared at seventeen campaign stops over two days with the candidate himself. Lord even put Roland back to work by ordering five thousand buttons, which would then be distributed across Ohio and the next state on the agenda, Michigan.

Lord prominently pinned one of the buttons to his own lapel at a factory gate in Toledo.

"I promise to wear this memento of Ohio for the rest of the campaign," Lord said. "Right into the White House." Mr. Roland made a similar vow.

Lord came off not only as the hero of a specific forgotten American, but a leader who was accessible and who could accomplish things. Dee Roland, after all, had gone from the kitchen table to Presidential politics in the space of ninety-six hours. And then Lord had created for him a job.

One of the television networks, broadcasting out of New York, reported the incident with unmistakable cynicism. Trouble was, most of the electorate didn't share that view of it. And thus another small public-relations victory had landed in Lord's column.

A short time later, so did much of Ohio. The Republican primary was closed to him, but his "phantom" votes were 10 percent of the total. And in the Democratic primary, Lord walloped the opposition, winning in some of the rural areas with as much as 60 percent of the vote. His overall total was 42 percent, with the front-running Democrat gaining 28 percent. He still, of course, professed no interest in the Democratic nomination.

At the end of the night, at the end of the Ohio campaign, Lord had challenged another myth: that he couldn't actually *win* in the North. The mathematics of the ballot boxes showed that Lord had captured more votes in the state than any other candidate.

On an incredibly ambitious and long journey, Senator John Lord had passed another milestone, leaving the accepted political wisdom in his wake. Michigan, however, was not Ohio. And the next significant state on the primary road would afford Lord's opponents ample opportunity to bring his lofty ambitions crashing back down to earth.

<<<< *8* >>>>

*T*O Paul Townsend, weekends were Fridays and Saturdays. Staffers pulled from other departments covered his page, unless something "significant" happened. More than once the death of a national figure—a politician, an entertainer, or an artist—had brought Townsend into the *Sun*'s offices on a day off. If he wasn't writing the obituary himself, then he had to oversee his page, as well as the creation of the death notices themselves.

On this particular Friday morning in May, however, no telephone rang in Townsend's apartment. The envelope containing the computer printout on Popov and Goleniewski sat unopened in a drawer in his bedroom. It had been Townsend's intention to read it the previous evening, but fatigue had overtaken him when he had returned home.

Home. To Townsend "home" was a term that was vague at best. When he was younger, how could he have imagined that he would pass his forty-ninth birthday living alone in a two-units-per-floor walk-up on Manhattan's Upper West Side? But in that way, he realized, he was no different from thousands of individuals he wrote about each year. Lives were not predictable. Few at forty-five were as they might have been anticipated at twenty-five.

Home: A source of considerable pride to Townsend was the fact that his building—in the eyes of the developers who were intent on gang-banging the neighborhood—was the "worst" on the block. That meant that it was the oldest, the smallest, and the most likely target for demolition. Townsend knew it would take at least one bulldozer and a handful of eviction notices to dislodge him from his current tenancy.

Townsend's set of rooms had once been part of a larger unit that comprised the building's entire fourth floor. There was a small entrance foyer and a long narrow living room which overlooked both 98th Street and Amsterdam Avenue. The living room had a low ceiling that was slightly convex. Townsend could stand on a chair and touch it at its center, but not near the walls. Idly, he sometimes wondered if the ceiling were about to collapse. Connected to this room was a windowless kitchen with appliances that dated from the building's last renovation in 1970. Off from the kitchen was a bathroom and Townsend's bedroom, complete with safe.

The bedroom was short, low, and cramped. Once, presumably, it had been a child's room, nestled alongside the small kitchen. There was a bed in it and a dresser, upon which there were some pictures of happier times when he had first been married and had worked for the *Philadelphia Bulletin*. There was also a neat rectangular table upon which sat a good desk lamp with a green glass shade.

The room was situated on the southwest corner of the building. If Townsend stood by a side window, he would have a clear view up and down Amsterdam Avenue. If he looked out the rear window, he could overlook the roof of the adjoining walk-up as well as downtown beyond the intersection of Amsterdam and 97th Street.

Despite the Spartan confines, Townsend liked the bedroom for reasons that would have escaped even the most studious observers. By some fluke of Manhattan real estate, no taller building or window afforded a view into his bedroom. Not, at least, for five hundred yards—beyond the range of accuracy, in other words, for the usual sorehead with a hunting rifle. Townsend had figured this out very carefully. No one could take an accurate shot at him—even with a long-range rifle—while he slept or sat at his worktable. In this room, even with his long list of enemies, he could comfortably sleep with the shade up. Or so he reasoned.

Recently, a new young couple had moved in next door. Townsend knew their names were Barbara and Jim Shields. First, he had met them on the stairs, and second—in a lingering spasm of paranoia after they had moved in two months earlier—because he had examined their mailbox and its contents.

Barbara and Jim both worked during the day. They appeared to meet each other somewhere after work and rarely returned home before ten. They were either newly married or had newly discovered each other, for they spent a good deal of their time making high-decibel love on the other side of Townsend's bedroom wall.

Amusing as this occasionally was, it was equally irritating. On account of the young couple's passion, Townsend had recently purchased a large box of foam rubber earplugs. Nonetheless, he still subscribed to the theory that anyone who wasn't covertly planning to kill him was essentially a good neighbor.

Townsend rose late on this Friday morning, showered, listened to the news on the radio, then went out for groceries. Sandwich supplies, ice cream and beer were the staples of his kitchen. He returned, sat in his kitchen over coffee and a pastry, and read the competing newspaper of record. The *Times* had three times the class and the *Sun* had two times the circulation. There was little overlapping, though Townsend felt his own obit page was the equal of anyone's. The *New York Times*'s necrologies, he told himself, read like granite inscriptions on gravestones. Then again, his friend Harry always liked to say, so did the *Times*'s sports pages.

Shortly after eleven A.M. on the same morning, Townsend paid a prearranged call at the Second Detective Division, Manhattan North. The newly reorganized division was housed in a new brick, steel, and concrete edifice on West 95th Street east of Broadway where a public-school playground had once stood. The building, completed two years earlier in 1994, served primarily as home for the Twenty-fourth Precinct, but a suite of offices on the third floor housed the detectives.

In a small conference room, Paul Townsend sat at a gray metal table with Detective Vincent Foliari.

"Thank you for coming by, Mr. Townsend," Foliari said. "I don't think I have anything new to tell you, though."

"I didn't really expect anything," Townsend answered.

"What do you think?" Foliari asked. "Is someone out to blow you up in particular?".

"It's not outside the realm of possibility," Townsend answered. "Let's face it. It wouldn't be the first time."

Foliari sipped from a styrofoam cup of tea. The label of the bag still hung over the lip of the cup.

"But you can't really name anyone, right?" Foliari asked. "I mean, okay. I understand. You've made enemies in your life. But nothing new, huh? Nothing that would set somebody off in the last few weeks?"

"Nothing that I know of," Townsend said. "But . . . Who knows really? People read things in newspapers, they take exception to imagined slights . . ."

Townsend shrugged.

Foliari made a sympathetic expression himself. He removed the teabag from his cup, squeezed the liquid from it, and tossed the bag into a green metal trash can.

"Yeah, I know what you're talking about," the detective said. "When you've been on the force as long as I have, you learn not to eliminate anything, either." He sipped the tea, grimaced slightly, then set it aside.

"Okay," Foliari said, "we're going to talk man to man. Just you and me and the four walls here, okay?"

"Go ahead."

"I've run your name past a few people on the NYPD," Foliari said. "People around here remember you writing about them. You got a few fans on the force."

"That's nice to know."

"The word is that you're okay. You never ripped any cops unfairly in print."

"I like to think I never ripped *anyone* unfairly."

Foliari allowed himself a trace of a smile. "In this building we only care about cops. And for that matter, *good* cops. If you rip a crooked captain or inspector, it's not on me."

"Keep talking."

"But I don't want to see anything in your paper that takes me by surprise," the detective emphasized. "Not about what we're gonna discuss. So what I tell you is between us, right?"

"I don't see anyone else," Townsend assured him.

Foliari waited for more.

"You have my word," Townsend said firmly.

"All right," Foliari said after a final moment of decision. "Let me show you something."

Foliari riffled through a stack of files on the left side of the gray table. He found the paper he wanted. He glanced at it for a moment, then handed it to Townsend.

"Take a look at this," the detective said.

Townsend accepted a sheet of paper. On it were four names combined with addresses in Manhattan. There were three men and one woman. The names were written in pencil by hand. The labored handwriting, Foliari said, was his own.

Townsend read the first three names and addresses.

Ivan Simoncez, 224 Avenue D
Veronica Rykell, 446 West 75th Street
Carlos Sanchez, 2134 First Avenue

Townsend's name was the fourth on the list.

"So? What's this?" Townsend asked.

"Know any of these individuals? Besides yourself, obviously."

Townsend searched his memory. "No," he finally said.

"You sure? You want to think about it? You want to go through your newspaper files?"

"I don't recognize any of the other three names. Why? Should I?"

Foliari looked thoughtful, though mildly disappointed. "Let's put it this way," the detective said. "All four of you used to own cars."

"Oh," Townsend said.

Foliari sipped his tea again. "Here's the deal," he began. "Your car was hit by a fragmentation grenade, set in plastic explosive, fused with a vibration sensor. It's not an unsophisticated device. We've seen all the components before, though not quite with this M.O. But it's a little unusual. Well, what I mean to say is, it used to be a little unusual. There is definitely the same bad guy out there who placed four of these devices into the vehicles owned by the individuals on that list. Yourself included."

"And?"

"So a total of four cars have blown up that way in Manhattan since April 8. Four so far. All in Manhattan. The bombs are all the same. The results differed. One man was killed when he started his auto in the morning. April twenty-nine. Five thirty A.M. That was the third bomb. Mr. Sanchez. The first two exploded the same as yours. No one in the car. Street vibration set them off. But there was one extra difference in yours."

"What's that?"

"The level of explosives was much, much higher. You got—or your car got, I should say—a double dose of plastic."

"Oh, gee. I'm honored."

Foliari shrugged. "There's a couple of ways to look at it. Someone wanted to kill this Sanchez guy. So to make it look random, our someone planted two other bombs before and one after. The other three cars have nothing to do with the intended target."

"Did Sanchez have enemies?"

"Nah. He was an innocent. Went to church, paid his bills, didn't gamble, didn't whore. Worked as a porter in a Park Avenue co-op for seventeen years. Then one morning going to work . . . Boom! Some mutt blows him up." Foliari paused. "The poor bastard's dead, but I don't think he personally was a target. Know what I'm saying?"

Townsend knew exactly.

"Sure," Townsend said, picking up on the detective's logic. "And that allows you to work your theory with a different spin."

"Exactly," Foliari answered. "Suppose *you* were the real target, Mr.

Townsend. Linking you as a victim with an Hispanic gentleman from East Harlem sends us and the guys on Homicide in the wrong direction."

"And then again, you have two more theories," Townsend continued. "All four explosive devices could have been random. The bomber doesn't even know his victims. Or all four could be linked. In a way that is not yet obvious to anyone."

Foliari took a long drink of tea. He gave Townsend a deeply appreciative look and a nod of approbation. "You're good at this," the policeman allowed.

"I used to do investigative reporting, remember?"

"Yeah, I remember. I never read any of the papers you wrote for, though."

"Too bad."

"Hell," said Foliari, shaking his head. "I got enough to investigate here."

In turn, Townsend nodded to Detective Foliari. He, too, knew how it was.

Several minutes later, their meeting concluded. Townsend stood. Foliari walked him to the door of the small room and opened it. Townsend took one step out of Foliari's office when he was stopped in his tracks by the firm touch of something hard—something that felt for all the world like the nose of a pistol—pressed against the base of his skull.

Unsmiling, Foliari stepped away from him.

"One move. One word. One smartass remark too many out of you, you hack newspaperman, and I'll blow your brains out," said a resonant and ominous voice behind him. "That's if you have any brains left!"

Townsend felt a hand of iron on his shoulder, and from the very corner of his eye could see the mocha tint of the skin. Townsend stood as motionless as a statue, his hands partially raised and carefully remaining in view. The body of the man speaking to him was unseen. Yet Townsend sensed a large, physically imposing presence, the bulk of a man large enough to fill a door frame by himself. Instinctively, Townsend broke into a rapid sweat.

"You'd *better* keep those paws where we can see them, mister!" the voice insisted. "Vinnie?" he snapped to Foliari. "Did you pat this guy down, Vinnie? He carries artillery sometimes."

"He's clean," said Foliari, still not smiling.

"Then let's lock him up."

There was something unreal about it. Everyone else who passed in the corridor hardly acknowledged what was happening.

"What the—?" Townsend began.

"Shut up, dude!"

The voice echoed with increasing familiarity. Townsend felt his mind speeding into overdrive, trying to place the voice. Then suddenly he had it.

"Jesus H. Christ," Townsend finally said, lowering his hands. He turned, recognizing the man behind him. "You dickhead!"

Finally, Vincent Foliari began to laugh, as did Townsend's benevolent assailant, Det. Sgt. Anthony Duncan, formerly of the Eighty-eighth Precinct in Brooklyn, now of the Second Detective Division, Manhattan North.

"You son of a bitch!" continued Townsend, as Duncan withdrew his extended forefinger from the base of Townsend's skull. Duncan laughed indulgently.

"If you weren't five inches taller than I am," Townsend vowed. "I'd deck you."

"Townsend, you couldn't break a friggin' egg."

"Screw you."

Townsend and Duncan warmly shook hands.

Their friendship—and it had once been a very firm one—went back a dozen years, first to Lower Manhattan where Duncan had drawn his first tour in the Fifth Precinct where Townsend was investigating high stakes dice games that operated with flagrant kickbacks to desk sergeants, judges, and ward captains. There Townsend came across Duncan, an articulate, self-educated young officer who had been born in Trinidad. They saw the corruption in the precinct as a common enemy, a retrogressive alliance that had no use for ambitious young black cops or reporters out to expose corruption. So, off the record, Duncan had pointed Townsend in the right direction. Townsend's expose in the *News* had resulted in resignations, transfers, two indictments, and one jail sentence—not to mention the usual death threats against the author of the evil tidings.

The youngest in a family of six, Anthony Duncan had moved as a child to Brooklyn. There he had grown up on the unrelenting streets of Bedford–Stuyvesant. He had never known his father. But an uncle whom he had liked in Port-of-Spain had been a policeman. So Anthony Duncan studied to be a policeman, too.

He passed the patrolman's exam in 1982 and went on the job fifteen months later. Assigned initially to Lower Manhattan, Duncan eventually was transferred to Brooklyn, where he worked as an officer on the same streets on which he'd spent his youth. There Townsend came across him again when Duncan and a Staten Island-born partner named Bill Neeley formed an ebony-ivory cop tandem and fought a relentless day-to-day war with the Jamaican and Colombian drug barons who brought plague to the new immigrant neighborhoods of North America. A kinship had been forged between the young immigrant cop and the surly Ohio-born reporter. Duncan admired a journalist who had the singular nerve to slaughter some sacred bulls around the city, and to print the truth as he saw it from the street. Townsend, in turn, admired a tough, disciplined kid who was not inclined to sidestep the tougher parts of his job.

But thereafter, Townsend had lost touch with his friend as Duncan spent his free time studying for a shot at the detective's exam. Meanwhile, Townsend was attempting to salvage his sanity after his nervous breakdown. Duncan had dropped him a note when he had heard of Townsend's difficulties, asking if he could do anything to help. Townsend had never answered.

"What are you doing out of uniform?" Townsend asked.

Duncan reached to his pocket and flashed a newly minted gold shield, that of a detective on the New York City Police Department.

"What's this?" Townsend asked. "You finally passed the exam?"

"I only took it once."

"You finally learned to read and write?" Townsend taunted.

"Jesus," said Duncan. "I knew I should have shot you on sight. You finished with this hunk of white bread, Vinnie?"

Foliari nodded.

"Then I'll get rid of him. Get in my office, Townsend," said Duncan, showing him the way, "and shut up. I want to show you what I'm doing these days. Otherwise, you won't believe it."

Townsend followed Duncan into a surprisingly modern office, complete with computer and fax. The room was cleaner and larger than Foliari's, with ample workspace and equipment resembling that which might be found in a darkroom.

"How you feeling these days?" Duncan asked. "I knew you'd had some troubles a year or two back."

"I'm alive," said Townsend. "That's a victory right there."

"Alive and working the death beat for Max Kohlheimer."

"Yeah. How'd you know?"

"I see your name all the time. People I know turn up on your page."

"More will," said Townsend.

"Just stay off it yourself for a while, you jerk," Duncan chided.

"I'm trying."

In the next few minutes of conversation, the men caught up with other details of each other's life. At the time when Townsend had begun work at the *Sun,* Anthony Duncan had graduated from precinct patrol to the Detective Bureau. He had first worked Missing Persons in the Bronx, then graduated to a busy homicide tour in Washington Heights. Eventually, as a result of some extensive work at John Jay College, which combined computer programming with photosynthesizing, Duncan had won an assignment to an arcane little sector of the NYPD called Special Services, which is where he was now.

"Does the term Photo Veneration mean anything to you?" Duncan finally asked.

"Should it?"

"Jesus Christ! Do you answer every question with another question?"

"Isn't that my job?"

"Photo veneration: I'm going to give you a six-week course in computer forensics in six minutes." Duncan paused as he eased into a swivel chair. "I'm guessing, Townsend. I say this would be completely new stuff for a nasty old fart like yourself. But for those of us on the cutting edge of technology—"

"Knock it off, you big, brown dickhead. What have you got?"

"PV portraits," Duncan said.

Seeing no reaction from his friend, Duncan sprung to his feet and crossed the room to a computer installation that filled half of a wall. He invited Townsend to look over his shoulder. Then Duncan showed him.

"Like I said: Photo veneration," Duncan began. "We use this mostly in missing persons. But you never know when it will turn up useful. A lot of bad guys disappear for a while, gain weight, lose weight, grow a mustachio, dye their hair, and so on."

Townsend still wasn't following.

"Take a look at this," Duncan finally said.

The detective opened some loose-leaf notebooks and gave Townsend a guided tour of his new deductive art. Each notebook was filled with photographs of individuals—mostly children, abduction victims, and those fleeing arrest warrants. All had been missing anywhere from two to twenty years. Duncan, with the use of an old photograph of the individual, could employ his computer to project how the departed individual might appear today in 1996.

"The technology has been around for maybe five to eight years," Duncan explained. "But the science has been rapidly perfected over the last two.

"The process can also work in reverse," Duncan said. "Give me a contemporary photograph of someone and I can work it back to childhood. I can see how someone would have looked as a kid or I can project how a child will look in seventy years. Give me a snapshot of you and

I'll show you how you'll look like an eighty-year-old, if you're lucky enough to live so long. You got a driver's license or did you lose it?"

"I got one."

"Let me have it. It's got your ugly mug on it."

Townsend declined.

"Okay, how 'bout I take a fresh picture of you," Duncan said, "and I'll work it back? See what an ugly kid you must have been."

"You can take my word for it," Townsend said.

"I'll bet your mother dressed you funny, too. Hey. Take a good look at this, man."

Duncan had performed the process upon himself. He showed Townsend an actual photograph of himself as a boy of eight and a picture of himself at present. Then he showed Photo-venerated portraits taken from each of the shots—one worked forward, one worked in reverse. The results were astonishingly accurate.

Then Duncan gave his guest a further demonstration involving an actual case. Duncan had that morning received a photograph of a teenage girl who had run away from home in Missouri in 1991. She was now believed to be in New York. Duncan ran her picture through and within ten minutes had a projection of how she might look currently. The PV-portrait came out of a machine that resembled a photocopier.

Duncan held up his work and looked at it critically.

"Females are more difficult than males," he mused. "Hairstyles. They change them more dramatically. One day it's 'big hair.' The next day they got a box-top crew cut like a dyke. But you'd be surprised what a PV-portrait can do. Want to see what the police commissioner would have looked like as a twenty-year-old kid with a 1979 Tina Turner fright wig?"

Townsend passed on this opportunity as well.

His computer could also analyze photographic portraits, Duncan continued. The bone structure of human faces never changed, he said. Thus he could compare a pair of photographs taken years apart and provide evidence admissible in a court as positive identification of a suspect or missing person. It was frontier forensic science and Townsend took note of it with interest.

"Okay, you old bastard," Duncan finally concluded. "I realize this is like outer space to a shoe-leather type of guy like yourself. But now you know where I am. If you ever need anything . . ."

"I appreciate it, Anthony. I'll call."

The two men shook hands again and parted.

* * *

In the afternoon, Townsend began to think of Leonard Wolik again. Yet he strongly felt the need to clear his mind from work—especially work that had no immediacy. So he walked down Broadway until he came to the West Sixties. He had lunch at an enjoyable but uninspired new place called Damon's that served hamburgers for sixteen dollars and pasta dishes for twenty. This was considered reasonable. His waitress was young and pleasant and wore a tag that proclaimed her name as Eileen.

She looked to be about twenty-two. When Townsend lured her into a conversation, Eileen revealed that she had recently left Barnard College to study acting. Townsend put in his usual pitch for the value of learning how to read, write, and think. The young woman seemed to be listening.

The atmosphere of the place was buoyant and the clientele eclectic. Even after two in the afternoon, the bar and dining room remained busy. It was filled mostly with people who were half Townsend's age and who—for some unseen economic reason—didn't seem to have jobs to return to.

Where, he wondered idly, do they come from? Despite the much-advertised decay and decline of the urban Northeast, why did this endless stream of young people flock to New York? Where did they live? Surely their salaries didn't afford them safe or comfortable lodging anywhere in Manhattan. How did they even survive?

Eventually, he felt alone in the midst of the crowd. Loneliness made him think of his wife and daughter. Though he phoned frequently, he hadn't spoken to either for several days. He would call that evening, he reminded himself, and sometime soon he would get together the money to visit. Even if Nora, his ex-wife, was drifting out of his life, his daughter remained part of it.

He left Damon's. Still on foot, he crossed Central Park and went to a movie in the East Fifties. Thereafter, out of curiosity, he browsed through a print shop and a pair of used book stores. He had a mental list of items for which he had been on the lookout for years but never seemed to find.

The biggest secret of the sixties. The thought kept pestering him.

When he returned home that evening, it was past seven P.M. He read a book for an hour, then telephone his ex-wife and daughter in California. Nora and Emily were on the way to a piano lesson and had to cut the call short. The communication left Townsend with a vaguely unsettled feeling. He yearned to know how well Emily was progressing with her music. And Nora sounded considerably less hostile than on previous calls. Perhaps their divorce was soon to become a fact of law. And perhaps the reality of it—allowing each of them to officially pursue his or her future—had eased many tensions.

He didn't know. That was one more thing, he mused, that he didn't know. So eventually he turned his attention to the telecast of a Mets–Dodgers game being played locally. The contest was a red-eye special, lasting twelve innings before the Mets emerged victoriously 2–1, thanks to a wild pitch. The winning run crossed the plate half an hour before midnight.

And now Townsend was wide awake.

He went to his refrigerator and found the rare roast beef he had purchased that morning. He made himself a sandwich on soft rye bread, spreading it thick with hot mustard. Over the next few minutes, two cold beers washed it down.

From the freezer he withdrew dessert: a pair of vanilla Popsicles, the thin, old-fashioned kind which now cost three dollars each. They were rich with ice cream and chocolate coating.

"Slow suicide through animal fat, alcohol, and cholesterol," Harry would have chided had he been there.

"Well, so be it," Townsend said aloud, agreeing with his absent friend. "What good is a health risk if you can't take it in triple doses?" Someday, Townsend reasoned, he would end up writing his own obituary—either figuratively or literally—and his pal Harry would be one of his pall bearers.

To make things complete, he then brewed some coffee—just what a wide awake newsman needed on an evening off.

At a few minutes before midnight, Townsend settled into his bedroom. As the evening died and as much of the street noise outside diminished to a low, constant rumble, he seated himself at the small rectangular table near his bed and within sight of the window. He turned on the desk lamp and a bright yellow light flowed onto the tabletop from beneath the green glass shade. From the drawer, he withdrew the manila envelope that bore his own name in his own handwriting.

After a day of low-key brooding and relative leisure, Paul Townsend was now ready. From the envelope, he withdrew the lengthy printout from the *Sun*'s official memory bank. He placed it squarely on the table before him, confronting himself with it.

With growing curiosity, he drew toward him the first pages of what he now thought of as his WOLIK file. Keeping a warm cup of coffee at arm's length, Townsend then leaned forward to begin the arduous task of collating Big Wally's memory with the words of Sarah's father.

As he did so, he had the eerie prescient sense of embarking on a long journey with an unchartable itinerary. He had a sense of such things after a quarter century of newsprint. He somehow knew that what was before him would never condense into a few columns and a few inches on even a busy news day.

*F*EW such stories have finite beginnings or endings. Most begin in confusion and end the same way. From the outset, Townsend knew that the story before him would probably prove to be no exception.

He reacted with no surprise when the first known reference to a Popov occurred in the year 1953, some twelve years before Leonard Wolik and Colbert Davies formed their Odd Couple act in Paris.

Nineteen fifty-three. The year Stalin died and the year the Soviet Union exploded its first hydrogen bomb. Eisenhower's first year as President, John F. Kennedy's first full year as a United States senator, and Lyndon Johnson's first as a majority leader of the newly Democratic United States Senate. It was a year when Nikita Khrushchev executed Lavrentii Beria and, not to be outdone, the government of the United States executed the Rosenbergs.

Nineteen fifty-three. Townsend remembered a large white house on a rural lane in Dublin, Ohio. He had been twelve years old at the time and in the seventh grade. His father had been the publisher of a small town weekly Ohio newspaper and his mother had made a home for a family of five.

Townsend nudged himself to stay within the professional limits of the pages before him. He began to read, and tried to picture the events as they must have occurred. . . .

* * *

In 1953, Austria remained occupied by the victorious allied armies of World War II, but already deep chasms had developed between East and West. The border cities of Eastern Europe—Vienna, Berlin, Zagreb—were focal points of intrigue.

Colonel Pyotr Popov of Soviet military intelligence, the GRU, was stationed in Vienna at the time. For reasons never entirely clear, Colonel Popov decided to offer his services to the West.

Colonel Popov volunteered his services by leaving a note on a car belonging to an American diplomat. Within a fortnight, Colonel Popov had become the first and only postwar penetration agent by the CIA within Soviet military intelligence. For his troubles and his risks, the colonel was to be paid $100 per month—the amount to be held for him in an escrow account in a West German bank.

In return, Popov delivered a witch's brew of secrets. Among them he had a list of cryptonyms for nearly four hundred Soviet agents who had infiltrated the West. One of these, a hair stylist named Irena, would put in motion events that would echo for several decades.

Popov had previously dispatched agents all over the world. He had sent them to England, France, Hungary, China, Singapore, Greece, Bolivia, Brazil, Cuba, and Japan. But he had never before sent one to the United States.

In Vienna, Popov personally prepared the woman with a suitcase filled with American clothing and cosmetics. Behind a vanity mirror in the suitcase was hidden her operating funds, several thousand dollars in various currencies. Irena was a shapely but plain brown-haired woman in her mid-thirties. Her mission was to travel to Manhattan in late 1954 and assume the identity of the "wife" of a Soviet agent already in place. She was fully equipped with a thorough cover story and a United States passport. The latter had once belonged to an American woman of Polish birth. It had been stolen from her hotel room on a visit to Eastern Europe. Now the passport had been elaborately forged and reissued with Irena's photograph.

The CIA's first and most lasting reaction to the Irena affair, as they learned of it from Colonel Popov, was to fervently wish that they had never known of it. Because she was a foreign agent on U.S. soil, the Federal Bureau of Investigation had to be notified. The CIA agents in the field drafted a memo to CIA Chief Allen Dulles. The fieldmen urged that the director of the FBI, J. Edgar Hoover, keep his meddlesome troops away from Irena. If she knew she was blown, suspicion would revert to Popov and the CIA would lose their best penetration agent within the structure of the Soviet military.

Logic followed their argument. Logic did not, however, follow the politics of Washington.

Dulles was sympathetic but committed to play by Washington rules. The FBI was informed, along with a personal plea by Dulles that FBI watchers steer clear of Irena. Hoover's office responded with its usual delicacy: twelve different agents, specially reassigned from the Chicago and St. Louis offices, were assigned to meet her flight from Paris when it arrived at New York's Idlewild Airport.

They stood a few feet from her as she changed francs for dollars. Two agents followed her onto the airport bus that took her to the East Side of Manhattan. Another team followed her taxi from the bus terminal to the Hotel Hewitt in Brooklyn. Such tan-raincoat, white-shirt, snap-brim fedora subtlety would make the Federal Bureau of Investigation famous.

The next day, other FBI agents broke into Irena's hotel room and searched it. The bureau's notes on the case maintained that the entry was done "with utmost care." Nonetheless, Irena recognized a break-in when she'd been the victim of one.

On her third day in the United States, she took a subway into Manhattan and spent six hours riding escalators and elevators in Macy's, Bloomingdale's, and Saks Fifth Avenue, attempting to discard her shadows. Or, more likely, she was trying to determine just how many she had.

Not only did Irena know she was blown, but the FBI knew she knew. Still, federal agents sat three rows behind her when she rendezvoused with her Soviet "husband" at a Broadway movie house showing *Moulin Rouge*. When she moved into his apartment, their phone was tapped immediately. Another FBI squad broke in to place electronic bugs in the walls.

This went on for several weeks. Then, Irena walked out of the apartment one day and disappeared. The FBI didn't even know she was gone until she turned up in East Berlin with a GRU inspector reassigned from Moscow. East Berlin was where Colonel Popov was now stationed and East Berlin was where—live and in person—she now accused Colonel Popov of being the source of her betrayal.

Popov protested his innocence. He insisted that Irena must have been stricken with cowardice in the United States. The GRU inspector was inclined to believe a man who was a senior officer over a woman who was in the field. The KGB, however, was not so readily convinced. Popov was escorted to Moscow for what was ominously described as "additional interrogation."

Popov had the opportunity to bolt to the West. But he declined, convinced that his status as a GRU colonel would allow him to tough things out. And in Moscow, he appeared to have reasoned correctly. The KGB had discovered that he had kept a mistress in Vienna, a revelation that might have been damning—except that it saved him by redirecting his inquisitor's attentions.

So as the months passed, Popov worked up the nerve to rekindle his contact with the West. A CIA agent working under diplomatic cover in Moscow served as Popov's contact.

Meetings with American contacts in Moscow were hair-raising events, even by the jaded standards of spies. Unlike Berlin or Vienna, there were no safe houses maintained by the West and no leisurely afternoons of food, drink, and political conversation. More than three dozen KGB observation posts encircled the United States Embassy in Moscow, with countless more on the streets beyond. Each was maintained with observers and cameras around the clock. A CIA officer or any American diplomat could count on a KGB pavement team picking him up any time he travelled out of the embassy. Thus, contacts with sources had to be confined to as little as a single word perhaps, or a frantic lunge to place a message in a dead drop.

Nonetheless, Popov served the West through the warm summer of 1959. Unhappily, he remained under KGB scrutiny. Then came a final contact with the West.

On October 16, 1959, Popov and his American contact attempted to pass notes to each other on a jammed Moscow bus. One reason the bus was jammed was that it contained fifteen Soviet police, all of whom pounced as a CIA man and Popov made their transfer.

The American was held for hours, threatened with life imprisonment, and forcibly interrogated. But he had spent many hours rehearsing for this grim eventuality. To his inquisitors, he said simply, "I am an American diplomat. I demand to be released immediately."

Immediately, no. Eventually, yes. Predictably, the United States government strongly protested the "harassment" of a member of its "diplomatic corps" and denied that he was in any way involved in espionage. Two days later, amid further protestations, he was removed from the Soviet Union.

His fate, however, was far preferable to that of his contact. An article in *Izvestia* which followed the arrests described the "treason" of Colonel Popov. It went on to "quote" the GRU officer.

"There are crimes after which it is impossible to live," the colonel was purported to have said. "At the end of a contemptible life, a bullet is a fitting punishment, as well as an act of mercy."

The "act of mercy" was an appearance before a firing squad at

Lubyanka Prison, around the corner from the Kremlin, before the end of the year. The colonel's body was then stuffed into the incinerator—maintained especially for such purposes—around back.

Townsend, at a few minutes past one in the morning, fumed as he digested this. He fumed just as the CIA must have thirty-seven years earlier. Hoover's heavy-handed meddling had apparently cost an excellent source his life. Equally, it had cost the country the benefit of a continued intelligence asset.

"Of all the pompous, blathering mid-twentieth-century frauds!" Townsend thought. "Hoover! The great G-Man who—"

Townsend froze. There were voices very close to him. His heart gave a wicked start and he sat very still for a moment. His thoughts leaped from Pyotr Popov and J. Edgar Hoover through to the present.

Voices. A man and a woman.

Where?

He broke a sweat. Then he relaxed.

It was only the couple in the next apartment. Barbara and Jim were speaking to each other on the other side of the common wall. They had returned home together and were having a noisy conversation—just a noisy conversation—in their bedroom.

Their first serious argument? Townsend mused as his nerves settled down. Had Barbara looked at another man, or had she slept with one? A simple lover's spat, or a breach in the relationship? Their voices drifted out of the neighboring bedroom, and as they did so, receded from Townsend's thoughts.

Townsend rose and walked away from his table. In his kitchen he reheated some coffee. Then he returned. He flipped to the next page of his long printout.

A new name appeared. The initial identification was SOURCE: SNIPER.

Sniper. Ruefully, he glanced to his own window and was reassured when he saw only dark sky and very, very distant buildings.

Sniper. His full attention was immediately arrested.

Back in December 1959, as the Central Intelligence Agency had been cursing Hoover, another penetration agent was already moving into place.

The new agent had first made contact in March 1959 with a letter, mailed from Zurich to Henry J. Taylor, the United States ambassador to Switzerland.

The correspondence was written in labored German. It offered "valuable information on Communist spy operations in the West." It was signed, "Sniper." Ambassador Taylor dutifully turned over the letter to the CIA station chief in Bern.

The station chief studied the letter. He sent photocopies by diplomatic pouch back to Langley for analysis. A German-speaking CIA officer noted that the syntax of the letter suggested that the author was not a native German. And as some of the initial content dealt authoritatively with Soviet operations in Poland, a tentative conclusion was drawn that the author was a Pole.

But everything else was a guess. Was Sniper a bona fide "walk in" defection or a Soviet agent of disinformation? Even an analysis of Sniper's typewriter and stationery revealed little. The best minds in the American intelligence service could only take the letter at face value, and proceed with caution.

Adhering to Sniper's suggestion, the CIA placed a classified ad in one of the Frankfurt newspapers. The ad, in veiled language, confirmed receipt of the letter. Thus began a lengthy correspondence.

The CIA opened a mailbox in West Berlin where Sniper could address future messages. He would use the same box to receive letters from the CIA. In those, instructions or questions would be hidden in secret writing beneath otherwise innocuous messages or advertisements. Similarly, Sniper was assigned a second letter drop in a repulsive public lavatory in Berlin's Tiergarten. He was also given a telephone number to call in an emergency.

The information from Sniper started as a trickle. Sometimes he was exasperating. Often he had names wrong. Frequently Sniper was misinformed on locations. And much of what he wrote was of little interest, even after extensive analysis. But occasionally he would drop a casual line or two, almost in passing, that would lead—given the proper exploration—into a vein of gold.

Example given: Sniper wrote that the KGB had taken over a Warsaw Pact operation from the Poles, with the payoff being the placement of a spy within the British Admiralty. Sniper came across with a maddeningly phonetic spelling of the spy's name. He wrote that the spy's name began with an "H," and that "H" had originally been recruited by the Poles while assigned to the office of the British Naval attaché in Warsaw.

That narrowed the field considerably. It narrowed it, in point of fact, to one man, Harry Houghton, a clerk at the Portland Naval base.

M.I.6 was notified. In June 1960, surveillance teams from Scotland Yard observed Houghton and his girlfriend, Ethel Gee, hand a package to a jukebox salesman named Gordon Lonsdale in front of London's Old Vic Theatre. Scotland Yard observed four additional meetings over the next six months. After each rendezvous, agents trailed Lonsdale to a working-class suburb of London called Ruislip. There he visited the home of Helen and Peter Kroger.

Christmas 1960 neared. Sniper, in the holiday spirit, suddenly dialed the emergency number given him by the CIA. He wanted to fully defect, he said, and would bring with him a wife and access to "extensive material" that he promised would be of interest to the West.

News of the defection went to the highest levels of Langley. Yet there were more skeptics than believers. Allen Dulles pronounced Sniper, "a bunch of crap," and advised his agents in Berlin not to spend too much time waiting for him.

Nonetheless, Sniper materialized in West Berlin at the start of the Christmas holidays, accompanied by—in a last second revision of plans—his mistress instead of his wife. He identified himself as Michal Goleniewski, an officer in Polish intelligence. Goleniewski had also worked for the Soviet KGB, betraying his own countrymen to the Russians.

He had planned his journey well, however. First, he would not be missed until after the long Christmas weekend. But second, and even more significantly, in a hollow tree trunk outside of Warsaw, Goleniewski had—in the months preceding his defection—gradually stashed microfilm of hundreds of pages of Polish and Russian intelligence documents, including extensive lists of names of operatives in the West.

Townsend rubbed his eyes as he read. It was past two A.M. He hit the bottom of his final cup of coffee.

Goleniewski fared much more comfortably than Popov. CIA operatives flew him to the Azores on a military aircraft. There Goleniewski and his lady friend pleasantly whiled away the time pumping nickels—courtesy of the American taxpayer—into slot machines at the local USO club. Meanwhile, their aircraft refueled. Then Goleniewski was flown to Washington. There a CIA interrogation team met him and escorted him in a three-car motorcade to a safe house in the Virginia countryside.

With the Pole in the United States, the hammer was about to come down for what London's Fleet Street would quickly name the Portland Spy Ring. Goleniewski was no longer at risk in being blown as a source. So on the first Saturday in January 1961, sixteen days before the snowy inauguration of John F. Kennedy, a pair of Scotland Yard detectives, a man and a woman, followed Harry Houghton and Ethel Gee as they strolled along Waterloo Road.

Before the Old Vic Theatre, they encountered their "friend," Gordon Lonsdale. Ethel Gee was carrying a straw bag. Lonsdale, ever the gentleman, asked if he might carry it for her.

When the bag changed hands, the Scotland Yard detectives pounced, assisted by another dozen backups. They arrested Houghton, Gee, and Lonsdale. An hour later, a meticulous search began of the home of their friends the Krogers, the happy suburbanites out in Ruislip.

Found, among other things, were a one time code pad concealed in a cigarette lighter, a one hundred fifty-foot antenna wired through the rafters of the house, and—beneath a secret trapdoor in the kitchen—a high-frequency transmitter concealed in a hidden chamber. But that wasn't even the worst news for the Krogers.

When the Krogers were booked, a set of their fingerprints was sent to Scotland Yard's Criminal Records office. Funny thing. A matching set had been on file since 1957 when they had been circulated by the FBI. The Krogers had previously been known as Morris and Lona Cohen of New York City. Their prints had been found in the apartment of Rudolph Abel, head of a Soviet spy network in the United States that had been rolled up four years earlier. The Cohens had been on the FBI's wish list since 1951 when they were named as accomplices of the Rosenbergs.

Townsend continued to read. The farther he went, the deeper the intrigue. While most human beings, at their summing up, had lived lives with a few secrets on the side, he knew that most lives were relatively straightforward. But not here. Not in the milieu of official governmental deception. Lonsdale, for example, wasn't even Lonsdale.

According to his Canadian passport and his work permit in the United Kingdom, Lonsdale had been born in Ontario in 1924. Within a few days, however, the Royal Canadian Mounted Police had located another thirty-six-year-old Gordon Lonsdale, working in Canada, and mystified by the sudden attentions of law enforcement.

The RCMP obtained Lonsdale's medical records. The real Lonsdale child had been circumcised shortly after birth. The man in London, observers readily agreed, had not been. Or at least not yet. The man in London, in fact, was eventually identified as one Conon Molody, an officer in Soviet intelligence. Molody had spent much of his life cultivating the persona of an agreeable Canadian functionary.

A team of British interrogators soon visited the safe house in Virginia, anxious to discover what else Goleniewski had to say. Specifically, M.I.6 wished to know how their assets in Poland had been compromised over the preceding years. In response, Goleniewski described the physical appearance and location of a double agent in Berlin who worked for Her Majesty's government but supplied information to the Soviets.

The double agent, the British soon deduced, was a man named George Blake.

Blake had been born in Holland, the son of a naturalized British subject, a Sephardic Jew from Egypt, and a Dutch mother. He had been named George in honor of George V and had been a heroic member of the Dutch underground during World War II. Taken aboard by the British during the war, Blake had eventually become the M.I.6 station chief in Seoul in the late 1940s. Communist insurgents had captured him in 1948 and he had spent three hellish years in a Korean prison. On his release in 1951, he had come home to London, again a hero, this time with a stopover in Moscow. That should have made his peers suspicious. It didn't. But then again, at the time the director of counterintelligence of M.I.6 had been one Kim Philby.

Following lengthy discussions with Goleniewski, M.I.6 agents confronted Blake over Easter weekend of 1961. Blake broke and confessed. Thereafter, he rallied his courage and bragged about the damage he had done to "Western imperialist interests, particularly the Americans." Once he had returned to London in the 1950s, Blake boasted, he had photographed everything to which he had access within the walls of M.I.6. What he hadn't been able to photograph, he reported verbally.

Through the 1950s, for example, the CIA had considered the Berlin "tunnel," a listening post burrowed under East Berlin, as one of their primary intelligence coups. Blake, through his clearance at M.I.6, had known of the tunnel in 1953 and had immediately warned his Soviet mentors. The West had received nothing through that post that the Soviets hadn't intended.

Townsend felt a headache coming on when he came to the next part, however. Blake's arrest put a completely different spin on the Popov operation, an operation which Townsend had thought he had understood.

In 1955, a British liaison officer in Berlin had been briefed by the CIA of the existence of Popov. The British officer had stashed several memoranda concerning Popov in an embassy safe. Blake, as the most junior SIS officer in the embassy, drew the task of locking the safe each night. Hence he had daily access to the safe's contents. The FBI's clumsy handling of the Irena affair in New York, the CIA thus concluded, had not been the actual compromise of the Popov affair. Blake had been. But the FBI had allowed the KGB a convenient way to terminate Popov without implicating Blake.

Townsend had enough experience as an investigative journalist to comprehend logic within a skein of illogic. Now, in a perverse, backhanded way at quarter to three on a Saturday morning, all of this began to make sense.

Then, however, the entire skein toppled and reversed upon him. Not just the Portland ring and not just George Blake and his network had been compromised by Goleniewski. There had also been a German, Heinz Felfe, of the West German intelligence service. He had been arrested and had confessed to supplying state secrets to the Soviets. The Felfe confession created a scandal within West Germany and almost led to a complete dismantling of the BDN, the West German intelligence agency. Yet, James Jesus Angleton, the head of the counterintelligence division within the CIA, insisted that Goleniewski was a disinformation agent. A setup by the Soviets.

Townsend continued to read.

"Whatever his faults," wrote another CIA Soviet expert in a hotly conflicting opinion, "Goleniewski is the best defector we've ever had."

Angleton's theory was almost too intricate for human consumption. Yet it began to chill Townsend as he continued his journey through the final pages of the Goleniewski affair, and as he labored to work Zarudni into the puzzle.

Goleniewski had written a total of fourteen letters to the West. The early letters had compromised both the Portland spy ring and Heinz Felfe. By Goleniewski's own eventual admission in Langley, he had been dropped as an agent in Poland prior to these letters. He admitted that he was writing to a CIA contact to gain a certain revenge on his former bosses. But after the first letters, the Soviets—again by Goleniewski's own admission—had picked him up again. Thereupon, he had begun sending information that bore a new tone.

Seen from this perspective, it followed that the Soviets might have realized that someone—they probably even knew it was Goleniewski—had been sending letters to the West. And they had been feeding information to him which they knew he would dispatch to his contacts. Unwittingly, according to Angleton's hypothesis, Goleniewski may have been a top-notch agent of disinformation, even though he was also passing on information of value that the KGB didn't know he had. When Goleniewski became suspicious of this himself, he panicked and fled. The Soviets, not wishing to acknowledge that they had been on to him for some time, permitted his departure, mistress and all.

Angleton's theory either collapsed of its own weight or went on to create entirely new vistas of deception, depending whether one wished to believe that Angleton remained a genius or had gone mad—a discussion that raged for the final ten years of his career at CIA.

Townsend drew back from the pages before him. His eyes were sore.

He had finished the body of the printout. But then he noted one of a series of addenda. This was a small article dated October 13, 1982, several years after all the events in question and more than seven full years after Angleton's resignation from the agency. It had originally been published in the *Washington Post*. Like the letters of Goleniewski, the addenda conveyed significant importance within a few lines.

A final missive from Warsaw, the *Post* reported, sent by Goleniewski shortly before he defected, provided tangible evidence that the Soviets knew of an operational step to be taken in Venezuela on January 28, 1961.

The undertaking, known as OPERATION: ARROYO, was a CIA attempt to kidnap a Cuban intelligence officer who was to be lured to Caracas by a ballerina. ARROYO had been formulated no earlier than November 26, 1960 by a Washington-based Maracaibo-born CIA operative. Two days later, the continuation of ARROYO had been approved by John and Robert Kennedy, the President-elect and the Attorney General-designate of the United States, in a special meeting with Allen Dulles. No allied parties—meaning English, French, or West German—had yet been advised. The Kennedys had been consulted by Dulles so that the CIA could move ARROYO forward without fear of cancellation by the new President. Dulles received the approval he wanted and had been pleased to learn that the Kennedys were even more enthusiastic about anti-Cuban operations than the Eisenhower administration.

The thrust of the *Washington Post* article had little to do with AR-ROYO, itself. Rather, what was significant was who knew about the article and when. The conclusion, if correct, was both staggering and inescapable. And herein also may have lain the greatest significance of the Goleniewski defection.

Goleniewski's letter was dated December 1, 1960. For such information to have blown back through Goleniewski within five days, the Soviets had to have had a high penetration agent in Washington. At cabinet level perhaps. Or within the highest echelon of the CIA. Or—most ominously—within the Kennedy brothers' closest circle of friends.

OPERATION: ARROYO crashed before it even flapped its wings. Yet this time there wasn't even latitude to blame the disaster on Kim Philby or M.I.6.

Similarly, for the Soviets to have given up Blake, Lonsdale, and Felfe to establish Goleniewski's credibility, the stakes must have been enormous. The prospect was even too terrifying to consider. What could possibly have been worth the loss of three established and valued networks?

That was a question which resounded in Townsend's mind as he closed the file. Several further newspaper references offered no satisfactory follow-up and no answer to the question. *How could information that sensitive have traveled that quickly? Who else, in December 1960, could have been a party to it?*

Townsend closed his files.

For several minutes he stared out his window into the night sky of Manhattan, gradually becoming more aware of street noises from the adjoining avenue.

As he had expected, he had forged through thousands of words only to arrive at an inconclusive ending. He moved his eyes and found himself staring at the blank wall of his bedroom.

Then Zarudni's words, related by Sarah's father, echoed again. *The greatest secret of the sixties.* What was it?

Zarudni had known something. Penetration of the CIA? A spy within the cabinet of the inexperienced young President? Just like OP-ERATION: ARROYO, Zarudni's proposed defection had been compromised, perhaps sustaining its own dire prophesy.

And compromised when? Townsend wondered. Almost immediately, he realized, after Washington had been alerted.

The logic circled back into the theories of James Jesus Angleton. Angleton had argued strenuously that the Soviets had a high penetration agent somewhere in Washington in the 1960s, and somewhere indeed high in the Kennedy administration.

But where?

And, of course, who?

"Obviously Lyndon Johnson," Townsend said facetiously and aloud.

The sound of his own voice jarred him after so many minutes of silent reading. Then the strange geometry of his facetious remark jarred him every bit as hard.

I always had this funny theory about the Kennedy assassination, Harry had said. *I always wondered whether Lyndon Johnson had something to do with it.*

And, *Lyndon's Man,* Sarah's father had called Colbert Davies. Davies who had sat astride the operation that had blown up in Paris in 1964.

And, *Obviously Lyndon Johnson,* Townsend himself had just said the name aloud. What was all this telling him? What, that wasn't patently absurd?

He continued to stare at the wall. The red letters on the time printout on his clock radio blipped from 2:59 to 3:00 A.M.

Voices again. Quiet at first, then louder.

Barbara and Jim. The neighbors one more time.

They were in the bedroom on the other side of Townsend's wall. In the silence of his own room, in the absence of most other noises of the city, he could hear them very clearly, almost word for word.

They were joking with each other, then laughing. Their voices settled for a moment, then came together in exclamations of physical feeling. There was no other way to say it: Barbara was one hell of a noisy lover.

Townsend left his bedroom, his mind churning much too rapidly for the hour. He retrieved a bottle of beer from the kitchen, then settled into a club chair in the living room. He was still deep in thought. Popov and Goleniewski. Lonsdale and Blake. James Jesus Angleton. Kennedy and Johnson. Wolik and Davies.

What a street gang.

He finished his beer. He returned to the bedroom at half past three. The room was quiet. Townsend climbed into his own bed and was asleep immediately.

Three days later, the other shoe dropped.

Bruce McMorris returned Townsend's call. McMorris—alluded to by Sarah's father toward the end of his long account of Paris, 1965—was still in the employ of a well-known company based in Langley, Virginia. McMorris would be more than happy—or at least agreeable—to meet in person.

Townsend arranged a meeting in Washington for the following Friday, which was his next day off. Staffers from the *Sun*'s city desk would cover the obituary beat for him. Harry, dependable old Harry, would oversee the editing.

McMorris agreed to a conversation on any reasonable nonclassified topic. As far as his agency was concerned, he warned, he hadn't been involved in anything interesting in years. And even if he had been, he said, he had nothing to hide.

As a reporter, Townsend felt a rush of enthusiasm. He sensed that he had a story. But better yet, now he had a contact.

< < < < **10** > > > >

THEY met in Washington at a the bar of the Hay Adams Hotel, diagonally across Lafayette Square from the White House. It was a few minutes past four on a cool, drizzly afternoon. The bar was quiet. At the tables in the rear, there were three people: a man and a woman at one table and a man by himself at another. Townsend, when he entered the bar, assumed the latter was waiting for him.

On sight, Townsend knew that Bruce McMorris was no one's fool. The veteran CIA man had a perfect view of the room and its entrance. He sat with a wall covering his left side, and nothing behind him.

The couple consisted of a man who, like McMorris, appeared to be in his mid-fifties. He was holding hands across a table with a much younger woman. She was in her late thirties, Townsend guessed, pretty with red hair. They had drinks before them and were seated four tables from McMorris.

Were they at borderline listening range, Townsend wondered, or just out of range? As a place of assignation, the bar of the Hay Adams was more unusual than most and unlikely at best.

McMorris had an untouched drink on the table in front of him, next to a small bowl of nuts. As Townsend first saw him, McMorris was plucking cashews from the bowl. Then when he saw Townsend, his long legs unfolded. McMorris stood, brushed his hands with a napkin, and extended an iron paw in greeting.

"I'm Bruce McMorris," he said. "You're Paul Townsend?"

Townsend accepted the handshake. The CIA man's hand remained faintly gritty from salt.

"Yes. How'd you know?"

"Central Intelligence is in the business of lucky guesses," McMorris said. "Didn't you know that? Occasionally a lucky guess proves right. You probably didn't know that, either." He laughed graciously. "That's life, right?"

Townsend seated himself and said that he supposed it was.

McMorris was a husky man about six feet three inches tall. He had sandy, thinning hair, glasses, and an angular but not unfriendly face. "What are you drinking?" he asked his visitor, barely pausing between sentences. He looked to the barman.

Townsend was parched from subways, trains, and taxis. "I'll have a beer," he said. In tweedy bars these days, the imported ones cost $6.50 a pop, thanks to the ever popular Excise Tax Act of 1994—which purported to protect the American breweries from a tidal wave of Asian suds. So Townsend specified domestic.

"How was your trip down from Gomorrah-on-Hudson?" McMorris asked. "I can't say I blame you for taking the train," he continued. "Those airports—LaGuardia, National, Dulles, Kennedy, the whole damned filthy lot of them—they're as deplorable as the cities they purport to serve."

"The train ride went quite well," Townsend said.

McMorris turned his attention to his drink. It had an amber color and was full. McMorris sipped it. Townsend caught the distinct aroma of bourbon. Yet there were a few dull, rounded vestiges of ice cubes remaining in it, meaning it may well have sat there for several minutes before McMorris had touched it.

Meaning, Townsend told himself, McMorris had arrived early to position himself comfortably in the bar. Meaning, Townsend concluded also, that McMorris wasn't ready to drink until he had company. Townsend noted that the drinks of the man and the woman at the nearby table were in much the same state.

Coincidence? he wondered. Or were they a backup team? Why, Townsend wondered, were all the old instincts and paranoia bedeviling him anew? It was the little things he was noticing again—like how long people had been waiting for him and where they sat around a room. He was, for example, completely cut off from both exits at this very moment.

Coincidence? he wondered again. Or had he taken the initial step to his next emotional breakdown?

A waiter appeared with a coaster, a mug, and a clear glass bottle of beer. The waiter also replenished the bowl of nuts. McMorris immediately attacked the new supply, working nimbly with long, sturdy fingers to pick out the cashews before any others.

McMorris bore the imprimatur of the proper church and universities, as well as the correctly influential elective contacts. He had served many years in Washington, as was readily apparent in his conversation. It was also clear that he had made friends along the years in sundry agencies beyond his own. He struck Townsend very much as a product of his times, what popular historians in weekend journals were already referring to the Republican Era of the tail end of the twentieth century.

Townsend, to friends, had already rechristened these years—1980 to 1996—as The Ass End of the Tremulous Century. McMorris fit neatly into the era, no matter what it was called. He looked ill at ease with nothing that he'd ever been a part of, and spoke in a faded Magnolia-tinged drawl that remorselessly suggested a birth in Arkansas or even deeper into the cotton states a half century earlier. After fifteen minutes, Townsend couldn't decide whether he liked McMorris in spite of himself or hated him for all the obvious reasons.

"So why are you here?" McMorris asked inevitably, sipping his bourbon a second time. "What's the story?"

"I don't have a story. Not yet."

"Hard to believe *that,*" McMorris retorted quickly. Two cashews perished in the midst of the sentence.

"Why?"

"You *always* have a story."

"Not today. Not a complete story."

"Come on," McMorris insisted. "You write investigative stuff, right? Big eastern liberal newspaper muckraking stuff. I know your name. Seen your byline. Think I just fell off the turnip truck? I know what you do."

"What's that?"

"You create trouble."

McMorris snorted as he munched. Townsend waited for more. He was not disappointed.

"Nothing personal, you understand, Mr. Townsend," McMorris said. "But I hate most of what you write. Check that. I hate all of it. I had a friend who was up for a federal judgeship during the early part of the Bush administration. Southern District of New York. You killed his nomination."

"Are you talking about Judge Frederick Perkins?"

"I am, sir."

"Judge Perkins ruled in four different cases in which he had obvious conflicts of financial interest. He was also reversed on appeal in more than forty percent of his decisions, usually on misinterpreted points of law or poor instructions to juries."

"Got a good memory, don't you?"

"Excellent. Judge Perkins killed his own nomination."

"Fred Perkins and I got a golf date every Saturday. I'll tell him you said so."

"Good. You can also tell him that I knew he kept a mistress for six years in Greenwich Village. But out of consideration for his wife and family, I didn't print that part."

"You're all heart, aren't you?" McMorris asked. He could be heard throughout the room. But the couple at the other table were too involved with each other—the man was kissing the red-haired woman's hand now—and took no outward notice of anyone else. The barman wasn't moved to look up, either.

"Why do you think I met you *here,* Mr. Townsend?" McMorris asked. "Can't invite a pariah such as yourself to my office. But I'm a sport. I want to know what you're up to. So tell me. What's on your mind today?"

"Well, first," Townsend began, "let's correct your misconceptions. I now write for the *New York Sun.* The *Sun* may be big and eastern but it's Max Kohlheimer's rag, which means it's not much more liberal than Louis the Fourteenth. As for muckraking, I had a nervous breakdown in 1994. I write obituaries now. Maybe someday I'll write yours. As for what you thought of my previous articles, I couldn't care less. I came here today to ask you some background questions. Off the record with no attribution. Not even an 'informed source' quote."

"About what?"

"There were several significant East-to-West defections back in the late 1950s," Townsend began. "Soviet intelligence officers. I'm sure you know the first of the important names. Popov? Goleniewski?"

"Yes. So what?"

"I want to know more about them," Townsend asked.

After a second, McMorris laughed. "Oh, God, Townsend," McMorris said. "Not that old mole-in-the CIA story?"

"That or something approximating it."

McMorris looked at him for another moment, then grinned. Townsend sensed a certain relaxation from across the table, like a tiny descent into boredom. "I suppose it stands to reason," he said, "that there still might be one stubborn old reporter left in the country chasing down that old canard."

"And I suppose I'm him. So what can you tell me?"

McMorris leaned forward conspiratorially. "I'll tell you something no one knows," he said. "I'll tell you who's suspected of being the high-ranking Soviet agent during the Kennedy years. Grew up in the slums of Hoboken, New Jersey, where he must have acquired his secret left-wing bent. Had personal access to every President from Kennedy through Reagan, yet had perfect cover. No one ever suspected. Want to hear the name?"

"Try me."

McMorris smirked. "Frank Sinatra," he said.

"Very funny."

"No, that's Bob Hope," McMorris said, continuing the joke.

"Frank's a good American and so is Bob Hope. It's you I'm starting to wonder about."

"Is *that* a joke?" McMorris asked, still amused.

"Yes. And every bit as lousy as yours. Now, what can you actually tell me?"

"Everything you already know," McMorris said, again speaking very routinely. "Look, there's been a detailed public record for years. All the major players are dead. And if there *had* been some traitor in the CIA or high up in the Kennedy or Johnson administrations, don't you think the dirt may have been shoveled onto him many moons ago? Who knows anymore? Who gives a shit? The old U.S.S.R. went out of business. Remember? Surely I can't present you with any special insight."

"But weren't you in Paris in the spring of 1965?" Townsend persisted.

"For the sake of discussion, let's say I was." McMorris had driven the cashews in the nut dish into extinction. Now he graduated to the macadamias. He was poised with an entire handful. "So? What then?"

"And you were friendly with a young diplomat named Leonard Wolik."

There was a pause. The CIA man grew slightly more serious. Then, "Sure. I knew Len Wolik," he said.

"When did you see him last?" Townsend asked.

"To talk to?"

"Yes."

McMorris pursed his lips. "I couldn't give you the exact date off the top of my head." Townsend waited as McMorris thought about it. "But Len and I were friends for a very long time."

"Even after Paris?"

"For many years after."

"When might you have seen him last?" Townsend asked.

"Last?" McMorris replied with something between a snort and a laugh. Then there was another uneasy pause. "It was at a church service in 1983. Here in the District. Nasty hot day in the mid-July, I'd say. Want the date? I could find it for you."

"Was it a Sunday church service?"

"The funeral of a friend."

"Did you talk to him?"

"Who?"

"Leonard Wolik. That's who we're talking about."

"I saw him. I didn't speak to him." More nuts, noisily. "Why? You talk to him these days, Townsend?" Something was changing in McMorris's attitude.

"Would you find it surprising if I did?"

"I might." McMorris's eyebrows were raised.

"Apparently you *are* surprised."

"All right, I confess. I am surprised. What did old Leonard have to say for himself?"

"He told me a story which took place when he was a young diplomat in Paris," Townsend said. "Wolik and the acting U.S. ambassador, a man named Colbert Davies, attempted to reel in a Soviet defector."

"Never heard of a Davies. The ambassador's name was Frank Merriman."

"Merriman was in the United States in February 1965. His wife was ill and he was attempting to resign. Colbert Davies was confronted by the proposed defection of a Soviet intelligence officer. Does this sound familiar?"

"No," McMorris answered, calmly sipping his drink.

"No?"

"No," McMorris said again.

"The defector's name was Alexi Zarudni."

McMorris hunched his shoulders. "I don't remember the name," he said.

"But you were at the CIA station in Paris at the time. You must have known about it."

"I don't."

Townsend assessed him for a moment. "I think you're lying," he said.

"Look, Mr. Townsend. It was long ago. So I'd let you have an off-the-record confirmation if it scratched your itch. But . . ."

McMorris munched another macadamia and seemed to lose himself in thought for a moment. Townsend watched him.

"Look, I suppose there could have been some Russian from thirty years ago that I don't remember," McMorris finally said. "Maybe we screened your Zarudni and didn't find him of any interest. It happens all the time. Most would-be defectors have their brain cells out of whack to start with, you know. They're sick. They're tempermental. They're strung out on booze or broads or drugs. They've got a grudge against someone. And most of the time whatever they have to say is worthless."

"But in this particular case you personally—"

"Townsend! Let me put a leash on you. Otherwise, you're going to run out on Connecticut Avenue and get hit by a car, right?"

Townsend gave him an offended look. As McMorris explained, his words formed an analogy, not a threat.

"I was at the embassy in Paris, right?" McMorris explained. "I was with the CIA station there from August 1963 until May 1966, right? And Len Wolik was assigned there with the Foreign Service for a portion of that time. Right? We agree on that much?"

"Yes, we do." Townsend leaned back slightly as he answered. He folded his arms.

McMorris continued. "Then listen closely: I don't remember a Russian named Zarudni. And I don't know of anyone in God's kingdom on earth named Colbert Davies. Period."

"My source says Davies was there for a very short time."

"Your source," McMorris answered skeptically. "Any damn fool can have a 'source.' At best, this 'source' is yanking on your trouser hose," said McMorris. "And at worst, some duplicit bastard is spinning a nasty, untruthful story to you. Look at this, Townsend. You come here and cite two names: Zarudni and Davies. You can't even prove that either man existed, right?"

For a moment, Townsend was uncharacteristically flustered. He recovered quickly.

"Dying men don't normally lie," he argued.

"Neither do dead ones."

"What's that supposed to mean?"

"It's a statement of very obvious fact," McMorris said, anger beginning to show. He gathered himself in his chair. He worked a final couple of nuts with his fingers, then popped them into his mouth. As a coda, he brushed his fingers on a napkin.

"Okay," Townsend tried next. "Don't confirm anything. We'll play a game instead. Let's pretend there *was* a Zarudni."

Townsend spoke as McMorris drained his glass. The remains of the ice cubes clinked against his teeth.

"And let's say Zarudni claimed that he could put other defections in order," Townsend pressed. "Such as Popov. Such as Goleniewski. Maybe others. And he further said he could provide the key evidence to a penetration at the upper levels of the Kennedy–Johnson administration. Would that be a queer thing to pretend?"

"By now, it's either public record or it's not," said McMorris.

"No. I don't think so. Zarudni was never part of any public record. Yet my source says there was a Zarudni and he wanted to defect. And when Colbert Davies contacted Washington," Townsend repeated, "Ambassador Merriman returned to Paris immediately. Davies was relieved of his duties and shipped back to the United States. Zarudni was returned to Moscow and shot."

"A fairy tale," said McMorris.

"Mr. McMorris," said Townsend. "Leonard Wolik cited you as the source for the latter. He said that you told him that an Aeroflot jet had taken a Soviet diplomat back to Moscow very suddenly. Zarudni disappeared from their consulate and a potentially invaluable source of intelligence never came to the West. As much as anyone, you were a witness to that. Wolik said," he concluded with emphasis, "that *you saw the airplane.*"

McMorris pondered it for several seconds. "Townsend," he said at length. "I'd be more inclined to help you if *you* told *me* the truth for a change." He paused. "Let's try again. Where *are* you getting this horseshit?"

McMorris's tone was suddenly pugnacious. Townsend knew he'd struck upon something. But what?

"I told you once already."

"Leonard Wolik?"

"Yes."

"Goodbye, Townsend. We're not going to do any business."

"So I'm on to a story, huh?" Townsend asked.

"Okay, you're onto a very minor story. But you have it inside out and twisted around. And it's not the one you think. Nor is it one you should touch. All right?"

"Which one am I onto? Which one do I think I'm on to? And why shouldn't I touch it?"

McMorris laughed and shook his head.

"I'll give you a very honest warning, Brother Townsend," McMorris said. "You're wading into journalistic quicksand. Popov, Goleniewski, and all those who followed broke more hearts and careers than any case I've ever seen. Thirty years after the fact it can still break yours. You want that?"

"How could it hurt me?"

"Think it's healthy to rattle yesterday's skeletons? That's what you're proposing."

McMorris raised his hand and signaled to the bar. "Waiter?" he called. "We'll take a bill here."

Townsend watched McMorris rise and reach to his wallet.

"Let me ask you a side question," McMorris said next, seeming to change the subject. "What do you think of this new Litvinov guy in Russia?"

"He seems like a reasonable successor to Gorbachev and Yeltsin."

The check arrived. McMorris unfurled a twenty-dollar bill, gave it to the barman and refused change.

"Yeah. That's what I think, too. We're living in 1996, right? Four years before the Third Millennium. You got sixteen to twenty countries out there in Club Nuke. But Uncle Sam is the only real superpower and Russian–American relations have never been better since the czar took a powder. So why, why, *why* in God's name, would you want to even take the chance of a small story stirring up the old unpleasantness of the 'Evil Empire' days? Why would you even dedicate one lousy column inch of your second-rate scandal sheet to something like that?"

"If no one cares anymore, what would I be stirring up?"

"You just answered your own question, Townsend. *Maybe* someone somewhere *does* care. It's not worth the risk."

McMorris gave his guest a final nod. Then he turned and was out of the bar, leaving Townsend behind with a snack bowl that had been reduced to a few peanuts, almonds, and soy crisps.

At the next table, however, the man and the woman laughed at some inane joke they'd shared. Then they too rose to leave. They left the bar, his arm around her waist. They proceeded not to the entrance of the hotel, but rather across the lobby to the bank of elevators which ascended to the hotel's rooms. Townsend watched—pondering Russians, Americans, and Paris in the 1960s—until the elevator door closed behind them.

On the same afternoon's late Metroliner from Washington to New York, Townsend stared out of his window. The train sped northward through the Maryland countryside, followed by the gritty railyards of Baltimore and Wilmington. Then the train eased its way through Philadelphia's Thirtieth Street Station and past the museum and the boat houses on the Schuylkill.

The cityscape of the Northeast fascinated him: Majestic old buildings laid to ruin by the cancer of urban slums. Neighborhoods where previous generations had flourished. Factories, boarded, broken windowed and crumbling, agonizing a death of ten, twenty, or fifty years.

Then his thoughts returned to McMorris.

Townsend steepled his fingers before his lips. He gazed tranquilly out the window as New Jersey flew past, accompanied by the steady steel churning of high-speed train wheels. He felt strangely complacent. All right, he told himself. He was an obit man now. He was tracking a story, but who cared? Who needed more trouble? He would drop the Wolik intrigue now.

There! There was his decision. He told himself he should feel good about it. He'd done enough time and suffered enough by tracking unpopular stories. Was he under some ethical obligation to track everyone who came his way? Of course not! To hell with this! He got up and left his newspaper across his seat. He would celebrate with a five-dollar Stroh's from the bar car.

Fifteen minutes later, as the train neared Newark, he was back, braced by a cup of domestic hops and two bags of pretzels.

So much for the previous decision. If he was onto a story, he told himself, revising his conclusion, he would follow it wherever it led. But he would do it on his own time. That was a practical compromise. He congratulated himself on his good sense.

A woman walked down the aisle, reeling slightly from the movement of the train. She held a small girl's hand. The woman was escorting her small clone to a lavatory.

Now a feeling of disappointment was upon him, breaking the buoyancy of his previous mood. Why did his own daughter and ex-wife live so far from him? But what could he do? He exhaled a long helpless breath. He was swept by a ringing sense of failure which lasted through the stop at Newark. Many minutes later, when his train arrived in New York, it was shortly after ten.

When he arrived home there were several messages waiting on the answering monitor that sat on his desk.

Among them, Harry.

"The Stuart woman called again," Harry said, carrying on his half of a dialogue with Townsend's machine. The LED screen on Townsend's machine pegged the message at 4:50 P.M.

Thinking of the flimsy wall that separated his study from the neighboring bedroom, Townsend reached to the machine and gently abated the volume. For all Townsend knew, Barbara and Jim, in the midst of slow, leisurely, and uncharacteristically silent coitus, might have been listening to every word.

"She left her number," Harry said more seriously, reducing his own volume at the same time. Townsend could tell. Harry was leading up to the main event.

Mrs. Stuart's father had passed away that morning. There would be a wake the next evening in Westchester County. Harry had an address and could be reached at home until midnight if Townsend so desired.

Townsend was tired. He didn't desire. Not that night.

Then Harry moved to the second part of the message. Two *Sun* staffers who normally worked the death page on Townsend's days off were suddenly unavailable. One had fractured an ankle playing softball in Central Park and wouldn't be at work until Monday. The other had been on jury duty for the week and was now sequestered unexpectedly.

Townsend sighed. There went his day off on Saturday.

The next morning, Harry Dubrow was waiting for him.

Harry had the address all written down, as well as the name of the funeral establishment. He also had a favor to ask.

"I know I'm only your old friend," he said. "I know that doesn't mean much in 1996. And I know that if I hadn't mentioned your name, Paul, you wouldn't be working here, much less be able to pay your rent."

"So maybe I owe you a favor, Harry. What if I do?"

It was one of those endearing 9:30 A.M. confrontations. Townsend was sipping black coffee, his jacket off, his feet up on his desk. Harry stood before him in shirtsleeves, sweat already breaking through. Invariably, by eleven every day, Harry smelled as if he'd put in two tough half hours on a handball court.

"So regale me," Harry demanded. "Make me laugh. Tell your poor struggling old buddy what the hell is going on."

"You don't really want to know, Harry. I can tell."

"Fuck you, Paulie. I mean it. Want me to say it in polite Quaker? *Fuck thyself!*"

"You really want to hear it?"

"Why should you get all the interesting stuff?" Harry paused and tried a softer tactic. "Look, I got all morning to listen to war stories. I'll bust my ass this afternoon, okay?"

So, against his better judgment, Townsend told him.

< < < < *11* > > > >

NEW ROCHELLE was about sixty creepy minutes from Manhattan on the cratered old highway that wove through Westchester County. Townsend knew the area well. He drove up from Manhattan in a rented car.

Marston's Funeral Home was a dreary establishment on an equally dreary street, a section of the central part of town that had fallen into decline in the seventies, grown worse in the eighties and—its economic base shattered during the spiral of municipal bankruptcies of the early nineties—tumbled further into ruin over the past two years. Yet Marston's was the anchor of its block, occupying two storefronts. It was flanked by a liquor store and an auto parts emporium, both of which left their window grates in place during daylight hours. Townsend did not need a sociologist to note the irony of a funeral parlor being the anchor of a decaying stretch of American suburbia.

It was really no place to be at a few minutes past seven on an otherwise pleasant Saturday evening in the spring. And even if the man who'd answered to the name of Wolik wasn't in much of a position to care, Townsend did.

Townsend had no trouble parking near Marston's. There were plenty of places on the opposite side of the street. That part of the block was shuttered and abandoned, the ruined old storefronts from the 1950s firmly bricked up, so as not to easily function as shooting galleries or homes for squatters. Two cars were already parked there. One was Sarah's.

At the funeral home, a single elderly man met Townsend inside the front door. He wore a black suit and introduced himself as Mr. Edwards. He directed Townsend toward the viewing room, then maintained his post for any other mourners.

Townsend entered the viewing room. There, the man whom Townsend had known very briefly as Leonard Wolik had found his penultimate resting place. The man who had poured out his story of youth and intrigue and Paris in 1965 lay before his final biographer in an open rosewood coffin. The late diplomat was still, silent and cold, just like the establishment.

For every death notice he had ever written, Paul Townsend thought to himself, somewhere there was a scene parallel to this one. Some were more elaborate than others. Some were brighter, some were darker. Some were punctuated by sad, uneasy laughter, most by sobs or tears. Some were tragic and before their rightful time and others, if actuarial tables could be believed, were years overdue. But inevitably there was this moment or its counterpart, then the funeral.

Townsend paused for a moment by the body. He looked down at the deceased, who looked smaller than Townsend had remembered him. But yes, it was the same man, he assured himself, and no, he was no longer alive. His many diseases had claimed him. Or he had been delivered from his many troubles. One could look at it either way. In any case, the dead man looked much more peaceful than Townsend had expected. It continually fascinated him how death managed to lift so many cares and worries from a human face.

The coffin was arranged simply. It was flanked by a minimal number of flowers. A simple wreath lay upon the dead man's body and a small scroll in gothic letters expansively identified the departed as Leonard Schofield Wolik.

May Almighty God Extend His Grace and Mercy, the same scroll continued in prayer, and Welcome His Humble Servant into the Kingdom of Heaven. Beyond the coffin, between an arrangement of silk orchids—machine made in Belize, Townsend guessed—there was also a small cross, but no crucifix. Wolik had been a Protestant, Townsend concluded, and probably a pretty casual one. So what else, he thought, was new?

Townsend looked to the rest of the room. It was a smaller chamber than he had anticipated, and he was equally surprised to see that Sarah Stuart was the only other mourner. He gave her an almost imperceptible nod of recognition. She raised one hand slightly to him in half a wave.

Sarah sat in the second row in an uneven semicircle of empty chairs that faced the coffin. She wore a dark dress—navy, not black—and a subdued print scarf. She wore glasses with a dark tint. Her face was drawn and tired.

Paul Townsend went to the second row of chairs, accompanied by the only sound in the building—his own quiet footsteps. He sat down next to her. Sarah's hands were gripped tightly together. There was a bedraggled handkerchief interlocked within her palm and fingers. Townsend placed his hand on hers. Her hands were chilly, tense, and unsteady.

"I'm sorry," he said.

"Thank you for coming." Her voice rasped slightly. Beneath the dark glasses, her eyes were red.

"How are you?" he asked. "It's never easy. You holding together?"

"I'm all right," she said.

"Is there anything I can do?"

She forced an appreciative smile, then shook her head. "Thank you, though," she said.

"Not much of a turnout."

"You're the whole audience," Sarah answered.

"Half of it. His daughter's here, too," he said, trying to cheer her.

She managed another smile. "Dad wasn't much for making close friends," she said. "He made a few, but they're all somewhere else." She managed a long sigh and her voice steadied. "My mother's dead. My sister . . . We don't get on that well with the rest of the family."

Townsend glanced at the rows of empty seats. "I guess that's a bit of an understatement."

"I didn't even tell the rest of the family," she said. "They wouldn't have cared. My choice, all right? I just want this to be over."

Townsend nodded. "It's your decision. You're his daughter, aren't you?"

"Yes," she said with a strange emphasis. "That's one thing I'm always sure of. I'm his daughter."

"What about your son?" Townsend asked.

"Away at school. Remember?"

It took Townsend a moment. "Yes. I'd forgotten," he said. "Boarding school in Connecticut."

She nodded.

Townsend withdrew a pencil and notepad from his jacket. "There are a few personal details missing," he said. "They'll just take a few minutes. I know this isn't the best time, but may I?"

"This is as good a time as any," Sarah said. "Ask whatever you want."

They spoke for several minutes of the background of Leonard Wolik—career and home, likes, dislikes, loves and hates, plus a few of the other things that mattered.

"What are you doing about burial arrangements?" Townsend asked at length.

"The people here at the funeral home handle everything," she said. "Thank God." Sarah turned toward Townsend. "Have you chosen what you're going to say?"

"Say?"

"Write," she said. "In the *Sun.* In my father's obituary."

Townsend leaned back in his wooden chair. "Often I don't decide till I sit down to write," he said. "Leonard Wolik isn't my typical assignment. Your father posed more questions than he answered."

"That assessment would have pleased him," Sarah said.

"I'm sure."

"Everything my father told you was the truth," she continued with surprisingly sudden emphasis.

"Maybe so. But not everyone agrees on it."

"What's that mean?"

"Your father's story fascinated me. So I went down to Washington. I found one of his old friends. Trouble is, his old friend suffers from a memory lapse."

She turned quickly toward him. *"Who?"* she asked.

"Bruce McMorris," Townsend said. "He's still with the CIA. Or, at least he says he is."

"You *talked* to Bruce McMorris?"

"Yes. In person. Why?"

She abruptly turned forward again.

"Something wrong with that?" he asked.

"McMorris is scum."

"He seemed like a genial sort to me," he said with obvious irony.

"You must know better than to trust those people in Washington," she said sharply. "They'll lie to you every time. That's if they don't stick a knife directly in your back."

"I don't for a moment disagree," Townsend said.

"Well, then . . . ?"

"There is such a thing in my line of work as a confirmation of sources," he said. "Your father told me quite a story. It was filled with implications and unanswered questions. The more I can verify, the more I can print. But I can't just hustle something into typeset without—"

"If you don't want to print what my father told you," she said, suddenly quite agitated, "you don't have to! You can forget the whole damned thing, if you like. But don't start dredging—!"

Townsend continued with the utmost courtesy. "Didn't you, or he"—here Townsend motioned with his head to the coffin—"think I'd try to confirm anything?"

She spoke very steadily. "You know what he told you. You know what my father's wishes were. That's all I can give you. I hope you'll follow through on that."

"I'll go with your father's death notice the way I see it," he said. "That's my standard procedure."

"Fine," she said abruptly. "That should be enough. Excuse me for a moment?"

She stood.

"Sarah?" he asked, making no attempt to detain her.

She waited.

"One doesn't have to be a genius to see that something's terribly wrong with this whole scene," he said. "I've visited more than my fair share of these services. Most of them fit into their proper place. They're like the write-ups I do in the newspaper. They fit the person and the occasion. This one doesn't, Sarah."

She looked away from him. "Why not?"

"Your father was a diplomat. He was an educated man. He was the head of a family. He knew people. He must have had friends. Yet, here we are: All by ourselves in a crappy bargain-basement funeral home in an incipient suburban slum. It makes you nervous that I would even do a little research. What gives, Sarah? What's wrong? What aren't you telling me?"

"My father made himself unpopular with his theories," she said. "As for this funeral home, it's what he told me he wanted. Just like getting in touch with you. It was not my idea. After twenty-some months of terminal disease it was what my father wanted. That's reason enough."

"Is it?"

She gathered her purse and moved away from him without answering. He watched her leave the room.

Townsend waited many minutes for her to return. He used the time to read through his notebook on Leonard Wolik. But when Sarah wasn't back by eight o'clock, his patience ended. Townsend stood. He left the second row of chairs and walked slowly past the casket again.

Townsend paused for a moment by the coffin. Yes, he noted again, Sarah's father looked very peaceful in death, and Townsend noted the irony. Whatever trouble the dead man had started—or continued—he was free of it now.

Slowly, Townsend ambled into the entrance hall. Mr. Edwards was sitting on a small chair reading—of all things—that day's *Sun*. Edwards quickly folded the newspaper and stood as Townsend passed.

"Small turnout tonight, huh?" Townsend remarked.

"There were a few others earlier," Mr. Edwards said.

"Family? Friends?"

"I have no idea, sir."

"What did they look like?"

"Sir?" Mr. Edwards fumbled. That, or he took the question as impertinent.

"Men? Women?" Townsend asked.

"A few of both, sir. Maybe more will come later."

"Yeah. Maybe. How late is the viewing?"

"Until ten o'clock, sir."

"Have a good evening."

"Thank you, sir."

Through the glass of Marston's front door Townsend could see that Sarah's car was gone. He accepted her departure as his own cue to leave. He nodded to Mr. Edwards and walked outside. He was no sooner on the pavement than he heard a bolt fall on the door behind him.

Townsend wondered. Were no further guests actually expected? Or was Edwards warding off the unwanted visitors who might prowl the block at dusk? It used to be, when Townsend was growing up, that the sounds of bolts falling and latches clicking into place were the prevailing music only in the cities. Now the tune was hummed everywhere.

There was only one car across the street now aside from his own. He assumed it belonged to the funeral director.

Townsend crossed the street. He stepped into his own car and started the engine. He locked the doors and turned on his headlights. He drove in the direction he had come.

He continued for about a mile. But then, as daylight finally expired, he made a decision to test his instincts. This was just for sport, if nothing else.

Who in hell knew why, but he was certain that the funeral director had been lying to him. So if there had been a lie, he would nail it. If not, he'd know his senses were out of whack.

He pulled into the parking lot of a shopping mall. From a large chain drug store, he bought himself dinner—a diet soda and a prepackaged sandwich. He dined, if that was the term for it, in his car. He listened to the Yankees on the radio. They were losing again, which made him think of Harry.

Townsend waited. When twenty more minutes had passed, he circled back to Marston's.

As Townsend expected, the funeral home was black. The block was deserted. Two of the overhead sodium street lights flickered, giving the whole scene an eerie, uneven bluish glimmer.

Mr. Edwards's car was gone. So, presumably, was Mr. Edwards. And so were any remaining doubts on Townsend's part that something very strange was happening.

He wondered again what it was. But he knew as well that—whatever it was—he hadn't even begun to understand it.

<<<< **12** >>>>

NORMALLY, this was her favorite time of the day.

Tina Hubbell walked by herself along a wide stretch of sand on Fort Myers Beach. She wore a T-shirt and a pair of blue shorts, a towel draped loosely across her shoulders. It was the type of gorgeous Florida morning that suggests that early summer will last forever. Blue skies. Clear water. A brilliant yellow sun, before the day's heat had begun to settle upon the gulf coast of Florida.

This hour, just after nine A.M., was the time of day that she had come to appreciate most, the window in each twenty-four hours that she left to herself. One daughter was at school, the other at day care. Her husband was at work. She had learned to use these hours to get some fresh air and some exercise, to maybe run a mile or two on the beach and maybe stroll another.

This morning, like other mornings, she had parked her car near the beach pavilion that sold sandwiches, hot dogs, and soda. She had run two miles and walked a third. She was feeling good about herself and good about life. Then, returning toward her car, feeling the warmth of the early June sunshine upon her, enjoying the invigoration of having completed a good workout, she saw him.

At first Allan was no more than the figure of a stranger who had pulled a car into a parking spot near hers. Then, as she approached, she realized that there was a familiar stance to the stranger who stood near her car. He wore a short-sleeve white shirt and a dark tie. He wore a beige summer suit, but the jacket was off, folded over his thick forearms. He was leaning against the hood of his own car, watching her.

He was waiting for her.

Yes, he was several years older than when she had seen him last. He had gained a few pounds. But he was still sturdy. The shape of his head was unmistakable, as was his frame. When she was a hundred fifty feet away, she knew who it was.

God damn him! she thought to herself. *Who the hell did he think he was dropping into her life like this! There were final chapters to everything—such as their relationship! Couldn't he understand that?*

She felt her resentment building as she walked toward him. Her car key was in her hand. This was no chance meeting and she wanted it concluded quickly.

He smiled at her when she was within twenty feet.

"Hello, Chris," he said amiably.

"First things first," she said. "No one calls me that anymore."

"Not even me? For old time's sake."

"Especially not you."

"Still hate me, huh?"

She didn't answer. She stopped a few feet from him and glared. He had positioned himself between her and her car.

"I'm Mrs. Hubbell now. My friends call me Tina. There's no Chris anymore. And I don't want you to call me anything."

He lowered his eyes for a moment.

"What are you doing here?" she demanded.

"I came to talk to you."

"Don't you take a hint?" she demanded furiously. "I don't want to see you! I don't want to talk to you! I don't want to have anything to do with—!"

"You've made that all very clear," he answered.

"Well, then—?" She made a gesture with her hands, an open, expansive one suggesting that he vanish. Then she stared at him angrily when he didn't move.

"Goddamn it! Leave me alone!" she insisted.

She bolted toward her car and he reached to her. He grabbed her arm firmly and held it.

"Allan," she said furiously, barely containing her temper. "I can break that grip of yours. I've had the same training as you. Want me to do it? I'm thirty-four years old and you're fifty-seven. Want me to put you through your car windshield?"

"I'm fifty-six," he said. "My birthday's not till August. And no. You needn't put me through a pane of glass."

He relaxed his grip on her arm. She pulled her arm away.

"I didn't come here to start anything between us again," he said. "But I have to talk to you," he said. "It's a matter of safety. Yours."

"I'm fine, thank you," she snapped.

"Please listen to me. I've come hundreds of miles. Just hear me out."

She drew a breath and looked toward him. Her husband was at work, she reminded herself. There was virtually no one else around. No one could see Tina Hubbell with her former lover. Her nerves settled and she relaxed slightly.

"You have one minute," she told him. "Make it worthwhile."

"I'm thinking about a certain death eleven years ago," Alan said. "I don't need to tell you which one."

She felt something jump inside of her, as if something out of her worst nightmare had suddenly leaped out into the daylight. And, in effect, something had.

" 'Mr. Carman,' " he said. "That's what you and I called the deceased at the time. Instead of his real name. 'Mr. Carman,' wasn't it?"

The terror crept slowly around her, like the long body of a snake, enveloping her body, then inexorably tightening its grip.

Mr. Carman. She hadn't heard the name spoken aloud for years.

"Oh, God!" she said bitterly. "Not this again."

He nodded somberly. "I'm afraid so," he answered.

"Eleven years," she said. She exhaled in disgust. "When I wanted it investigated further back then, no one would listen to me. 'You're crazy, Chris,' everyone said. 'Behave like one of the guys,' they demanded. 'Typical girl!' And, 'Forget it.' Now when *I* want it to go away, it won't!"

"Maybe it will disappear eventually," he said. "Maybe this will be the end of it. I don't know," he said. "But I do know that people are starting to ask questions again."

"Who?" she snapped. " 'People'? Who do you mean by that?"

"*I* don't even know," he said. "I can only guess. Same as you. They've come around. They don't identify themselves. You know how they work. I don't ask to know the details."

She knew too well. She was quiet.

"Have you ever talked to anyone about the case?" Allan asked her. She shook her head. "Never."

"Not with your husband? Any friends?"

"No one," she said. "I got the message loud and clear in 1985. I didn't need another clue to shut up."

"That's good," he said. "See, you *shouldn't* talk to anyone," he said very succinctly. "Even now. It won't do any good. It won't help anyone. It won't help the man who died. And you'd only endanger yourself." He paused. "As well as your family."

She looked him squarely in the eye.

"You're not here to threaten me, are you, Al?" she asked.

"You know the answer to that," he said gently.

She nodded almost imperceptibly.

"Honestly," he said. "I know I hurt you. I know you hate me. But I never did it intentionally. I never wanted—"

"Let it drop, Allan," Tina Hubbell said. "All right?"

He did. For a moment, he gazed uneasily at her.

"See, the thing you have to understand is this," he said. "It was never me that made any waves about the case. It was you. That's why they'll leave me alone, I suspect. And that's why you . . . Well, that's why you have to be careful." He paused. "You're the one who was threatening to talk to newspapers."

She looked at her former lover with building anger. "So that's it?" she asked with a lowered voice. *"That*'s why you're here?"

"I came here to warn you," he said evenly. "You wouldn't answer my letters. You wouldn't call me. I'm only concerned about your safety. I'm not going to bother you again."

"Why . . . ?" she started to ask, feeling a surge of anger as well as emotion and resentment. "Why can't this just go away?" she said. "I didn't ask for any part of this. I don't want any part of this."

"None of us did."

"How will they find me?"

"They'll find you," he assured her. "Count on one thing in life, *they* will find you."

For a second or two, her eyes settled on something much more pleasant: a sailboat on the horizon. When he spoke again, her gaze shifted back to him.

"Do you still have . . ." he asked euphemistically, "a way of defending yourself?"

"Allan? What are you suggesting?"

"Well," he answered. "It strikes me that you were a bit of a nuisance back when Mr. Carman died. And it strikes me further that we're dealing with people who never used to play by anyone's rules. So why should they play by any rules now?"

The expression on her face was collapsing in fear. And he could see it.

"No!" she answered resentfully. "I don't keep an arsenal in the house! I have young children!"

"You might," he said, "make a change in that situation. You might find yourself something. Please. Take some precautions. For your own good." He paused awkwardly. "If I can help you—"

She shook her head.

"Just go," she said.

She stood before him in shock. Allan nodded. Then he leaned to her and kissed her on the forehead. She remained too stunned to even resist him.

"Goodbye, Tina," he said. "Consider yourself warned. I won't see you again."

Could he, Townsend asked himself, have any perspective? Could he do his job with honesty? There was always an edge to writing the death notice for someone he had known.

Leonard Wolik: In the end, who was he? How was Townsend to balance one strange incident into a man's lifetime or into a career that spanned almost a quarter century? And yet, as he knew well, often a lifetime is defined by a single moment or action.

Neville Chamberlain, for example. Orville Wright. Benedict Arnold. Charles Lindbergh. Bobby Thomson. Lee Harvey Oswald. Jack Ruby.

At a few minutes after nine o'clock on Sunday morning, Townsend looked at what was on his desk. A hotel executive from Connecticut was dead at seventy-four. The former president of a local university had died of cancer. Townsend knew immediately he needed eight column inches for the latter, or he'd hear from disgruntled alumni. There was a Manhattan lawyer and a New Jersey banker. Five inches each, one column. He farmed those two out to staff writers. A theatrical stage manager who had been prominent in the 1950s had also died. Five more inches. Already it promised to be a busy day, but he would use Wolik to anchor the page.

Harry walked into the office. "So?" Harry asked.

Townsend, preoccupied, looked up after several seconds. "What, Harry?" he asked.

"Too busy for a friend, huh?" Harry asked. "The Mets want to buy Strawberry back from Los Angeles for ten million dollars and make him a playing manager next year."

"What?"

"Forget it. It's just bullshit. The ruminations of a disgruntled senile sports editor. But now that I have your attention, want to have lunch out today?"

"No, Harry. I can't."

"So I'll never come back. Never bother you again. You Scotch—Irish jerkoff."

Harry, who seemed to be in excellent spirits, vanished.

"We'll send out for sandwiches," Townsend said, calling after him.

Townsend looked back to his desk. He turned to the typewriter, thought for a moment, and tried to construct a headline:

> LEONARD WOLIK, 64;
> NEVER SOLVED SPY
> MYSTERY

No good, Townsend thought. It didn't tell enough. It didn't have enough flair. And it presupposed that the "spy mystery" really existed. So far, he had no corroboration. But at least he had something on paper.

He tried again, this time across two columns:

> LEONARD WOLIK, 64; EX-DIPLOMAT
> MYSTIFIED BY SOVIET DEFECTOR

That was closer, but still wrong. Zarudni never defected, as far as anyone knew. Townsend put up a third heading, this time over a single column.

He tried another angle:

> NEAR SOVIET DEFECTION POSED
> LIFELONG MYSTERY FOR—

He stopped. No good at all. This was an obit, not a news story. Or was it?

Was it what? he thought to himself.

In anger and frustration, he broke a pencil in his hand. Damn! He wasn't even thinking right. His telephone rang. It was the son of the university president. Townsend talked to him at length. When he was finished, he made two follow-up calls on the same man. By eleven that obituary was complete.

He returned to Wolik. But the phone rang again. The lifelong companion of the theatrical designer was on the line, sobbing. Townsend gently went over some clippings from the morgue with him. When

Townsend was finished, he had enough to complete that job. He wrote the man's notice in a single draft with one light edit. But it was now one o'clock.

"Okay," Harry said, appearing at the door. "Sandwiches. But just this once. After all, we're not friends anymore."

"It's the third time this week, Harry."

"So I can't count. Nobody's perfect. I'll call. What do you want? American cheese on white with ketchup?"

Townsend asked for a pastrami. Harry ordered a fruit salad. "Real food and moose food," Harry said. "But mooses live a long time. You got to clean up your diet someday, Paulie." Health was an occasional kick with Harry Dubrow.

Townsend felt the need to escape his desk so they ate in Harry's office at half past one.

"You know something, Paulie?" Harry said over lunch. "You're the Death Page Man, this should interest you: See that pink fatty substance in your sandwich? That's spelled suicide. If all the numbers were added up correctly, I think pastrami has probably killed more of my people than Hitler."

Harry paused. Townsend continued to eat. Harry tried a different angle.

"You should have a special column on your obituary page about people who die from lunch meats or gooey desserts," Harry said, continuing his case. "For example, 'So-and-so passed away today from acute triglyceride poisoning. He was thirty-eight and was home alone in the kitchen at the time. His death was witnessed by a bag of cookies and a six pack of Coca-Cola Classic.'"

"No jokes today, Harry."

"So who's joking?" Harry asked, working on a slice of pear. "What gives? Are you Mr. Sunshine today or what?"

"Wolik. I can't get it."

"What can't you get?"

"The handle."

"Oh. That's all, huh? Just the handle?"

"I don't know whether this defection ever took place. Or even the conversations he alleged in Paris in 1965. Look at these."

He showed Harry his attempts at headlines.

"Yeah?" Harry asked. "You got three headlines here, none of them very good. Did he die three times?"

"None of these is accurate."

"That's because you're missing the point, Paulie. You want me to get serious about this? Help you figure what to do?"

"Sure," Townsend said.

"All right. You don't know from any Russian defector. All you know is the story your man Wolik told. See what I mean? I can't believe you don't see this. You're a reporter. You met a man, he told you his story." Harry shrugged. "In court, they call it hearsay and they don't even listen to it. So why should anybody read it? And that's all you got. A hearsay death notice. You know that and that's your problem, Paulie. If you were smart you'd just drop this unsubstantiated defection stuff and run a regular obit. Who cares, anyway?"

Townsend thought about it. *"I* care," he answered. "And maybe I'm not so smart."

"This is news?" Harry arched his eyebrows, paused for several seconds, then continued.

"I'll tell you something else," Harry said gently. "You're too close to this material because it's the father of a friend. You got no objectivity. It's written all over you. You're in danger of making mistakes all over the place."

"Just push me in the right direction," Townsend answered. "Let's do the headline."

"Okay," said Harry. "This is the *Sun,* not the *Times,*" he said. "So you don't have to be smart. You don't have to be objective. On most days you don't even have to be accurate. You got a hearsay obit? So that's what you write, pal, your hearsay account. See? You got to make that your angle."

Townsend thought about it and began to smile. "Thanks, Harry. You're right."

Harry frowned and finished his salad. "You catching a case of terminal dumbness from the J-schoolers, or something? I'm surprised at you, Paulie. You know everything I just told you."

"I needed to hear it from you."

"Hey! So you owe me one, right?"

Townsend waited.

"Next time this Sarah Stuart pokes her face around here, I want to see her.

"Why?"

"Call me curious."

"Why else?"

"Well, you know, this investigative stuff. It's interesting. Sports is . . . sports."

"This is just an obit," Harry."

"Yeah," said Harry, finishing his lettuce. "And I'm a candidate for Pope. If you're not hiding a piece of investigative work in the death page, then what are you going to Washington for? Or going to funeral parlors? Or riding around with strange women in cars." Harry mimicked the voice of a radio announcer, circa 1948. "Stay tuned, boys and girls, for the further adventures of hard-bitten, three-fisted newsman Paul Townsend who, hotter than a cheap pistol, will pursue and incarcerate a galaxy of sleazeball malefactors from high and low across Gotham City."

Townsend laughed. "I ain't a superhero, Harry," Townsend said, responding to his friend's incantation.

"You heard it, boys and girls!" Harry persisted. "Townsend claims he's no superhero. But *we* know better." Harry paused. "Hey, Paul, do me a favor."

"What's that?"

"Let me have a piece of it sometime."

"A piece of what?"

"A piece of the action. A piece of an investigation. Let me help you. Let me play Tonto to your Lone Ranger. If this story turns into something, let me at least carry your car keys some night."

"Maybe, Harry. Sometime, I guess, but—"

"I got retirement coming up. I don't have forever."

"Sometime soon," Townsend promised.

"Okay. That's good."

Townsend packed up his notes and prepared to return to his office. "See you later, you old goat," Townsend said.

"The Yankees play an exhibition game tonight against their West Haven, Connecticut, farm team," Harry said. It was his turn to call after Townsend. "They've lost a dozen in a row now. This is their big chance. Class A! The Yanks have a shot at this one!"

But Townsend was already far away. Now, as he sat down at his desk again, a new headline came into focus:

LEONARD WOLIK, 64;
RETIRED DIPLOMAT;
TOLD OF SPY ENIGMA

It was still cumbersome. And one column didn't seem right. He would extend the headline and go for a second column. But he had the angle. He opened his notebook to the pages on Wolik and began a draft. The account would need dignity with a certain amount of mystery. Couldn't be too flip. Or too cute. No Parachutist-Dies-in-Fall stuff.

As his concentration sharpened, Townsend worked undisturbed at his quiet corner of the *Sun* from two o'clock to four thirty. Then he edited and polished what his staffers had written on their assignments. Fortunately, their copy was clean. He returned to the unfinished Wolik draft by five. He dismissed his staffers and worked till six. Harry waved goodbye and went home.

At six thirty, Townsend pulled the results from his typewriter. He reread it. Two minutes later he made a minor change in the headline.

Wolik's passing would be noted across the top right of the necrology page. Two columns by eight inches. The space worked perfectly. Townsend juggled his stories, cut a column inch off the New Jersey banker, and assessed the new layout of his page. Now everything fit, even the advertisement for a mausoleum in Connecticut. Townsend was finally pleased.

Now, with the text complete, he had his headline. Wolik's passing was ready for the typesetter.

LEONARD WOLIK, 64; EX-DIPLOMAT
TOLD OF WOULD-BE SOVIET DEFECTION

By Paul Townsend
New York Sun

Leonard Wolik, a career diplomat who served during the administrations of six American Presidents, died Friday in New Rochelle, New York. Mr. Wolik was 64 and succumbed after many months of ill health. Surviving Mr. Wolik's passing, however, is an enigma of which Mr. Wolik spoke at length through the final days of his life and which harkens back to the cold war days of the Kennedy and Johnson administrations.

Leonard Wolik was awarded bachelor's and master's degrees from Columbia University. He worked briefly for the late Senator John Pastore, Democrat of Rhode Island, then was hired by the U.S. Department of State in 1959. He served a quarter century in the Foreign Service, including tours in Panama, the Dominican Republic, France, Finland, West Germany, as it was then known, and Canada. The focal point of Mr. Wolik's life, however, and the mystery which remains after his passing, evolved from an incident which Mr. Wolik recalled from his tenure in Paris from 1964 until 1966.

As Mr. Wolik related, he accompanied an acting American ambassador, whom he knew as Colbert Davies, to a remote café on Paris's right bank. There they met a man whom Mr. Davies identified as a would-be defector from the Soviet Union to the United States. Mr. Wolik was introduced to the would-be defector by name and knew him to be a Soviet diplomat.

The defector alleged being in possession of vital Soviet intelligence documents. The documents purported to contain a key to a series of previous Soviet defections, some fraudulent and some legitimate, that would mystify the Central Intelligence Agency for two generations. The defector maintained that he could provide the answer to the greatest intelligence secret of the 1960s. But Mr. Wolik maintained the defection was abruptly compromised through a leak in Western security. Mr. Davies was replaced within hours, and the defector vanished.

The unanswered questions surrounding this incident perplexed Leonard Wolik until the day he died. He had cause to believe that the Soviet diplomat had been returned to Moscow and executed. Mr. Wolik further suggested that incident contained the key to, as he termed it, "the greatest conspiracy of my generation." But officials in the Lyndon Johnson era gave it little credibility, as did any subsequent administrations or agencies.

Mr. Wolik died before he could personally prove his theories. And as recently as this past week, CIA sources informally denied the existence of any such proposed defection. Agency sources further maintained that no Colbert Davies had ever served as acting ambassador to France.

Mr. Wolik is survived by a daughter, Sarah Stuart of New York. Funeral arrangements are private.

In Monday morning's edition of the *New York Sun,* the account of Leonard Wolik's passing appeared in a position of prominence on the upper right-hand side of page 34.

Townsend, breaking with his custom, purchased the first newsstand copy of the *Sun* that he saw on his way to work. He immediately turned to the obituary for Wolik and, standing at the northwest corner of Ninety-sixth and Broadway, reread it in its entirety.

Then he folded the paper under his arm, wondering how many days or hours or minutes would pass before the fallout from the article rippled back to him.

<<<< **13** >>>>

*F*OR the final two days before the Michigan primaries, Senator John Lord rode a specially hired whistlestop train from Flint in the east of the state to Niles in the southwest, down near the Indiana border. It was a route pockmarked with middle-size cities and frequent small towns. President Harry S. Truman had traveled the route while running for reelection almost half a century previously. Gerald Ford moved along a similar path, with less spectacular results, twenty years earlier in 1976.

The two days of whistlestop campaigning were at no small expense to Lord's treasury. But similarly, they were no small success. John Lord was raising the devil and a whole lot more in the upper territories of America's heartland.

There were stops in Ann Arbor and East Lansing. Lord wanted these venues because the university towns would provide hecklers. Lord liked hecklers. They helped them to get his message across.

Lord had 123 reporters aboard, most of them from the North. About a third were from Michigan and about half of them came equipped with cameras, microphones, recorders, and two-person sound crews. About two dozen, maybe more, were considered Hostiles, including a brace of newcomers from Washington, two network types from New York, and three from the West Coast.

The train was a comfortable, streamlined, six-car Amtrak special, and it would travel through small-town midwestern America. Lord casually wandered through the train while it was in transit from one Michigan town to the next. He sat on the arm rests of aisle seats in the three press cars and shot the breeze with the eager laptop battalions. In rolled-up shirtsleeves and a loosened regimental tie, he'd sip a diet Dr Pepper while the newsmen sipped beer. Jerry Huddleston, his paunchy press honcho, kept him advised who among the reporters was new to the campaign.

Lord would make a point of personally welcoming newcomers, no matter how bellicose that person's organization had previously been to his candidacy. It was almost as if every new face, every new microphone, and every new notepad was an incipient challenge. Damned if this didn't work, too. Damned if close up, Lord hardly seemed quite the ogre that many perceived from afar. And damned if the national coverage wasn't starting to reflect that.

The candidate had help now, too, softening up his west Texas image. Eugenia Lord made all the dais appearances with her husband. She made her presence known in the press cars as well, following her "official" introduction to the newer members of the press.

"This is in case anyone still thinks I'm too Down Home and Folksy," Lord cracked, standing before reporters in Flint with his arm around his wife. "I've brought Eugenia along to give the campaign some good northeastern nastiness."

'Sho' 'nough," Eugenia Lord remarked with a mock curtsy and a pretend southern simper. She was a sturdy, attractive, good-humored woman with dark hair and a large frame. And "nastiness," of course, was a joke.

She was a woman of charm and grace, the daughter of a family once influential within the Democratic party, though she raised eyebrows when she married a rough diamond like Lord. While many in the press had difficulty projecting John Lord as President, there might be little difficulty seeing Eugenia as first lady. It was just difficult sometimes to imagine her as *his* first lady. But, like Vice Presidents on hastily conceived tickets, John and Genie came as an unlikely package.

And in the end, Lord answered all the familiar questions. He'd even make a joke out of the unmentionable.

"What's today's date?" he asked in Battle Creek.

"June seventh," someone shot back.

"This is the first day since June third that no one's asked me about the Ku Klux Klan."

There was a nervous silence, then a smattering of laughter. Jerry Huddleston looked stricken. How could his candidate joke about the Ku Klux Klan? The gaffe squad among the Hostiles were poised and ready. Lights went on and a few cameras quickly began to roll.

So, seizing the moment, one of the most incorrigible of Hostiles, Lee

Ellis of ABC News, called out, "Do you still completely renounce your Klan membership?"

"Lee," Lord answered with a perfect deadpan, "I've gotten in so much trouble with sheets, that I don't even use them anymore when I sleep."

After a nervous moment, between Three Rivers and Kalamazoo, much of the car convulsed with laughter. Then Lord turned the tables.

"How 'bout you, Lee?" he called to the newsman, who was from Boston and had graduated from Harvard in 1970. "You renounce your membership in the 1968 Peace and Freedom party yet?"

Here was a telling aspect of the new John Lord. He had learned how to defuse issues instead of detonate them and how to volley them back in the direction they'd come. He was learning to loosen up. But the incident also showed more. It demonstrated Lord's uncanny mastery of facts and how to pitch them around. Some found it scary.

But in a day of techno-campaigns and media blitzes, the whistlestop express was a political coup and a publicity bonanza all at once. It was pure gimmick. Pure camp. Pure theater. It was old-time religion and other candidates made fun of it—which only made them look small and jealous—while privately they wished they had thought of it. And the whistlestop campaign worked. Here was one candidate who—as he appeared nationally on the evening news—looked as if he really took the trouble to travel through small-town America. And during this time, he polished his new theme. From "The Forgotten American," he had moved one step further:

"Forgotten America, where people still clean their pavements and go to church on Sunday . . .

"Forgotten America, where good people scrub their front porches daily and pay their taxes in cash . . .

"Forgotten America, where people respect the flag, have paid-up insurance on American-made cars, and"—applause rising to John Lord's oratory again—"are damned tired of a load of expensive *bull* from the Democratic and Republican parties."

It was a theme that hundreds of thousands of people—good, hard-working, loyal American people—turned out to hear along the route in Michigan. Obligingly, Lord stood on the rear platform of his train at every single stop and gave his growing audiences what they wanted.

Meanwhile, the front-running candidates of the two major parties could barely get their suitcases unpacked in the state.

The leading Democrat moved from city to city, trying to expand his largely black following into liberal or progressive white areas. In party meetings, he arrived soliciting support, and spent most of his time fighting a rear-guard action. Incessantly, he battled the suggestion that if only the Democrats would nominate a "less controversial" candidate—meaning a white candidate—maybe they could win the Presidency for the second time in thirty-two years. In reality, if examined closely, the Democrat held the most traditionally democratic views. Yet he was seen as a Bolshevik, the destroyer of the party. It was classic political doubletalk.

The incumbent Republican Vice President campaigned in conservative suburbs, at country clubs, and at wealthy bastions of commerce, never comprehending that he was repeatedly seeing the same people at all three locations. He shook hands and kissed babies among the minority of people in the state who were content with the status quo. He was successfully defeating the more moderate candidates in his own party, though his media handlers usually had one "spin" or "clarification" problem every other day. And in trying to appear reassuring and dignified, he lulled voters to sleep at best. At worst, he did nothing to dispel his reputation as an air-head.

In Michigan, both leading candidates of the major parties began to share a sense of impending disaster. Both were suffering a strong sense of campaigning against a man who wasn't there. John Lord could only burn them in their own primaries. They couldn't defeat him even on their own terms. But he was able to wound them on his.

It was at this time in the 1996 campaign that fund-raisers—as if they didn't have enough to worry about—began to notice something else. With Lord's showing in New York, New Jersey, and Ohio, hundreds of thousands of small contributors—the ten- to fifty-dollar folks—were skipping the major parties and sending money to John Lord. Senator John Lord, Fort Worth, Texas 76101, was one of the best-known addresses in the country.

By primary day, things were bubbling along quite nicely in Michigan for Senator Lord. It was a fine state, complete with decayed, crime-ridden cities, racial problems, and 12 percent white unemployment. It was generally agreed by most people in the state, that white people avoided the state's main city. It was the type of place where John Lord's message, that of the Forgotten America, could find an audience. Hence, as the Amtrak special moved from station to station on the final days of its swing through the state, the mood was upbeat among the senator's staff. The candidate himself was high on life, itself. And prospects for a victory in November had never looked better.

"This whole rail caravan through Michigan is so damned buoyant and infectious, and Senator Lord himself exudes such confidence," reported CBS correspondent Freida Carruthers one night on the network news, "that sometimes even the most skeptical of us start wondering. Maybe, just maybe, this candidate actually knows what he's talking about. And that maybe, just maybe, Jack Lord will be elected President of the United States."

"Maybe, just maybe, I will, Freida," Lord graciously replied in a handwritten note to the same newswoman.

Lord had gorgeous handwriting. Bold, symmetrical strokes with a deep blue ink from a fountain pen. The contents of the note were duly leaked to the rest of the press during a stop in Ann Arbor.

Right up until the end in Michigan, the Hostiles among the press corps kept trying to catch John Lord in a gaffe. "Senator, why do you think your campaign has caught on with people who have never voted for a third-party candidate in their lives?"

That was Lord's cue. "It's caught on," Lord explained patiently, "because I'm the only guy who understands the Forgotten America. I didn't grow up among country clubs and get a suck-butt draft defer- ment. And I'm not a big city guy, either." That, in the veiled language of politics, reminded certain segments of the electorate that he wasn't a privileged son, a crook, a heroin smoker, a black, a Jew, or any unfortu- nate combination of the four.

This was the closest he came to a gaffe. But it didn't turn into a gaffe. Instead, it probably translated into twenty thousand extra votes. People in the media, the big shots who wrote editorials or got their pretty faces on television, may not have liked it, but the guy who went to work from seven to four thirty each day understood what the senator meant.

"Don't you think you're a spoiler candidate?" he was asked again during a rally before his true believers.

Other men might have grown angry when they kept hearing this one. Not Lord. It just provided him another chance to explain his version of the new math,

"I'm not a spoiler at all," he said. "I can win. If three and a third people out of ten vote for me in Michigan, I can carry the state. Right now three people out of ten are for me. So if one of my three voters talks one friend into voting for me, there's my margin of victory."

He pointed to his lapel and smiled. He was still wearing his GET A FRIEND TO VOTE FOR JOHN LORD button from Ohio.

"Do you think the voters are confused?" asked Jim Kornbluth, a Washington correspondent for NBC News. Kornbluth had flown to Michigan to observe the Lord caravan firsthand.

"No," Lord said. "You ladies and gentlemen in the press, with your Ivy League diplomas and your pointy-headed politics, are confused. The voters know exactly what they want."

Thunderous applause. On a roll, Lord couldn't help but add something.

"You know, Jim," Lord said. "if the government had been looking out for The Forgotten American for the last generation, instead of euchring him or her on taxes with nothing in return, I wouldn't have any voters at all."

More applause. Lots of it.

On primary day, the polling places were busy in Michigan. The evening they closed, a lightning bolt hit the American political system.

In the Republican primary, where the Vice President had run virtually unopposed, Lord racked up 36 percent of votes cast, all on write-ins.

In the Democratic primary, Lord had drawn 32 percent, leaving the black front-runner in second place and the rest of the field fragmented. Yet other polls showed that many low-income white voters, who were traditional Democrats, hadn't voted that day. They were waiting instead to vote for Lord in November.

Lord had done it again. Hereafter in the campaign, analysts would have to take him seriously. Two days later, for example, an editorialist in the *New York Times* had the unthinkable on his mind.

Is Senator Lord the first overtly Fascist candidate who could actually be elected President of the United States? If so, are there not men and women of the mainstream in both the Republican and Democratic parties who could not now announce their candidacies?

The *Times* provided a short list of names of people the newspaper would have liked to see run. One of eight could have been categorized as conservative. Then the editorial concluded.

These are not normal political times. It is morally imperative that these men and women announce their availability now, before it is too late.

"Too late" meant before You-Know-Who from Texas had his boots propped up on a desk in the Oval Office. Lord got a big laugh out of that one. He was in the habit of occasionally breezing through the opinion pages of the *Times* whenever he wished to be amused by some squishy-soft liberal thinking.

But then he realized that this time the unsolicited opinion of the *New York Times* was worth more than just a good laugh. It was valuable. He clipped it and folded it into his pocket. He would present it to some of his money people in the business community. It would help convince them of his campaign's credibility, and that with their help he could establish an administration which really could declare war on such tired, misguided concepts as minority rights, affirmative action, abortion, support for Israel, accommodation with the remnants of the Soviet empire, and so on.

"Curious, isn't it?" Lord asked a few of the Laptoppers in an impromptu session at his hotel. "My constituents have been under represented in Washington for fifty years. No one says a thing. When it looks like I could become President, editorial writers don't like democracy very much. They'd just as soon my campaign jet fly into the side of a mountain."

Then, in response to questions, a few more good quotes.

On his third-party candidacy: "There's nothing in the Constitution that mentions two parties, Republicans or Democrats," he said.

And on the subject of federal matching funds: "The American Revolution wasn't financed by matching funds from the crown." Maybe not, but following his showing in Michigan, Lord would be eligible. Quite eligible. Millions of dollars in tax money would now be given to him, which would only help him spread his message.

The Republican and the Democrat staggered out of the state. Senator Lord's combined vote had buried the other two. The Vice President returned to Washington. The Democrat flew in the general direction of the West Coast. Both remained front-runners for their own party's nomination. And both were now seen as highly vulnerable to a third-party attack in November.

Lord and his wife Genie packed their bags in Detroit and set out for California. The Golden State primary had been the biggest prize in American politics for almost a generation now. It was here that Lord now planned to deliver a crippling blow to his two likely opponents in November, pegging them as losers and convincing the rest of the American public of the inevitability of his Presidency.

Seen from a reasonable perspective, it was all terribly frightening.

< < < < *14* > > > >

*H*ARRY DUBROW was waiting for Townsend. He stood halfway between his office and the end of the fourth-floor corridor of the *Sun* Building. When he saw him, Harry looked greatly unsettled.

"I think," Harry said, "you got some trouble this morning."

"Probably," Townsend replied cheerfully, making light of the warning. "Why? What's—"

Townsend stopped in midsentence when a man he didn't recognize stepped out of his office. The man was tall, clean-cut, square-shouldered, and in his early thirties. Townsend, who was quick to make judgments in such situations, thought he had a cold, heartless face. So he didn't like the look of him any more than Harry did.

"What's going on?" Townsend asked.

"There are two of them," Harry Dubrow said. "They've been here since before I arrived. And I was here early. About eight fifteen."

"Paul Townsend?" the man inquired.

"Yes."

The visitor reached crisply to the breast pocket of his suit jacket and produced a small black case the size of a wallet. The case held his identification, a gold shield nestled within what had been the skin of a once-endangered reptile.

"I'm Special Agent Michael Flynn, Federal Bureau of Investigation," the man said. His intonation was dry but polite. "Could I speak with you for a few minutes?"

Townsend paused, assessing what confronted him. If he had $100 in the bank for every time an angry stranger had come looking for him, he might have retired already.

"Why not?" Townsend said, after a moment's hesitation. Already his indignation was growing, as was his instinct for battle. "Come into my office, even though you've already been there."

Townsend stepped past Flynn. There was a second FBI agent already stationed in Townsend's office, standing with his arms akimbo. The second man was shamelessly looking through an unruly maze of unrelated photographs and clippings that adorned Townsend's wall.

The second agent said nothing, throwing only a sidelong glance in Townsend's direction. He was unable to wrest his eyes away from a clipping about a beach volleyball tournament in California. The accompanying photo, with which Townsend was in danger of falling in love, showed a tall blond woman in a pink one-piece bathing suit leaping high to block a shot.

"What brings this honor upon me?" Townsend asked.

"This is my associate, Special Agent Grodine," Flynn said. Silently, Grodine offered identification and a solid handshake. He muttered a greeting. Special Agent Grodine was a smaller, darker man than Flynn, but with a thick frame and wide shoulders. The sleeves of his suit jacket were tight around his biceps.

Harry stood nervously in the doorway.

"You guys have some sort of warrant?" Townsend asked.

"Not yet," Flynn said.

"Then you shouldn't be in my office. How did you get past reception?"

"We were invited past."

"By whom?"

"It's *Sun* policy," Harry said softly and tentatively. "Cooperation with all police agencies."

"Says who?" Townsend snapped.

"The Big Guy." By that, Harry meant Max Kohlheimer.

"They can let these bozos loose in the corridors," Townsend answered. "But not in the offices. That's my policy."

Harry rolled his eyes. He could sense all the artillery being wheeled into place.

"We've been standing here waiting," said Special Agent Flynn. "We're not prowling, we're not poking around. We haven't touched or examined anything."

"If you're in my office," Townsend shot back, "you're doing all of those things."

For a moment, an ominous silence gripped the room. Flynn tried to defuse it.

"We want to ask you a few questions," Flynn began. "It will take less than ten minutes."

Townsend glanced at Harry.

"We don't want a problem any more than you do," Flynn continued.

Townsend pondered it for a moment. Then he pulled off his jacket and hung it on the back of his chair. "Harry, you stay. You're my witness," he said. He looked to the special agents as he sat down. "So? What's on your mind?" he asked.

"May we sit?"

Townsend motioned that they could. They did. Flynn settled into a chair. Grodine made himself comfortable on the edge of a metal side table.

"Leonard Wolik," Flynn said.

Townsend could have guessed ahead of time. "Yeah?" he asked. "Nice man. What else about him?"

"I assume you wrote the article that appeared under your byline."

"That's the way it normally works," Townsend answered.

"Was that article some sort of bad joke or something?" Flynn asked. "What did you run that story for?"

"What the hell kind of question is that? The man died. After a man dies, we sometimes print an obituary."

"Where did you obtain your information?"

"Personal interviews. And public record. *Why?*"

Without saying anything, the two federal agents fell silent and waited for Townsend to grow uncomfortable and say more. Townsend knew the tactic and waited with them.

"Leonard Wolik was a very private man," Special Agent Grodine said, finally finding a voice. "There isn't any public record on him."

"Then there is now," Townsend answered.

"What sort of personal interviews?" Flynn asked next.

Townsend thought about it for a moment. "A private source which will remain unnamed," he answered

The FBI agents waited silently a second time. Again, Townsend waited with them and offered a thin, apologetic smile. At the doorway, Harry's brow glistened with sweat. When half a minute passed, Townsend picked up some wire service clippings that had been left on his desk by a staffer. They were the beginnings of the day's roster of the dead. Townsend began to glance through them.

"You're welcome to sit there and rest for a few minutes, gentlemen," Townsend said, barely looking up. "But I have a day of work to begin."

"Do you have notes from your interviews?" Flynn asked.

"Do you have a warrant for my notes?" Townsend asked.

After a moment, Flynn answered. "We could have one by noon today."

"But you don't have one now?"

The agents were silent.

"None?" Townsend asked. "No warrant at all?"

"No," Flynn admitted.

"In that case," Townsend said helpfully, "I'll be happy to show you the notes."

A small wave of relaxation went around the office. The agents seemed temporarily pleased.

Townsend rummaged through a shelf behind his desk and produced a battered memo pad. He sat down at his desk. At the corner of the desk was just what he needed, a ceramic bowl, sometimes used for writing utensils or flowers. He removed a few ballpoint pens from the bowl.

Townsend glanced into his memo pad and found the appropriate pages. He tore them out of the notebook and glanced them over.

"Please remain seated, gentlemen," he said.

He reached into his desk drawer. As the FBI agents watched in mystification, Townsend produced a bottle of bourbon. He poured about half an ounce of it into the bowl.

He looked up at the agents and grinned. Grodine's brow was furrowed. Flynn's eyes were sharp. Townsend grinned again.

Townsend sealed the bourbon bottle.

"Hey, Paul! No!" Harry said suddenly.

Townsend smiled to him. Then, quickly, and from nowhere that the special agents anticipated, Townsend produced an ignited match. He dropped the match into the bowl. The bourbon caught fire with a loud, dramatic whoosh. A flame shot upward.

"A warrant," Townsend announced amiably, "won't be of much use three hours from now. My notes are *none of your fucking business.*"

Townsend crumpled his notes and dropped them into the flames. As Flynn suddenly realized what Townsend was doing, he sprung to his feet and charged the desk. Flynn lunged toward the fire with a bare hand, but Townsend deflected Flynn's entire arm away from the burning paper.

There was no time for a second lunge. And Grodine was on his feet too slowly. The makeshift incinerator consumed the notebook pages in tight yellow flames and a cloud of black smoke.

"You son of a bitch!" Flynn snarled.

"I don't have to do you any favors, and you guys didn't come here to do me any!"

Flynn and Grodine stared angrily at the embers of blackened paper settling into the bottom of the bowl.

"Listen, Townsend!" Flynn said, retaining an icy decorum. "We could still have a warrant by noon today. I was hoping that could be avoided."

"I don't know what made you hope that."

"If we get a warrant," Grodine added, "you'll need to accompany us down to the federal court house. We'll also make sure that it's sixteen hours of questions, instead of ten minutes. You have your choice."

Townsend looked from one of them to the other, then back again. "Let's get to some specifics," Townsend suggested. "Why don't you tell me exactly why you're here."

"You wrote an obituary containing material straight out of a classified government document," Flynn said. "You had no legal access to that information. You had even less right to print it. We'd like to know how you had access."

"Access to what?" Townsend asked. "Which information?"

"Relating to the deceased Mr. Wolik's Foreign Service career."

"You and I have some basic differences, guys. My feeling is that I have the right to print anything I like."

"Answer the question. Did someone *give* you the information in the obituary of Leonard Wolik?"

"Yes. *He* did."

"Who did?"

"Wolik. He wanted to make sure I ran it."

Both Flynn and Grodine looked at each other.

"When?" Flynn asked.

"Last week. Just before he died. We had a nice chat."

Grodine was suddenly animated. "That's bullshi—!"

"In your article," Flynn tried, "you alluded to Mr. Wolik speaking of the incident in Paris. You said he spoke of it up until a few days ago. You're talking about last week? Do we understand that correctly?"

"I know this might shock you guys, but what you read in the *Sun* was accurate." Townsend looked them back and forth. "I don't owe you any explanations beyond that, particularly since you still haven't explained why you're here."

"We just gave you an explanation."

"No, you told me *what* you wanted to know. You didn't tell me *why* you need to know it. There's still time, fellas. I'm waiting."

They offered nothing further. With a palm, Townsend made a slight waving motion and chased away a small cloud of smoke which hung over the ashes in the ceramic bowl.

"If I printed something from a classified document, so what?" Townsend mused aloud. "How sensitive could Leonard Wolik's story be after thirty years?"

"We can't tell you that."

A strange realization was upon Townsend. "Then it is, huh?"

"Is what?"

"Hot. Sensitive. There's still something going on, isn't there? If there weren't, you dickheads wouldn't be here." Townsend looked them back and forth again as he gathered momentum.

"What office do you guys work out of? Manhattan? Brooklyn?" Townsend asked.

Again, they didn't answer.

"I've had more than a few run-ins with your bureau over the years," Townsend continued. "I know the ground rules. You're required by law to identify yourselves. That includes which outpost you call home."

"Washington," said Flynn.

Townsend exchanged a glance with Harry. Harry, like a large, faithful dog, remained stationed at the door.

"Is that right?" Townsend asked. "And you were just in the neighborhood so you thought you'd drop in on me?" He looked hard at them. "No? That means you made a special trip. And that also means you were assigned to this by someone in Washington. Say, I'm flattered." He paused. "How would you feel about telling me who assigned you?"

"Mr. Townsend," Flynn continued, "we're not here to answer your questions. And we're not here to start trouble for you. But we can if you don't cooperate. Which is it going to be?"

Townsend folded his arms.

"We just want to know your source," Grodine said. "We know it wasn't Leonard Wolik."

"That's the one thing I *have* told you. Just like you read in the newspaper. It *was* Wolik.

"What else did your 'source' tell you?" Flynn demanded.

Townsend was silent.

"What about the name of the defector in Paris?"

"What about it?"

"You didn't print it," said Flynn.

"Why would I print his name?" Townsend answered sharply. "He may be alive, despite what anyone says. Why would I want to compromise him?"

"Zarudni was shot by his own people," Grodine said. "That's a fact. Isn't that what your 'source' told you? The KGB executed him."

Flynn's eyes were set on Townsend like a terrier's, anticipating a reaction. Townsend gave him one.

"Thanks for the confirmation," he said slowly. "If you'd visited me two days ago, I could have used it."

"How much more information do you have that you didn't print?" Flynn asked.

"None of your business."

"A lot more than you printed?"

"Refer back to the previous answer."

Grodine spoke again. "What about this Sarah Stuart? Where would we find her?"

"Why should I tell you? Call IRS. You guys snitch information from tax records all the time."

"Do you have her telephone number?"

Townsend shot him a disgusted look.

Flynn exhaled a long breath, which matched Townsend's in general disgust.

"Townsend," Flynn finally said. "You're just going to make it difficult for everyone, especially yourself. Is that what you want?"

"I'm sorry, gentlemen," Townsend said. "I'm not in a position to help you."

Flynn considered it for several seconds.

"All right," Flynn said at length. "We don't need a warrant. We have other ways. Remember that you had the chance to cooperate."

The two agents filed past Harry and out the door. Harry retreated into the corridor and, to considerable relief, watched them disappear down the hall.

"Jesus," Harry said when they were gone. "Feds. I don't get Feds on the sports desk." He paused. "Paulie, you're working on something big, aren't you? What is it?"

Townsend shrugged. "I've told you everything I know, Harry. I wrote an obituary for a dying man. I interviewed him myself. Did I look for trouble? Did I go out of my way? I wrote what I believed to be accurate."

Harry was shaking his head. "You got this black cloud that follows you around," he said. Dubrow shook his head again and departed.

Townsend sat quietly on the edge of his desk for several minutes, attempting to understand the morning's visit—where it had come from and where it might lead. His eye settled on the bottle of bourbon. He uncapped it and took a sip. He tried to uncover logic where none was apparent.

Then, in the afternoon, he called the single telephone number that he had for Sarah Stuart. This time an operator came on the line.

The number had been disconnected, the operator said, at the request of the customer. And the account had been terminated.

<<<< **15** >>>>

TOWNSEND hated trips to the sixth floor of the *Sun* Building. The sixth floor was the lair of management and its minions. There was an entire swarm of Business Board toadies on Six, close to upper management in both geography and philosophy.

Most of them were male. They studied charts, wandered purposefully down corridors studying printouts on clipboards, and they looked upon newswriters as nuisances. Frequently, these business and marketing people didn't even recognize their own reporters. Yet they thought of themselves as "newspaperpeople," though in a millennium they could never have made a living writing headlines or covering fires.

In two ways, Townsend had arrived at the conclusion that they served no useful purpose. One, they took long lunches. And two, they didn't realize when a reporter was staring out a window, he or she was actually working. In turn, the Business Board people couldn't figure out why the remaining newspapers in the city couldn't pool all information by a single team of reporters and let young rewrite people—fresh out of J-school—punch up the stories with the particular perspective of the individual newspapers. It seemed to the businesspeople a staggering waste of resources to have so many different people out on the street.

Confronted with this mentality, Townsend tended to avoid the floor, except in instances like today. His telephone had rung shortly before lunch and he had been summoned. He was to attend a three o'clock meeting: a cozy twosome, Townsend and one K.N. Shaw II.

K.N. Shaw's name was prominent on the upper masthead of the *New York Sun,* where it was listed as managing editor. The name—and the position—sat fourth from the summit, below Max Kohlheimer's listing as publisher and those of two coexecutive editors. As managing editor, Shaw oversaw the day-to-day operations and publication of the *Sun.*

Townsend reported at the designated time. Three obituaries for that day's edition remained open. He waited for several minutes in a receiving room outside Shaw's office, accompanied by a secretary who made and screened Shaw's calls. At quarter past the hour, Townsend was admitted to the managing editor's office.

Shaw was a balding, beatific-looking man who appeared a decade older than thirty-eight, which is what he was. He was a veteran of nonunion Kohlheimer papers in Oklahoma, Georgia, and Florida. He had a large, flat nose, a receding fleshy jaw, very white teeth, and a benign expression that frequently misled the uninitiated. Friends—and he had at least half a dozen—called him Ken. His parents had given him the Christian names Kenneth Nelson, the same name born by his uncle, who had been a respected editor of children's books in the 1960s. Reporters in Oklahoma City, Atlanta, and Miami, every place where Shaw had worked, swore that the K.N. stood for Knows Nothing.

As Townsend entered, Shaw was seated at his desk in white shirtsleeves and red suspenders. In a corner behind his desk there was a squash racket, intended to prove that K.N. was one of the guys. It hadn't moved since the day the *Sun* published its first edition in 1994. Townsend had once asked Shaw if he knew which end to hold. Shaw had not appreciated the joke, if it had been one.

Shaw leaned back in his leather swivel chair. He folded his hands behind his head. "How are things down in obits, Paul?" he asked regally.

"Considering the way the city, country, and world are going," Townsend answered, "we're predictably busy."

"I'm sure you are. Sending people off to hell in good style, I see. Nothing like a good literate write-up before burning in the devil's own fire for an eternity."

"Nothing like it."

"How are things at home?" Shaw tried. "The family?"

"My wife moved to California. My daughter's with her."

"Ah! That's right. Sorry," he said with something that might have passed for sincere regret. "I'd forgotten."

Shaw was not a master of small talk. Townsend knew the managing editor had already exhausted his supply for the day. So Townsend offered nothing. There was no point to prolong the meeting. Townsend's gaze traveled behind Shaw's desk and settled for an instant upon the squash racket, which—were it not for the army of Guatemalan cleaning ladies who roamed the offices by night—would have been a-tangle with cobwebs.

"Look, I'll get right to the problem, Paul," Shaw said. "You may be busy down there in obits, but I doubt if there's much need to run a death notice of someone who didn't die."

"Who are we talking about?"

"Come on, Jack," Shaw said, peering up from a series of papers on his desk. "You know."

Jack. Shaw had long held this mannerism. He would call all news-people "Jack," interspersing it with a writer's real name in an apparent attempt to be one of the guys and ingratiate himself. All real newspeople had long since learned to ignore it. In keeping with the professed egali-tarian philosophy of the *Sun,* Shaw had recently taken to calling female reporters "Jack" as well. Even more recently, they too had learned to ignore it.

"I know what?" Townsend asked, after a pause.

"Who we're talking about."

"I want to hear it from you."

"Leonard Wolik, Jack."

"The Feds, huh?" Townsend answered. "My friends Flynn and Grodine, they stopped here after they left my office? Or did they come here first?"

"That's not really important."

"No?"

"Paul, they didn't do either. I haven't seen your federal acquaint-ances and, for that matter, I haven't even spoken to them. But my telephone has rung more than once."

"Who called?"

Shaw studiously ignored the question. "What did you have as back-ground when you ran that story?" he asked.

"It wasn't a story, it was an obituary. And I had more than I usually do. I had a daughter and a dying man. He was terminally ill. I visited him in his final few days. Now, who called?"

"Would you be patient? Which side of this damned desk do you think you're sitting on?"

Townsend seethed. "The only side I'd want to be sitting on," he answered.

Shaw missed Townsend's implication. His face wrinkled. "Now, you say *visited* this Wolik? How am I to understand that? You mean you knew Wolik personally?"

"I've known his daughter for more than a year," Townsend said. "I didn't take fingerprints and I didn't ask to see everyone's passport. It smelled clean."

"Where did you and the deceased meet?" Shaw asked in an overly theatrical voice.

Townsend was silent.

"Come on, Jack," said Shaw disdainfully. "You and I are allies. We both work for the same newspaper." One of his stubby fingers drummed the desktop, a constant tapping on the same spot.

"If I tell you, I don't want it going any further than this room."

"It won't if I can help it."

"Damn it!" Townsend snapped. "What does that mean, Ken? That's not a promise. That's a statement of conditions."

"Please answer me," Shaw said evenly.

"A family home somewhere in New York State. Is that sufficient?"

"Not really. Who's family?"

"Wolik's, presumably."

"How did you know how to get there?"

"I was led there."

"By whom? And when?"

Townsend explained.

"Isn't all this a bit unorthodox?" Shaw asked.

"It's an unorthodox business."

"How do you know this man you saw actually died?" Shaw pressed.

"Ken, I saw a terminally ill man. Then I saw him lying in his coffin. I don't hallucinate. What would you like me to do when I go to a wake? Stick a pin in each corpse to see if it jumps?"

"You might consider it in the future," said Shaw with an unusual attempt at wit.

Townsend didn't respond.

"Look. You saw someone lying in a coffin," Shaw said. He was gathering momentum and a definite tone of reproach was creeping into his voice. "How do you know who this man was?"

"Ken . . . ?" Townsend asked impatiently. "What's the old newsman's saying? 'We don't print the truth. We print what people tell us.' I've been through two thousand death write-ups and I probably did more background on this one than on nineteen hundred ninety-five others."

Shaw grunted. From a jacket pocket he produced a battered pipe. From a side drawer to his desk he pulled a tobacco pouch and flipped it onto his desk. Then he absently searched the rest of his pockets for matches as an uneasy silence enveloped his office.

Kenneth Nelson Shaw, managing editor. The M.E. For some silly reason, while Townsend was watching Shaw fumble for a light, he thought of Harry. Harry always called attention to the fact that M.E. stood for both managing editor and medical examiner. Harry insisted there was more to this coincidence than met the ear.

Finally, Shaw spoke again.

"I know this is heresy, Townsend," Shaw suggested heavily, "but did it ever occur to you, perhaps in your wildest flights of fancy, that you just might—surely for the first time in your life—have made a mistake?"

Shaw found a lighter instead of a match.

"My source looked good. I printed what people told me," Townsend said.

Shaw rubbed his chin and pursed his lips. "Max Kohlheimer wants us to run a retraction, and possibly an apology."

"What?" Townsend was on his feet in anger.

"Sit down! This is not my decision, Paul!" Shaw stuffed a generous pinch of his own specially blended tobacco into the bowl as he spoke.

"How the hell does Max Kohlheimer come into this?" Townsend was beside himself. But he settled back into his chair.

"Apparently the FBI contacted him. And you'll recall that Mr. Kohlheimer's signature appears on your paycheck." Shaw's voice attempted to soothe, then paused for emphasis. "The FBI is quite angry with you, as is Mr. Kohlheimer. Paul, listen to me. The boss plays golf in Palm Springs with the present director of the FBI. He has also played with three former directors of that agency. This is one story," he said, dwelling on each individual syllable, "that you cannot fuck with."

Townsend stiffened in his chair. "I stand by what I wrote," he said adamantly.

"I figured you would," Shaw said sullenly. He paused, as if mentally he were turning over each facet of the situation. He lit his pipe and a low cloud of smoke enveloped him and then rolled over the desk. The aroma from the pipe smelled midway between burning leaves and a bad tropical punch.

"I'll tell you something, Jack," Shaw said generously and making an an admission of sorts. "There have been many times when I have not been a fan of yours. Like when somebody dies and you print the truth. You know, that the guy was a real shit. Other times, well, your stuff's okay. Not my cup of tea." He paused again. "But you have your following and your department runs efficiently. It even turns a little profit, in case you didn't know. Usually the obit page flies at a loss. And, Christ knows, I've heard the stories: you've paid your dues."

Townsend sat listening to this. Shaw took another drag on his pipe. His eyebrows shot skyward and he exhaled something that looked like a storm cloud. He stared imperiously above Townsend's head, then his gaze settled into Townsend's eyes again.

"You worked at the *New York Post,* didn't you? Back during Dorothy Schiff's ownership?" Shaw asked.

"I worked at the *News,*" Townsend answered, "back when the paper's Chicago ownership started union busting."

"Yes. Of course. Well, that's your opinion of it," Shaw said, as if preparing to say something further. "So you did. You worked at the *New York News.*"

Shaw, Townsend recalled, was a native of the Southwest, where he had first started climbing up the slippery pole of the Kohlheimer publishing conglomerate. Shaw remembered none of the defunct New York City dailies and could have cited no distinctions between any two.

So Townsend waited.

"Look," Shaw said cheerfully. "I don't like giving orders to a reporter. Even an obit man." He was at his most fulsome and patronizing worst. "I'd rather give assignments and let our people do their jobs." He paused again. "I can give you a day or two to turn around. Maybe even three days. Mr. Kohlheimer is in Japan, fortunately for all of us. It would be worse if he were right on our doorstep."

"The FBI called him in Japan?"

"Not just the FBI, Paul. The director phoned him in Tokyo," Shaw said. "Last night, our time. My phone rang this morn—"

"The *director?*" Townsend heard his own voice rise very suddenly. "Ken, you fancy yourself a newspaperman and you don't see something's strange about this? How the hell does an alleged mistake on an obituary page, in a paper that's not read by anyone with a triple-digit I.Q., get all the way to the head of the FBI?"

"It's not just our paper," Shaw said, missing the point. "Other papers picked it up from us."

"Doesn't this bother you, Ken? Won't you lose a few minutes of sleep tonight *wondering* what's so important about this?"

"Frankly, no." He shrugged. "There are some stories you learn to stay away from. I wish to remain employed here. I'm not sure, but I'd guess you do, too."

"You got a real instinct for news, Ken," said Townsend at his abrasive worst. "I don't know why one of the television networks hasn't hired you away to cover the Presidential campaign."

Shaw's voice rose predictably with the provocation.

"Paul, you stumbled across something best left alone, damn it! Don't you see that?" He was shouting, his voice echoing out the half-open door of his office. "If you're smart, you'll go with a retraction in today's edition. Get rid of it. Drop it. Make everyone happy. Then that's the end of it, all right?"

K.N. Shaw stopped to gather his composure, but his eyes, amid the pipe smoke, remained ablaze. "I'm doing you a favor. Don't you see that, you damned stubborn fool?" Then he paused ominously. "Don't make us fire you and run the retraction ourselves."

Townsend felt like charging the desk, hurtling it and throttling his managing editor. Not for the first time. Instead, he maintained a complete stillness in his chair. He felt his hands wet with sweat. He supposed the Scottish and Irish components in his blood had turned his face crimson with rage.

"There will have to be a quick resolution to this," Shaw said, calming rapidly. "And I assured Mr. Kohlheimer that there would be one." He paused and waited. "There *will* be a quick resolution, won't there, Paul?"

"I stand by my story," Townsend said again.

Shaw sighed. Through the cloud of pipe smoke his eyes were intent upon Townsend. He folded his hands and glanced down.

"Give me a chance to prove it, Ken," said Townsend. "For the paper's sake if not mine. We all look like dorks if we run a major retraction."

Shaw looked as if he were in pain.

"All right," Shaw finally muttered. "Can you prove your account within forty-eight hours? I can buy you that amount of time. No more. I can put it in the budget as a special assignment. No loss of pay, obviously. No reprimand or anything."

"And if I can't prove it?"

"The alternative is clear, isn't it? Retraction and apology. Or your resignation and we do the retraction and apology. Mr. Kohlheimer owns the paper."

Townsend thought about it. "Yeah. It's clear," he grumbled. He stood, then turned to go.

"Paul?" Shaw asked as Townsend arrived at the door.

Townsend turned, expecting the worst.

"Just because I work on this floor, you think I'm your enemy. Is that it?"

"I'm not used to having friends in upper management, Ken," Townsend answered. "If it ever happened, it would be a new experience for me."

Shaw pulled thoughtfully on his pipe. "Then maybe you should cultivate it a little more," he said.

"What does that mean?"

"I don't mind having you on this paper," Shaw explained, spending a moment at his fulsome worst. "You're not quite my favorite flavor, as I said. But I really have nothing against you, either. You provide something different for the *Sun,* which is good for all of us." With surprisingly conciliatory tones, Shaw continued. "I think of you as a 'fast format' Boswell," the managing editor said. "You know: Boswell. The Scotsman who wrote about Johnson. That's James Boswell and Samuel Johnson."

"Yes. I know."

" 'Literary journalism,' " Shaw proclaimed, forging ahead. "Isn't that what the *Columbia Journalism Review* calls it when a man writes intelligently for a daily deadline?"

"I wouldn't know," Townsend said, wondering as he spoke if his tone of voice conveyed the proper irreverence.

"Well, *I* would," Shaw retorted cheerfully. "What I'm saying, Paul, is that all in all, you're an asset for this paper. You do things well. Your work is appreciated even in places where you wouldn't expect." He paused. "So don't get your knickers in a twist over something that doesn't pay. There aren't that many newspaper positions out there in this city. So don't blow the one you have. Okay?"

"I'll try my best."

As Townsend departed, Shaw picked up his phone. Townsend heard him call Herb Frederick, the city desk editor. Shaw pulled a pair of writers—one from sports, one from a New Jersey beat—for the next two days. Without saying anything, Townsend had apparently agreed to the forty-eight-hour deadline.

Strangely, Laurie had been worried about her mother for the past two weeks. Her mother had fallen silent at times in the day which normally were the most enjoyable. Mom had even forgotten the little games that they played. Dolls and puppets, for example. The little jokes that they normally shared had vanished. Worse, her temper seemed short and she argued with Laurie's father more.

And now, this . . .

Seven-year-old Laurie stood at her bedroom window and looked down to the garden below. What was Mom doing? What kind of plant or vegetable could she have been digging a space for? What, under a nearly full moon at ten minutes past two in the morning?

Perhaps it had been the strange wavering light outside, the light from Mom's flashlight, that filtered up through the trees and into the bedroom she shared with her sister. Perhaps it had been the sound of shovels and rakes at that hour. That wasn't a usual sound in the Hubbell house. Nor was it usual that Mom should be out in the garden with a flashlight in the middle of the night.

Tina Hubbell carried a shovel. She knelt by the edge of her backyard vegetable patch and laid the shovel on the ground. She seemed to be studying its position, then to be aligning it. Perhaps with the driveway. Perhaps with something unseen to Laurie, like the spire of the church which rose between the houses across the street.

Tina Hubbell picked up the shovel and began to dig, right where the head of the tool had been.

Buried treasure! Laurie thought with a burst of excitement. *Mom had found a map from pirate days in old Spanish Florida! Mom was looking for a chest of gold right there in the Hubbells' own backyard!*

Tina wore jeans and a sweatshirt. She dug for several minutes until the shovel clanked against metal. Then she set the shovel aside, went to her knees, and began to push the dirt away with her hands.

Mom found it! They were rich! They were rich! Laurie could barely keep herself from crying out with glee.

Tina wiped her brow with her forearm. She pulled from the earth a strangely shaped box which looked to be the size of a small toaster oven. It was wrapped in black, however. She knocked the loose dirt from it and set it aside. Then she picked up the shovel again. She worked very quickly, as if she feared being observed. Twice she looked back over her shoulder to see if anyone from the Hubbell house was watching. Twice Laurie looked away just in time.

Mom filled in the dirt in the garden. She patted it down with her hand and turned the flashlight off. From the moonlight, Laurie could still see. Mom carried the hidden treasure under one arm and hurried back to the kitchen. She set the shovel against a tree.

Laurie couldn't wait. She wanted to see the gold and jewelry that were buried in the pirate chest. It would all be so beautiful, she was sure, sparkling and glistening like in a movie.

She tiptoed from her room without waking her sister. Her father was asleep. She could hear the snoring in her parents' bedroom. Mom was so brave going out to hunt for treasure by herself.

Laurie tiptoed down the stairs. The light was on in the kitchen. Mom came into the house and locked the door. Quiet as a church mouse,

Laurie scooted across the dining room to the kitchen door, where she peered around the edge of the door frame. She was sure Mom had heard her, but no. Mom was locking the screen door and had heard nothing.

Laurie peeked into the kitchen. A radio was softly playing an oldies station from Tampa, presumably to cover the noise of Tina Hubbell at work.

Tina Hubbell had spread newspapers across the kitchen table. Now she was unwrapping the treasure. The treasure was wrapped in a big plastic garbage bag. Mom pulled a smaller metal box from it.

Funny thing was, the box was steel and rectangular. It was no longer than a loaf of bread and it looked very modern. It didn't really resemble the type of thing a girl saw in pirate movies. It was more like one of the fireproof metal boxes in which her parents kept their bills, their tax records, and their bank statements.

Tina Hubbell produced a key. She fitted the key into the lock on the small steel box.

Mom opened the box. Laurie was still peaking from the darkness of the dining room into the kitchen. And Mom was so intent on what she was doing that she paid no attention to anything outside the room.

Tina lifted the lid. The box opened. Laurie squinted to see. But there were no gleaming gold coins or fancy necklaces. No silver and no bracelet or pearls.

Instead, Mom's hands worked quickly, gathering from the box what seemed first like capsules, then like a handful of tiny pencils. These were yellowish with a shiny, coppery glint. She scattered them on the table. Then she reached to a much larger, heavier item from within the box. It was wrapped in an old dish towel and bound tightly by heavy brown string. Mrs. Hubbell's hands treated the object with clear respect.

Tina Hubbell cut the string with a kitchen knife. The binding fell away. So did the dish towel. Out came something that was black and very heavy, judging by the way Laurie's mother hefted it in her hand. Initially, the mysterious object looked like a wrench.

So that was it! Laurie thought. *Mom has hidden Dad's birthday presents! She's giving him some little pencils, which she has to wrap separately. Some pencils and a big black wrench for his basement workbench. And she's keeping the presents hidden so that he—*

But Jim Hubbell's birthday wouldn't come until the other end of the calendar. And what Tina Hubbell held was not a wrench. Laurie's excitement went to consternation and then straight to fear as she watched her mother for several seconds longer, and as the "wrench" suddenly took a more sinister form.

Tina Hubbell opened the black snub-nosed .38-caliber revolver and held it in her right hand. With her left, she gathered what looked like five of those tiny pencils. She was quite methodical and concentrated on her task.

Laurie was horrified!

The pencils turned into shiny bullets as Mom threaded them into the chambers of her revolver. And Mom's face, tired, drawn, and tense, suddenly looked very old—suddenly quite unlike her mother—etched as it was with an apparent fear. It was a fear that matched that of her unseen daughter who was already hurrying through the living room— the sound of her footfall covered by the kitchen radio—and scrambling up the stairs.

Some of the steps creaked as the child fled.

But by the time Tina Hubbell came to the kitchen doorway, revolver in hand, Laurie had landed safely in bed. There she pulled the covers up high around her shoulders. She trembled and closed her eyes tightly, lying as still as her sister, who had never awakened.

Mom finished whatever she was doing in the kitchen. The lights clicked off downstairs in the Hubbell house.

When Tina appeared again in her daughter's bedroom, she was wearing a nightgown and had nothing in her hand.

Laurie looked at her through eyes that were almost shut. The light from the moon lit the room with a blue glow.

Mom looked so pretty again. She was back in her nightgown. She left the room.

Laurie kept her eyes closed. Then, for a moment, she rose again and looked out the window, down toward the garden where everything was now still and quite.

Maybe, she told herself, it had all been a dream. A strange nasty dream. She was convinced of that as she settled back into her bed, closed her eyes, and tumbled back into a deep sleep.

She was convinced of that, too, the next morning when her mother seemed in quite good spirits again, fixing her breakfast and getting her ready for the school bus.

So it *had* been a dream, Laurie decided. She held that conviction right up until the moment she left for school via the kitchen door of the Hubbell home.

Mom's sneakers, caked with dirt, still rested on the flagstone path outside. And the shovel, the one that had drawn that ghastly box up from the ground, was still propped against a tree. It was exactly where Tina Hubbell had left it in her daughter's dream.

<<<< **16** >>>>

*T*HAT same morning, Paul Townsend rented a car in Manhattan and retraced the route Sarah had driven on a rainy evening three weeks earlier. Now it was a Friday morning in June, however. Daylight considerably brightened the trip.

He easily found Route 120, and with it the right turn past the picket fence. He drove about two miles on the unmarked two-lane road. But then where was the next turn? Where were the guideposts? He knew he had to have been within a few miles of the house where he had met the dying man. Where was it?

For an hour in the late morning, he searched. Then he gave up temporarily. He drove to New Rochelle and found Marston's Funeral Home.

He parked across the street and tried the entrance. It was locked. He cupped his hand over his eyes and leaned against the glass door. There was no activity within. He rang a bell. No one answered.

He stepped back from Marston's. This was the first warm day of the month and the sun was starting to beat on him. He removed his sports jacket and held it folded over an arm.

There was a burst of heavy machinery and metallic noise from the auto parts establishment next door. Townsend, now in a white short-sleeved shirt and a tie, walked to its entrance.

Townsend could see that a new Toyota sports coupe was being chopped for parts. Two men belligerently turned to watch him as he looked their way. No, this was no place to ask questions, he decided. He went instead to the liquor store which flanked the other side of Marston's.

There was a handpainted sign on the door that said, OSCAR'S LI-QUORS. Townsend walked past it. There was a single clerk in the store. He was a beefy man who had slicked-back black hair, deep jowls, and a massively fat frame. He wore a billy club, which hung at his belt on the right side. Clipped to his shirt pocket was a red New York State pistol permit, but no firearm was within view.

JUNE'S DRINK OF CHOICE—VODKA proclaimed a large sign behind the clerk's head.

There were two refrigeration units filled with beer. Hard liquor took up most of the wall. There were a few wines in bins on the floor. The most exotic was Chilean. Townsend studied the choices.

"Help you?" the man said.

Townsend stood before the refrigerator case, pondering the beer. He found a six-bottle pack of Miller High Life and took it to the counter. He glanced at the pistol permit and read the man's name. This was, not surprisingly, Oscar.

"Dollar a bottle. Comes to six bucks sixty-six with the tax. The man spoke in a low growl. "Six sixty-six."

"The devil's number," Townsend said affably, making a joke of it. He put out a ten-dollar bill.

"What is?" Oscar asked.

Townsend knew he shouldn't have bothered. "Nothing," he said.

"Did I miss something?" the fat man asked as he put the six-pack in a paper bag, then picked up the ten-dollar bill and made change. Townsend smiled and shook his head.

"Mind if I open one?" Townsend asked. Townsend pulled one cold bottle from the bag.

"Don't drink it in the fuckin' store, duke," Oscar said.

"Whatever you say."

Townsend accepted his change.

"You don't know who owns the parlor next door, do you?" Townsend asked. "Or who operates it?"

"I might."

"Would you tell me?" Townsend asked with the utmost civility.

"Why do you want to know?"

"I got a sick friend."

The clerk raised his eyes. "An old man named Marston. Raymond Marston. He's half Jew, half Nigger."

"Is he a friend of yours?"

"Would I have a friend who's only a fuckin' one-quarter white?" Oscar ranted.

"You might," Townsend allowed.

Oscar smiled. One front tooth was missing. The other looked like an inverted tombstone. His eye teeth looked like they had been borrowed from a malamute. "Yeah, Ray's okay people," Oscar said. "Why?"

"Does he do much business?"

"You an asshole from IRS or somethin'?"

"You really want to know?" Townsend asked.

"Not really."

The fat man scanned his cash drawer, then slammed it shut. Behind him, next to his liquor license, was a diploma conferring upon the same man a bachelor of science degree from an accredited university in the state of Pennsylvania, embossed and made out to the man's name: Oscar Skowdenski. Some things never ceased to amaze Townsend. Here was Archie Bunker with a university education.

"My uncle's funeral service was held there last week. I want to know where the burial was."

"Your uncle, huh?"

"Last—"

"Saturday, bubba."

"How did you know?" Townsend asked.

"It was the only service old Marston has done in a month. And I hear only one guy came to it."

"Is that a fact?"

"That's a true fact, pal. How'd ya like that? You die and only one guy comes to your fuckin' funeral." Oscar shook his head, genuinely moved.

"A real shame," Townsend said. "But I'm sure that if more people had known—"

Oscar forged ahead. "Marston don't do much no more." The fat man looked at Townsend suspiciously, as if to weigh carefully the content of what followed. Then he decided he could safely continue.

"Marston does queers mostly," Oscar said. "Was your uncle queer?"

"No."

"That's what everyone thinks about their uncle. Anyway, Marston stays in business because no one will embalm queers these days. Disease, you know what I mean? I wouldn't touch a freakin' queer, either. Marston does it for the money. Who the fuck else would have a funeral service on this stinkin' block? No offense, you know." The man clucked a loud laugh. "But this ain't the greatest, see what I mean?" He motioned to the world beyond the grates on his window.

"I think I know what you mean." Townsend paused.

"Marston does Niggers, also," Oscar said, continuing remorselessly. "Sometimes Mondays and Tuesdays are busy days for nigger funerals if the welfare checks came in on Friday. Know what Ray's specialty used to be when he was younger?"

"What's that?"

"Bullet wounds. Knife wounds. Head, neck, or face. Ray could fix up a body really fine within a few hours. Hey, this one time Ray had a big Irish kid who'd eaten his own pistol. This is back when this was a Mick neighborhood. Anyway, this dumb young Harp blew a hole out the rear of his skull. Ray patched him up, fooled the priest, got the kid a fuckin' Catlick funeral and—"

"Does Mr. Marston make his own appointments?" Townsend asked.

"Yeah."

"Know where I can find him?"

"Ray Marston? Yeah. I know."

"Will you tell me?"

"Your friend ain't a Nigger. So I bet your friend's a fairy, ain't he?"

"Does it make a difference to you?"

"Not to me. I don't notice those things."

"Tell you what," Townsend said. "Just give me Mr. Marston's address. I'm sure he lives around here, doesn't he?"

"Not too far away. How'd you know that?"

"Lucky guess."

"No," the man insisted. "That's amazing. Tell me how you knew."

"You said he was old," Townsend said. "An old man wouldn't travel that far to run a part-time business in a decaying neighborhood. I took an educated guess."

"Pretty smart," Oscar said. "What'd you say you did for a living?"

"How would you feel," Townsend pressed again, "about giving me the address?"

"I'd feel," Oscar said, "like a first-class American citizen."

Townsend had a pencil and notepad available. He wrote down an address in nearby Mount Vernon. Then he thanked his new friend and departed.

Townsend found Raymond Marston at the latter's home early the same afternoon. Marston lived in a row house on a decaying block which looked to Townsend to be in an entirely black working-class neighborhood. A parking space was open in front of Marston's home.

Raymond Marston was a small man who appeared to be in his eighties. He had slicked-back white hair, tortoise-shell glasses too large for his narrow face, leathery skin, and glassy brown eyes that looked as if they had seen too much and forgotten nothing. When Townsend found him, Marston sat in a cushioned white wicker lawn chair on the shaded front porch of an old house. He was neatly attired in a pair of beige slacks and a golf jacket. He puffed a cigar. A cane leaned against his chair. He looked like what he was: a semiretired undertaker.

Marston was too old to lie or connive. He barely cared to know why the visitor might have wanted to know where the remains of his most recent customer had gone. Marston rose from his porch. On his feet, he looked much more frail than when seated. He was no more than five and a quarter feet tall. Arduously, Marston carefully stretched out his legs to ward off stiffness.

"Come on inside," Marston said to Townsend. Mildly surprised, Townsend followed. "Let me go a few steps ahead. I have a lifetime companion. Name's Clyde. Clyde gets upset if someone comes in too quick unannounced."

"I understand," Townsend said. Townsend only thought he understood. He actually didn't.

Marston, even at his great age, was not a totally guileless man. "Clyde," Marston announced loudly, "we have a friend to see us."

Clyde, an immense black Doberman, carefully inspected Townsend as he entered. Clyde, an easy hundred ten pounds of fang and muscle, conducted the inspection at a distance of under two inches—an attentive black wet nose to Townsend's bare wrist. Clyde scrutinized guests carefully, ever vigilant for the scent of threat or fear. Townsend was relieved to pass the uncompromising judgment of Clyde's warm nostrils.

Marston led Townsend to a desk where he poked through an assortment of loose papers.

"The client's daughter done signed the burial order certificate," Marston said. "I has a copy here somewhere."

Next to Marston's desk was a standing file. The undertaker rummaged through it. "Here," he finally said.

Marston produced a document. And although the name of the deceased had carelessly not been filled in, the signature of Sarah Stuart appeared at the bottom. Townsend noted that the remains had been sent to a crematorium in Manhattan's Yorkville section, on First Avenue in the upper eighties. Townsend wrote down the establishment's name and address.

Townsend thanked the old man and returned to his car. He resisted the temptation to drive directly to Manhattan. Instead, he retraced his route from that morning. Back in New Rochelle, he bought a map of Westchester County. He returned to the area where he suspected the Wolik residence had been. He began to prowl the back streets and country lanes.

Methodically, Townsend checked off roads and lanes from his map as he drove them, so as not to repeat one or miss another. The discovery was not upon him until late in the afternoon, following two frustrating hours of search. And then it was on him with astonishing suddenness.

He saw the large, rambling house rise out of the trees on an isolated road called Hillside. He recognized, even in the sunlight, the distinctive lines of the roof. He quickly turned into a driveway that he might otherwise have missed. Townsend's tires made the same noisy impression on the gravel driveway. To make things complete, the same dog from the next residence barked when Townsend stepped out of his car.

He had a premonition of what he would find. He had worked enough cases, tracked down enough individuals who didn't wish to be found, explored the aftermath of enough swindles or homicides to sense a departure even before it was evident. And so it was with the Wolik house.

Townsend went to the back door, again following the identical path as on his previous visit. But this time the rear door was hooked tightly from within. Shades were drawn and the house was still.

He knocked and there was no response. He called aloud. The only response was the echo of his own voice. And that echo only underscored the stillness within the house.

He walked around the building, discovering a For Sale sign on the front lawn. He returned to the rear, an area in which he was not visible from the street. He drew a breath and looked in every direction. Then, under the circumstances, he took the only logical next step for a dedicated member of the working press. He broke in through a ground-floor window.

Never had Townsend experienced such a strong feeling of trespass. Sliding through the window, planting his feet on the wooden floor, he found himself in a clean, empty room. It was as spartan as a pine coffin, as quiet as a tomb. He had a sense of having violated an order higher than his own. As all the shades were drawn, the outside world was unconnected from this place.

He walked through a parlor, followed by the sound of his own steps. There was no furniture. Then, passing through to the sitting room where the deceased had so recently entertained him, he found that room empty, too. So was the kitchen. So were the kitchen cabinets. So was every room downstairs.

Townsend's heart began to pound when he mounted the uncarpeted wooden steps. Even though he was walking up the stairs, he had an overbearing, almost sickening sense of walking down deeper into something—some place where he was not welcome.

But he continued. He stood at the second-floor landing and sniffed.

He tangibly sensed death but couldn't smell it. One of his old-fashioned migraines was starting to move into place at the forefront of his skull. He wanted to be out of this house soon. He also wanted to pick up a bat, or a fire poker, or anything, to carry. He felt—no, he knew—there was something there to ward off, something horrible lurking in his near future.

He could almost taste it.

He walked into each empty room upstairs. Gingerly, expecting the worst, he opened each closet.

Nothing. Silence and emptiness.

His pulse began to ease.

The house had been picked clean. No furniture. No clothing. Not even a scrap of paper. Wolik had been dead for seven days and his house was already empty.

Or, Townsend wondered, had it already been empty? All except the rooms to which he had been shown.

At the top of the steps, Townsend blew out a long breath. He walked downstairs. He paused for a moment, then let himself back out the window.

He returned to his car and leaned against it. He pulled out another bottle of beer. His mouth was parched, his pulsebeat was still rapid. The drink was lukewarm now, but he downed it anyway.

He stared at the house. He walked around it again and stopped at the realtor's sign on the front lawn. He wrote down the agency's name, Singer Realty, and their telephone number in nearby White Plains. Then he went to the adjoining properties. He rapped on the doors of both neighbors, but no one answered. The dog, a large golden retriever tethered to a post within a large mesh corral, went crazy with an orgy of barking.

His visit concluded, Townsend got back into his car.

What was he looking at? What had he seen? It was right before his eyes and he still didn't know.

He considered the pieces:

The greatest secret of the 1960s. The FBI still active, following Wolik's death notice. A house picked clean of any sign of its previous occupant. A disconnected telephone for Sarah Stuart. Popov and Goleniewski.

Somewhere in that melange, something had to fit together.

Townsend drove to White Plains. He found Singer Realty in a small, white Cape Cod house on a side street off from the center of town. There was one associate broker on duty when he walked in the door just before closing hour. Her name, according to the marker on her desk, was

Esther Mueller. She was a platinum-haired woman in her late fifties. Without inhaling, she puffed a cigarette in a small tortoise-shell holder.

Already, as Townsend walked to the door, he felt his facility for deception starting to return to him.

"I work for the *New York Sun,*" he said, showing his press card. "I'm looking for some old friends of mine. The family's name is Wolik. They used to have a home on Hillside Road."

Mrs. Mueller apologized and shook her head.

"I believe it's the house you represent for sale," he said.

She thought for a moment and then linked his request with the proper home.

"*That* house," she said. "Number Thirty-six. What was the name of the people?"

"Wolik," he said. "W-O-L-I-K."

Mrs. Mueller shook her head again. "I'm afraid the name doesn't mean anything to me," she said. "When did they own Number Thirty-six?"

"I thought up until very recently."

"No. You're mistaken," she said. "Not that house in any case."

"Why are you so sure?"

"Well, number Thirty-six . . ." she said. "I don't know. I don't ask questions."

"About what?"

"It used to belong to a lovely family named Reed," she said. "Their children grew. The family sold. I think Mr. Reed died. Mrs. Reed, her name was Eleanor, I think, moved to New Hampshire or Vermont. Or maybe she went to Florida. But the property was sold privately. Owned by an out-of-state company."

"A *company?* What sort?"

"A *small* company," she said, as if that were the explanation Townsend sought. "And I have no idea what they do."

"You must have an address."

She said he could call her Essie. Everyone else did. And she also said she had an address. Somewhere. She went to a book containing her listings and came up with the name of F.C.T. Holding Company. There was a mailbox in Dover, Delaware.

"What if the house sells?" Townsend asked.

"We're authorized to accept any offer above a certain amount," she said. "Of course, I can't tell you that amount," she laughed. "We're to execute the sale with a local attorney of our choice. Papers are to be sent to the company in Delaware. The secretary of that company will execute the proper papers on their part."

"I don't suppose you would have a name?" he asked. "Of the secretary of the company."

She didn't.

"Have you ever met the man?" Townsend asked.

"It's a woman," Essie said proudly, as if striking an ardent blow for 1990s feminism. "The secretary of the company is a woman. We spoke on the telephone once."

"But you don't know the woman's name?"

She thought about it for a moment.

"It was a Mrs. Reeves," she said. "Or maybe it was a Mrs. Padula." Her brow furrowed. She shook her head apologetically. "I'm sorry," she said. "It was about a year ago. And I'm terrible about names." She snuffed out the remains of her cigarette and extricated the butt from the holder.

"The name wasn't Stuart, was it?" he asked. "A Mrs. Sarah Stuart, perhaps?"

She pursed her lips, then shook her head again. "I just don't remember," she said. "You see, it wasn't really very important. We were to take the listing for the house and communicate with the corporation. That's all." Essie leaned forward slightly and glanced sidelong, reassuring herself that the walls of her office didn't have hidden ears. "It's all legal. But it's some sort of big business secret," she said. "That's what my husband figured out. But who knows?"

Who knew, indeed, Townsend wondered. Certainly no one else in the office, Esther Mueller informed him after his obvious next question.

"Essie, look," Townsend tried. "If I told you someone was using that house about two weeks ago, what would you say to me?"

The woman laughed. "I'd say that's quite impossible," she said.

"I was there myself. The lights were on, people were in the house, and the downstairs was at least partially furnished."

"You're mistaken," she said. "You must have been somewhere else. Why, we had strict instructions from the company. A letter from Delaware. *No one* was to be in that house, even realtors, for a two-week period. The company even changed the locks. The period ended yesterday, when we got a new key."

"Is that right?"

"It is."

"And you received the new key without actually seeing anyone, I assume. Such as by private courier. Or by mail."

"Yes," she said, surprised that he would know. "By Express Mail."

"As I suspected," Townsend said.

She was in an expansive mood and enjoyed talking to the younger man. So she was anxious to help him. She rose from her desk and produced exactly what she had received. She showed him the remains of an Express Mail envelope. It bore no return address, and contained only the new key plus a handwritten, unsigned note explaining that this new key would be needed for admittance to 36 Hillside Road. Townsend didn't recognize the handwriting. He knew it was not Sarah's.

Townsend examined the envelope. From its markings, he could determine its point of origin.

"But this didn't enter the postal system in Delaware, Mrs. Mueller," he said. "It came from northern Virginia. Just across the Potomac from Washington."

"Did it?" she asked, genuinely intrigued.

"Does that make any sense to you?"

She shook her head.

"And why do you suppose," he mused, "that the owner would have mailed you the key? He or she could have dropped it off in person. Obviously, someone was on the premises locally if the lock was changed."

Essie Mueller hunched her shoulders. "Sometimes," she said, "I just don't know why people do things."

"Me, neither," he said.

Townsend smiled and thanked her. Essie Mueller gave Townsend her business card. He graciously accepted it.

It was six P.M. now. Townsend found the highway that led back into Manhattan. His anger growing, he drove back to Manhattan at a mad speed, knowing ahead of time what he would probably find next.

He drove down the East Side of Manhattan and came to the block of East 53rd Street between First and Second avenues. He dumped his car in a metered space on Second Avenue. Then he set out on foot, carrying a copy of the *Sun* under his arm.

He knew her building well enough to have recognized its soft spot in residential security. He stood near a magazine kiosk across the block until seven thirty. At that time, he knew, Sarah's evening doorman took a twenty-minute break for dinner. His backup was the porter from the service elevator. But whoever was on door duty was frequently called to the back elevator on an intercom. Townsend watched the building entrance carefully. When the porter was called away, Townsend walked into the building.

He knew he had about half a minute to get into a front passenger elevator. None was there as when he arrived at the elevator bank.

One elevator descended slowly. The other was stopped at the twelfth floor. Around the corner in the lobby, he heard the porter returning.

The descending elevator stopped on the second floor.

Townsend opened his newspaper and held it up, as if to read it. He shielded his face from the porter. The porter strolled slowly in Townsend's direction. Townsend could tell from the man's footfall.

The elevator began to move again. It went to one, then to the lobby. There it opened.

A man and a woman stepped out. Townsend didn't know them, but they greeted the porter by name, distracting him for a moment. Townsend stepped past them and into the elevator. He punched the button for Sarah's floor. Eight. The door closed.

Less than a minute later, Townsend stood before the door to Sarah's apartment. But Townsend's instincts had again proven correct. The lady was in the midst of a vanishing act, or at least playing hard to find. He could tell before he even knocked at her door. There was evidence of a fresh lock cylinder where her key would normally fit, and a second new cylinder added below the first.

Nonetheless, he pushed her doorbell. He heard the buzzer within her apartment. He knocked. Then he tried something resembling a coded knock—three raps, then two, then four—just in case.

Nothing. No answer from within. It struck him that everywhere he looked for Wolik or daughter, he was met only by silence and emptiness. He was starting to spot a trend.

He rang a final time. Still nothing. He belligerently eyed the locks, then realized in frustration there was no way he could break in without a drill. Four minutes later, he walked out of the building. The evening doorman was back on duty. The man barely glanced up from *El Diario*.

Townsend walked back to his car and stood next to the driver's side for several seconds. He blew out a long breath. Then, in fury and frustration, he stepped back and violently kicked his car door, leaving a dent in its side.

"Son of a goddamned bitch!" he cursed bitterly. A few bemused passersby glanced in his general direction as if he were crazy. But in keeping with Manhattan etiquette for dealing with the deranged or emotionally disturbed, none looked directly at him. And no one stopped.

All right, he realized. For the first time in his career, he'd been duped. He'd been truly had and he knew it. Leonard Wolik wasn't Leonard Wolik, Sarah Stuart wasn't his daughter. The house in Westchester probably wasn't theirs, and who in hell now knew about the story that the dying man had so convincingly told?

Townsend had been set up and knocked over like a bowling pin and considered himself just about as smart.

But just who *was* the man who had died? What did it have to do with the FBI or the CIA? What had there been in the story he had told? Was Sarah Stuart really Sarah Stuart? Did she really have a son in prep school and had she really been married to the doctor?

He fumed, arms folded across his chest, as strangers passed by without further noting him. Traffic briskly moved on East 53rd Street, ignoring him totally.

In his mind, all sorts of possible deceptions unfolded to him, expanded, then reformed in endless now-obvious patterns of deceit.

How *long* had she been setting him up, he wondered. He had dined with her and gone to movies with her. Many times, they had shared ideas, thoughts, and a bed. Was it all part of the same grand pattern of deceit? Or had something arisen during the life of their relationship which had moved her to this action?

He didn't know. Worse, he had no idea. Nor, looking back on what had transpired so far, could he find any clue that he had missed, any indication—however faint—that he should have known what was coming.

"Goddamn!" he cursed again.

Maybe he should have known that something was wrong, he told himself, when she sought an audition for the dying man's death notice. Normal people don't do that.

He stood against his rented car, arms across his chest, feeling himself the biggest sucker in the city. He was also, he added in further self-rebuke, the most incompetent newswriter ever to paste together a story.

He let all this sink in. And, as he stood there watching the city grow dark around him, he didn't much like the feeling.

<<<< **17** >>>>

A MONG Sunday morning's necrologies, there was a violin maker, a woman in her nineties. There was also a former state police lieutenant and a Broadway chorus dancer. The main obit on Townsend's page, however, had already been laid out for a man who had been a particularly acerbic movie critic in the sixties and seventies. The deceased critic would be worth a full column. Normally, the challenge would be finding someone with something nice to say about such a man. Townsend didn't bother. He printed some of the nastier things said of the critic. Even his family, Townsend soon discovered, had disliked him.

For Townsend this was a slow morning. But it had been a strange one. Three times his phone had rung while he was putting together his write-up of the critic. All three times there had been no caller on the other end.

Malfunctions in the new multimillion-dollar phone system? Or someone keeping track of Townsend's whereabouts? Shades of the old days, he told himself. Shades of the old paranoias.

Then, at lunch hour, Townsend again found himself in the unfriendly climes of the sixth floor. There, K.N. Shaw wore a pained expression as he peered across his desk. Unlike other trips to the sixth floor, this was one that Townsend had solicited.

"What are you trying to tell me, Jack?"

"I'm telling you I was set up," said Townsend.

" 'Set up,' " intoned K.N. Shaw, dwelling on the phrase. "Mind telling me how?"

Much of what Townsend had to say was a rehash of their previous meeting, though Paul Townsend now admitted that there still was no evidence suggesting who had really died and what was going on. Townsend talked for several minutes.

Shaw could think of only one approach.

"We have to do a retraction of some sort," he said, harkening back to his point of the previous meeting. "That much is clear. I assume," Shaw said carefully, "that you're willing to write it. Your forty-eight hours are up, after all."

"What do you want me to say, Ken?" Townsend asked.

"What do you mean, 'What do you want me to say?' " Shaw asked, as if it were obvious. "The director of the FBI is whispering in Max Kohlheimer's ear and you admit that you had the story wrong. We have to retract the Leonard Wolik obituary of June—"

"Whoa, Ken," Townsend said. "I don't know if I have the story wrong. I just suspect the wrong man died. Plus, how do we retract an obituary, Ken?" Townsend asked pleasantly. "Is the real Leonard Wolik complaining? And where is the real Leonard Wolik? I know one existed because I contacted a CIA source. Further, what's going on? Someone faked a death. Someone faked an identity. Someone wanted an ersatz Wolik obituary in our paper and someone equally wants it out."

Shaw pursed his lips as if the act were laced with pain.

Townsend leaned forward. "Ken, use all of your faculties on this. Doesn't it seem to you like a news story is lurking somewhere here?"

"I know *this,* Jack," Shaw said ardently. "I know that Max Kohlheimer is lurking no farther than the other end of my phone line."

Shaw's pipe came out again. The first bowl of the day, and Shaw fingered it carefully from pouch to pipe, packing it with his thumb. Then he lit it as a silence held the office.

"There's something else I don't understand, Paul," said Shaw as the inevitable cloud of smoke rolled forward from his desk like an industrial fog. "Did you come up here today to tell me something or ask me something?"

"Both," said Townsend.

"Clarify it for me. What might each be?"

"I came up to tell you where this case stands and to tell you that a retraction of sorts is likely."

Shaw waited. "And?" he finally growled.

"Well," Townsend said cautiously, "we both agree that if something is going on, this is a news story. A news story on which the *Sun* has an inside track due to the events we've already discussed. Correct?"

"I suppose." Shaw had made a career of being cautious.

"I want it," Townsend said.

"You want what?"

"I want this story as an ongoing investigation."

Shaw's brows furrowed into a dark, ominous frown. It was both uncompromising and unpromising. That, apparently, was his entire initial response for he uttered no sound. He only stared and drew on his pipe.

"Look," said Townsend. "I'm prepared to run a signed column on the death page under the heading, *I goofed, but* . . . I'm going to tell what happened. But I'm also going to bring our readers into a mystery. Then I'll continue to follow up the story."

"On your own time?"

"In addition to my current duties on the *Sun.*"

Shaw removed the pipe from his mouth, cupping it in his palm. "Paul, you haven't done straight reporting for several years. You've never done it for this paper."

"It's less than two years. And so what?"

"So you got yourself in a mess of personal trouble last time you took it up. That's if I understand correctly."

"You do. And again, so what?"

"So how the devil do you know the same thing won't happen this time?"

"I don't."

"Then what do you want this for?"

"I don't care much for being duped. And seeing as how I write for your paper, you shouldn't like it much, either."

"I don't. Neither does Max. Image is everything, you know."

"There's a matter of circulation, too, Ken," Townsend said soothingly. "This is a scoop, after all. Here's a case that the whole city could be talking about, given a few more leads. And it's our story. It's a *Sun* exclusive."

More smoke. More furrowed, turbulent brows. Then, "What do you want from me, you troublemaker?" Shaw asked.

"You're the managing editor. You make assignments."

"Ah," Shaw said skeptically, drawing gently on the briar. "I don't know . . ."

"Come on, Ken. Have some balls for once."

"What about the retraction, so to speak?" Shaw asked, choosing to distance his hearing from Townsend's insult. "When will it be included? When will we make Mr. Kohlheimer happy?"

"Monday. Tomorrow's edition."

"Then I suppose you can do your follow-up. If you're so damned hell-bent to do so."

Townsend stood. "Thanks," he said.

"Paul?" Shaw asked, as Townsend got to his feet.

"What's that?"

"Don't make a fool out of yourself. Or the paper. All right? I know Max Kohlheimer better than you do. He'll see you crucified if this gets fucked up any further."

Townsend nodded. "All right," he agreed.

Townsend took the elevator down to the fourth floor, still hyped from the events in K.N. Shaw's sanctum. When he passed the open door of Harry's office, Caryn DiCarlo—complete with midthigh skirt and a problem with a feature article on a female tennis player—was with Harry. Townsend knew better than to interrupt. The Yankees were in last place, having now lost seventeen in a row—a franchise record—and a visit with Caryn DiCarlo would sooth Harry's spirits.

When Townsend walked into his own office, he found three telephone messages on his desk. All were in Harry Dubrow's Midwood High School handwriting. Two pertained to obituaries in that day's edition. His eyes froze upon the third. But when Townsend looked up from his desk, Harry was already at his door.

"You just missed her on the phone," Harry said. "Ten minutes ago. Your mystery dame."

"You talked to her? Sarah?"

"If a rushed conversation that took a quarter of a minute can be viewed as 'talking,' yes. I talked to her."

"Where did she call from?" Townsend asked.

"Paul, everything I know is on that message. She wants to meet you tonight and there's some great secrecy involved. Urgency, too, judging by her voice."

"What the hell does this say, Harry?" he asked. He saw a pair of initials—*S* and *F*—and an address he didn't recognize in Brooklyn. Then something marked "Unit 012" and the time: one A.M.

"She says she needs to meet you," Harry said. "It's urgent. Said she won't even be able to call back." Townsend looked at the initials and the address again. He thought of the three times that morning that he had answered his phone, only to find no caller on the line.

"I don't suppose she left a number?" Townsend asked.

"Hey, I tried for one. But—"

"Yeah. I know."

"S and F is a warehouse," Harry said. "One that's been converted into self-storage units."

Townsend's eyes rose to meet Harry's. Harry continued talking. "She said the front door of S & F will be unlocked at ten minutes before your meeting time. Go to the basement storage area. She will meet you at unit oh-one-two. She said everything that has happened so far will make sense."

Townsend's mind raced, searching for further meaning or a sense of what this was. Several scenarios passed through his mind—most of them not good—at speeds which had no measurement in terms of time.

"Uh huh," Townsend said skeptically. "That or I get my head blown off, right?"

"Well, don't get pissed at me, damn it! That's all she said."

"You know Brooklyn, Harry," said Townsend, still trying to get a grip on the message. "What kind of neighborhood is this?"

The sports editor rolled his eyes. "Pretty grim."

"Did it sound like her real voice?" Townsend asked.

"Paulie, I should know? I've taken three phone messages in my life from her for you. A lot of women call you. I don't separate the ones who are buying a coffin from the ones who want to mail you their panties."

Townsend looked at the address again. And the time. More uncertain scenarios danced before him. Harry read his thoughts.

"Listen, Paul," Harry said. "Let me go with you."

"No way, Harry."

"Come on, Paul," said Harry. "Look, it's better for you if someone's there to back you up."

"Harry, look . . ."

"*You* look," Harry said, growing angry. "Let me back you up on a good story, would you? I spend all my time writing about overpaid, ungrateful assholes stuffing balls through hoops or trying to throw a ball past someone else. Let me be part of some hard news. Once before I retire, okay?"

Townsend blew out a long, dispirited breath. "Harry, I promise to include you at the right time. But this isn't it."

"Why not?"

"I just can't let you, Harry. Not this time."

"*Why?*"

Townsend assembled his excuses. "It could be dangerous."

"The drive home on the BQE is dangerous. The corned beef from the West Harlem Delicatessen is dangerous. So is the gas range in the kitchen in my home. Give me another reason."

"I mean *really* dangerous. I don't know what I'm dealing with here, Harry. Who the hell knows who's going to be at this location?"

"It's supposed to be this woman. Your Sarah."

"But who knows?"

"Well, if we both go, then we both know."

Townsend was resolute. "I can't let you do it, Harry."

"Why? If she *doesn't* show, at least you'll have someone to talk to."

"It's not a good idea," Townsend said, weakening.

"Then let me watch your car for you on the street. You want to come back in ten minutes and find it up on cinder blocks with all four tires gone?"

Townsend wavered. "No, Harry. I can't do it."

"Why the fuck not?"

"If for no other reason than the presence of someone unexpected— you, in other words—could clam up whomever I'm meeting. These things are delicate. And second, as I said, I don't want to be responsible for your safety."

"Oh. So I'm an old fart and can't protect myself, huh? Is that it?"

"Harry . . . Come on."

"You come on! I'm responsible for myself," Harry answered indignantly.

For a moment, Townsend wavered again. "The answer remains, no," he finally said.

"Prick," concluded Harry. "That's what people warned me about with you. Out to grab all the glory for yourself, huh?"

For once, Townsend didn't know if his friend was kidding or legitimately angry.

"That's not it, Harry. And you know it."

But Harry wasn't listening. Caryn DiCarlo appreared at the door, holding in her hand a printout of a sports feature and a miniature tape recorder. She was on her way to an interview.

"Harry, can I talk to you?" she asked. It was an inappropriate time for Townsend to notice, but unlike her brother Lou, who had a voice like a klaxon, Caryn had a purr. It was something like velvet.

"The trouble with you, Paul," Harry said, gathering some pent-up momentum, "is you're a selfish ingrate. I don't like to bring up favors. But I did you a big one to get you on this paper. Now I'm asking you for one in return—the one I *want*—and you don't know me."

"Yeah, but Harry, try to underst—"

By now, Harry was furious. "We had a promise, you and I," he said. "You said you would let me do an investigative piece with you. We had a promise and you just broke it. Remember that."

Then Harry was out the door. Townsend was too astonished to answer. Caryn DiCarlo gave Townsend a dry smile of sympathy, then disappeared with Harry.

Later in the day, Townsend discovered how steamed Harry really was. Harry never spoke to him all afternoon and left without saying anything further.

Then, just before leaving for the day, Townsend called K.N. Shaw. Citing the impending rendezvous in Brooklyn, Townsend asked Shaw for another day's hedge before running a retraction of the Wolik obituary.

Shaw responded with a long, agonized silence. Townsend could have sworn that he smelled the tobacco smoke in the telephone. Townsend held the silence, too. Then, very grudgingly, Shaw gave his consent.

"I was wondering why I hadn't seen it in the layout," the managing editor grumbled portentiously.

"That's why," Townsend answered.

"See that it's in tomorrow," Shaw said. "Max the Knife won't wait forever, much less another twenty-four hours."

Townsend was about to agree, but Shaw hung up too soon. For a moment, Townsend sat again in silence. Like old times, indeed: his friends angry at him, his bosses skeptical, his love life shattered, a mystery meeting past midnight in an outer borough, and—thinking back to the bomb in his car—possibly at least one person in the city trying to kill him.

The last thing Tina Hubbell needed was another visitor. Yet that's what she was on guard against. As the sun set across the Gulf of Mexico, as another beautiful Florida day died, she walked by herself along the tidal line, the waves from the water occasionally lapping at her bare feet. And as she walked, she studied faces.

She watched people when they drew near her and she watched them when they were approaching from far away. This stretch of Fort Myers's beach was quiet. But there was a smattering of other people. Evening bathers. Other mothers with children. Couples in their late teens or early twenties. Everyone else seemed to have not a care in the world. Yet Tina felt like she had the weight of the century upon her shoulders.

She watched her children, Mindy and Laurie, dart ahead of her and play games with the tide as it rolled in and out. Well, she concluded, at least no one looked like a threat. Not tonight at least.

Tina's life had become a lonely type of existence over the last weeks. Lonely because she had been forced to turn inward. There was no one she could tell about her terrible secret. No one she could tell, and yet this was the one thing in the world that others might wish to know. It was the one thing, in all her years on this planet, that she had been witness to that could actually change lives—even rough up accepted history a little bit—and she couldn't even whisper to anyone about it.

Damn, she thought. She knew how important it had to be. Otherwise, how could it have stayed alive for so long?

She sighed. Wouldn't it be nice if in every woman's life one fantasy could come true? She would have liked to have been twenty years old all over again, ready to live her life over.

A second chance at life! That was it! All she wanted was a second chance. Was that such a sinful thing to ask for?

Well, she told herself angrily, she would never choose the same path twice. *Never!* She would never have become involved with the police. She would never have taken Allan as a lover and she would—

As her reverie continued, thoughts rushed at her. Her current husband? Would she marry him again? Maybe. Probably. Jim was fine. He was a good man. A solid man. But, she realized, he was also part of her problem. She could never confide in him about certain things that had happened before they met. Thus, she could never tell him what troubled her so deeply. He would never understand. He just wouldn't. So he could never be permitted to know.

She walked by herself, her arms folded across her chest. Ahead, her two daughters played in the shallow surf. An upstart wave hit Mindy across the legs and the four-year-old began to laugh. Laurie only smiled and glanced tentatively back toward her mother. Tina worried about Laurie. Over the last few days it almost seemed like her older daughter sensed something—or *knew* something—of the danger that lurked. But how could she? How could she *possibly?*

Tina walked with her car keys in her right hand and scanned every face ahead of her. Occasionally, Mrs. Hubbell—ordinary Florida housewife to all who knew her—would look defensively over her shoulder.

Tina kept her car keys ready. Even the Chevy Corsica was a problem of logistics now. Tina's revolver was under the front seat, right where she could grab it in a hurry. It was loaded. It was ready. So was she. And, by God, she knew that she wouldn't hesitate to use that weapon if it meant defending herself.

But, of course, the presense of the weapon had also turned the vehicle into a time bomb. She couldn't let her daughters anywhere near the car without her while the pistol was in it. Never. Life was so complicated.

The only thing uncomplicated, it seemed to her, were her walks by the shore. Once in the evening with her girls. Once in the morning by herself.

Each day, the walks allowed her to unwind. They sure beat this brutal new insomnia that plagued her nightly, and they were a lot nicer than the way she now conjured up new routes to drive to familiar places—always to disguise her daily path. And the walks along the shore sure beat the tension of hanging around the house all day, wondering when and if a volley of bullets was going to come through the window.

The walks were brackets within which Tina Hubbell structured her day. Even though Allan had ruined one of them, they were two points of relaxation around which she could live and breathe. And in that manner, even though she didn't completely recognize the fact, they had become the only predictable part of her daily routine.

That evening before going to Brooklyn, Townsend telephoned his ex-wife and daughter in California. He wanted to say hello just in case this turned into his final chance.

Nora was in a strange mood. She dwelt on their imminent divorce with a newly found ambivalence. Emily, his daughter, was in a strange mood as well. She dwelt on how little she saw him and extorted from him a promise to come visit as soon as possible.

He took his pistol from the safe in his apartment before he left. And as he drove, he chided himself again for making a promise that he had no idea how he was going to keep.

<<<< *18* >>>>

S & F Self-Storage was a converted warehouse in Bensonhurst in a desolate stretch of the city, a block glowing with mercury lights, chain-linked fencing topped with concertina barbed wire, and sidewalks strewn with broken bottles. It was the type of place that Townsend had seen too many times as an investigative reporter. He arrived in the area at midnight, amid a steady humid drizzle. From the mercury lights and from the rain, the whole neighborhood was a bluish gleam. He had the impression of visiting a war zone.

In his rented car, he slowly circled the renovated warehouse. S & F appeared to have only one entrance. Townsend parked a block beyond it, then cut his auto lights and his engine. He had carefully chosen a location in which he could see in every direction for at least fifty feet. He knew how quickly the creatures of an urban night could pounce. He kept the key in the car's ignition. Then he slumped low in his seat. He adjusted his rearview mirror so that he could see behind him. He held his eyes open and sharp.

Something was making his heart pound. By now there was no mistake. All the old instincts and fears were back upon him. He felt himself sweat and he wondered anew what he'd touched upon to bring a pair of Feds to his office.

Grodine and Flynn. Typical of a pair of Feds, he told himself. They wanted answers but wouldn't give any. He wondered when a federal court order might arrive to coerce him to talk. He further wondered if he would obey it.

He grinned. He already knew. He would obey no such thing. What the hell were a reporter's rights all about? What did confidentiality of sources mean? What was the Bill of Rights there for?

So put me in jail, damn it, he thought grandly. He wouldn't be the first reporter to see *durance vile. Damned federal dickheads,* he thought further.

In his rearview mirror, he watched the entrance to S & F. The radio played softly in his car, and the atmosphere made him think of the night he had driven to Westchester County to visit the dying man.

Wolik. Sarah's father. Or whoever he was.

Townsend nudged the radio a little louder and began to scan the dial. There was no traffic, no movement anywhere on the street. No sound other than his radio. If it had been pitch black, the night couldn't have been more imposing. He was glad he had brought his gun. But he wished that he wasn't here.

From the radio, he found a country station. Willie Nelson's plaintive voice soothed him only slightly. Willie sang of faraway Texas, southwestern drifters, Lone Star belt buckles, and long, desolate highways. To Townsend, Nelson's voice made an appropriate counterpoint. No Robert White tonight. No John McCormick. And both baseball clubs were finished for the evening.

Townsend watched and he waited. As the time slowly passed, it became his notion that if Sarah were to show up at all, she was already within the warehouse. Yet, it further occurred to him that this was not the type of location that a woman would choose under any circumstances. He hardly expected to see her. So who had really called? Who was he meeting?

Nervously, for the tenth time, Townsend checked his own weapon. It was loaded and ready, just the way it had been the previous nine.

Then, as he checked, the rain came down more steadily. It drummed on the roof of his car. The sound might have been soothing, but the showers made it more difficult to see or hear, making his anxiety all the worse. Time dragged. Townsend was conscious of his shirt being already soaked with sweat.

At a quarter hour before one A.M., another car eased its way through the rain and down the block. It came to a stop under a street lamp across from S & F's entrance. But in the glare and in the rain, Townsend couldn't manage a good look at it. Then the car pulled back half a block and parked behind a stripped vehicle. Townsend turned his radio off and watched. He sat low in his seat so that his head couldn't be seen.

For a moment a tiny wave of relaxation overtook him. Surely the man in that car was not adept at this sort of thing. He was right there in the open. Surely he had to know he would be spotted. There was nothing subtle about his movements, nothing that couldn't be picked up completely by a professional.

The man Townsend watched sat in his driver's seat for less than five minutes, then stepped from his car. Townsend squinted as he couldn't see that well. The man had wrapped himself in some sort of long coat and wore a hat upon his eyes. Then he moved quickly to the warehouse, tried the door, and was quickly inside. Townsend saw a light go on, then go off. Townsend almost had to laugh. The man was an amateur of the first rank.

Townsend looked at his watch. Ten minutes to go. The music was gone now and he was aware of his heart. He drew a deep breath. Decison: should he go in a few minutes early, or wait to the appointed time?

He had waited this long, Townsend reasoned. He would wait the final few minutes.

He gnawed on the nail of his left index finger. Then it was time. He checked his weapon again and made sure he could grasp it quickly. He reached for the handle of his car door.

Then he froze again. Two men whom he couldn't see well were leaving the warehouse. Townsend studied them. Their actions were not calm but slow and methodical. But they seemed to be *locking* the warehouse, not opening it. One man was about six feet, Townsend guessed.

The other was shorter and stockier. But Townsend's vision was obstructed by rain and shadows. He couldn't even tell if they were black or white.

Then, once they had left S & F's front entrance the way they wanted it, the two men turned quickly in a direction away from Townsend. They moved hurriedly down the block and around a corner.

Perplexed, Townsend stared at the wet summer darkness into which the two apparitions had disappeared. What was this? The changing of the guard? A link in a contact?

Or was he making more out of this than reason demanded?

He backed his car through the intersection. He left it poised on the end of S & F's block. He left the doors open and checked a backup key that he had sewn against the inseam of the seat. He slid a small flashlight into his pocket and checked his weapon a twelfth time. Then he stepped from the car. For a moment he froze, remaining perfectly still, listening to the ominous silence of the city.

Despite the rain, it was now a hot, sticky night. Other than the rain, there was no movement anywhere. Townsend drew a deep breath. It was time to go in.

He turned and walked to the warehouse door. There he stopped. He stood for a moment and glanced down the block. His heart fluttered. He could finally discern the configuration of the car that had parked behind the stripped chassis.

Sure enough, he recognized it. Suddenly—horribly!—what he had witnessed made sense.

"Oh, Jesus! No!" he said aloud.

His hand went to his pistol and his heart kicked in his chest. He turned, went to S & F's entrance, and yanked at the door. It was locked.

"Fuck!" he bellowed. He yanked it again. When it didn't give way, he stepped back, furious. He stood to the side and pointed his pistol at the lock. He fired. The metal on the door exploded as sharp fragments flew in all directions. Townsend bolted to the door and pulled at it again. With a tremendous effort, it opened.

An alarm blazed in his ears. He stood in an entrance area. There was a door which led past a security window. When he tried it, it opened. He moved through it, nose of his pistol first. He found himself in a passageway that led to stairs.

Up for units 200—400, said a sign. Down for 01—199. He went down a dark set of concrete stairs. The air was mildewed and dank. Still the alarm rang. No matter. If the police were in the area, he could use them. More than likely, however, this was an area abandoned by the police many years earlier. He reached a door which led to the basement.

A low-wattage bulb cast a faint light within the stairwell. Townsend descended to the lower level, keeping his weapon aloft and ready to fire.

Townsend knew this was a disaster. He could only pray that the worst hadn't already transpired.

He pushed open the door to the basement. Darkness. He stepped into it. This time he would be shot, he reasoned, when he put on the light switch. He stayed away from it. He reached to his pocket for the flashlight and felt his way along the edge of the wall. His hand eventually settled upon a light switch.

Nothing. No sound other than his own heartbeat. He turned the light switch on and the entire corridor went brilliantly bright. Townsend bolted across the corridor and stood flush against a wall of gray aluminum storage lockers. He turned his head in each direction. He saw no one. He heard nothing.

He glanced at a sign above him, which directed him to his left for unit 012. Townsend, gun still ready, moved to his right. If this unit was like any other, he reasoned, there was an entrance and exit at the end of each row. He would take the less likely route, better to surprise anyone who might be lingering in wait. As he moved he also scanned the lockers. He searched for any that were not sealed. It was out of just such a hiding place that a gunman might step.

He moved with a cautiousness that was painful. Sweat cascaded off his brow into his eyes. His hands were soaked, particularly the palm against the handle of his gun. Outdoors and upstairs, he had been swift and eager. But now, in this clammy cavern, all too cognizant of what he might expect, he was cautious and apprehensive.

He moved to one corner. He safely rounded it, assured himself he was still alone, and proceeded to the next.

There was still no living being anywhere near him. The lockers were divided one on top of the other. Townsend continued to scan for an unlocked unit.

He turned the corner to the final row of lockers. The corridor was unlit. He stopped in midstep, heard nothing, and reached to another light switch. He turned it on.

He waited. By now his heart was sinking and he knew he was alone. Alone with his thoughts and alone with the tragedy about to befall him.

"Oh, God," he said, almost crying, as he looked ahead.

Several feet before him he saw—as by now he knew he would—a splattering of blood against a wall, as well as a deep dent in a locker that Townsend recognized as a bullet hole. But it was not a clean hole—it was a jagged one, as if made by a bullet fired at close range but partially spent.

He knew the rest. He dashed to the area. There was blood on the floor. Some of it was spattered, much of it was a long streak, as if something—like a bleeding body—had been dragged. It had been dragged into locker number 012 and the door had been pushed shut. Not locked, just shut.

"Oh, God. Oh, Jesus," Townsend muttered to himself. It was half curse, half supplication. He tucked his pistol into his belt.

He reached to the locker door, as a man might when opening a tomb in a nightmare. But this was real. He braced himself and gingerly opened unit 012.

The lifeless body of Harry Dubrow slumped slightly toward him. Harry, unable to stay away from a story that enticed him, had been shot in the head. It had all been tragically apparent as soon as Townsend had recognized the overeager Harry's car out front.

Harry's words of that same afternoon rung back with a hollow echo. *Listen, Paul. Let me go with you.*

"Oh, Harry, no!" Townsend blurted aloud. He reached into the unit and embraced Harry's body. He struggled to pull him out. Harry's clothes were soaked with blood, particularly in back. The blood flowed freely onto Townsend's arms.

Let me back you up on a good story.

"Why couldn't you stay away?" Townsend struggled with his composure.

Out to grab all the glory for yourself, huh?

"Oh, God, Harry. Why couldn't you have understood?" Townsend said, fighting back tears, holding his friend in a long, shuddering clasp. "No, no, no. This wasn't the story. This wasn't for you."

Even the three phantom telephone calls of that morning, the times Townsend had lifted the phone to find no caller, now made sense. Someone other than Sarah wanted to leave a message. Townsend would have recognized her voice. Harry didn't. It was a another setup, pure and simple. What the opposition hadn't figured was that Harry would appear in Townsend's place. Appear and get a fatal look at them.

Harry Dubrow had been executed cleanly. Whoever had done this— the two men leaving, Townsend assumed—had ambushed him, one in the front, the other in the back. Harry had been hit with two shots to the back of the skull. In his last moments of life, he may have understood what was about to happen, that he had walked into a trap meant for Paul Townsend. But surely he hadn't understood why.

Townsend's tears began to flow. He sobbed with anger, fury, and helplessness. For all the villains Townsend had ever challenged, for all the criminals he had battled, for all the principles he had defended, when it came right down to it, he hadn't even been able to keep his best friend from getting killed.

Poor Harry. Poor Everyone.

Townsend cursed Sarah Stuart and the vile old man posing as Leonard Wolik. He cursed the *Sun.* He cursed his fate. But he saved the most vehement, violent, and profane curses for himself.

Then he stood. He propped his fallen friend against a clean wall. For a moment Townsend closed his eyes against the pain. Deep within him he nourished a wish that someone would leap from a locker and shoot him, too. Townsend was convinced that he wouldn't even draw his pistol to defend himself.

But there was no such neat ending, no such nicety or convenience. So Townsend trudged back upstairs and looked for a telephone. The alarm was still ringing shrilly and he barely heard it.

He went to the front entrance area and found a pay telephone. He lifted the receiver. He was just coming to grips with the fact that the telephone was out of order when he saw movement near the front door he had smashed.

"Police! Don't move!" a voice barked.

Townsend froze, his arms raised, his hands visible. Someone shone a heavy floodlight upon him. As was the custom since the Revised NYPD Firearms Procedures of 1995, the police came into such situations with flak jackets and heavy weapons—a response to the relentless firepower that had been thrown at the police in the late 1980s and early nineties. Tonight this took the form of shotguns drawn and pointed at anything that moved. Townsend was the only thing that moved.

"I'm a reporter for the *New York Sun,*" Townsend said. "You've got a homicide downstairs."

The police were both methodical and rough. They kept two heavy firearms trained upon him, one a foot from the back of his head. They shoved him headfirst against the wall. They frisked him and stripped him of his weapon. They pulled his pockets inside out, retrieving his wallet and his identification, including his pistol permit. And for good measure, they handcuffed him with his wrists behind his back.

Only then was Townsend allowed to begin his explanation of who he was, what he was doing there, and—most significant of all—what had happened.

The murder of Harry Dubrow fell under the jurisdiction of the Second Detective Division, Brooklyn. Two NYPD detectives arrived at half past one A.M. Their names were Newman and Cheney. To

Townsend, they seemed to have the opinion that in their borough there wasn't much unusual about finding a freshly murdered man in a self-storage unit. And, why not? The previous night, Townsend eventually learned, Cheney and Newman had found the mutilated corpses of three Bolivian children at the bottom of an elevator shaft in Bay Ridge.

After talking to Townsend for several minutes, Cheney ordered Townsend's handcuffs removed. A few minutes later an ambulance pulled before the warehouse. A doctor arrived toward two A.M. and Harry Dubrow was officially pronounced dead.

"Do you know who his family was?" Cheney asked.

"I know he's widowed. He had no children," Townsend said. "Next of kin of some sort would be listed at the *New York Sun*." Townsend said he would notify the proper people. It was at that time that Newman connected Harry's name with the newspaper.

"There's a guy there who writes a sports column," Newman said, as if in revelation. "You're not telling me that—?"

"No more columns," Townsend said.

A few minutes later, medical technicians packed Harry's body onto a stretcher. Harry was on his way to the morgue at Kings County Hospital.

Detective Cheney examined Townsend's weapon. Thirty-eight calibre. Harry had been murdered at close range with a twenty-two.

"What do you carry this thing for?" Cheney asked him.

"Personal protection."

"Yeah," Cheney said. "Don't we all!" He found Townsend's permit to be in order, confirmed over the police radio that it was legitimate, and returned the weapon to Townsend. He took a further statement from Townsend as to what Townsend had seen and heard leading up to the slaying. When Townsend began to describe the complicated events leading up to the meeting in the warehouse, Cheney stopped him. Instead, he asked him to come by Brooklyn homicide the next afternoon to make a complete statement.

"Yeah. I can do that," Townsend said.

"All right," Cheney said. "You can go."

Townsend left S & F Self-Storage like a man in a trance. The rain had relented to an intermittent drizzle, but Townsend was hardly aware of it. Equally, he was fatigued to death, but knew he would never be able to sleep.

He got into his car as other teams of detectives and forensics units arrived. They would put the crime scene on videotape, dust for fingerprints, retrieve expired bullets, and so on. Townsend felt the exercise was probably futile—the same as the investigation of whomever blew up his car.

The ambulance to Kings County Hospital pulled out at the same time as Townsend. He followed it for part of its journey, creating his own mini-cortege and starting Harry off on his final journey.

Townsend had no idea what to do. He felt lost. Stunned. Shocked. Completely adrift. He felt as if a rug had been yanked from beneath his feet, but he was still suspended in air.

An urge was upon him. He would embark upon a world-class drinking binge, an experience in self-destruction even greater than his last. He thought of the Old Dublin on West 86th Street in Manhattan—where his last great binge had begun—and realized that the bar would still be busy. The Old Dublin stayed open to seven A.M., then—in theory at least—closed for an hour and reopened at eight. No emporium of serious boozing would want to miss the early-morning barflies. He knew that the beer and vodka would be ice cold and plentiful.

But Townsend temporarily nixed the idea.

Instead, he followed the ambulance for ten minutes along the Brooklyn-Queens Expressway, dozens of conflicting urges before him and the desire for a drinking binge looming all the larger. But solace in liquor would have to wait, he finally decided. For now there was only one place to go, considering the circumstances. There was really only one request that poor old Harry would have.

Townsend drove to the *Sun*. He parked his car in the subterranean lot beneath the *Sun* Building and took the elevator to the deserted fourth floor. He slowly walked the corridor to his office. He paused for only a moment by Harry's door, then continued to his own desk.

He sat down at his typewriter. He would be damned if he would see any of what he knew appear first in the dull gray "newspaper of record" or the upstart middle-brow Long Island tabloid.

"Fuck them both," Townsend snarled aloud. "Fuck *New York Times* and fuck *New York Newsday*. Fuck Ken Shaw and Max Kohlheimer. And fuck whoever killed Harry."

Townsend was now propelled by adrenaline and blind anger—and he was self-conscious enough to know that those two qualities were what had once made him the best news reporter in the city. He punched out a painful two-column headline for the lead obituary of the *Sun*'s next edition.

HARRY DUBROW, 59; FRIEND,
AND SPORTS EDITOR OF
THE *NEW YORK SUN*.

He pulled the paper from his typewriter and tacked it to his wall. Then he punched out a headline for the first news page.

MURDER OF *SUN* SPORTS
EDITOR TIED TO ERSATZ
OBITUARY OF JUNE 12.

He pulled that heading from the typewriter and hung it next to the obituary. Working in the solitude of his floor, he stared at the two of them for several minutes. Then he returned to the obituary. He spent an hour getting it almost exactly the way he wanted it. Then he spent another half hour revising it.

The account of Harry's murder was easier, at least on its surface. It was straight true crime reportage. Townsend could do it almost by rote.

He finished his copy and polished it. Then he polished it some more. But he wasn't finished. Townsend was breathing fire now.

Any writer on the *Sun* could submit a piece of opinion related to any newsworthy topic. Townsend had never submitted one. Such pieces had to waltz past Ken Shaw. Their eventual appearance in print largely depended upon the vagueries of Shaw's moods.

But Paul Townsend had something to say. So he said it angrily straight onto a clean sheet of paper.

He titled it,

A DEATH IN OUR FAMILY

And then he wrote,

Harry Dubrow, who was murdered early Wednesday morning, was more than a beloved friend to everyone who knew him. He was also one of the best sportswriters to ever pound a typewriter or cover a game or profile an athlete in our decaying city.

Yet when his life came to an end in a Brooklyn storage warehouse in an as yet unsolved homicide, Harry was still aspiring to do what he considered grander things—as if his own craft and brilliance were not rare enough.

Harry wanted to be part of what we in journalism still stubbornly and egotistically call a "hard news" story. But rather than merely uncover or report such a story, Harry has now become a central part of one. Yet—in an irony he would have appreciated—in slaying a kindly widower nearing retirement, his assailants have signaled the beginning of their own rapid demise.

Journalists are here to report news and inform the public. Naturally, we are human. We make mistakes. We sometimes offend or infuriate those whom we attempt to serve. That is part of the journalistic process.

But we are, after all, not here to become targets any more than any other citizen. Any homicide is intolerable. No human life weighs more than another. But in the murder of Harry Dubrow, the citizenry of this city has been attacked, from those who report the news to those who spend fifty cents to purchase a newspaper.

Thus, it is a given that the resources of the *New York Sun* will be fully dedicated to exposing the killers who took our colleague's life. Similarly, the pages of this newspaper—and hopefully other newspapers around the city, state, and nation—will in time be alive with the full sequence of events which resulted in our colleague's death. This is a trail which will be exposed no matter how far it leads or how far into the past it travels.

The *New York Sun* is pledged from this day forward to provide a solution to this horrendous case.

Townsend left Harry's obituary on his own blotter. He dropped off the crime report with a stunned night editor at the city desk. Then he walked to K.N. Shaw's office on the sixth floor. He left his "opinion piece," as Shaw would patronizingly call it, on the managing editor's desk. He knew the odds were perhaps fifty-fifty that it would even see the light of day. Shaw had a condescending way of pronouncing such pieces "intemperate" or "overly emotional." He would then spike them. But who knew? Shaw was unpredictable. So Townsend left the text on Shaw's desk nonetheless.

Then he returned to his car. He would go home. He would sleep for two hours then return to work. It was only on his way home, when he heard the baseball scores of the previous evening and learned that the Yankees—Harry's team—had finally broken their long losing streak, that he lost composure completely.

Thereupon, he pulled to the side of the West Side Expressway. Then, for several long, painful minutes, he cried a second time for his friend of many years who had been murdered in his place.

<< << *19* >> >>

*I*T occurred to Paul Townsend that he was seeing too many funerals from too close a perspective. Nonetheless, he noted a brilliantly taste-less touch to Harry's memorial service—one that would have had Harry slapping his thighs in laughter had he not been deceased.

The lid was closed to the coffin in which Harry lay. But along the lower rim of the coffin, the manufacturer had bolted a plaque: 100 percent copper. Had Harry been able to move his cold, lifeless hands, he would have ripped the plaque right off. Townsend flirted with remov-ing it for him, then rejected the idea.

Harry. He would have been the best-dressed person in attendance. Everywhere there were bad suits and toupees on Harry's male peers from the old neighborhood. There were bleached hair, size eighteen dresses, and too much red lipstick on the women. There was the scent of cologne or elevator perfume, combined with the stench of cigarette smoke from the outside hallway, often accompanied by a cardiac cough.

Why were these events, Townsend wondered, so often like this? Deaths were so final and simple. It was lives, he had long since realized, that were complicated, multidimensional, and vibrant.

Harry's brother Bernard was there, looking stunned and leaning against a post. He had a kindly, tired face and kept repeating that he had just talked to Harry the other day. People still told him he bore a resemblance to the late Adolph Menjou. And distantly, he did. Bernard was long divorced from a wife named Barbara whom everyone still asked about. Another brother named Seymour lived in Florida. Or so everyone had thought. Cy had been in "import-export," whatever that meant, but no one had been able to contact him for years. An older sister named Gertrude had predeceased Harry, but another sister named Pearl was providing food at her house in Forest Hills after the burial. There was an array of nieces and nephews, mostly in their teens and twenties.

There was a contingent from the *Sun* as well, a population distinct from the family and friends. The people who had known Harry via the press box and the sports desk over the years drifted in and out: writers, editors, copy boys, mail room people. An occasional retired athlete showed up as well, creating a stir and an occasional awkward request for an autograph. Whenever Harry had voyaged, he had left friends in his wake, and this was never more evident than the day after he died. Townsend wished he had twenty dollars for every time he heard someone follow Harry's name that afternoon with, "May he rest in peace."

Plenty of old faces from the *New York Daily News* showed up, too. At various times, Townsend stood in an anteroom and exchanged gossip. Typical of Harry, too, Townsend noted. Bringing old friends together even in death. Harry would have laughed, too, at seeing his Irish and Italian friends wearing yarmulkes at his service. *So! I've finally made some converts,* Harry would have teased. But everywhere, instead of laughter, there were the recurrent questions.

Why? And *Who would have done this to Harry?* For most of the afternoon, faced with such questions, Townsend kept his own counsel.

Caryn DiCarlo showed up midway through the viewing, dressed appropriately in black and a knee-length skirt. She sat quietly in a corner, her hands in her lap. Townsend nodded to her and acknowledged her presence. She nodded back. They didn't speak directly, but Townsend felt her gaze upon his back several times.

K.N. Shaw showed up, too, making a half-hour appearance. He shook hands, made the properly solemn pronouncements, and placed his hand on several shoulders. Two or three times, he took *Sun* employees aside to talk a few minutes of shop with them. Caryn DiCarlo was among them. As Townsend watched the two of them, she seemed surprised by the tenor of the discussion.

Marginally, Shaw's stock had risen with Townsend over the last twenty-four hours. The managing editor had astonished everyone— perhaps even himself—by breaking Townsend's tortured editorial on page one. Townsend's heading, A DEATH IN OUR FAMILY, had been the front-page bold-type shocker that had screamed out to the entire city.

"It was the least I could do for Harry," Shaw explained to Townsend in a sanctimonious purr. Shaw shook his head. "The poor old man."

"He was only eight years older than you are, Ken," Townsend reminded him.

Shaw had this way of asking questions and then ignoring the full thrust of the answers. "I don't think poor Harry had ever been on a front page in his life," he intoned sadly.

"Harry broke front-page sports stories at least a half-dozen times on the *Daily News*," Townsend answered.

"Is that right? Well, I was in Miami then," Shaw explained, almost by way of suggesting that nothing really happened if K.N. Shaw hadn't been in New York to witness it. "And it's the least I could do, anyway," he concluded.

It *was* the least. It was also the most. Because the *Sun* had hawked the story to the city, complete with something that purported to be an Extra edition, the rest of the print and broadcast media had picked up on it. Yet Townsend still felt that he held the crucial cards. He alone was acquainted with all the hidden dynamics that underlay the slaying, the facts and the background that he had carefully withheld from print. Part of the trail, he reasoned, only he could pick up.

"We have some things to discuss, you and I," Ken Shaw said to Townsend before departure. "I suppose this isn't the time or the place. You were so close to Harry. Come up to the sixth floor as soon as you can, Jack." His eyes darted quickly in both directions to guard against eavesdroppers. "What are you doing tomorrow?"

"Sleeping off a drunken spree, I'd guess."

Shaw again chose to hear only selectively. "You're still following this case, aren't you?" Shaw asked next.

"What the hell do you think, Ken? You must have read what I wrote. You fucking printed it."

"Good." Shaw nodded conspiratorially. "That's good." He grasped Townsend on the arm for a second, as if to indicate support and approval. He removed the yarmulke he had been given when he entered.

"I never thought I'd see the two of us wearing skull caps," Shaw whispered. Why was it that Shaw always provided a reason to be disliked, even when he was doing the right thing? Townsend felt his temper near a flashpoint, despite the time and place.

"Ken?" Townsend demanded. "What do you have to say that you can't say to me right here right now?"

Shaw paused for a moment before deciding to talk.

"I'd like to make some changes at the *Sun*," he finally confided. "But I don't want a lot of backbiting. I want to do this with as much good will as possible."

"What's that supposed to mean?"

As Townsend pursued him, Shaw returned the headwear to an assistant funeral director. But he stopped just inside the front door.

"I want to take you off obituaries," Shaw said. "You're wasted there. It was a fine place for you to get your feet steady on the ground after your crack-up—I'm allowed to call a spade a spade, aren't I?—but I want you back doing investigative work. That's what you do best, damn it. Any fool can see that." He paused. "I'll ask you point-blank: Have you got the guts for it again full time?"

Townsend was shocked. "What sort of investigative work?" he asked.

Shaw turned and motioned to the room that held Harry's body. "The story you yourself asked for," Shaw said. "The story you've already begun on our front page."

"Since when do we even do investigative reports?" Townsend asked.

"Since this morning," Shaw said, "when we sold an extra four hundred fifty thousand newspapers." Shaw stared at him. "Oh, don't look so shocked," he snapped. "You mentioned circulation yourself in my office. Now stay with it, Jack. For our sake, Harry's, and your own."

Townsend remained incredulous. "I'll do it under one condition," Townsend said.

"What's that?"

"I want a few days off. Right now."

"What the hell for? You're sitting on top of a big story."

"I've got some personal business to attend to. If I'm going to immerse myself totally in a single assignment, I've got to have a few days first to get loose."

"Why?" Shaw huffed. "Family?" his eyebrows furrowing with accusation.

"Personal business. That's the only explanation I'm giving."

"Secretive fucker, aren't you, Jack?"

"Yeah. Guess I am."

"Someone will have to watch the case for you while you're gone. And you'll have to remain on call in case anything major falls out of God's blue sky."

"Fine, Ken, fine."

Shaw snorted again. "Oh, all right," he said finally, awarding his consent. "Might lend you a damned bit more objectivity if you do get out of here for a few days," he concluded. "You could use it sometimes, you know. Objectivity. In some circles—and I decline to name which—it is alleged that Paul Townsend doesn't even know what the word means."

"Since when is a Max Kohlheimer rag objective, Ken?"

Shaw raised his brows again in his best one-of-the-guys expressions. "Got me there, Jack." He shrugged. "Look, just come back from wherever you're going refreshed and ready to bite everyone on the ass. Your usual cheerful self, in other words."

Then K.N. Shaw disappeared outside. He climbed into a waiting black Ford sedan with a chauffeur. The driver would guide him in comfort back to his desk in Manhattan.

An hour or so after the memorial service, the cortege following Harry Dubrow's hearse arrived at Mount Zion Cemetery in Park Slope. The funeral director ushered everyone toward the gravesite. As he had been in departing the funeral home, Townsend was a pall bearer.

When the rabbi was finished, the flowers were set in place. The casket was lowered. After the first shovels of dirt had been tossed, the funeral director spoke again. He reminded everyone that food was to be served back at Pearl's house. Pearl had a voice like a clapper in a new bell. Fortunately, she was too overcome to talk and only cocked an eyebrow.

It was almost sunset. Townsend's gaze settled into the middle distance. There, another coffin followed by another congregation of mourners moved into place in an adjoining plot at the cemetery. As Harry's service concluded, another casket neared its final resting place and—if any of these rituals could be believed—another soul began its journey into the afterlife.

< < < < **20** > > > >

*I*T was evening when Townsend crossed into Manhattan over the Brooklyn Bridge. The bridge was condemned now as one of the most dangerous in the northeastern United States. That, in turn, resulted in only two lanes being open in each direction at any hour, which resulted in a traffic jam at any time, day or night. Tonight the delay was only fifteen minutes.

There were feelings within Townsend which fought with each other and thrust his tangled emotions in different directions. Harry's death had torn a hole in his life. He had again a sense of personal loss and catastrophe, a sense that no matter what he did now it would make no difference.

Harry had been his best friend in the world. And Townsend had been to some degree responsible for Harry's death. Why hadn't he just let Harry come with him?

Ridiculous, he told himself. Then they both would have been gunned down. What good would that have done?

Then a second feeling coiled around him. He had a sense of a pair of unseen eyes watching him. And why not? Why shouldn't someone be watching him? He remained the target, after all. Harry's death had done nothing to detract from that.

He scanned in his rearview mirror as he crossed the bridge. He tried to discern any pattern within the armada of headlights behind him. He found none. Still, this feeling grew upon him until it was unbanishable.

He drove uptown on the F.D.R. Drive, left it suddenly at Forty-second Street and drove west past Second Avenue. Yes, indeed. At least two other cars seemed to veer off after his. He accelerated and turned north onto Third Avenue. He lost the headlights that seemed to pursue him. Or at least he thought he did. He continued north cautiously, continuing to scan for any pursuer.

He figured he had lost his tail. Or maybe there had never been one. He drove to 86th Street and turned west. There were distant headlights behind him as he traversed Central Park.

But now another feeling was upon him, one that came from within. He recognized the urge and he knew where it would lead. But he did nothing to control it. Giving in would be as easy as falling off a log. It would begin with one cold beer, continue with a few more, and who in hell knew where it would end?

And, for that matter, who cared?

He found his way to the West Eighties, ignoring anyone's headlights now. He crossed Amsterdam Avenue. He parked his car on the north side of West 86th Street. He sat in the car and waited. His pistol was under the seat. He reached to it and put it beneath his jacket in his belt. No point to leave it in the car. Street thieves can smell booty like that. It would be gone by the time he returned.

He stepped out of his car. In the gutter at curbside, he easily found some discarded beer cans. He nudged them along with his foot, forming a geometric pattern along the underside of his car. No bastard was going to slide underneath and leave an explosive surprise wired to the undercarriage without dislodging the cans. Townsend memorized how he had the cans. If an intrusion occurred, he would detect it easily when he returned. With that done, he set out on foot.

Like the night when Harry had been murdered, this one was unseasonably warm and sticky. But when he entered the Old Dublin Bar, the air-conditioning was upon him like a set of fresh clothes. He made his way to the bar, sat down, and ordered a draft beer.

One world-class drunk coming up. One Olympic-caliber drinking spree. This one's for you, Harry, he thought to himself. One for the road. One to send off a dear old friend.

Harry would have been horrified.

The beer arrived. It felt good in his hands and on his lips. It felt even better going down. It was gone in less than a minute. He ordered another as he felt someone slide into the seat next to him. But he never looked to his side. It could have been Santa Claus and it could have been someone sent to execute him. It made no difference at the moment. His drink arrived.

"You're a rude son of a bitch," a woman's voice said after several seconds. "Aren't you even going to say hello, Paul?"

The voice was familiar. At first something flashed inside him because he thought it was Sarah Stuart. But then the flash subsided because he knew it wasn't.

He turned toward the woman. He looked Caryn DiCarlo squarely in the eyes.

"Much better," she said.

He looked back away from her. "I *knew* someone was following me," he said.

"Hell of a turn you took on Third Avenue. Do you always hang them that sharply?"

"Only when I'm trying to see who's after me."

"Maybe we should have shared a ride. Would have been easier for both of us."

She ordered a diet cola from the bartender.

"What are you doing here?" he asked, turning away and looking forward again.

"We need to talk," she said.

"Do we? About what?"

"About you and me and the newspaper we work for."

He sipped his beer. "Why's that?" he asked.

"I get the impression you don't like me," she said.

He thought about it for a moment. He had an impulse to verbally rip into her. Then he eased off.

"Personally," he said, "I don't really know whether I like you or not. I haven't decided."

"Then what is it?" she asked. "There's something you don't like and I need to know."

"It's not you personally," he said. "I don't know anything about you personally. I just suppose . . ." He found himself momentarily pondering the point.

"I'd love to hear it," she said. "We've worked two offices away for eighteen months. Not once have we sat and talked."

"Did we ever have a reason to?" he asked.

"Probably not."

"I guess I'm an old fogy," he said. Through the mirror behind the bar, he watched the entrance. That creepy sense was still upon him. "But I'm not at home with the way news is reported today," he said. "It's done differently. It's glib. It's superficial. It's a four-color print version of show biz. To me, you people don't cover events so much as you write stories and filter them through a computer. You scratch the surface, you come up with one fact, you build your case around it. You don't dig deep into a story. You don't hit hard. You just splash some words together with some color picture and the day's work is done."

She was silent, listening attentively with not the slightest bit of resentment. He gathered momentum. He wondered if anything he was saying was registering. "Tell me a few things very honestly," he said, looking back to her.

"Yeah?" Her drink arrived. She sipped it as he ordered a third brew for himself. "What do you want to know?"

"How old are you?"

"Thirty-one."

"How long have you been writing for newspapers?"

She had worked for the *Hartford Courant* for two years, she said, and the *Boston Globe* for three. In Hartford, she had been first assigned to local high school and minor sports at college level. Then she was reassigned to health and consumer affairs. In Boston, she was on a city desk and did her fair share of crime reporting, mostly the scene-on-the-street kind. Then two years ago, in 1994, she had moved to the *Sun,* hoping for a better assignment with more responsibility. She'd ended up back on sports, but with a sexier beat: local universities, plus professional hockey and tennis.

"Do you think that any story you've written," he asked, "has ever given anyone a sleepless night? Do you think there's anyone out there who'd like to tear your head off for something you've printed?"

She thought about it. "Maybe not," she said.

"Well, then, Ms. Caryn DiCarlo . . . As a reporter, you stink."

Finally, she recoiled slightly.

Townsend continued. "There's enough crap going on each day out there," he said, pompously motioning to the city beyond the door, "to fill up any number of newspapers. How the hell do we expect people to care about anything if *we* don't care, if *we* don't bombard the uncaring, apathetic, stupid-assed citizenry with the dirt about the people who affect their lives?"

He paused, not even mildly embarrassed by his own self-righteousness. She held her gaze upon him.

"Know what else I think?" he finally asked.

"I suspect you're going to tell me whether I ask or not."

"I think what most of you J-schoolers do is junk. You can quote me."

"I don't have to," she said.

"Why's that?"

"Harry used to."

It took a moment to register. Then he laughed. "Harry used to what?"

"Quote you. All the time. He idolized you, you pompous nitwit. Don't you realize that? As a writer, as a reporter, you're everything Harry wanted to be."

He was suddenly uneasy with the direction of the conversation, and Townsend stared ahead. "Spare me the maudlin stuff, all right?" he asked.

"No way. You don't deserve to be spared. What's the word you like to use? 'Dickhead'? That's it, isn't it? Well, you're one yourself."

"I never said I wasn't."

"Harry used to amuse me with anecdotes about you. 'Paul Townsend Stories,' he called them. He always had something good to tell me," she said. She drained her glass and motioned to the bartender for a refill.

"Office chatter, huh?" Townsend asked.

"Not at all," she said. "Social chatter. Off hours. At my place and Harry's."

Astonished, he looked back to her. "What are you talking about? *You and Harry?*" he asked, stunned.

"Not like you think," she said. "Harry and I were friends. Friends in a different way than you and he. Once or twice a week I'd cook dinner for him at his place. Maybe once a week, he'd come over to mine. I live on West Eighty-fourth Street." She motioned with her head to the neighborhood outside the bar. "I live two blocks from here."

"I thought you lived in the Bronx."

"Used to," she answered. "Moved away to go to university in Michigan. Haven't lived in the Bronx for a dozen years. And not that it's any of your concern, but it was Riverdale, not Belmont Avenue."

Townsend pursed his lips and thought about it. "A coarse guy with jagged fingernails like your brother? From Riverdale?" he asked.

"Lou works at being coarse," she said. "He's got a master's degree in journalism from Temple University."

Townsend rolled his eyes and shook his head. "Should have known," he muttered. "Used to be a guy like that on the *New York Daily News.* Used to walk around the office talking trash, masquerading as a tough Irish kid from Queens. It turned out he'd gone to Deerfield and Brown." Townsend took a long drink of beer, then moved the subject back a step.

"So what are you telling me?" he asked. "You and Harry had intimate dinners *à deux.*" He paused, then angled his question as he trained his eyes directly on hers. "And eventually I became the pillow talk?"

She laughed. The bartender set a fresh drink before her.

"No pillow talk," she said. "Just shop talk." She sighed. "I knew Harry was coming on to me a little. I've been around a bit. I couldn't mistake it."

Townsend chuckled. "So Harry was after your body, huh?"

"He would have liked it."

"Can't say I blame him. How did you put him off?"

"I told him I had a lover."

"Do you?"

"Several. Or maybe none." Caryn DiCarlo smiled sweetly. When she did, she was very pretty. For the first time, Townsend began to understand why Harry had been so smitten. "What's the phrase you used with your FBI visitors?" she asked. " 'None of your fucking business'?"

"That's the phrase. How'd you know?"

She smiled sweetly again, as if to let him arrive at his own conclusion.

"Oh. That's right," he realized quickly. "Harry told you. The FBI visit became a 'Paul Townsend Story.' "

She nodded. "I know all about you from Harry," she said. "I know enough to guess that you're probably in here to tie on a drunk that will last for several days. Right now, you probably don't even know whether you'll turn up at work tomorrow."

"And you followed me to save me," he concluded.

"No," she said. "I came in to talk to you while you were still sober. You're useless to me once you've got a load on."

"*I'm* useless to *you?*" His sarcasm was evident.

"As well as to yourself," she said.

"Then start talking."

"I hear you've been taken off the death page," she said.

"News travels fast, doesn't it."

"Ken Shaw told me, himself," she said. "I thought you were a happy man among the death notices."

"I was."

"Then why did you let him move you? You could have protested."

"Could have, yeah," Townsend said edgily. "Might have even talked Ken into letting me stay put."

"They why didn't you?"

"If you must know," he said, "I figured it's what Harry would have wanted me to do. How's that sound?"

"A closet sentimentalist, huh?" she asked.

"I have my principles. I compromise them as much as anyone, but I have them."

He looked her up and down, suddenly conscious of the fact that she was the focus of attention of almost all the other men in the Old Dublin. She was, in point of fact, quite beautiful. Perhaps he had always stood up too close to her, or too far away. He hadn't seen the full canvas of Caryn DiCarlo.

"Know something else?" he asked, starting to talk too much. "I used to tell Harry that with all the crap I'd been involved in, I only had one regret: my marriage breaking up. Now I have two. Harry was my pal. And I didn't come through with what he wanted in his lifetime."

Caryn DiCarlo searched for the right words of consolation. She couldn't locate them.

"Ah, but what's all this mean to you?" Townsend then asked sharply. "Why are you asking me all this?"

"Ken Shaw offered me the sports editorship of the *Sun,*" she said.

He bristled. Then, instinctively, Townsend felt himself start to seeth. "Harry's job, right?"

"I'd be the first female sports editor of a New York daily," she mused. "One of the first female sports editors in the country and certainly the one with the largest circulation."

"Congratulations," Townsend said sourly. "And I'm sure that in terms of cheap publicity, Ken Shaw will milk it for everything it's worth."

"Of course he will. But that was only one of two alternatives he gave me," she said. "Want to hear the other?"

"Sure."

"He said I could work with you on the story to which you're currently assigned. The fraudulent obituary. Harry's death. And so on."

"He said *what?*"

Caryn DiCarlo repeated. Townsend let it sink in, as she explained.

"Ken said several things. He thought the story might be big, very big, and you could use some help. He also knew that I'd spent time with Harry. I've heard from Harry what you were working on." She sipped her drink. "Ken also thought I could use some toughening up for New York," she said. "Apparently, you would agree. He said there was no way to get experience faster on the *Sun* than to work with Paul Townsend for a few weeks."

"That dickhead said that, did he?"

She nodded.

"I've never worked with an assistant or a backup in my life," he said.

"You've never worked on a paper like the *Sun* before." Again, the beguiling smile. "I also suspect Ken wanted someone smart to keep an eye on you. In case you fall on your drunken ass."

"He told you that?" Townsend asked sharply.

"I surmised as much."

"Well, you're going to take the sports job, I hope. That's where the prestige will be. Plus the money. Plus it's easier. And there's an added bonus. No matter what you write, no one will put a pipe bomb under your car."

"I understand all that. I've already made my decision."

"Good," he said, looking away.

"I'm working with you."

"Oh, come on . . . !"

"No. For real. That's what I came in here to tell you."

"What if I don't *want* assistance?"

"You get it anyway."

"What do you hope to gain by this?" he shot back angrily. "What are you doing this for?"

"I gain plenty, in terms of experience. I don't get a fancy title, but that can wait. And who cares, anyway? As for what I'm doing this for, that's obvious, too, isn't it? Harry warned me about getting pegged on the sports desk. Do something else, he always told me. Do something bigger, grander. Said he always wanted to, but it passed him by. Harry was my mentor. Now you've inherited me, like it or not."

Townsend contemplated his empty beer glass.

"There's a final reason, too," she said.

"What's that?"

"I figured this is what Harry would want me to do."

He gave it several seconds of consideration. "So. You're a closet sentimentalist, too, huh?" he asked, looking back to her.

"Did you think you were the only one?"

"It felt lonely from time to time," he said.

She slid off the bar stool, her purse in her hand.

"If you go on a drunk and don't turn up at work for a few days, I take your story and proceed without you," she warned. "Ken's orders."

"I'm sure," he said.

"I'll see you tomorrow," she said. "Or whenever you come in to work again."

She turned to go. The bartender arrived to fetch Townsend a fourth beer. Townsend put his palm up to indicate that he wanted no more. He left several dollars in tip money near his glass as he stood.

"Caryn?" he asked, stopping her. She turned.

"I'm going to be out of the city for a couple of days," he said. "Personal business. Important, long-standing commitment. Think you can keep current on anything new in the case while I'm away?"

"For a 'J-schooler' I'll try real hard," she said.

"I'll leave a number where I can be reached," he said. "In case anything big turns up. I wouldn't leave now except I've got a promise to keep. And I have to get my thoughts together as well."

"I'll keep the pilot light on for you," she said.

He moved closer to her. "There's one other thing, too," he added. "I've already lost one reporter on this case. I'd prefer not to lose another quite so soon. Let me take you home."

She smiled. "I accept. Thank you," she said.

He led her as they stepped outside. It was not yet late. The street and sidewalk remained busy.

"If you're working with me, the first thing you have to remember," Townsend said, "is look both ways after you go through a door to the street."

She stopped on the sidewalk. With an exaggerated gesture, she did just that.

"Like this?" she asked. She laughed.

He laughed, too, for the first time since Harry died. "Almost," he said. "You got a bit to learn, but you're catching on."

They both laughed. He took her arm and showed her to his car. The beer cans were still in place. No one had tampered. He explained what the cans were and why they were there. And he studied the comprehension in her eyes as he spoke.

Yes, he was concluding, Caryn would make an excellent student. A disciple, as it were. *And, yes, Harry,* Townsend said to himself. *This is in fact what you would have wanted.*

< < < < *21* > > > >

ON its descent into Los Angeles, the Delta 757 from New York hit turbulence. The entire airliner shook as it dropped two hundred fifty feet in two seconds. The aircraft steadied, then shook even more violently. This second time, the flight crew looked around apprehensively.

Townsend was not a carefree flyer. He knew his fears in the air were illogical, but not unreasonable, either. He had written too many obituaries of persons who died in air accidents to dismiss the possibility of becoming one himself someday. As a result, he rarely flew without giving his own mortality deep consideration. Pockets of extreme turbulence didn't help.

Want to plan your life? a terminally ill friend had once said to him. *Envision your death and work backward.*

Somehow the phrase had been recurring to him a lot recently, almost every few hours since Harry's murder. *Envision your death and work backward.* What would be said about him in his own obituary? He should have been able to figure it out. What would he say about himself? What were the great moments of his life. The triumphs? The defeats? The joys? The sorrows?

With a pen and paper, he began working on his own headline. He wrote,

PAUL TOWNSEND, 49

What next? He let his imagination ramble. He continued to construct his notice until he had it:

PAUL TOWNSEND, 49
WRITER FOR THE *SUN*
SHOT TO DEATH IN NYC

Well, why not?

How many friends would show up? Who would send flowers? What would he list as his own single, greatest accomplishment? Had there ever been one? He decided that there hadn't. Then would there ever be one?

He decided that there would. Yes, he told himself, definitely. He would make sure there would be . . . as long as this flight from New York to L.A. set down safely. He carefully folded the paper with his headline into his notebook.

He was in a window seat. Down below he saw the mountains. Placing his head near the window by his seat, he could see the skyline of Los Angeles up ahead, shrouded as usual by smog.

Several minutes later the aircraft was on its final approach to Los Angeles International Airport. The flight passed directly above Hollywood Park and the Great Western Forum. Horses, hockey, and roundball: Harry would have been titilated. The landing which followed sixty seconds later was smooth as silk. And why wouldn't it have been? Had there ever been a moment's doubt?

A stranger watching Townsend's arrival might easily have mistaken him for a family man returning from a business trip. He was greeted at the airport by Nora and his daughter.

Emily was first to spot him coming through the arrival gate. She left her mother and ran to him. Townsend hoisted his daughter and hugged her. He was amazed how much she had grown since last he had seen her.

Nora followed. There was no embrace. But after an awkward moment she leaned toward him and he kissed her on the cheek. She led him to her car.

Townsend had reserved a room at a hotel in Pasadena. Nora drove him. She and Emily waited while he registered, changed clothes, and washed quickly. That evening, Townsend took his estranged wife and daughter out to dinner. Afterward, Nora invited him to come over to the house she now owned—she and the mortgage company. Townsend read to his daughter before bedtime. He found two hand puppets in Emily's room—a possum and a raccoon—and put on a brief show for her before he kissed her good night.

He then sat with Nora in her living room.

"I finally received the papers," she said.

"Which ones?" he asked, thinking she meant newspapers.

"From the lawyer. For the divorce decree," she said. "You and I."

She paused for a moment. "You know, I never really thought it would happen. That's why I didn't do anything 'official' for so long." She sighed. "Now it's after the fact and I still can't believe it."

"Here were are sitting around like old friends," he said, "and we're about to be divorced." He shrugged. "Life's weird," he said. "But we both already knew that."

"I guess that's what we are now," she said. "Old friends." They both pondered it for a moment. "Well," Nora finally said. "Could be worse, I suppose."

He allowed that it certainly could have been.

Townsend glanced in the direction of the papers in question. They were in a manila envelope on an end table just inside the front door, as if they had arrived and been examined. Then Nora had left them untouched for several days.

"All each of us has to do is sign," she said. "Then it's official." She paused. "Do you have your copies?"

"Not yet," he said.

"Then I guess I get to sign first."

"If it bothers you," he said, "wait for my papers to arrive. *I'll* sign first and call you. You can sign second. Then you're free to remarry or whatever you have in mind."

"I guess I will be," she said.

The moment was awkward. Nora changed the subject.

"So," she said. "The *Sun*. How is life for a man working on the *New York Sun?* I've never seen a copy."

"It's not a paper you'd read, Nora," he said. "It's a lot like the old *New York Daily News,* all tarted up for the mid-nineties. It's for people who move their lips when they read."

"Do you still enjoy working there?"

"I don't mind it."

"And you're still on obituaries?"

"Pretty much."

"What does 'pretty much' mean, Paul? I was your wife for fifteen years. I know your methods of avoiding questions."

" 'Pretty much' means that occasionally an obituary will lead to a side story of some sort," he said. "Like a feature."

"That's all?"

"The *Sun* is not terribly strong on investigative reports, if that's what you're wondering. If anyone is still after me," he said, "the likelihood is that it's from the bad old days."

"Are you sure?"

"Shouldn't I be?"

"I'm just inquiring," she said defensively. "I still care about you, Paul. I still have bad dreams about you getting shot in the back some night."

He grimaced. "So do I," he admitted. He shrugged. "Well, it won't happen," he said agreeably. "All right?"

She nodded. "All right," she said.

Then the topic changed to people they knew from the old days and the times they had shared in New York when they were younger—back when the city was more innocent and when personal catastrophes didn't lurk around every corner. They laughed a lot and didn't flirt with any of the subjects that had led their marriage into ruin.

Nora made some coffee. Townsend stayed until ten thirty when she began to yawn. Then he excused himself and returned to his hotel.

Nora was a branch manager in her bank by now, but had arranged a personal day off. She let Townsend drive her car, and for the next day Paul, Nora, and Emily were a family again. They drove northwest from Pasadena until they came to the coast, then Townsend drove along the highway that bordered the Pacific. Neither of them had ever done it, and at least Emily could see this stretch of the ocean with both parents.

It was a day that made Paul Townsend recall why he had fallen in love with Nora in the first place.

The first time he had ever seen her had been while waiting for a flight from Minneapolis to New York. She had been a flight attendant with the airline, but traveling on her own time. She had had one of those cute, perfect faces of the American northwest. But on the first day he saw it, it was cut into an owlish puzzle by a pair of huge sunglasses, behind which her eyes could not be seen. And, since it had been summer, her light brown hair had been gloriously streaked with sun.

He remembered also, she had been wearing a gray sweatshirt that had been many sizes too large for her. When she stood, it had hung almost to her knees over faded blue jeans. The sleeves, which must have been made for a basketball player, were pushed up from the bracelets on her tan wrists.

Townsend maneuvered his way next to her in seating. When, shortly into their flight, she took out a book of nineteenth-century romantic poetry, he struck up a conversation. She finally removed her sunglasses, he looked into her eyes, and—for the first time in his life—had taken the first step toward tumbling hard in love.

Later he would joke to friends that he had "picked her up" on an airplane. This was almost true, but wasn't really. She wasn't the type of woman whom one successfully hustled in a public place. The truth was that Townsend had just finished a murderously difficult investigation into racketeering in the air freight business, a report that had immersed him in work for weeks on end. Nora, when he first saw her, was the prettiest girl he had seen in many months. He would be damned if he would let her get away.

As it happened, his timing had been excellent. She had broken up with a boyfriend of many months—the original owner of the gray sweatshirt—two weeks earlier. Discovering this over the course of the next few times he saw her, he hoped that she would be receptive to his advances, if he didn't rush the relationship.

She was. He didn't.

Her airline allowed her to relocate from Minneapolis to New York. He did all the appropriate things. While raising living hell as a reporter for various perpetrators during the daylight hours, he was the endless romantic in the evening, with carriage rides, flowers, and quiet evenings at her place or his. They married a year after they met.

It had been a wonderful time, they both agreed, that time many years ago when they were newly in love. It had been an era for finding new restaurants, for going out on pleasant evenings in New York—seeing Baryshnikov at Lincoln Center, Dwight Gooden at Shea Stadium, movie stars strolling down Fifth Avenue, and the laughably insufferable Mayor Koch anytime one raised one's eyes. It was the type of relationship that Townsend had hoped he could kindle with Sarah Stuart many years later when he first met her. But it had been a naive wish. Relationships like that, times like that, came along not every few years, but once in a lifetime—*if* one was very lucky.

Townsend had been lucky. For a while. But he could equally accept that it was now over.

And her body?

Townsend drove north on the highway that overlooked the ocean and wound north from Santa Barbara toward the Santa Ynez mountains. The presence of her in a car beside him recalled the physical pleasures of his marriage to her. He remembered how much he had loved to hold and touch her, and make love to her far into the morning hours. If he thought about it enough, it could torture him that other men could now have what she had once shared with him alone. From the corner of his eye, he took a long look at her. She still wore those big owlish sunglasses and, courtesy of southern California, her hair was now permanently streaked with sun.

She remained, in fact, an enormously attractive woman—just as she had been the first time he had seen her.

But, he reminded himself, it *was* over. So he pushed it out of his mind as best he could.

They lunched in a terrace restaurant near Isla Vista. Then they spent an afternoon showing their daughter the mountains. They returned to Pasadena by ten in the evening. Then on the next day, Townsend shamelessly took his daughter to Disneyland. She had never been. Neither had he. Nora worked that day. They met again in the evening. He wondered again why he so much enjoyed being with her again, and then he knew.

This wasn't the real world. While Harry had passed through his thoughts from hour to hour, he had left the Wolik–Dubrow case behind him on the East Coast. This was the most legitimate getaway he had enjoyed in years. He found himself even feeling good about life.

Inevitably, it ended that evening. The telephone rang. Emily answered, listened, and came to her parents.

"It's a lady to speak to Daddy," she said.

Townsend went into the bedroom where he could talk privately. He picked up the telephone.

"Having a good time?" a female voice asked.

"It could be worse," he said. "What's new, Caryn?"

"A couple of things," she said. "I thought I'd better call. Want to hear about it?"

"Probably not. But tell me anyway," he said.

Ken Shaw had run the retraction of the Wolik obituary, she said. It had been labeled as a "Correction" and buried near the comics. Max Kohlheimer was apparently appeased as he had said nothing further.

Caryn had also been catching some odd bits of work on the fourth floor, she said, including obituaries. One of the most notorious Wall Street manipulators of the Reagan Era, recently paroled, had died while in the sauna in a Long Island mansion. Caryn had his obituary in front of her. She had written it.

"Everyone agrees he was a greedy sleazeball," she said.

"He was," Townsend answered.

"I mean, it's beyond opinion," Caryn said. "It's statement of fact."

"A statement of fact, in our opinion," he teased. "But I'm still with you."

"I'm calling him 'a greedy sleazeball' in print. Is that okay?"

"That's what makes our death page famous," he said. "We're fine as long as the greedy sleazeball doesn't come back as a ghost. Chances are he won't." He paused. "Did you run it by Ken Shaw?"

"Ken says 'sleazeball' is fine. He's worried about the 'greedy.' "

"That's K.N. Shaw for you."

They both laughed. Then her tone changed. "Do you want to go out to a phone booth," she asked, "or is this line secure?"

He sobered. "As far as I know the line is fine. Why?"

"Here's the real reason I'm calling," she said. "Someone named McMorris called you from Washington this afternoon. I said you were on vacation. I didn't elaborate where or why or what. Know him?"

"I know him," Townsend said.

"McMorris wants to talk to you in person as soon as you can. Wanted me to relay that message as soon as you returned, or if you called in." She paused. "I have a phone number. Want it?"

Townsend did. He took it. "You done good, kid," he said.

She laughed again. Townsend rang off.

An hour later, Townsend drove to a telephone booth in Glendale to counter any attempt to trace his subsequent call. He telephoned the number in Washington that Caryn DiCarlo had provided him.

Bruce McMorris answered his own line almost immediately.

"Paul Townsend," McMorris said grandly. "I've been thinking about you a bit."

"I'm honored."

"I'm sorry about the tragedy on your newspaper," McMorris said.

"Is it anything you could have prevented?" Townsend asked.

"No," McMorris pontificated. "But I'm starting to think you and I have some common goals. I'd like to explain things. In person. Where are you?"

"Out of state."

"Can you come to Washington?" McMorris asked.

"You'd have to give me a good reason."

McMorris promised him two. First, he was now in a position to shed some further light on the whereabouts of the dear departed Leonard Wolik.

"I understand what must have happened to you," McMorris said. "We're ready to help you."

"Who's 'we'?"

"My employer."

"Uh huh," Townsend said.

"Oh, don't be so damned cynical. We're on your side, you know. We're part of the United States government."

"That's why I'm so cynical."

McMorris forged onward. Second, McMorris said, he would open up some CIA files to Townsend. On the Q.T., of course. Nothing could be printed. Nothing was for attribution in the press. This could steer Townsend further in the direction of Harry's assassin, McMorris said, as well as explain the setup that had already been chronicled in the obituary pages.

"It's your story," McMorris said. "Take it or leave it. But I'm not giving it to anyone else. So it's either yours or it doesn't exist."

"And I'm supposed to suddenly trust you?" Townsend said.

McMorris seemed quite affable on the telephone.

"You can if you want. You can hang up if you want. The choice is yours. If you're secretly the pensive type, you can ponder your options and call me back."

"What's in it for you?"

"Enough to make your intolerable presence worthwhile," McMorris said. "You'd clear up a mystery for us as well. That's the only way I could authorize letting you in here."

Silence on the line. Townsend blew out a long breath.

"If the offer can stand for a couple of days, I'll call you from Washington sometime next week," Townsend said. "How's that?"

"That's excellent!" McMorris enthused, sounding quite pleased. "I'll have things ready for you," McMorris said. "This will be worth your while, Paul, if I may call you that. Honest Injun. You'll profit by this."

Senator John Lord was profiting as well.

On the same evening that Townsend sat with his family in Pasadena, Senator Lord was a hundred miles to the north in Bakersfield, surrounded by an array of country music singers who supported his candidacy. They were putting on a fund-raising performance for him. They had sold out a muggy auditorium of slightly less than ten thousand seats at twelve to twenty-five dollars a pop.

Cracker music, the people up north in San Francisco liked to call it. Okie music, the people down in Beverly Hills and Hollywood called it. But to John Lord, these were his voters, these blue-collared, voting-age boys and girls who were the grandchildren of the Great Depression and whose lot had rolled them into southern California.

There was one singer there named Charley Bovis who came as close to being an embarrassment as anyone. Charley was the son of an oil roughneck who'd lost his home when petroleum had crashed in Houston in the late 1980s. His old man's failures were the type of things Charley found suitable for music. Well, that was one sort of thing.

Like his roughneck father, Charley was a high school dropout. But he wrote songs nonetheless. The songs carried a predictable ideological slant. He'd straightened up his act and had gone a bit mainstream, meaning he didn't perform two of his early underground hits, "Are You Sure You're Sure the Pope Ain't A Pollack No More?" and a slightly less subtle work titled "All You Jews and Niggers Better Watch Out."

Now, however, Charley had a song he wrote called, "My Folks are Red, White, and Blue." Rednecks, white skin, and blue collars, the song went on to explain, and one hundred percent proud of it. This one was controversial, but just within the bounds of taste that country music stations would play. So it was also a hit.

Some observers from the national media noted that the thrust of the song was mildly racist. "Whadaya meanin' by 'mildly'?" Charley once guffawed. The press had that comment on tape, too. So the Laptoppers were all set to pounce if the song were performed in front of John Lord. It was a built-in trap for the candidate. If he disavowed it, he antagonized his most fervent constituency. If he said nothing, the national press, in addition to the Republicans and Democrats, could get after him for weeks, claiming he wasn't part of the nation's democratic mainstream.

It was no wonder then that very quietly the Republican National Committee had made sure that a conflicting concert date for Charley in North Dakota had been canceled, and that a "wealthy fan" had provided Bovis a first-class plane ticket to Los Angeles so that he could perform for Senator Lord.

So the Laptoppers were ready. The only problem was that Eugenia Lord had smelled it coming. The candidate's wife mentioned the potential problem to her husband. He ran it past Jerry Huddleston, the campaign manager. Charley Bovis thus found himself in musical limbo before he knew what had hit him. *He* could be heard. But his freshest material couldn't be.

Charley started to get indignant about his treatment. On the day of his planned performance, he found himself a Coors suitcase, retired to a Winnebago he'd leased for the journey to Bakersfield, and threatened a walkout. The Lord campaign had a problem on their hands—woven out of thin air—three hours before the music was supposed to start.

"Let him be the opening act," Eugenia Lord eventually suggested. "Let him sing the National Anthem."

"He can't really sing, ma'am," Jerry Huddleston answered.

"He's got a voice like fingernails on a blackboard," her husband said. "Ever heard him?"

Eugenia shook her head. Despite the fact that the phrase "loves country music" appeared on her campaign biography, Charley Bovis wasn't played on the stations Eugenia Lord listened to. She was from the East, after all. Her father had even been a United States ambassador.

"No one will hear him tonight, either," Eugenia said. She smiled. Mrs. Lord had a grand plan.

Charley was honored to sing the "Star Spangled Banner" to open the evening's festivities. And as his rasping, untrained vocals assaulted the anthem, much to the entertainment of his audience, Eugenia and her children, who were teenagers, made an unexpected appearance in the aisles and in the balcony of the theater. They handed out little four-by-five-inch cloth flags made by a local factory. They told the television people ahead of time exactly what they were going to do. So as Charley Bovis hacked away at the "S S B," the Lord family stole the moment from him. The prevailing TV sound byte of the evening was Eugenia, regal woman that she was from the old New England family, handing out flags to enthusiastic Americans in the balcony.

It was great politics. Great theater. Outstanding media manipulation. Townsend watched it on the local CBS affiliate in Pasadena, and marveled at Eugenia Lord's grace and presence.

Idly, he wondered how she'd ever gotten mixed up with such a man as her husband.

$$< < < < \ \mathbf{22} \ > > > >$$

ON Monday morning, Townsend was awake early. He had the pleasure of walking his daughter to school. As he dropped Emily off at the playground entrance, she turned to him.

"Are you going to come see us again?" she asked hopefully.

He stooped down to her eye level. "Real soon, angel," he told her.

"Promise, Daddy?"

"I promise," he said.

She hugged him and he reciprocated. He stood, then he leaned over to give her a final kiss on the forehead. Then she turned to go to school.

He lingered on the sidewalk and watched her as she crossed the playground. Just before she went into the building, she turned and waved to him. Very gently, Townsend bit his lower lip as he watched her disappear. He didn't see her enough to please either her or himself. He wondered when he would see her again. And he wondered what he could do, living on the other side of the continent.

He walked back to Nora's house. He offered to take a taxi, but Nora insisted on driving him to Los Angeles International Airport for his noon flight. They talked amiably on the way to his plane.

"It wasn't you, you know," she said. "It was the situation that made the marriage fail. I understand that now."

"The 'situation'?" he asked, knowing the answer. "You mean my job?"

"Your job," she affirmed. "And what you turned your job into."

Nora drove southbound on the Pasadena Freeway. Townsend was amazed at how well she had adapted to West Coast driving. Nora was a woman, he remembered, who was unable to wrestle a Volkswagen into second gear when she was twenty-two.

He said nothing. He looked at the sunshine drenching downtown Los Angeles. For some reason he was reminded of the contrast of driving to Westchester on a wet spring night with Sarah Stuart to meet Leonard Wolik's impersonator.

"I couldn't take the life-style," she said. "You being frazzled all the time. The threats. The phone ringing at any hour of the night. But there was never anything wrong with you as a husband. You understand that?"

"I do," he said. "Thanks."

They rode in silence for several minutes.

"I might as well tell you," he said. "I don't want to mislead you." He drew a breath and continued. "I'm getting into another investigation. There's this one case."

She made no outward gesture of disappointment. But he thought he felt it, anyway. "The whole thing again?" she asked. "Criminals? Threats? Bullets? Two A.M. phone calls?"

"I didn't go looking for this," he said. "It was an outgrowth of a death of a man I thought I knew. An obituary, actually. So, maybe just this one final time . . ."

He didn't point out that there had already been two deaths. Two and counting.

"You always used to say that," she said evenly. " 'Maybe just this one final time.' "

"Did I?"

She nodded, taking her eyes off the road for a moment.

"Well," he concluded, "this really may be the 'final time.' "

"Sure," she said. She clicked her turn signal on and took a ramp which guided her onto the Santa Monica Freeway. The Santa Monica would lead toward the airport. "Well," she concluded, "in the end it's your life, Paul. You make your own choices."

"I guess I do," he said, looking away.

After several more minutes, she spoke again. "Mind if I ask you something?"

"Go ahead."

"Who called you the other night? The woman?"

"Someone I work with."

"On the case you just mentioned?"

"Yes."

Several seconds, then, "So you have an assistant?"

"My managing editor assigned one to me," he said.

More silence, then, "Is she nice?" Nora asked.

He actually had to think about it. "In fact, she is," he concluded. "I don't know her that well," he added for some reason. "As I said, I work with her. That's all." Nor did he bother to point out that Caryn DiCarlo was eighteen years his junior.

At the airport, Nora guided her car off the access ramp and toward the short-term parking lot.

"You can drop me at the departures terminal," he said to her. "You don't have to see me off."

"I'd like to. I'll walk you to the gate," she said. "Okay? For old time's sake."

He looked at her curiously. "For old time's sake," he allowed.

She parked and they walked together through the departures terminal. He wondered what had changed. This wasn't for old time's sake at all. Her attitude toward him had softened. He wondered when and why it had happened. He figured he would probably never know.

"What's your flight?" she asked.

"United 273," he answered. It was 10:45 A.M. Their arrival at the airport was perfectly timed.

"Is that direct to New York?"

"No," he said. "I'm going to Washington. I have to change planes."

"There are direct flights to Washington," she said.

"I don't want one," he said. "And don't tell anyone who calls, okay?"

"Okay."

She looked at the departures board and studied it. Then it dawned on her. This visit had been the nicest time they had passed together since before the marriage collapsed. But even on this day, Townsend was changing planes in Kansas City just to make life more difficult for anyone tracking him. Nor, he confided to her next, was he flying under his own name.

When United 273 was called, Nora leaned forward. He held her for a moment. The touch of her seemed so familiar and sparked so many of the old physical feelings, making him long for what he was missing. He kissed her on the cheek.

"Paul," she said. "I guess it would be best if I signed the papers. You know, making the divorce official."

He nodded. "Best for both of us, I guess. We'll talk. I'll visit Emily as much as I can. I know you can't take the life-style that comes with me. What can I do?"

"Nothing," she said. "Don't try.'

They embraced a second and final time. But she wouldn't let go of his hand. "Paul," she said. Her voice was nearly breaking. "I was really hoping you'd stopped trying to change the world."

He shrugged.

"You keep doing it," she said. "You are physically unable to stop. You make enemies of the most dangerous people in the country. Eventually, one of them is going to—

"Nora . . ."

She gathered herself.

"I know you won't make any promises," she said. "And I know you won't stop." She held back tears. "God bless you, Paul. I don't want to come to your funeral. I don't want to see you buried."

He gently kissed her again. "Bye," he said lamely. She waved bravely. Then Townsend turned to go.

He passed through the metal detector and walked down the ramp to the United Airlines departures. He felt her eyes upon his back, but he never looked back. Why would he? She still had the divorce papers to sign. With a few strokes of the pen she would be a free woman. Within a few weeks or months, she might officially be someone else's. In the end, that was what she wanted and what would be best for her. And he knew there was nothing he could do to stop it.

<<<< **23** >>>>

*T*OWNSEND arrived in Washington at half past eight in the evening, Eastern time. He rented a car at Dulles Airport and drove toward the Capitol. He checked into a Marriott on the Washington side of the Key bridge.

At the hotel, he called Caryn DiCarlo in New York to report where he was. She had no new information, other than the fact that several other reporters were working on the Harry Dubrow case. But they had no leads. The story, as murders sometimes do, was starting to disappear from the front pages.

"Fine," Townsend said. The last thing he needed was a spotlight. More could be accomplished without one.

Later that evening, Townsend drove to Georgetown and ate dinner alone. He tried to put his thoughts together. So many trails led in varying directions. His thoughts remained a maze of facts leading to some indecipherable end.

He was back at the hotel close to eleven o'clock. He stopped at the bar. He fell into conversation with a woman who said she was traveling alone on business. She said she was divorced and mentioned her room number.

Townsend answered that he was separated from his wife. She waited. He made no move. Eventually, she invited him to her room. He declined to join her, though he couldn't even figure out why. Some good recreational adult sex would have felt just fine right around then. She seemed disappointed and Townsend was on the verge of changing his mind and ordering a bottle of champagne. But she quickly accepted his refusal and excused herself. He didn't see her again on his stay.

* * *

The next morning, Townsend telephoned McMorris at the CIA. He arranged for a noon meeting at McMorris's office.

"Where in God's name are you?" McMorris asked affably.

"At the other end of your telephone line," Townsend said. "I'll see you at noon."

"I guess you will," said McMorris. "Know how to get here?"

"All too well."

"I'll leave written authorization at the main gate in Langley for you to enter. Otherwise, your car will be riddled with bullets."

Townsend was silent.

"Just kidding," said McMorris.

Townsend hung up.

It took only a few minutes for Townsend to break free of District of Columbia traffic, cross the Francis Scott Key Bridge, and take a short ride through the Virginia countryside. After a few miles, he easily picked up the green and white signs directing him toward the Central Intelligence Agency. For an institution dedicated to secrecy, the numerous signs were a glaring contradiction of purpose.

The agency's headquarters had been situated since the late 1940s on one hundred forty acres of what had once been farmland. The building itself, as Townsend grew closer, was enormous even by governmental standards. It was surrounded by trees, a strange touch of landscaping, with an oblong two-story base that occupied—Townsend recalled from previous research—a full nine acres, including inner courtyards, offices, and cafeterias. Five sturdy, thick-connected oblong towers of predominantly white-reinforced concrete interspersed with glass rose from the base. Almost fifty years old in 1996, the building was at once retro and newfangled, modern and dated, like the agency it housed. It was a Taj Mahal of monotonous and remorselessly middle-brow bureaucratic architecture and yet it housed intelligence arsenals on the brink of the twenty-first century.

As Townsend made his way past the final guard box and was admitted to the parking lot, he had an air of quaintness and an air of intimidation, each fighting with the other.

In the ground-floor lobby, Townsend presented himself to a long desk of "reception specialists." He gave his name and whom he was there to see. He was immediately assigned a "guide" to take him to his destination.

The guide was a woman named Helen. She engaged Townsend in small talk as she took him to the fourth-floor office in the south wing where he would find Bruce McMorris. She was an attractive woman with very short brown hair. She wore a jacket and dark skirt. She was from Alaska, she said, and enjoyed living in Washington. She offered nothing more.

Townsend was kept waiting in a fourth-floor reception area for less than five minutes, Helen remaining with him the entire time. Suddenly, the door to an adjoining office flew noisily open. When Bruce McMorris appeared, Helen quietly departed.

"Hello, Townsend," McMorris said to his wary guest. "Welcome to the belly of the beast. Come in here, would you?"

McMorris was quite affable this time. Almost cheerful. Townsend took the mood change to be proof that McMorris wanted something that only Townsend could provide.

McMorris guided Townsend into an office that was grand even by governmental standards. McMorris seated himself behind a massive desk that bore not a single shred of paper. Through the venetian blinds behind McMorris, there was a view of trees and sky. An American flag stood to McMorris's right. There was a portrait of the President of the United States on the wall to the left. Prominently displayed on a side bookcase, McMorris had several framed photographs of himself. The portraits chronicled his career, as they were all of him taken with famous people. He was photographed at various ages with every American President, Townsend noticed, since Johnson, with one exception.

"No Jimmy Carter?" Townsend asked, assaying the collection as he seated himself in a leather chair before McMorris's desk.

"Carter wasn't exactly popular in this building," McMorris said. He paused and spoke in a lowered voice. "If it puts you at ease in any way," McMorris said, "I *have* a picture of myself with President Carter. I just don't display it."

"Pity," Townsend said. "History will probably judge him more favorably than all those others." Townsend noticed a picture of McMorris with the current head of the Federal Bureau of Investigation. That reminded Townsend of another unpleasant morning.

"What about those two FBI goons?" Townsend asked.

"Who on earth are you talking about?"

"Special Agents Flynn and Grodine. Working out of a District of Columbia office. That means FBI headquarters. Or at least that's what they said. Are they working for you?"

"That's a different agency, Townsend. I can't comment."

"You just did," Townsend said. "If you know who I'm talking about then they have something to do with you."

"Take it as a 'nondenial denial,' if you wish," McMorris said. "That's the term you fellows use, isn't it?"

"That's one of them," Townsend said, tiring of the banter again. "Now come on. What's the pitch? Why am I here?"

McMorris folded his arms, drew a deep breath, and began. "Well, I told you on the phone. If you help us, we help you. Just confirm something for me first: I'm correct in assuming that you're still involved in this Leonard Wolik affair?"

"Yes. I am," Townsend said.

"Why *you?*"

"What do you mean, why me? The case came my way."

"But it's not just an obituary anymore, is it? Your paper launched an investigation, naturally following up on the tragedy in Brooklyn as well. But why not give it to a writer who's not emotionally as close to it?"

"Maybe the powers that be consider me the best writer on the paper," said Townsend.

McMorris chortled. "Best writer on the *New York Sun.*" He laughed. "That's a little like first-class passage on a Greyhound bus, isn't it? Best sailor on the *Titanic.*"

"Worse newspapers than the *Sun,*" answered Townsend, "have brought down governments."

McMorris saw no humor in the remark. "Is that supposed to imply something?" he asked.

"No," he said, losing patience, "other than the fact that we're wasting each other's time. Do we have something to say to each other or not?"

"Are you working with an assistant?" McMorris asked.

Townsend stared him in the eye and thought of Caryn. "No," Townsend lied smoothly. "Now start talking to me."

"Goddamn it, Townsend," McMorris said, grimacing and shaking his head. "You put us in a damnable position. You're on to something, sure. *We,* this agency, don't even know what it is. But we're going to help you find it, if you let us." He paused. "Problem is. We have to trust you. And vice versa."

"I still don't know what you're talking about."

"You will," McMorris said, getting to his feet. "Time to let you in on your first official secret," McMorris continued. "You're an obituary writer. You should appreciate this." He motioned to the doorway. "Come along."

"Where are we going?"

"The big graveyard," he said. "But not just any big graveyard. You'll see."

"How are we getting there?" Townsend asked.

"We're going for a drive."

"You and me?"

"Just us."

"I'll follow you in my own car."

"Oh, don't be melodramatic," McMorris scolded.

"I'll follow in my own car," Townsend repeated.

McMorris sighed and shook his head in exasperation. "As you wish," he said.

Finally, Townsend stood.

Townsend returned to his car in the parking lot. He started the engine and waited. Several minutes later, McMorris's car came around a turn in the parking area and drove alongside Townsend's. There it stopped. Both men lowered their windows.

"We're going south on the George Washington Parkway," McMorris shouted over the low rumble of the two automobile engines. "If we get separated—"

"We won't."

"—If we get separated, get off the parkway at the Key bridge. Take the Jeff Davis Parkway to Arlington. Meet me at the entrance to the national cemetery."

Townsend rolled up his window. McMorris proceeded out first. McMorris's car was typical of a governmental functionary. Beige, new, and nondescript. It bore a Virginia plate with the first three letters AHN. Townsend memorized the entire plate, then followed close by.

McMorris was at the parkway within five minutes. He proceeded south at a reasonable pace. The trip was short. There was little traffic. Checking the rearview mirror was almost a religion now to Townsend, and he did so continually. Again, he saw no indication that anyone was following.

McMorris arrived first at the entrance to Arlington National Cemetery. He put his flashers on and continued to move slowly. He passed the signs which directed all traffic to parking lots and proceeded to a guard's position.

A uniformed United States Marine stepped from a booth. Townsend's car followed McMorris's, almost bumper to bumper. McMorris held the marine in conversation for almost half a minute, producing identification as he spoke.

Whatever McMorris said, whatever he produced, satisfied the young guard. The marine stepped back for a moment, gave McMorris a salute, and waved him past. The guard looked to Townsend, saluted, and indicated that he, too, could follow.

Townsend followed slowly. The two cars traveled at fifteen miles per hour, following the narrow asphalt roads that snaked through the national cemetery.

At first, Townsend thought McMorris was driving toward the Kennedy tomb. In fact, he was. Then he turned away from it and traveled through a section of burial ground reserved for war heroes. But McMorris clearly knew where he was going. Townsend followed, watched carefully, and kept his eyes occasionally on his mirror. No one followed. Townsend's hands were wet, but he began to relax.

Several minutes later, McMorris was where he wanted to be. He pulled his car gently to the side of the road, his tires up on the grass. He left his flashers on. Townsend pulled into position behind him.

McMorris stepped out of the car. It occurred to Townsend that there was no other human being anywhere in sight. They had arrived at an isolated strip of the cemetery, surrounded only by grass, granite markers, and trees. Townsend was aware how vulnerable he was.

Nora spoke from somewhere within his memory: *I don't want to come to your funeral.*

McMorris came to Townsend's door, buttoning his suit jacket as he walked. "The rest of the trip is on foot," he said.

Townsend opened his car door and stepped out. Still no one else was visible.

Nora again: *I don't want to see you buried.*

It was a hot day, one of those humid summer killers for which Washington and Virginia are notorious. Townsend could feel the sun pounding upon him almost immediately.

"Where we going?" Townsend asked.

"I'm taking you to see someone," he said. "We'll be there in half a minute."

"We're going to have a conversation here?" Townsend asked.

"The 'friend' has been dead for ten years," McMorris said. "But that shouldn't bother you, Townsend. You commune with the deceased very well."

Townsend let the comment pass. He followed McMorris by a few paces as he climbed a path up a small knoll. Mercifully, it cut through some shade. There was even a faint breeze.

If this was a spot of rendezvous, Townsend concluded, it was a hell of a secretive one. They were within a few seconds of meeting their contact, and Townsend saw no other living being.

"Here we are," McMorris said finally.

McMorris stopped at a tombstone. He pointed down toward it.

"I don't know who you think you met," McMorris said, "but you can see why your government was a trifle miffed."

Townsend's eyes darted about until his gaze settled upon the name and dates chiseled in granite.

LEONARD BARNES WOLIK
JAN. 10, 1932–FEB. 8, 1985
REST IN PEACE

McMorris let the vision sink in. Then after several seconds he spoke.

"You wrote a good obituary for the man," said McMorris. "It's just that you wrote it eleven years too late." He paused. "And, of course, you had the cause of death wrong, as well as surviving relatives."

Townsend stared, stared, and stared. He groped for words and eventually found some.

"How do I know you didn't put this stone here a week ago?" Townsend asked after several seconds.

"Does it look it?"

No, it didn't. There was moss on it and it showed a decade of weather.

"How do I know who's really down there?" Townsend asked.

"God Almighty, you're a suspicious bastard," said McMorris. "What do you want me to do? Get shovels from the car? Dig down and bring up some bones?"

"I need to see more than a tombstone."

"You will," said McMorris. "You're going to see a complete file. *Several* complete files. Come along. We're finished here."

McMorris guided Townsend by the shoulder.

"Look, Townsend," he said. "Wolik was a good man. A dedicated nephew of his Uncle Sam. That's why we're being a little bit possessive about him. All right?"

They walked back toward the cars. There were several seconds in silence as they moved through the heat. Townsend removed his jacket. McMorris kept his on.

"Wolik," said McMorris. "The real Leonard Wolik died in a traffic accident eleven years ago. I can give you all the documentation you need."

"When?"

"Tomorrow," said McMorris. "If you're willing to come into the CIA to examine it. If you're willing to sit quietly in a reading room for a few days. And if you're willing to approach all this with an open mind."

"How open? And what do you want?"

"First, you have to get this damned chip off your shoulder,"

McMorris said with suppressed disgust. "We are not your enemy. I keep telling you that and you don't believe me. You and I, you and Central Intelligence, have a common purpose, as you'll see."

"What's that?"

"You were set up by an impostor. You ran a fraudulent obituary of a former diplomat. Well, that doesn't happen every day, does it? We'd like to know who did it and why. Same as you. Similarly, your friend. The sports editor. He was murdered. It's all related, Townsend. So you help us solve a riddle," McMorris concluded, "and we help you solve a murder."

"Then what?"

"We turn the evidence over to the district attorney in Brooklyn for prosecution. We help in any way we can. Unofficially, of course."

"And what about the story?" Townsend asked.

"It's yours when it's complete. May you land a Pulitzer."

"All of it? The whole story?"

"I think so," McMorris said. "I think we can get it declassified, but only on its completion. And there's another ground rule or two."

They were close to the cars again. The faint breeze had turned into a memory. The sun was scorching them. McMorris stopped walking in order to talk.

"You cannot print anything you see in our files," McMorris said. "You'll have to sign an agreement in advance, and we'll sue if you break it. Anything you can find on your own, you can go on. We point you in the right direction, in other words, we give you background, and you do the digging. It's that easy." McMorris looked at him expectantly. "Well? Do we have a deal?"

Townsend felt the sweat beading beneath his hairline. He considered the proposal for what seemed like half an hour. It was probably closer to five seconds.

"You have a deal," Townsend said.

"Good. *Good!*" McMorris exclaimed. "Wise choice." McMorris smiled. "Now let's get to hell out of here," he said.

He touched Townsend lightly on the arm. The two men walked the final few paces toward the cars.

Townsend left Arlington first. And, if anything, he studied his rear-view mirror twice as studiously upon departure as upon entry.

<<<< **24** >>>>

NO fewer than sixteen men and women in the Brooklyn and Manhattan detective bureaus were assigned to the Harry Dubrow case. Many of these cops knew Paul Townsend personally and recognized a special interest in the assignment.

"He may be a detective to you," Harry had said during his lifetime about some of Townsend's friends on the NYPD. "But to me he's only a dick."

More than once since Harry's murder, Townsend had laughed anew at Harry's sentiment. Often, Townsend had repeated it to members of the police force, who were equally amused. Yet, no one on the side of justice would have been laughing had he known that all sixteen men and women on the Dubrow investigation were doomed to failure and frustration. Not only had the man who had pulled the trigger on Harry quickly departed from their jurisdiction, but he had left no trail behind him.

There were dozens of stories in the New York media on the case, put together by scores of newswriters above and beyond the new team of DiCarlo and Townsend—bylines were always alphabetical at the *Sun:* company policy. Yet all the accounts reduced to one conclusion. There were no new leads. Even Paul Townsend and Caryn DiCarlo, working together by telephone during Townsend's absence from New York, were—in print at least—no closer to breaking the story than anyone else.

And no wonder. The killer was currently ensconced in considerable comfort in a motel in Florida. Poised to complete his next assignment, he had taken a $90-a-day room at the Trade Winds Motel on Fort

Myers Beach. He was on the second floor of the building and liked to sit out on a small private terrace. There he could enjoy the morning and early-evening sunshine. There he could watch the water and the beach. More importantly, he could also watch whomever walked on the beach.

He had arrived three days after Harry died. He hadn't moved since. He remained in contact with his usual associate in New York, however, who had supplied him with the next tools of his trade. The killer understood his mission and knew whom his next target was. He had already seen her twice, in fact, which was why he had taken a room at the Trade Winds. The name she now went by was Tina Hubbell. She was married to some sort of hardware merchant, didn't look terribly happy, and took walks on the beach twice a day, sometimes with her children, but frequently without them.

Unlike the execution of Harry Dubrow, who had shown up instead of the real target, a handgun would not be used to murder Tina Hubbell. Something more sophisticated would be needed. Well, mused the killer, a job was a job, wasn't it?

That evening, Harry's murderer settled in to his next assignment. He had already noted where Tina Hubbell normally parked her car when spending time at the beach. He had watched her from a distance as recently as late that very afternoon.

But now the killer strolled to the strip of sand that Tina favored. When he was at the area where she began her walks, he measured with his eye the distance between the beach and the parking lot. Then he turned and looked back toward the Trade Winds Motel. He looked directly at his room, which was third from the end on the second of the motel's two floors.

But he needed more of a landmark. Looking around on the beach he spotted a child's sand bucket, a white one covered with blue and yellow stars. It had been abandoned during the day. It would now well serve the assassin's purposes.

The killer picked up the bucket and placed it in the center of the beach, as close as he could to Mrs. Hubbell's usual path. He turned the bucket on its side and weighted it with rocks. Then he returned to his motel room. It was 8:45 P.M.

He locked both the door to his room and the door to his private balcony which overlooked the beach. He drew all the window shades.

There was one table in the room. The killer removed everything from its surface. Then he opened one of two suitcases with which he traveled. From it, he drew several smaller bundles, all wrapped tightly with chamois cloth. He methodically placed the bundles on the table.

He began to unwrap them, starting with the largest. It was, as could be readily seen when uncovered, the breech and barrel of a firearm. As an entity, it was about twenty-four inches long, made from black chromium steel and surprisingly lightweight. There was a bolt on the rear of the barrel, just above a piece of curved, well-sanded wood which formed the grip. There were two holes drilled in the grip for attachment to a stock, which was also of wood. Harry's murderer unwrapped this part next.

The killer examined the instrument carefully, playing with the bolt, clicking it in and out of place. There was a small inverted magazine above the barrel which could house two bullets in addition to one which needed to be chambered manually. This was part of an instrument designed for a specific purpose—a long-range kill. Piece by piece, the assassin put together a weapon that acquired the contours of a normal rifle.

But when that part of the assembly was finished, three cloth-bound packages remained unopened. These were the facets of the weapon that would separate it from the ordinary.

First, the killer unwrapped a clamping mechanism. It was very much like a heavy steel vice, attached to a tripod which could be adjusted in height from three inches to a foot. On the feet of the tripod was a rubbery, nonskid substance that would hold the weapon in place despite the inevitable kick when it was fired.

Then there was an eight-inch tubing that was thicker than the actual barrel of the rifle. This was the silencer. It screwed tightly onto the nose of the weapon, but hung off like an ominous black hot dog.

Then the killer came to the third and most sophisticated of his instrument's final components: the sighting mechanism. This took the form of a scope with cross hairs that attached to the uppermost part of the rifle. But it was also a newly developed technology for a weapon of this sort. It was computerized. It combined the principles of the auto-focus on a fine camera and the "lock-in" computerization mechanism used on the warheads carried by modern attack aircraft. When properly wired into the trigger mechanism, it allowed a rifleman to take his mark on a target, lock in on it, and fire a small caliber bullet a great distance with unerring aim. Squirrel hunters across the world, among others, would have loved it, had it not cost upward of twenty-two thousand dollars per sight.

The killer threw a sheet over the weapon to protect it from any unwelcome eyes. To pass the evening, he watched television.

The lead story was the final day of campaigning in the California primary. The killer watched this with disgust. With the exception of John Lord, who spoke the truth about the American condition, the assassin hated politicians. Maybe someday he would get to shoot one of them, too, he mused. The other stories, labor conflicts and student demonstrations against nuclear power and animal exploitation, disgusted him, too. He checked the index on the motel's television listing and opted for a semipornographic movie.

As he watched, he ate a pair of sandwiches and drank some warm beer in his room. Once or twice he stepped out on his balcony. He kept the weapon assembled overnight.

He arose before dawn the next morning. He stepped to his balcony and looked at the deserted beach. It was a few minutes past five A.M. The toy bucket was still in place. There was no one on the beach.

"Good," he whispered to himself.

He went back into his room. He left the door slightly ajar. He moved the table with the weapon upon it closer to the door. Through the partial opening, he sighted the weapon, drawing an aim on the child's bucket.

He locked in on it. He squeezed the trigger twice.

He felt the weapon kick softly and exude a dull *phrump* sound with each shot. Through the sight, he could see the bucket, about two hundred yards in the distance, fly up in the air with the impact of the first shot. Then it tumbled several yards down the beach. The lock-in computerization had stayed with the target and sent it tumbling with the impact of the second shot.

The killer closed his door and shrouded his weapon. There was no other human sound anywhere.

Minutes later he went to his door. Looking like any other early riser from the motel, he emerged to the beach in a jogger's warm-up suit. He strolled casually until he came to the bucket. He nudged it with his toe.

Clearly, it had been hit twice. He could tell by the patterns with which the bullets had ripped, sliced, and cut through the plastic. Imagine what two similar shots would do to a woman's head or torso.

Imagine? Well, he knew.

He returned to the motel. The morning television stations were calling for sun early in the day, with clouds coming in later. The forecast proved accurate, and affected the killer's routine.

When Mrs. Hubbell arrived that morning, the beach was crowded. Despite the fact that the killer was confident that he could have successfully lined her up and hit her, his instructions were clear: the possibility of witnesses was to be kept to an absolute minimum.

So he didn't take his shot. Instead, he completely disassembled his weapon, locked it away, and spent the afternoon sightseeing in the Fort Myers area.

That evening, he didn't get the shot he wanted, either. Nor did he have it the next morning. But the killer patiently remained in wait. And the battered toy bucket on the beach lay undisturbed by scavengers.

The Central Intelligence Agency's reading room for the former Soviet Section was accessible through the third floor, south wing, at Langley. Townsend, bearing a pass bestowed upon him by Bruce McMorris, made his way through a gloomily antiseptic light-green corridor that passed through several doors and then down a second corridor with a conspicuous closed-circuit camera.

He was met at the end of the last hallway by a U.S. Marine sergeant, part of a cross-departmental security unit adopted in 1995. The guard abruptly stashed his reading material at the advent of Townsend's footsteps. Townsend wondered if the youth had been absorbed with a Danish naturalist magazine, or worse. When he was close enough, Townsend read the young soldier's name: Kawachi. James W. Kawachi.

Kawachi was dark haired and narrow eyed. He was seated at a gray steel desk. Kawachi wished Townsend a good morning, took Townsend's pass, and immediately ran a computer scan to verify its validity. The computer took fifteen seconds to confirm the authorization, during which Townsend tried to figure out whether the soldier was Asian or Native American.

"You're limited to D Section, Alcove Sixty-five through Sixty-seven," Kawachi asked, not lifting his eyes from the computer screen. "You aware of that, sir?" His gaze finally rose to meet Townsend's.

"Is D Section part of 'Soviet Registry'?" Townsend asked.

Sargeant Kawachi reacted almost indignantly. "I have no idea, sir," Sargeant Kawachi said.

Townsend guessed that he didn't.

"Don't you know what's back there?" Townsend asked.

"I only check authorizations, sir," Sargeant Kawachi continued, his only elaboration of the morning. "I'd be subject to court-martial for going back there unless directly ordered. How many reference requests do you need, sir?" He motioned to some yellow requisition slips.

"Can you give me a bunch?"

"There's a limit of four, thank you, sir."

"Give me four."

Onto the slips, the marine filled out Townsend's name directly from his authorization pass, plus the date and time. He tore off stubs and fed them into a computerized file.

"See the archivist next please, sir," Kawachi said. He motioned toward the twin swinging doors which were padded with brown leather and which stood motionless behind him. The doors gave the quaint impression that one was entering a gentlemen's club. Sargeant Kawachi indicated that Townsend could pass through them. As Townsend did, Sargeant Kawachi returned to his copy of *Car and Driver* magazine.

Townsend was now in the windowless main reading room. There were three dozen reading tables—no fronts, no drawers, just legs and tops—before him, four rows of nine perfectly flat open surfaces, about half a dozen of which were occupied by readers scattered around the room. All the desks faced the front of the chamber, where an archivist sat at a larger desk on a raised area.

The room had the tone, feel, and almost the look of a study hall at a boarding school. When Townsend pushed through the swinging doors, the archivist, whose name turned out to be Johnson, raised his eyes and peered critically above the lenses of his glasses at the latest intruder.

Townsend knew already what he was looking for. His memory harkened back to the reports he'd written on this same agency in the 1970s, and then to the names that had passed through his typewriter at the time.

The same names that had passed through Sarah's father—or whoever he was—the night in Westchester in the last weeks of his life.

Popov and Goleniewski.

James Jesus Angleton.

Golitsin. Nosenko.

"Yes?" Johnson asked. It was half past ten in the morning and he was already cranky. He was either an old man with a young face or a middle-aged man with an old body. Townsend couldn't tell which. But with his white hair, craggy face, and crooked head, he had the bearing of an old New England parson working on a Lenten sermon.

"I have authorization for a section of files," Townsend said. He had memorized the numbers. He wrote them on the requisition slips.

Johnson took the slips and via computer entered their numbers, the time and date and Townsend's name into his own log. Presumably, Townsend figured, someone's computer somewhere would dutifully reconcile this log to that of Sargeant Kawachi. Then Johnson climbed painfully to his feet and told Townsend to follow. Johnson seemed to be afflicted with an arthritic condition and had trouble walking.

The archivist slowly led Townsend to Alcove 65 of D Section. There, on wide metal shelves, shelves that were as deep as a wide receiver's arm, was the cumulative political intelligence of several generations and countless lives. Files stood in sealed folders of various colors—pinks, greens, blues, yellows, beiges—one after another, row after row with no marking on their spine. Occasionally they were separated by a wire panel.

There was some method to what was where, but Townsend couldn't figure it out. Johnson, presumably through years of service, was the master of it. Deftly, Johnson picked through the shelves and found the first of the four files Townsend had requisitioned, taking at random the one on the top of Townsend's list. He pulled the file from the shelf and replaced it with Townsend's requisition slip.

"One at a time," the archivist snapped. The spectrum be damned; the file envelope that Johnson had arbitrarily selected was a pale fuchsia.

Townsend reached for it. Johnson ignored his hand, returned with painful, teeth-grinding slowness to his desk, and sat down again.

"You know the rules?" Johnson asked gruffly. "No cameras. No notes. No recorders. If I see any behavior I don't like I can revoke your reading privileges. Everything better be back in here in the same order when the file is returned or you sit and wait for the security officer."

"I know the rules," Townsend said.

"Hope so." Johnson's skepticism was palpable. "Had to call security twice last week. Theft."

"What a shame," Townsend said, attempting to be congenial.

"Shame? *Shame?*" the archivist snapped, seizing upon the word. "It's a scandal, not a shame. They let anybody in here. That's the whole problem."

"I can take a hint," Townsend said.

"See that you do," Mr. Johnson said.

The archivist opened the file. There was an inventory of material on the inside flap—four photographs, six numbered long reports, memos labeled A-1a through Q2-4f. Johnson breezed through the list, flipping pages, checking referenced titles, comparing what he saw to what the inventory listing told him he should see.

Townsend studied him. He couldn't tell whether Johnson was senile and perfunctory or brilliant. Or either or both.

"We check these *in,*" Johnson said icily, "and we check these *out.* Your requisition slip remains on computer call for the duration of life of this planet. If anyone in the agency asks, we can supply a list of who's seen which file and when he saw it. If anything's missing we know who took it. But it doesn't go that far. Every photograph, every shred of paper, every paper clip better be in its rightful place in this envelope when you bring it back. If anything's missing, we don't hesitate to arrest and prosecute."

"I hear you," Townsend said.

Johnson shoved the file shut again, this time with something that resembled carelessness. "Take Reading Table Twelve," he said. He nodded in a direction where no one else was sitting. Table 12 was directly beneath a surveillance camera.

"Thanks," Townsend said.

Johnson's silence suggested that when it came right down to basics, Townsend was not welcome. Nor was anyone else.

But Townsend accepted the file anyway and retreated to Reading Table 12. He seated himself and opened the material. He drew a deep breath and prepared to dig in for several days if necessary. Thereupon, he began the long, tedious task of attempting to reconcile his own memory of Popov and Golitsin to the official version that was now before him.

<<<< **25** >>>>

I*N* California, Senator Lord littered the political landscape with bodies.

In Los Angeles, moderately heavy Democratic turnouts in the black and Hispanic wards of Watts and East L.A. rolled up respectable numbers for the black Democrat who remained the front-running candidate. San Francisco and its surroundings also provided a base of votes for his candidacy. But in other areas of northern California, a liberal white candidate—a U.S. congressman from the Northwest—eroded the black voters' support. Senator Lord, meanwhile, ran well in all other sections of the state, particularly among conservative white Democrats in the southern third of the state. It was enough to give Senator Lord 38 percent of the vote and a win in the primary. It sent the Democrats to their convention with their front-runner pegged with a CAN'T WIN label. Second in Democratic delegates was John Lord, who wasn't invited to the August convention and had announced he wouldn't attend anyway.

Lord also scattered some carnage in the Republican primary where he had petitioned his way onto the ballot. There he had exactly the situation he desired: a head-to-head contest with the sitting Vice President. The latter had been stubbornly running six points ahead of Lord in the party polls in the Golden State.

But the incumbent Vice President hadn't been content with a slim lead. He had seen fit to attack Lord as "a political amateur" in the final days of the campaign, then gaffed further by declaring that a southerner hadn't been President since the Civil War and probably wouldn't "until the next century."

When the press reminded the candidate that James Earl Carter had won the Presidency two decades ago and asked for a clarification, the Vice President expressed the thought—which would be amended in a press release later the same afternoon and which attempted to assert that the candidate had been "joking"—that Jimmy Carter had been from Annapolis, Maryland. Maryland was a "border state," not southern.

No, the press—particularly the Hostiles—pointed out again. Carter had graduated from the United States Naval Academy *at* Annapolis. He was *from* Georgia, which was widely conceded to be a "southern" state.

This gave Lord all the ammunition he needed, and it gave it to him twofold. First, Lord ballyhooed the remark as an "insult to all southerners," of which there were plenty who had been transplanted to California. Then, in the last forty-eight hours of the campaign, Lord attacked the Vice President with a ferocity which stunned even veteran political observers.

"The Veep's a pretty boy, an air-head, and a wimp," Lord declared. "He has no knowledge of history, no ability to govern, and no sense of the needs of The Forgotten American. He looks like the third lead in a back-to-the-beach movie, but frankly, if he were cast as such, I don't think he'd be smart enough to remember his lines. He certainly can't remember the ones the Republican party is feeding him now. He's a dolt and unfit to be President."

On this final pair of points, no one leaped to accuse Senator Lord of giving away state secrets.

The Vice President, in response, said that he "resented" the attacks. And in trying to remain calm, he sold the electorate on another idea that Lord had been insisting for many weeks—that the Vice President didn't have the "guts" to really go bare knuckle in politics, either domestic or worldwide.

Then the voters spoke. Lord beat the Vice President in California by seven percentage points. That left Lord in an even more ominous position in the Republican party. Uninvited to their convention as well, Lord was sitting very closely behind the Vice President in the actual count of delegates. And there was a considerable rank-and-file support for him in the party, much to the chagrin of the leadership, where his thoughts weren't too far from the party's actual agenda. If Lord had wanted to go into some back rooms and make deals, he would have found some Republicans ready to listen.

This thought was expressed to him by one of the 178 reporters who covered Lord's "victory" statement at the Adams Mark Hotel in Los Angeles.

"I don't make deals with the politicians who have run this republic into the ground," Lord answered boldly, a fierce grin from ear to ear, as wife Eugenia stood next to him, his arm around her. "That's why my candidacy comes from *outside* the existing political system and that's why we're going to go to Washington, throw all those expensive bureaucrats out of their soft jobs, and stop giving money away at home and abroad to people who don't deserve it."

Vintage John Lord, once again, citing the purity of his candidacy and how it flowed directly from the will of the American electorate. And once again, many of the Hostiles among the Laptoppers had a more cynical analysis. Running as a Republican or Democrat, Lord was less likely to win, as it would force all the moderate opposition to him to galvanize behind the other party's candidate.

Running simultaneously against a weak Republican *and* a weak Democrat would allow Lord just want he wanted. There were enough states where his strength could be maxed out at 36 to 39 percent, with the two major parties splitting the difference.

So, of course,

wrote political analyst Jim Geiberger in the *Los Angeles Times,*

Senator Lord wants nothing to do with a major party label. Not only would it make him part of the establishment, but it would make him less likely to win. In short, Senator Lord has the political system by the short hair.

This town appreciates a good script. And with the primaries finished, Senator Lord has perfectly followed the scenario which he wrote for himself, his own starring vehicle. It's a perfect script for him. When will the country wake up and realize that by November it will make him President?

As was his bent, Senator Lord sent Jim Geiberger a friendly note in that gorgeous bold penmanship:

Jim:

If you're alleging that I'm an actor, I deeply resent it. Haven't we already elected one actor too many as President and aren't we still paying for it?

Come on, pal! Loosen up!

Your friend,
John Lord

But as Senator Lord savored his triumph in California, Tina Hubbell, who paid little attention to electoral politics, stepped out of her car at seven minutes after six the next evening. She was intent on her evening walk along Fort Myers Beach.

Tina was alone again. It was her husband's day to stop at the supermarket after work. Laurie was with him. Mindy was still at a friend's house. Tina would just have time for her evening stroll, her chance to unwind, before returning home to make dinner for her family.

The evening was partially overcast. There were fewer people than normal on the beach. She parked her car and locked it.

Ever since Allan had shown up in this place, she had been apprehensive. It was bad enough, still carrying all those secrets from the old days. The fears, the suspicions. The knowledge that an innocent man had been killed and she had been witness to an official cover-up. But to have *actually seen* someone so closely associated with those bad old days . . . Well, that had made them all the more real. That had pulled them into the present. As, of course, had the warning Allan had given her.

What was it about the whole mess that kept it in her mind these days? The whole episode, vague as it was, was like a recurrent toothache, throbbing within her while she was incapable of dispelling it.

She went to the strip of sand along the shore. She took off her sneakers and held them in her hand, appreciating the satisfying tactile sensation of the warm sand against the soles of her bare feet.

How this place comforted her. . . .

Near the spot where she normally began her walk there was a plastic bucket—a child's beach toy decorated with yellow and blue stars. It lay in shreds, torn apart. She supposed that it had been attacked by some small-time malevolent force like an obstreperous child . . . or a dog

. . . Or maybe the bucket had become lodged in the blades of an outboard motor. If the bucket had been in better condition, she would have taken it home for her daughters.

Tina looked at it and smiled. How malevolent a force, she mused, could there be in such a beautiful strip of beach? Fort Myers at least was finally feeling like home to her. She reckoned that she could easily live there for the rest of her life.

She reckoned correctly. She nudged the bucket with her toe. It was weighted by rocks. She stood for a moment, then began to walk south. Part of the overcast parted and the evening turned bright. She stopped again a few feet beyond the bucket and put on her sunglasses.

She walked south about three hundred yards, her usual distance. Then she turned. She wondered how soon her children would be old enough so that she could leave them for an hour. These walks, she reasoned, would be so much more fun with someone she loved. She made a note to ask Jim to come with her next time. The fresh air would do him good as well.

She was halfway back to her starting point. She could see the torn bucket up ahead of her. Beyond it, a long stretch of sand. Then the road, some houses, and the Trade Winds Motel.

There was a fishing boat way out on the gulf. It looked like a shrimper. Her eyes settled upon it as she walked. On and off she watched it for several minutes.

Then her foot brushed something plastic.

She looked down. She had already returned to her starting point. Her foot had brushed the damaged toy bucket.

Tina Hubbell, feeling good about life for a few moments, stretched out her arms to get her blood circulating. She drew a deep breath to clear her lungs.

Not too far away, there were some children playing and a teenage couple strolling.

Tina Hubbell never heard a sound. Instead, very suddenly, she felt the impact of something of tremendous force striking her through the left breast. She convulsed with the impact and staggered. In the moment or two of consciousness that remained for her, she clutched the area of pain. She looked all around her to see who might have bumped her or who might have thrown something.

But then she was aghast to feel blood, soaking through her blouse in a torrent.

"My God!" she started to think. "Shot! I've been—"

Jim Hubbell's wife never finished the thought. Thoughts emanated from the brain. Less than two seconds after the impact of the first shot from the Trade Winds Motel, a second bullet found its mark.

The shot hit Tina in the left temple, pierced her skull and fragmented within her head. For her, everything was blackness by the time her body hit the sand.

<<<< **26** >>>>

*A*S *an impostor,* thought Townsend in a very intellectual fashion, *Sarah Stuart's father rates among the best I've ever seen.*

In his time as a newsman, Townsend had seen many frauds. Art forgers. Dealers of French antiques manufactured during the reign of François Mitterand. Ersatz counts and dukes—Eurotrash, in other words—trying to marry American money. But Sarah's father had been in a category by himself.

Reviewing the files and their multiple cross-references on Leonard Wolik, former diplomat and career member of the Foreign Service, Townsend found little that had not been ably represented by the terminally ill man who had sat before him. Sarah's father had known Wolik well. Yet who was he really? And why did he wish to die as someone else?

And where was Colbert Davies? True to what Bruce McMorris had said, to all intents and purposes, Davies did not exist. At least, he did not exist in any file to which Townsend was privy in the Soviet Registry. That begged a larger question. Why did the official version of Wolik's life merge perfectly with what Sarah's father had said—with the exception of the Paris incident of 1965. In Sarah's father's version the incident existed. In Langley, it didn't. In Sarah's version, Leonard Wolik was dying in front of him. In the official version, Leonard Wolik had died of multiple fractures to the skull in a Baltimore motor vehicle accident on a snowy February morning in 1985. Townsend even found the death certificate, signed by a Dr. Schmidt, the assistant medical examiner in Baltimore County.

Motor vehicle accident. Multiple fractures to the skull. Townsend focused on the two phrases.

Then Townsend searched thoroughly for Colbert Davies's name. He couldn't find it anywhere. He tried to access it cross-referenced by pulling any available files on the late Ambassador Merriman, who had died, he noted, in July 1973. Davies's name again eluded him. Nor, in the accounts of Merriman's tenure in Paris, was there any reference to a trip back to the United States in February 1965. No Zarudni, either.

That wrapped up the first morning. Townsend left the file he was reading on Mr. Johnson's desk, went to a cafeteria open to visitors, and ate lunch. He returned at one thirty P.M.

What was he doing here? he began to wonder. Why had the CIA allowed him in? Better yet, what were these files? Token accounts, with the sensitive stuff carefully purged? He began to suspect so. But in that case, where was the good stuff kept?

There was a moment in the afternoon when he absently gazed upward from reading. Mr. Johnson was staring right at him. *A real Congregationalist hammer, this guy,* thought Townsend, who immediately shifted his eyes back to his work.

At four in the afternoon, Townsend opened the final file of the day. Like one earlier, it was a file that centered on Leonard Wolik and any work he might have done or known about during his tenure with the Department of State. Fifteen minutes into the file, however, Townsend stopped short.

There before him was a three-by-five-inch photograph. He stared at it for a moment. It did not resemble the man Townsend had met in Westchester. But the photograph was about thirty years old. Paris in the 1960s, Townsend guessed—a likeness of the man during the purported Zarudni contact.

Townsend turned the photograph over. It was inventoried in dark blue ink with the item number and file code.

"Damn," Townsend said softly to himself. Mr. Johnson glanced up. Townsend put the picture back in the file. But a bad idea was now upon him. He would, for more reasons than he could even have elaborated upon, have loved to get hold of that photograph. To have it outside these agency walls.

Get hold of, in his current frame of mind, meant *steal.*

Absolutely impossible! his common sense screamed at him. *And the risk? Don't even try to calculate the risk! You think these people let their stuff just amble out the door?*

Don't be an idiot! he warned himself anew. He raised his eyes and stared at Johnson. Townsend counted silently.

One one thousand. Two one thousand!

Come on, Johnson! Read my mind! Look up!

Four one thousa—

It took Johnson less than five seconds to sense a foreign karma somewhere in the room. The archivist raised his eyes and was scanning all the readers.

The man is unholy, Townsend told himself. *Don't even think of stealing something from here. Don't even think about it for a second!*

Townsend looked at the back of the photograph again. He memorized the index numbers as well as the manner in which they were written.

Then he closed the Wolik file and called it a day.

That evening he drove to a telephone booth on Constitution Avenue. He parked his car where he could get quickly back into it, if necessary. Then Paul Townsend telephoned a number in New York.

Three rings. Four rings. He prayed for an answer.

"Hello?" A woman's voice answered. Pretty. Short dark hair. Long legs. A way of carrying herself that could catch a man's eye. All of this he knew well.

"Hello, Caryn," he said. He paused. "You alone?"

"None of your business. Where the hell *are* you?"

"Is your phone secure?" he asked.

"Why wouldn't it be?"

"Your name appeared on a newspaper article with mine two days ago," he said. "That automatically gives you hundreds of enemies, some who invade NYNEX junction boxes. Do you live near a good phone booth?"

"I just got out of the shower," she murmured.

"Wrap a towel around your hips and get out the door. It's New York. No one will notice."

"It will take fifteen minutes," she said.

"I'll wait." He gave the number of his booth and asked her to call him back.

"You're lucky," she said, "that I wasn't in the middle of something."

She hung up. He stood in his booth, watching the formations of headlights coming down Constitution and telling himself—trying to convince himself—that no one was after him at that particular moment.

Caryn. Come on, Caryn. Call me back.

As he waited, he wondered what she had meant by "something."

Do you have a lover? he had once asked.

Several. Or maybe none. None of your—She had deflected the question well. He gave her credit for it. He kept thinking about her. He could see why Harry had been smitten. Had Townsend not been coming out of a broken marriage and if he hadn't been involved with Sarah Stuart, he told himself, he, too, might have—

The phone rang again. He picked up.

"Hi," he said.

"What's new?" Caryn DiCarlo asked.

"I'll ask you first."

She brought him up to date. Nothing new in any other branch of the New York media. Harry's murder had slipped to secondary status.

"What's new there?" she finally asked.

He told her of the files he'd read. He told her of the absence of Zarudni's name as well as that of Colbert Davies. Then he moved to the point of the call.

"I need something," he said.

"What's that?"

"Go to the photo department of the *Sun* first thing tomorrow morning. Get a head shot of a man. He should be dark haired, no glasses, no facial hair. He should look straight in a 1965 way. Don't get anyone recognizable and don't get cute by finding one of me. Have the lab run up a three-by-five print. Tell them to put it on the oldest paper they have. Then send it to me by courier as soon as you have it. I'll be here for another two days at least. You writing this down?"

She repeated it to him, word for word.

"All right," he said. Then he gave her the name of his hotel and the name under which he was registered. She said she'd take care of the photo by nine the next morning.

Then, "Anything else?" she asked.

"Nope."

"Come on, Paul. Give me something. You can't do it all, even if you're a monomaniac and think you can."

He thought about it for a moment.

"How are you at locating people?" he asked.

"Are you kidding?" Caryn DiCarlo laughed. "I'm the meanest lady on the East Coast."

"For real? You know how to find people who might be missing?"

"I used to work for a collection agency in Hartford, Connecticut," she said. "I did 'skip traces' on deadbeats."

He moaned. "You're one of those nasty people who call up and try to squeeze money out of folks who've lost their jobs, huh?" he asked.

"No," she said. "I never phoned anyone. I just traced people who blew out stolen cards. Used to find ninety percent of them."

"I love discovering hidden talent," he said. He gave her an assignment. He asked her to find Lt. Billy Hamilton, last heard of at the United States Embassy in Paris in 1965. He was the one, according to Sarah's father, who may have actually *seen* the phantasmagoric Colbert Davis—if such a beast actually existed. Sarah's father claimed the young lieutenant had taken the acting ambassador to the airport.

"And while you're at it," Townsend added. "See what you can find on one Sarah Stuart."

"Who's she?"

"An acquaintance of mine." He gave the background and her most recent address.

There was a pause on the line. Now he *knew* she was writing things down. "Is this second inquiry personal or professional?" she asked, coyness wrapped around her tone of inquiry.

"Professional," he said.

"See that it remains so," she teased.

Townsend rang off.

It was twenty minutes later, while he was driving back to his hotel, that a bizarre thought hit him. It was so obvious that he didn't know why it hadn't come to him before:

His estranged wife was considering a reconciliation. That was why she hadn't signed the divorce papers. That was why she was inquiring about what he was doing. That was why he and Nora had gotten along so well again. That was why she wanted to know who had phoned. That was why—

"Oh, Christ," he said aloud in the car. Nora had been hinting all over the place and he had been so preoccupied that he had completely missed it. And now that he realized it, he didn't even know what his reaction should be.

He would never understand women, he told himself. One walks out on him and a second one sets him up. Then the first one flirts with the idea of coming back.

He was still thinking about this as he pulled into the parking lot of the Key Bridge Marriott. He wondered what kind of spin all this put on the other woman currently in his life. The one he didn't see all that much, had never even touched but who was spending more and more time in his thoughts.

Caryn DiCarlo.

Just stick to the investigation before you, he told himself. *Keep your mind on your business and your eyes over your shoulder.* The last thing he needed, he concluded, was any more personal complications.

The last thing, indeed.

<<<< **27** >>>>

*F*ACTS, Paul Townsend demanded of himself, now in his second day of reading. He was finished with Wolik and the fruitless search for the names of Colbert Davies and Alexi Zarudni. Now Townsend settled into the file on Popov and Goleniewski.

The biggest secret of the 1960s. That's what Sarah's father had promised.

Again, what were the facts?

How did this tie in to Zarudni and Wolik? Colbert Davies, also known as Lyndon's Man.

Townsend began to wade through the first file. Was it a token file? Or was it complete? Where, if anywhere, was the rest of it? Why, for that matter, was Bruce McMorris allowing him to see it?

Facts. He always tried to return to facts.

Townsend spent a solid day plus the next morning on the first dossier he had requisitioned. It left him no further into the Wolik mystery or the Dubrow murder than he had been when he began. An enervating sense began to grip him and he wondered if that was the goal McMorris had sought. Throw so much flotsam at the troublesome reporter and Townsend's investigation would collapse.

Nonetheless, by noon he had reviewed Popov and Goleniewski. The old names came back. Blake. Lonsdale. The Krogers. The Portland Spy Ring. With a few small discrepancies, the CIA file—if it could be believed—matched the knowledge Townsend already had. In short, defector Michal Goleniewski had blown several of the highest level operations launched by the KGB against American and British interests. Yet James Angleton, the Idaho-born Yale graduate who became the CIA's chief of counterintelligence, had insisted that the Goleniewski defection was a put-up job. Goleniewski's defection was allowed by the Soviets—Angleton's theory here—so that the much larger issue at hand would not be revealed: namely that the CIA had been penetrated somewhere near its own top level or at the Presidential level by a Soviet superspy.

"If such (a mole) existed," noted one of the deputy directors of the CIA reviewing the file in 1976, "he doesn't exist anymore. And if he did exist he had to have been as American as burger and fries, as wholesome as white bread."

Townsend mused upon the metaphor. How wholesome *was* white bread, anyway?

Nineteen seventy-six: The director of the CIA had been George Bush. It had been an era, Townsend recalled, when Bush and his counterpart, Yuri Andropov, a pair of ambitious political insiders, were both destined to rise from CIA and KGB directorship to be heads of their respective countries. What light did that throw upon the power politics of the seventies and eighties?

Townsend moved to the cross-referenced files.

The biggest secret of the 1960s. A Soviet mole in the CIA or in the top echelon of the United States government? Well, that could fit the description.

He requisitioned another set of four related files. Sitting at the bare tabletop a few yards before the surly archivist named Johnson, who still insisted that only one file leave the shelves at a time, Townsend then plunged into the further depths of official deception.

The first new file on Townsend's second afternoon began with a KGB major named Anatoly Golitsin, who, in 1961, defected to the United States and appeared to confirm Angleton's darkest fears.

Golitsin—code-named AE/LADLE within CIA files—was labeled "a HumInt bonanza" by those in the agency who believed in him. HumInt—the word ran persistently through the files—referred to solid intelligence obtained from human sources, as opposed to photographic or technological means.

Golitsin spoke of a Soviet agent with the code name of SACHA who had been planted within the CIA. Golitsin also told of a Soviet "master plan" to provide disinformation to the CIA. He warned further that subsequent Soviet defectors—dispatched by a previously unheard of agency called the KGB Disinformation Directorate—would arrive to discredit him soon after he began to talk.

Golitsin told of Soviet agents across the globe—in England, France, Canada, and almost anywhere else where there were Western interests. With Angleton as Golitsin's number-one fan, officers from friendly intelligence sources beat a path to Langley, Virginia, to hear what Angleton's new star had to say.

He said plenty. He warned of a "ring of five" at the highest levels of Britain's M.I.5. A note in the file dated 1983 suggested that Burgess, Philby, Maclean, Blunt, and Hollis were very probably the five Golitsin had held in mind. However, the file Townsend examined continued with another dozen "probable" names and two dozen "suspects." Both lists had been revised over the years. The latest entries had been in 1994. Philby himself defected less than two years after Golitsin had named him. Philby also would have been pleased to know that six years after his 1988 death, the CIA was still pushing his name around its lists.

Townsend read a summation memo written in 1991. Soon after Golitsin defected, the memo recalled, he demanded thirty million dollars to help organize counterintelligence networks in the West, plus a meeting with President Kennedy. He was turned down for the money. But James Angleton did secure for Golitsin a meeting with Robert Kennedy, then attorney general of the United States. Townsend read the exchange of letters between Angleton and R.F.K. arranging the meeting.

"It is a lousy A.G. who doesn't personally understand the nature of the threat," Angleton had argued waspishly.

"I understand the threat perfectly well, Jim," Robert Kennedy had written back in his own hand. "You call me about it seven times a week. But I'll meet with your Russian love interest, anyway."

With access to the President's brother, Golitsin revealed that a KGB penetration—code-named SAPPHIRE—was operating within the French cabinet. He made a convincing case. With Angleton standing as Golitsin's character reference, President Kennedy sent a personally signed warning to President de Gaulle. The result was the unraveling of the SAPPHIRE network—later to become better known in spy film and fiction as TOPAZ. Although the biggest fish in the SAPPHIRE ring arrived safely back in the USSR, the operation was broken. Once again, Golitsin's information had been excellent.

It looked excellent again in 1962 when, almost like clockwork, two more Soviet agents defected. Two were from the Soviet United Nations delegation in New York. They were coded SCOTCH and BOURBON by the FBI and AE/SALT and AE/PEPPER by the CIA. Both, as Golitsin had predicted, sought to discredit Golitsin.

It was not till Townsend was on his third day into the files, however, that he came to the main event—the defection in 1964 by KGB Lt. Col. Yuri Nosenko. Nosenko's defection would reverberate through the walls of Langley for the next thirtysome years. He was known in the files as AE/FOXTROT. Here was another good hard dose of HumInt. The problem was that it contradicted some important HumInt sources that were already taken as gospel.

Nosenko—who had been feeding information to the CIA since 1962—claimed to have firsthand knowledge that the KGB was not involved in the assassination of President Kennedy. He further insisted that the KGB had never successfully penetrated the CIA. But Golitsin convinced Angleton that Nosenko was a false defector. Angleton sided with Golitsin, despite the fact that virtually all other aspects of Nosenko's information turned out to be good.

"This is crap! Giveaways! Worthless pap!" screamed a strangely intemperate memo from Angleton to the director in 1965. Angleton claimed that Nosenko's leads led to "small fish" only. Not long afterward, dissenting opinions began to appear in the file.

"So this is a small-time fish?" angrily wrote someone named Viktor Chyshychi from Eastern Bloc Information Analysis in 1966. The message was to the director in the unmistakable fractured English of a post-WWII recruit. "Then please, sir, where's the damned 'big time'? To give away all that FOXTROT has, where is he then the king tuna that he's protecting? Tell us that!"

It was a noble sentiment, almost poetic in the subgrammatical way it was phrased. But apparently Angleton no longer cared to respond— perhaps because he couldn't produce the big-time mole, SACHA, that Golitsin had "confirmed" for him. Instead, Angleton began to *ignore* Nosenko's leads. As chief of counterintelligence he was perfectly empowered to make that decision, but it was one that infuriated scores of subordinates.

As Townsend read over the next day and a half, Angleton—perhaps irrationally—never relented from his belief in Nosenko. Nor did he waver in his conviction that the CIA had been penetrated by a Soviet mole. And when he couldn't find sabotage from outside the CIA, he turned within it with a vengeance. Over the next sixteen years, until Angleton's retirement in 1980, defectors, agents, sources, and the CIA's own staff were set up for particular scrutiny.

Some four dozen officers in the Soviet Division were labeled "suspects." A dozen and a half of them were "seriously investigated." The only grounds were Angleton's hunches, their Russian surnames, or Golitsin's vague allegations.

Townsend continued to read. Over the ensuing years, three senior CIA officers who learned that investigations into their backgrounds—while proving nothing—had greatly hindered their careers. They sued the agency and received six-figure settlements, the bill going to the usual sucker—the unwitting American taxpayer.

No one was safe from the quiet witch hunts of the 1960s and '70s. If a CIA employee was zealous in his pursuit of the mole in Angleton's behalf, the enthusiasm was frequently interpreted as a suspicious attempt to divert attention from oneself. If one dragged one's feet and argued against the very existence of such a penetration agent, it was construed as a lack of desire to find the alleged mole—the motivation being "obvious."

Angleton's pursuit of SACHA created a ripple effect down the line. CIA field agents found their best recruits discredited in Langley, thus making it that much more difficult to create new recruits. And to many observers—here Townsend went through sixteen memos, all to the same effect—the Soviet Division was doing absolutely nothing, tied up as it was for many years chasing its own tail.

"Jim Angleton fell in love with the defector who told him what he wanted to hear," wrote William Casey, D/CIA from 1983 to 1987. "He couldn't see beyond that. He kept looking for Mr. Big."

"Mr. Big." Sacha. The mole. The penetration agent. Golitsin and Angleton took a final lunge at him—if he existed at all—in a disaster whimsically named Project BRONTOSAURUS.

"BRONTOSAURUS was Jim Angleton's final undoing, both personally and professionally," William Casey testified to a closed U.S. Senate committee on Intelligence. "Like its namesake, it wouldn't fly, it didn't eat meat, it was big and dumb and it couldn't survive."

Neither did its creator.

BRONTOSAURUS, Townsend read, was the investigation of another Golitsin lead, one that was vague and flimsy. But it was 1965 and Nosenko was already doing considerable damage to the Angleton-Golitsin believers in the CIA. So Angleton was grasping at straws, following any path upon which his man would send him, hoping to score a big Soviet agent.

According to BRONTOSAURUS, Golitsin had described a man from a wealthy family who had been recruited by the Soviet Union in the 1930s. The place of the recruitment was said to be England while the man was visiting on family business. The Soviet Union had supplied the man a Soviet "wife" by whom he was said to have an illegitimate son. Golitsin claimed to know the boy personally but, as Townsend searched, the boy's name was not entered in the file.

Years passed. The agent worked for the Soviet Union while he held several important jobs—elected and appointed—in the United States. Then during the end of the Stalin Era, the man had a falling out with his Soviet controllers. After Stalin's death, however, the man returned to the fold. He became a United States ambassador and began supplying information again to the Soviet Union.

Angleton analyzed this take from Golitsin and decided that the description fit only one man: Averell Harriman, an intimate of Roosevelt, Truman, Kennedy and Johnson. Harriman was the scion of an immensely wealthy family, had been governor of New York, secretary of commerce and—conveniently—ambassador to both Great Britain and the Soviet Union. Thereupon Angleton launched a long investigation of Harriman. The investigation proved futile over the course of several years. But that still didn't deter Angleton, who in 1968 pressed the new CIA director Richard Helms to "warn" President Johnson about Harriman. Helms steadfastly refused.

The memos, in fact, were acquiring a nastier edge all the time.

"While we're investigating Harriman," wrote someone named McKerndrick from internal investigations, "why not look into Thomas Jefferson as well? After all, he consorted with colored people and founded the Democratic party."

Townsend looked at this one for several minutes, trying to figure out whether it was a joke. If it was, it failed, for it had earned an angry rejoinder from Angleton, whom it had not been addressed to. Angleton—it occurred to Townsend—must have been setting aside a little time every day back then to read everyone else's mail.

But the fact was, Golitsin's fan club was growing smaller all the time. On top of the Harriman investigation, Golitsin maintained that the Sino–Soviet split was a ruse to trick the West into a false sense of security. So was, Golitsin maintained, the unrest in Czechoslovakia in the Dubcek spring of 1968.

"The so-called unrest in the Czecho republic is staged for the benefit of the West to lure America and Britain into trying to exploit unrest that is not there," Golitsin said in March 1968. The comments were in a transcript of an interview contained in file 67SU12a.

Then events undid both Golitsin and his mentor. U-2 photographs of the Sino–Soviet border, showing weapons and troops on both sides, indicated that the rift was no fake. And the invasion of Prague by Soviet troops in August 1968, showed that the Czech uprising was something far more than a staged event.

"The audience for this kook is growing smaller by the day," wrote a deputy D/CIA in 1969. Golitsin's remaining adherents were dubbed the Flat Earth Society within the agency. Linked closely with the bum steers on Czechoslovakia and China, Project BRONTOSAURUS collapsed into an agency tar pit almost instantly.

Much of Angleton's clout within the agency collapsed with it, with one final death spasm.

One theory arose that all that Golitsin had accomplished with his cries of a mole was to throw the CIA into havoc for years. The theory was advanced that this is exactly what Moscow would have wanted.

Yet Golitsin couldn't have tied up the agency without help from within, someone whose handling of his defection would give it the credibility it needed to tie up the staff. Theorists looking for a culprit, wishing for a Soviet agent, felt their eyes slowly settle upon the one man who was in a position to guide Golitsin's defection in that manner. The one man was James Jesus Angleton.

Townsend ran his hand through his hair, closing the file. Only in the CIA, only in the world of espionage, could an image turn on itself in such a manner: The finest spy-catcher in American history ended his career under suspicion as a Soviet agent.

Ridiculous! Or was it? Like the smile of the Cheshire cat, the whole intrigue receded as Townsend approached it. Then, to some degree, it became academic. Angleton was sacked in 1980 and died in 1988. Out with him went his bathwater—Golitsin, in other words—and all the other Flat Earth theories which they expounded.

Nosenko was in from the cold. The Sino–Soviet split was a fact of history. The tombs of the Czech students and workers, who died in 1968, had gathered snow for more than two dozen gray winters in Prague.

And Project BRONTOSAURUS, the unlikeliest of all the Angleton–Golitsin brainchildren, had developed an in-house case of leprosy. It had gone the way of its blundering prehistoric namesake, stumbling clumsily into oblivion and was no longer to be seen by any intelligent eyes.

"BRONTOSAURUS is totally unfit for HumInt consumption," cracked DCI William Casey himself in 1981, also known as Year One of the Evil Empire days. And with those comments, the project was spiked into extinction.

When Townsend returned to his hotel that evening, there was a couriered letter waiting for him. He took it upstairs and opened it.

Within it, there was a small white envelope. Within that, when he opened it, he found a three-by-five photograph—a head shot of a man, just as he had requested of Caryn.

Townsend stared at it for a moment, then laughed. Where she had found an old picture of Ken Shaw, he had no idea. But the photo would fit his purposes perfectly.

He reached for a dull ballpoint pen. Then he turned over the photograph and, working from memory, wrote the file and index number of Leonard Wolik's photograph within his CIA file.

He stared at what he had done.

No good, he thought. *The picture looks too new.*

He considered it for a moment, then borrowed a trick from a counterfeiter he had once met, a man who needed his freshly printed money to look "old" very quickly.

Townsend opened a can of cola and poured some in a glass. He immersed the picture for sixty seconds, dried it, then repeated the procedure.

He did this three times, handling the photograph roughly so that it would show wear as well as discoloration. Finally, he had it the way he wanted.

He dried it carefully and put it in his jacket pocket. The next day his options would be clear.

He would successfully pull off a clever theft from the nation's top intelligence agency. Or he would land in jail for the attempt.

<<<< **28** >>>>

MR. *JOHNSON'S* line repeated on him like the previous evening's bowl of Texas chili: *If anything's missing, we don't hesitate to arrest and prosecute, mister.*

Townsend drove back to the CIA the next morning. His pass still worked at the gate. Several minutes after parking his car, he walked past Sargeant Kawachi and into the reading room for the Soviet Registry.

Mr. Johnson's head rose in the usual manner—one long, slow inquiring motion, narrowed eyes peering above the glasses—as he entered.

He spent the morning and early afternoon reviewing the files on Angleton, Nosenko, and Golitsin—concluding with the ill-fated Project BRONTOSAURUS. In the early afternoon, he went to the cafeteria, braced himself with some coffee and returned. His business was finished. What he had on his mind now was larceny.

Butterflies? Instead of monarchs fluttering in his stomach he felt like he had a couple of crows shifting around. But it barely mattered. He filed a new requisition slip for the Wolik file and returned with it to Reading Table 12. He hung his jacket over the rear of his chair.

Once again, he reviewed the file. He made himself busy so that each time Johnson looked up Townsend appeared studiously at work.

Gradually, the hour approached. Townsend's shirt was so wet with perspiration that he felt as if he'd been hosed with warm water. He felt the heat rising.

He reached to the right side pocket of his jacket. He found the photo of Ken Shaw within. Keeping his hand in his pocket, Townsend worked the photo up the cuff of his shirt.

He lifted his gaze. No one was watching him. It was only the surveillance camera that bothered him now. But that camera, providing a lasting record, might prove trickiest of all.

He reached into the file material for the photograph of Leonard Wolik. He took it into his right hand. He slid his arm in as natural a motion as possible across the file. The Shaw picture came free of his cuff. He returned his hand to his right pocket and dropped the Wolik picture within.

He brought his hand out again and tidied the file before him, as if nothing had happened. He could hear his own heartbeat. He looked around.

Nothing stirred. He wondered what was on the other side of the closed-circuit camera—a tape storage unit or a live watcher? Or several live watchers. Were alarms going off right then in places he could only imagine?

If so, he could only fantasize about them. Nothing in his immediate area happened.

He killed another twenty minutes on the file. His anxiety level rose. He felt tight enough to explode.

He realized: now was the time to take the next hurdle. Now or not at all. Despite the efficient air-conditioning, the sweat was rolling off him. In his own mind's eye, he looked guilty. He wondered how many years in a federal prison theft of a CIA document would land a newsman.

Fifteen minutes later, he assembled the file. He set it in perfect chronological order so as to give Mr. Johnson less to think about. He rose and approached the front desk.

Never, he thought to himself, *had his nerves been jangled like this.*

He stood before Johnson and handed back the file. "I'm finished," Townsend said.

"Everything back within?"

"Perfect order?"

"Yes."

"You're sure?"

Without flinching, "Yes," Townsend answered. He had expected the question.

"Well, let's have us a look then," Johnson said.

Was there an extra edge of suspicion in Johnson's voice today? Townsend wondered. Or was he imagining it? He'd soon know. He stood before Johnson and felt a bead of sweat roll down from his left armpit.

Johnson opened the file. Even if his legs were slow, his hands were not. *How about his mind?* Townsend wondered.

Johnson held the file open to its inventory sheet and began to cruise through the file's contents.

"You do this on every file returned?" Townsend asked.

"My job," said Johnson. He went through three reports in a matter of seconds. His eye was keen for this sort of thing, Townsend realized, keener than Townsend had imagined. Johnson found a pair of pages out of order—an unintentional error by Townsend—and was sharp enough to see it immediately and flip them back.

I'm sunk, Townsend concluded hastily.

"How many's that a day?" Townsend asked.

"What's that?"

"How many files a day?"

A pause. Johnson didn't look up. "How many files do I check a day?"

"Yes?" Townsend inquired politely.

"Why do you want to know?"

"Just being friendly," Townsend said.

"Don't bother."

There was no fooling this man, Townsend now told himself. Sneaking this dummy photo past him will be like trying to sneak a pork chop past a wolf. Townsend wondered which prison he would land in.

Keep him talking, Townsend said to himself. *Any distraction will help. You have to keep him talking.*

"Damned hot outside, isn't it?" Townsend said.

"Haven't been out. Don't go out," Johnson said.

Johnson's hand came to the photograph. He held it betwixt thumb and forefinger for several seconds, stared into its black-and-white, cola-stained eyes, and gave it more attention than all of the other material combined.

"I don't remember seeing this before," Johnson said.

Oh, Jumping Jesus, Hot and Holy! Townsend thought. *He's spotted the substitution. He was on it like a cat. He's got me. He's got me!*

Spur of the moment, Townsend desperately groped for something and came up with a truly inspired distraction.

"You any relation to the former President?" Townsend asked.

This—*this finally*—caused the archivist to look up. "What?" he asked.

"Are you any relation to the former President?" Townsend asked.

"Which former President?"

"President Johnson," Townsend asked, still sweating like a pig, as if it were obvious.

"There were two," the archivist said, cantankerous as ever. "Andrew or Lyndon?"

"Well, either," asked Townsend.

"No," Johnson said blankly. "Neither." He looked back down to what he was doing. He turned the photograph over and compared the penned coding—and its handwriting—on its back to the item number in the file inventory. Then he looked up abruptly. He stared at Townsend.

"Only one person's ever done something famous in my family," the archivist volunteered lazily. "I had a very distant cousin you may have heard of named Howard Johnson."

"The hotel man? Of course!"

"No, this Howard Johnson played baseball. New York and Detroit, I think. Don't know. Maybe he still plays. I never payed much attention to sports."

Johnson glanced back to the photograph for a final second. "Ugly bastard," he said in unwitting reference to Ken Shaw, looking at the photo and returning it to the file. Then he inventoried the next set of papers. From somewhere, Townsend thought he felt a breeze. Then, seconds later, Johnson flipped shut the Wolik file and sealed it.

"Anything else today?" the archivist asked.

"No. Thank you."

"Be back tomorrow?"

"Maybe. I'm not sure yet."

Johnson gave him half a nod. Townsend turned to leave.

Townsend waited for heaven to fall upon him, for crotchety old Johnson to spring lithely to his feet, reveal himself as the Security Man from Hell, blow a whistle and point. He waited also for Sargeant Kawachi, bayonet in hand, assisted by two larger men with leg irons and manacles, to explode through the swinging doors, thunder in his direction and virtually put him brains-first through the wall before they hogtied him and applied the electric clamps to his genitals.

But it didn't happen. None of this. *Nothing happened.*

Townsend could practically feel his knees shaking in his pant legs. But he was flying! He made a point of not looking upward at the security camera.

He passed through the swinging doors. Sargeant Kawachi glanced up and paid him no notice.

I'm free. I did it. I'm almost out of here.

Townsend was almost singing to himself as he went down the corridor. His spirits soared on the main floor when he came out of an elevator. He was only a minute from the building's main entrance. Then his heart practically spasmed to a stop when he rounded a final corner and found himself looking into the unfriendly blue eyes of Bruce McMorris. It appeared to be chance encounter in the hall.

"Hello, Townsend," McMorris said.

"Hello, Bruce."

McMorris stopped. "Things going well?"

"So so."

"Got anything to tell me?"

"Should I?"

"I'm just wondering."

The encounter was awkward, the exchange stilted. Then Townsend noticed that the large figure that hulked into view behind McMorris, a Virginia State Police sergeant was his acquaintance's escort.

Townsend decided to bull it all the way through. "Frankly, I'm kind of disgusted," Townsend said.

"Why's that?"

"Your damned files aren't telling me anything that I don't already know. You sure they're complete?"

McMorris laughed and opened his hands in a gesture of futility. "Freedom of information," McMorris said. "You fellas in the newspapers have plundered us for years. Why should we have *anything* left."

"I was hoping it would be somewhat *more* productive."

McMorris shrugged, starting to move again. The trooper followed him. "You staying for more? You need a new pass for tomorrow?"

"I'm going back to New York," Townsend said. "I have a job to keep. If I can't find a damned thing to write about in your files, I'd better find something somewhere else."

"Taking the train, are you?"

Townsend began moving away from him. "Does it matter?"

"Do I know where to contact you?" McMorris asked. "Once you're back to New York?"

"Care of the *Sun.*"

"I assume your paper will be in business," McMorris said, finally continuing onward. "Max Kohlheimer's scandal sheets have a sort of a tacky staying power."

"They do, don't they?" Townsend agreed, grateful that he now appeared home free. He was out the door two minutes later and into his car five minutes after that. As he drove from agency property, the picture of Leonard Wolik in his pocket, he enjoyed a miraculous sense of relief. And, at the same time, the sense of being followed had remarkably lifted as well.

By six P.M. that evening he had nailed at minimum one CIA lie. From his hotel, he telephoned the Baltimore County Medical Examiner's officer. The death of Leonard Wolik was confirmed. The actual date of death was confirmed and checked with the certificate on view in the CIA file.

Within this truth, if it was a truth, lurked inconsistencies. Wolik's name had never popped up in the search Townsend had run on him through Big Wally, the computer, in New York. And calls to local libraries in Washington and Baltimore confirmed that Wolik's death had never received any obituary notice at all.

For an obituary writer like Paul Townsend, who knew the significance of a man and his obit, this struck Townsend as inconsistent.

But more telling was the response from the M.E.'s office when asked the current location of Herbert Schmidt, M.D., whose signature adorned Wolik's death certificate.

There had never been a Dr. Schmidt.

A woman named Molly, a very solicitous lady who sounded to be in her fifties, had worked for the M.E.'s office since 1976. She had lists of the doctors and had known all of them in her career, at least by sight. There were five valid signatures for February 1985, she said. The surnames were Penrose, Siegel, Eksmann, Young, and Bauerman.

"Are you sure?" Townsend asked.

Molly was sure.

"What about Dr. Schmidt?"

"No Dr. Schmidt. Absolutely."

Therein, Townsend had bracketed the type of inconsistency that normally surrounds a lie. No obituary for a man who from all indications was prominent. His death certificate in CIA files, at least for show purposes, very possibly contained a fraudulent signature.

"I wonder, Molly," Townsend said, "if you would be kind enough to check your files. Here's the name and date of death. You tell me whose name appears on the bottom of it."

He gave the name of Leonard Wolik and the time of death. Molly said she would call back. Townsend said he would hold. He did. For five minutes while the telephone line was tapped into a local "E-Z listenin' " station. As Townsend waited, a chorus of spritely, anonymous studio singers found new subtleties in the chorus from Beethoven's Ninth.

When Molly returned something strange had happened, something she'd never encountered before.

"What's that?" Townsend asked.

"We keep our files very carefully here," she said with an edge of defensiveness. "Both the originals and the index."

"And?" Townsend asked.

"The name Wolik is listed in the index," she said, which meant that it was in the computer, and yes he died in Baltimore County on the date given. "But as to the original," she said. "That seems to have been misplaced."

"What does that mean, Molly?" Townsend asked.

"It means someone took it and never put it back," she said indignantly.

"How long ago might that have happened?" Townsend asked.

There was a silence on the line. Molly conceded that the document might have disappeared a day ago or as long ago as the time of the man's death. There was no way to tell. And no way to put a trace on the document, either.

Townsend set down the telephone. He was still thinking of the implications of the previous conversation when the phone rang inches from his hand.

The sound jarred him. He picked up on the second ring.

A call back? he wondered. *Bruce McMorris to demand the picture back?*

"Hello?" he asked.

"It's Caryn," a pert voice said.

"Oh, hello," he said.

"How did you do?" she asked, meaning the theft of the photograph.

"Fine," he said. "You?" He meant Billy Hamilton, the former marine guard at the embassy in Paris in 1965. Or Sarah Stuart, late of East 53rd Street.

"Excellent!" she said.

It took him a moment. "Which one?" he asked.

"The man."

"You *found* him?" he asked, astounded and impressed. *"Already?"*

"I told you," she insisted. "I used to do skip traces in Connecticut."

"Don't say anything specific. The phone may not be secure. But he's alive? Accessible?"

"One day from New York," she said. "You coming back soon?"

"Flying out tomorrow morning. I'll see you then."

She rang off.

Flying out tomorrow morning. That was just for the listeners, in case he had any. Townsend packed his bags immediately and went to his car. He loaded himself with coffee, stopped for burgers at a drive-in, and drove through the night to New York.

A reporter developed a sense through the years, knowing when he had the scent of a story or when he was close to picking it up.

Townsend had the latter now. He knew it. And he wasn't going to let it slip away.

<< < < **29** > > > >

"WHO is he?" asked Det. Anthony Duncan of the NYPD. He gazed at the photograph that Townsend had lifted from the CIA file on Leonard Wolik.

"A career diplomat," Townsend said. "A man named Leonard

Wolik. Maybe. Would I be here talking to you if I knew all the answers?"

"Dunno," said Duncan. "You might be."

Duncan smiled to his friend. Caryn DiCarlo stood a few feet away from Detective Duncan's desk in the 24th Precinct, fascinated by the photographs on Duncan's bulletin board and the assortment of photographic and police equipment on a side table.

"Photo veneration," she said admiringly. "That's a new one on me, too."

"What can I tell you?" Duncan said to her with a smile. "Here at the Two-Four house we're on the cutting edge of forensic science." He looked from Caryn to Townsend and back again. "Well, what the hell? You came to me today, right?"

"We did," said Townsend.

"Let's get on it," Duncan said. "Oh, wait a minute," he said, rising from his desk. You wanted to see 'Horse,' too, didn't you?"

"Who?"

"Joe Smallhorse."

"He's your sketch man?" Townsend asked.

"Our one and only."

"Yes," Townsend said.

Duncan picked up his telephone and called an office down the hall. He placed the photograph of Wolik next to his computer. Then he led Townsend down the hall, past Vincent Foliari's busy but frustrated office, to the cluttered enclave of Sgt. Joseph Smallhorse. Smallhorse, a sturdy, stocky, ruddy-faced man, was of the Huron nation, Brooklyn, and the NYPD's Special Assignments Squad, in that particular order.

Smallhorse was a police artist. When no photograph of a suspect or a missing person existed, Smallhorse would take descriptions from witnesses and, working with pencil, paper, his imagination, and instincts, put together a sketch of any individual in whom the NYPD had an interest.

Smallhorse, a quiet, good-natured man who was meticulous about his work, would do anywhere from three to ten such projects a day. He always refined an assignment till he had it perfect, frequently working with Tony Duncan and the photo computers.

Sometimes a case would begin with a sketch of how a suspect looked today. Then Duncan would venerate Smallhorse's sketch through the computer, add facial hair, take away facial hair, put on glasses, change glasses, remove glasses, push up a receding hairline, add fifteen pounds, take away twenty pounds, remove a scar, break a nose, cap some teeth, pluck some eyebrows or whatever, until he had a ten-year-old image of a suspect. The circulation of such pictures to other departments and law-enforcement agencies around the world had led to positive identification of suspects or missing persons in countless cases.

Arrests had followed many times, even in locations as far away as Hawaii, Australia, Switzerland, and India. Certain malefactors had been left to wonder—and curse—in the enforced leisure of their prison cells just how their flawless new identities had been undone by a Huron cop and a West Indian cop in a distant metropolis.

Duncan introduced Townsend to the artist. "Our own 'Man called Horse,'" Duncan said. Joe Smallhorse grinned and pumped Townsend's hand. A radio in the corner softly played a jazz station. A few minutes later, with Duncan returned to his own office, Paul Townsend sat before the police artist and described in detail the man who had appeared before him with Sarah Stuart in Westchester several weeks earlier.

The project—as Miles Davis and Branford Marsalis played in the background—took an hour. Eventually, Smallhorse had a very good likeness.

"You can go back to Tony Duncan's office if you want," Smallhorse said. He spoke with a strong Brooklyn patois. "I'll tidy up the picture and bring it down."

Townsend thanked him. Returning down the hall, he poked his head into Vincent Foliari's office to inquire about any leads on the destruction of his car. Townsend didn't expect any leads and made the inquiry more out of courtesy than anything else.

Foliari, who was on the telephone, knew what Townsend wanted without Townsend asking. Foliari gave Townsend a sympathetic shrug and an open gesture of the hands, meaning nothing was new. Townsend nodded. He continued back to Duncan's office to find Caryn in handcuffs.

"I'm trying them on," she said as he came in the door. Duncan was just releasing her. "Like them?"

"Did you request the cuffs or did Tony make a collar?" Townsend asked.

"Just fooling around," she said. Townsend tried to figure whether Caryn was flirting with the handsome Duncan or vice versa. Both, he decided, and he tried to suppress a twinge of jealousy. He had walked Caryn into this place. What damned business did Duncan have trying to—?

Something on Duncan's desk caught Townsend's eye. Duncan handed it to him. It was the result of the photo veneration of the CIA picture of Leonard Wolik. Duncan and his computer had added the age.

The new portrait looked nothing like the man in Westchester who had claimed to be Wolik.

"What's this?" Caryn then said, appropriating something from the clutter beyond Duncan's computer. Both men looked.

"NYPD surveillance equipment," Duncan said, settling behind his desk. He lounged back, with his feet up. "Item number PE-92-34. Like it?"

"Love it," she said.

From somewhere among the tools of Duncan's trade, Caryn had found a small camera. It was a subminiature, measuring no larger than half the size of her palm. It was flat and about an inch thick, except for the lens, which could telescope out or lie as flat as the camera frame.

"In plain English," said Duncan, "it's a spy camera."

"This *is* a piece of work," she said, admiringly. She held it up to her eye. From ten feet away from Duncan, she focused in tight on his eyelash. Then she pointed it toward Townsend. "Paul, you need to shave," she said.

"Let me see that thing," said Townsend, starting to consider other possibilities for it.

"Toys for kids of all ages," Tony Duncan said in his rich baritone. "Come to Tony Duncan's West Harlem Bazaar. Open seven days a week, twenty-four hours." He glanced at Townsend. "Do you remember a men's clothing store in Union City that used to be open all night?" he asked. " 'Money talks, nobody walks.' Damned place used to be all over the all-night radio. What I always wondered was who the fuck— 'scuse me, Caryn—"

"Doesn't bother me," she said, without looking up. "I know what the word means."

"—who the fuck," Duncan continued, "buys a suit at four o'clock in the morning?"

"Is the store still in business?" Townsend asked.

"Nah. Long gone."

"What kind of detective are you? There's your answer, Brain-o. *No one* buys a suit at four in the morning."

They all laughed.

"Guess not," Duncan agreed. He watched his guests examining the camera. "You want to borrow that?" he asked. "You got some neighbors you want to get some cozy pictures of?"

Caryn laughed again. Townsend looked at the camera and found a more immediate use for it. *"Could* we?" he asked. "Borrow it, I mean?"

"Sure. I got a couple of them. You're not going to bring it back with a bullet hole through it though, are you?"

"Not if I can help it," Townsend said.

"I mean, we know what happened to your car, man. Poor Vinnie Foliari in the next room still has that file cluttering up his desk. That piece of crap you drove was worth seven hundred bucks. Now we're spending thousand of dollars of police time trying to find the guy who cashed the car in for you."

"Nobody puts bombs on the undercarriage of cameras," Townsend assured him.

"I don't know," Detective Duncan said, somberly shaking his head. "This is New York. Just when you think you've heard of everything—" He could no longer keep a straight face. He laughed. "Go ahead. Take the camera. Bring it back when you're finished, unless you're so clumsy that the subject of your photography exercise blows you away."

"How 'bout a pair of cuffs, too, Tony?" Townsend asked.

"What? For real?" the detective asked.

"Yeah. For real."

Caryn looked at him in mystification.

"Is the *Sun* taking prisoners these days."

"I'm not kidding, Tony. I might need a pair."

"Hey," said Duncan with mock seriousness, "we got standards in this department. We got firm *rules,* man!" He yanked open a bottom drawer of his desk, in which there must have been a dozen pairs of NYPD handcuffs. "What color do you like. Red? Steel? Black? Steel? Avocado? Primrose? Steel?"

"Steel would be good."

He grabbed a pair of cuffs and tossed them to Townsend, who caught them. A pair of keys were attached on a separate ring.

"Hey!" Duncan said. "You're not going to do something funny with the lady and those cuffs and a bedpost, are you?"

To this Caryn looked up. "If he were," she said, not missing a beat, "he should have asked for four pair."

Townsend and Duncan both laughed. At which time, Joe Smallhorse appeared in the office.

"Hello, Horse," Duncan said. "What've you got?"

"Sorry to miss the party," Smallhorse said, "but some of us have been working."

"What a grouch," said Duncan.

Smallhorse had a drawing of Wolik's impostor that was now nothing short of remarkable. Both detectives then went to work with Townsend.

They fed Smallhorse's drawing into Duncan's computer. With some effort, and in response to Townsend's request, Duncan brought out a picture of how the man might have looked thirty years earlier. Townsend filed this photograph carefully into an envelope with the drawing and with the original pictures of Wolik. He was about to leave when he spotted several other head shots in Duncan's waste basket.

"Who are these guys?" Townsend asked.

"Dead guys," Duncan said. "I don't need them anymore in certain parts of my files."

"Then you don't mind . . . ?" Townsend asked, leaning down to select a few.

"Help yourself," Duncan said.

Townsend did, taking six.

It had been a good morning. The *Sun*'s new investigative team of DiCarlo and Townsend—the paper's *only* investigative team—now had strong visual material to support their search.

From that point, their paths would diverge again. Caryn DiCarlo would attempt to pick up the trail of Sarah Stuart from her last known whereabouts on the East Side of Manhattan. And Townsend would head south again, in pursuit of former U.S. Marine Lieutenant Billy Hamilton. Caryn had provided the name and address of a boat yard in South Carolina where, until recently, Hamilton had been part owner.

Caryn drove Townsend to the airport that afternoon. There he would board a flight to Charleston, South Carolina. En route, he gave Caryn a copy of the key to his apartment, in case he needed someone to go in for something while he was gone.

She accepted it.

"Keep it separate from any other keys to men's apartments you might have," he teased.

"Oh, stop it," she said amiably. After another half mile along the Northern State Parkway, she added, "I'm never sleeping with more than two men at a time," she said. "And I never get the keys confused."

"Very funny," he answered.

"Actually, I practice the 'New Chastity,' " she said next. "I'm sure you saw the article about that in the *Sun* last week. Remember that? The premise: Mature adults don't screw strangers anymore, like the indiscriminate way they did in your generation. In fact, diseases are so bad that you can't even safely screw people you like thanks to—"

"I don't read most of our paper," he answered irritably, "and I don't care what you do with your private life."

"No?"

"No!"

"Then how come you were steamed off when your friend Duncan was flirting with me?"

"I was *not* 'steamed off,' as you put it," he snapped at her. "I didn't even notice. Was he?"

She smiled sweetly. "It was all over your face, Paul."

He was about to lose his temper and argue the point. Then he relaxed. The problem was, she was too damned perceptive. He watched Shea Stadium, now in its final two years as home to the New York Mets, as they drove past.

"We were not there on a social occasion," Townsend said, retreating a piece. "I didn't think it was appropriate." She took the exit ramp for the airport.

"I'm a big girl. I can handle it," she said.

"I'm sure you can."

They rode in silence.

"So you think I'm sexy, huh?" she finally asked.

"Caryn—?"

"It's all right. I'm right up front about these things. I want to know what you think."

"Jesus. Who's interviewing who?"

"I asked you a question," she sang out.

"Yes," he said. "You're sexy. The problem is that you know it."

"Ah! A *really* honest answer." She laughed.

More silence.

Never more than two men at a time.

Or, the *"New Chastity."*

Well, which was it? he wondered. Caryn DiCarlo could be such an enigma. She told two conflicting truths, was credible with either or both, and left him wondering where she really stood, having answered no question and every question at the same time. He had half a mind to start working her into some of his more bizarre theories of what was going on surrounding Wolik.

But that's silly, he told himself. *Isn't it?*

They arrived at his departure terminal. He stepped out of the car. She looked at him from the driver's seat and a sly smile crossed her face.

"Paul?" she asked.

"Yeah?"

"I didn't mean to get on you. Okay?"

He nodded. He mustered a smile. "Understood," he said. "You too, okay?"

She nodded. "We stick strictly to work from now on, right?"

"Right," he said.

"Watch your back," she said to him. "You know the address in South Carolina?"

He nodded. He reached into the car. She offered her hand. He took it and squeezed it to say goodbye.

"Good luck," she said.

Then he turned. As he watched her car pull away, he was triply accosted. A porter wanted to know if he needed help with his overnight bag, a college student was collecting money for preservation of marine vegetation, and—nastiest of all—a surly foreign-born agent for New York Air Terminal Parking Enforcement pointed to an ABSOLUTELY NO STOPPING sign that had been in effect for at least two days. With the verbal admonition in fractured English, as Caryn's car weaved into moving traffic, came a summons and a $40 fine to any passenger discharged.

<<<< **30** >>>>

IT was only late June. But on the next morning the summertime heat in South Carolina was already crushing. Townsend, having driven north following an overnight stay in Charleston, began to sweat the moment he stepped out of his rental car in front of the Benson Boat Yard. He would continue to sweat for many hours.

Billy Hamilton, he thought to himself, *please be home.*

The boat yard was located at the foot of a dead-end road on the Atlantic coast of South Carolina, just south of Myrtle Beach. The yard itself was about two acres, filled with drydocked speedboats, cabin cruisers, wrecks, and fishing boats towed in for overhauls.

There was a single large building which resembled a hanger for airplanes. There was an office in the front but no one was there. Townsend rang and knocked. There was still no answer. So he took a dirt path through some weeds, grass, abandoned tires, and boat parts and walked around back.

As he approached a work area he heard the sound of hammering, metal to metal, as well as the occasional hissing whine of a gas-and-flame torch. He came to a corner at the rear of the building.

Someone, working hard presumably, was here somewhere.

Townsend rounded the corner and found himself in an open work area, shaded by a tin roof. Simultaneously, Townsend saw a hulking bald man with a broad bare chest which gleamed with sweat. He wore tight cutoff jeans and a pair of leather work boots. He was sweating profusely, crouched down as he was, laboring on an outboard engine attached to a rear of a forty-foot racing boat. There was no fan, no breeze. Just heat and humidity, both of them in megadoses.

The man mopped the skin on his head and brow with an oil-stained towel. Everything flexed. Arms, thighs, calves. Pecs. Lats. Delts. The muscles in the man's neck rippled. Then he saw Townsend.

The man stood. The large frame straightened up to even greater proportions than Townsend expected. The man must have been six feet four, two hundred forty pounds. But he was also a big, well-developed—almost steroided—six four, two forty with biceps as thick as fireplace logs. When Townsend studied his face, he realized that despite the powerful physique, the man was not as young as Townsend originally thought. The man's fiftieth birthday was probably history, Townsend guessed. Same age that Billy Hamilton would be.

"Yeah?" the bald man demanded.

"I'm looking for a fellow named Billy Hamilton," Townsend said pleasantly. "Maybe he calls himself Bill Hamilton now. Ex-Marine. Heard he works here. I wonder if you'd know where I could find him."

The workman assessed Townsend critically. Then he went back to his labor. "Who wants to know?" the man asked.

"I do."

"Who're you?"

"My name is Paul Townsend. I'm a writer, for the *New York Sun,*" Townsend said, carefully avoiding the word, "reporter."

"What's that?"

"A newspaper."

"Never heard of it," said the man. "Never heard of you, either. And I hate anythin' from New York." The man was not a southerner, judging by his accent. He was more mid-Atlantic or midwestern, Townsend guessed.

Townsend reached to his folder and pulled out a copy of the *Sun.* He showed it. The day's headline surrounded an ongoing financial scandal at the Board of Education.

"Well, here's the paper," Townsend said affably, "and here *I* am.

Now you've heard of both of us and seen us as well. And if it makes any difference, I was born in Ohio."

The man ignored Townsend. He pulled on a pair of dark goggles and picked up an acetylene torch. Working close to the rear of the boat, he shot a blue flame toward a rudder flap on the outboard motor. He held the flame in place for several seconds and completed the connection of one piece of metal to another.

Sweat poured from his muscles. There was a cobra—blazing eyes, fangs exposed, naturally—tattooed in black, red, and yellow on the man's left shoulder. The snake seemed to stare at Townsend while its owner worked.

"Fuck," the man finally said, finishing. "Time for a butt."

He groped for a pack of cigarettes, pulled out a single smoke, and used a final spurt from the torch to light it. He inhaled deeply, then hacked a rough cough.

He stood. He again inhaled deeply and pushed the goggles upward on his forehead. He looked critically at the outboard motor. Then, with one massive arm, he easily picked it up from where it hung on the back of the boat, held it at shoulder height, and walked it—all one hundred fifty pounds of it, Townsend guessed—across his workshop and hung it on a steel mount.

Not even breathing heavily, he returned to confront his visitor, which he did from a position about two feet in front of Townsend's toes.

"So?" the man asked.

"So I'm looking for Mr. Hamilton," Townsend said. He spoke pleasantly again. He was close enough to feel the heat radiating off the sweating man's body. But Townsend refused to back up.

"Okay, look, duke, let's get it straight. You ain't lyin' or nothin', right? You ain't from no bank or finance company and you ain't no lawyer, right?"

"Nope."

"I mean, I'll be pretty fuckin' gonzo mad if you start bein' on my ass about money or somethin'. I mean, so help me, I'll fuckin' light that torch and put it to your fuckin' stones if you are." He clearly might have enjoyed it.

"I used to own this yard," the man continued. "Bank foreclosed on me, took every dime of equity I had, then hired me to work for them. So if you're here to shove some sort of papers at me—"

"I'm just a writer," Townsend reassured him sympathetically. "I work for a living. Same as you."

The man looked at Townsend for another instant. He was only four or five inches taller than Townsend, but seemed—when he was positioned there in Townsend's face—like he was a yard higher. He also seemed to be about as wide as the speedboat.

The bald man suddenly reached to Townsend's copy of the *Sun* and took it. He flipped a few pages. His eyes settled upon a Max Kohlheimer trademark—a beach scene from Australia featuring two yummy twenty-year-olds named Cindy and Lacey who purported to be budding model/ actresses. The photo was a quarter page in full glorious color and, as millions of readers knew, Max Kohlheimer's papers were state-of-the-art on female flesh tones and small, bright bathing regalia. On the same page was a flattering story about Jodie Foster and her new husband.

"Hmmp," the man grunted. "Nice paper." He apparently meant it. Townsend wasn't used to receiving compliments on the *Sun*. "Awright, I'm Billy Hamilton," he said. "So what do you want?"

"I wonder if we could talk?"

"About what?"

"I'm doing a bit of a research project for my newspaper," Townsend said. He didn't exactly lie. Rather, he allowed the truth to wrap itself around a convenient misinterpretation. "It includes a few personal details on a man named Kenneth Merriman. He was Ambassador to France in 1965."

Hamilton leaned against the boat. He extinguished his cigarette by nipping off the end of it with his teeth and spitting it quickly onto the floor. He crushed the glowing ember with the toe of his worn boot.

"Oh, yeah," Hamilton said, nodding after a moment's reflection. The name rang a bell. "Jeez. Way back then? You want to ask me about way back then?"

"If I may."

Hamilton shrugged. "I don't believe this. Thirty friggin' years ago! Shoot. Go ahead, duke."

Townsend was tickled to death. He continued. "Mr. Merriman, I believe, was ambassador while you were stationed at the embassy."

"Yeah. That's right."

"You knew him?"

"Not personally. I didn't mess with no big shits. I was with the marines." Hamilton, loosening up, laughed. "Us jarheads kep' to ourselves, know what I mean? I was mainly s'posed to stand at the doors and shut up. Act like a dummy. Shut up and follow orders. Know what I'm sayin'?"

"I know exactly."

"Seemed like a nice man, Mr. Merriman. Class guy, I guess. Real aristocrat, Hamilton said, puffing himself up a little. He attempted to make a regal nose-in-the-air expression. It failed. Up close, Hamilton, who was fair complexioned, didn't appear to have shaved that day. Or the previous day, either. "But he was a gentleman. Never gave the jarheads no trouble." The former lieutenant paused. "I understand he knew all the famous people. All the Presidents."

Townsend nodded.

"Rich old guy, too," Hamilton recalled. "That's what everybody said. Didn't lord it on like a lot of them do."

"Ambassador Merriman was very wealthy, yes," Townsend agreed.

"Ah, all those big-shot guys are rich," said Hamilton as a populist streak took hold of him. "It's all a fix, you know. Guys with big money and everybody else. Should be two political parties. The Big Money party and the Everybody Else party. Then you'd really see something. The Big Money guys would have a tenth of the votes and they'd win anyway."

From an open area within the boat, Hamilton found a jar of room-temperature Gatorade. He knocked back a third of it with one long, noisy swig. "Right now you got two Big Money parties, but no Everybody Else party," the boatman said after drinking. He wiped his mouth with a forearm. "For the average Joe, it sucks."

Townsend wasn't sure of Hamilton's grip on mathematics, but he did start to sense the makings of a John Lord voter. Yet Hamilton's memory was proving excellent. So Townsend chatted amiably for a while until subtly nudging the conversation to its hidden destination.

"Mr. Hamilton, I—"

"Hey, call me Billy, duke." He thrust a sweaty palm at Townsend. Townsend accepted it. "Want a butt?" Hamilton then asked, breaking out the smokes again. Townsend declined.

"Billy," Townsend began, "I wonder if you might remember a funny incident back in February 1965. Almost like a game of musical chairs among ambassadors. Mr. Merriman went back to the United States. Something about trying to break up a romance his daughter was having. There was another ambassador named Davies for a while. Then Mr. Merriman came back and—"

Billy Hamilton started to laugh. His weather-beaten face creased with amusement. "Yeah, sure. I remember that real well."

"You do?"

"Davies. A Texan." He laughed again. " 'Lyndon's Man.' People called him 'cause Johnson had sent him personally."

"That's right. You saw him?"

" 'Course I saw him. My job was to stand at the door. Like a cigar-store Indian. Didn't have nothin' to do but watch people."

"You talked to him, this Davies?"

"Sometimes. Bit of a cowboy. Seemed okay, I guess."

With a feeling bordering on disbelief, Townsend listened. Praise God Almighty, he had a source! A live, talking, reliable source!

So Colbert Davies did exist! He was flesh and blood after all. God bless you, Billy Hamilton, thought Townsend. *Beneath the thick brow, the bald head, the pecs, the lats, the delts, you are the perfect witness! God bless you and keep talking.*

"I'm sure he was," Townsend said, following up quickly once he gathered himself. "What might you have talked about?"

Hamilton finished his smoke. "Oh, I don't know. Small talk. Hey, it was thirty years ago." For an instant Hamilton's gaze disappeared into the distance, then flashed back. "I think he used to ask me about the French broads. You know. Whether I was gettin' anything at night."

"Uh huh."

"Nothin' much beyond that. I didn't talk embassy shop with him, if that's what you mean."

"But Colbert Davies was definitely there and definitely serving as an acting ambassador?"

"Yeah. I guess that's right."

"What about a younger diplomat?" Townsend pressed. "A man named Wolik. Leonard Wolik."

Again Hamilton searched his memory and the past. And again he came back with an answer.

"Yeah. Young guy, right?" Hamilton asked.

"That's correct."

"Maybe in his twenties at the time."

"He would have been about thirty," Townsend said. "He may have looked younger."

"Wolik was kind of a brainy fucker. I didn't know him that well."

"But you remember him, too?"

"Yeah," Billy Hamilton asserted. "I remember them both." He shook his head. "Jeez, you know sometimes it seems like yesterday. And here it is. Thirty-some fuckin' years."

Townsend was glowing. He sought to underscore what he had gained. "Like that day in February," said Townsend. "Ambassador Merriman came back, then you were supposed to take Davies to the airport. Am I correct? You were sort of his 'guard,' shall we say?"

"You could say that."

"You were in charge of making sure he didn't talk to anyone. Isn't that correct?"

"How did you know that?"

"I've done some research. I talked to Leonard Wolik once."

"Yeah? But how'd Wolik know what the ambassador told me to do?"

"What do you mean, Billy?"

"The ambassador—"

"Merriman?"

"Yeah. Mr. Merriman called me into his own office when he came back to Paris. Davies was sittin' right there in front of him. Looked real mad. Told me to get Davies out to the airport, pronto. He was recalled immediately. Wasn't s'posed to talk to *nobody,* 'specially embassy staff. So how's this guy Wolik know the orders?"

Townsend was temporarily perplexed. "I suppose," he hypothesized, "Wolik could have communicated with Davies after the fact. Davies could have told Wolik much later what the orders were."

Billy gave a shrug. "I guess," he said. Then he gazed curiously at Townsend. "Say, what're you askin' me all this for? Why don't you find Davies or Wolik? Ask them. Or the ambassador, himself."

"I can't find Davies. Wolik is dead and so is Merriman."

"Oh," said Hamilton, as if it barely mattered.

Then Townsend had one of those moments. Or rather, as it turned out, he had a couple of them right in a row. Not knowing where to go further with his witness—yet not wanting to let him go, either—he reached to his jacket pocket.

"I want to thank you, Billy," he said. "You've been very helpful. Maybe now," he said, "you could just confirm everything by identifying a photograph for me. Do you mind?"

"No. I don't mind."

Hamilton grabbed the oily towel again and dried his hands.

"This is just so I'm sure I know who we're talking about," Townsend said. "I'm going to show you eight pictures. Six have nothing to do with anything. One man appeared before me shortly before his death and claimed to be Leonard Wolik. The other one, according to a government file, *is* Wolik. That's what I want to confirm."

Hamilton shrugged. It seemed like a game to him. He grinned. "Okay," he said.

Townsend unveiled the packet of head shots: Wolik, swiped from the CIA file, and his impostor—computer venerated from the NYPD and taken back thirty years. Then there were the six assorted dead felons that Townsend had plucked from the trash in Anthony Duncan's office.

Townsend laid out the eight photographs on the only clear space he could find—a worktable otherwise littered with tools, oil cans, and outboard motor parts. Hamilton looked at the eight photos and did something that astonished Townsend. He immediately separated the six extra felons from the two faces that were relevant.

Townsend stared at Hamilton.

"These are the six phonies," Hamilton said.

With a thick forefinger, Hamilton pushed the six ringers aside. Townsend gathered them together. Hamilton looked casually at the two that remained.

"Leonard Wolik," said Hamilton next, correctly indicating the CIA photo.

That left a single head shot on the table, the man who had appeared before Townsend in Westchester several weeks earlier.

"Trying to trick me, huh?" asked Hamilton, looking at it. "That's Colbert Davies."

Townsend gazed upon his witness and started to feel a ripple of goosebumps. He looked at the photograph again. "Billy," he asked in a low, astonished voice. "What are you telling me?"

"That's Colbert Davies," said Hamilton. "That's the guy who was acting ambassador."

Several seconds of stunned silence passed before Townsend spoke again. But it seemed like five minutes to Townsend. Hamilton filled it by reaching for his smokes and setting one on fire.

"Billy, I have to tell you. This is for high stakes. You're not jerking me around, are you?"

"No, I ain't kiddin'." Hamilton laughed, as if dealing with a likable but slow child. "Hey, look, pal. I was at that friggin' embassy. I know who was who."

Out came the forefinger again. Hamilton stabbed it first at the photograph of Wolik. "That's Leonard Wolik," he said. Then he thrust it at the other picture. "That's Colbert Davies. Anybody who gives you somethin' different is givin' you bullshit. Okay?"

"Yes, okay," said Townsend, speaking slowly and coming around to this newly found truth. "Thank you, Billy," he said, taking up the photographs and filing them together in the same envelope. "You've been a tremendous help. Thank you."

So, Townsend said to himself as he flew back to New York that same evening, what did he now know? What had Billy Hamilton told him?

There had been no explosion of lights, no music cascading down from heaven. But Hamilton had given him a breakthrough. Billy had identified the man who had appeared before Townsend in Westchester.

Colbert Davies.

Why hadn't Townsend considered that before? If the stars of the story had been Davies and Wolik, and presuming that the unfortunate Zarudni had disappeared into the furnaces of Lubyanka Prison, who else better than Wolik to know the ins and outs of the dying man's tale?

Who else, indeed, if one considered that Wolik had died in 1985?

Yet every time a question seemed answered, six new questions posed themselves, opening up new vistas of deceit.

Why had the real Wolik died, for example? And *how?* Were there witnesses to the death as well? To Townsend, suspicion surrounded this like a glove, considering that at least one aspect of the death—the medical examiner's signature—was a forgery.

Multiple fractures to the skull, he recalled. *A motor vehicle accident.* Says who?

Further, *why* was Colbert Davies impersonating his younger mentor? Why would a man want to a tell a convoluted story under a false identity in the final hours of his life?

And what was his connection to Sarah Stuart?

Townsend arrived back at LaGuardia Airport shortly past eight in the evening. He took a taxi home. The fare was twenty-eight dollars, plus tip.

When Townsend walked through his own front door, the lights of his apartment were on. His gaze wandered around the room until it settled upon a woman's purse in the front entrance alcove.

There was loud music playing from the radio in his bedroom. The FM station was entirely too young for him—Cool Punk or New Funk, whatever they called it. By any name, it was All Junk to him. But then he recognized the purse.

"Caryn?" he called out, closing the door and moving to the living room.

The music subsided and she emerged from his bedroom. When he saw her, for an instant she struck him as being so young and pretty that he wished he came home to her as a matter of course. Then it further occurred to him—as it had already on several occasions—that she, like the music she played, was too young for him as well.

"I wouldn't get too comfortable if I were you, Paul," she said. "We've got a bit of a drive tonight."

He looked past her. There was a small suitcase on his bed. One of his. It was still open, but she had already packed for him.

"Where are we going?" he asked.

"Your woman Caryn has been successful again, Paul," she said. "I know where to find Sarah Stuart."

<<<< **31** >>>>

*P*AUL TOWNSEND reached to the car radio from where he sat on the passenger's side. He turned down the volume. These kids—and that's how he thought of Caryn, in spite of himself, as a thirty-one year-old kid—always played their music too damned loud. A man couldn't even think in a car. *How can they drive,* he wondered. *How can they hear other traffic? Or don't they care about things like that anymore?*

"Okay, talk," he said when the decibel level dropped. "I'm packed. I'm in a car with you. I'm tired. I'm cranky. At any moment, something nasty may come after us out of the rearview mirror. So tell me."

Caryn smiled from the wheel of her car, a blue Mazda Miata. She glanced toward him and winked, then looked back to the road as they flew through the stretch of Interstate 95 that rolled through Westchester County.

"Let me just ask you a question about ethics first," she said. He groaned and she continued without hearing him.

"Suppose there's, like, this reporter for the *New York Sun.* Suppose she's real eager to do well on a big investigative case. So she misrepresented herself. Or suppose she poked her curious nose into a file that actually didn't belong to her and no one had granted her permission to look into. Would that be a breach of professional ethics?"

He glanced heavenward. "Caryn. What are you saying? And what the hell do you think? You're smart enough to know the answer to that."

"Okay. The answer's yes, isn't it?"

"The answer's yes. Is that what you did?"

"Yes."

She was moving into the speed lane on 95. She had a firm foot on the accelerator and the car moved between seventy and seventy-five miles per hour. A sign welcomed them to the state of Connecticut. He wondered how long it would take before she became acquainted with the Connecticut State Police and their radar.

"Is that a bad thing to do?" she asked.

"Probably. Did it work?"

"Yes. Ever done it yourself? Like 'borrow' something? Or snoop around where you have no right going?"

He was silent. "I don't have to tell you that," he said. He crossed his arms.

"No?" she asked.

"No," he said firmly. "I can compromise or refuse to compromise my personal ethics in perfect privacy if I see fit."

"Not anymore," she sang out.

"Why?"

"Because if I obtained the information unethically," she said, "and if I tell you that I did, that means you have to make a decision. Would you like to be party to it, the information, and the ensuing lack of ethics at the same time?"

He looked at her. She held her gaze on the road now. It was dark within the car but he could see her well in the reflected lights of the turnpike, as well as the occasional brush of headlights from across the lane. She was, as always, very pretty in profile. He felt himself inheriting Harry's fixations as his male eyes followed their own instincts and, against every other professional ethic he had ever known about working with a female peer, found his gaze drifting downward to where her breasts seemed to perfectly fill her blouse and to where, as she was positioned in the driver's seat, her skirt came to an inviting halt several inches above her knee.

"Well?" she asked. She suddenly glanced over at him. She caught him assessing her and pretended she hadn't.

"You're asking me if I want to compromise myself by asking you about the information that you obtained by dubious means? Is that it?" he asked.

"That's it."

They were in Greenwich. Her foot was still steady.

"Silly question," he said. "Just tell me, damn it."

She laughed. Then she did.

She had gone back to Sarah Stuart's apartment building, she said, just to snoop, just to see what she could scare up, just to see if she could run into a talkative neighbor. Instead, she had come up with a bit of inspiration of her own at the building's entrance.

She had whipped out her wallet, showed her identification, and told the doorman—the same one whom Townsend had encountered—that she was Sarah's sister. So what that they didn't look alike, so what that they didn't have similar names? It didn't seem to bother the doorman.

"I told him I knew Sarah was going on a trip, and I wondered whether she had left yet," Caryn explained. "I was all smiles and everything. You would have loved it, Paul."

"Yeah, I'm sure."

"Well, he was real tight-lipped, the doorman. He said that she'd gone a couple of weeks earlier and wouldn't be back. I asked if he'd seen Sarah's son. My nephew. He said the boy hadn't been around at all, either. So I collapsed into tears."

Again, he stared at her.

"You did *what?*"

"I started to cry. I'm real good at it. Can do it on a minute's notice if I psyche myself up. Want to see?" she offered.

"No!"

"So I stood there crying. Really miserably. He didn't know what to do. The doorman's on duty and he's got a bawling babe on his hands."

Had Townsend not been forty-nine years old he would never have believed this.

"I told him that Sis and I had had a big argument for the first time ever back in May. I said I was hysterical because it was all my fault and I wanted to make up. Then I accused him of not being helpful, not wanting to help our family patch things up. I said I knew he must have some sort of clue as to where she was."

Townsend waited. Caryn grinned. "And?" Townsend finally asked.

"He insisted that he had no idea," he said. "So I started crying all the harder. He's getting a handkerchief out for me and tenants of the building are walking by, staring. They think he's got girlfriend problems, so now he's anxious to get rid of me."

She paused for effect.

"So he gave me the name of Sarah's travel agent," Caryn said. "He remembered the bill arriving along with some airline tickets. She used a travel agent on Second Avenue, right around the corner."

"God Almighty," Townsend said with admiration. "I guess that stopped your crying."

"Within a few minutes," she allowed.

Her next stop was the travel agency. She went in, she said, all perky and dry-eyed again, just before closing time the same day. "I told them that my sister had recommended a representative with their agency but I couldn't remember the agent's name. 'What's your sister's name?" the secretary asked. 'Sarah Stuart,' I said, loud enough for everyone in the whole place to hear. I got lucky. It was a man. His name was Herm. He poked his head up right away from a desk in the rear and says eagerly, 'Mrs. Stuart is *my* client.' Don't you love it, Paul? A minute later I'm sitting down at the desk of a man who knows exactly where Sarah is."

"I love it," he said. He did.

"I leaned forward to put my purse down and I caught him trying to look down my blouse. That's when I knew I'd get the information that I needed." Caryn smiled. "I told him that I wanted to meet Sis during her trip, but I'd lost her itinerary. 'Where will she be on July tenth?' I asked. Nothing special about that date. I figured it was close and served our purposes."

"This guy didn't smell a rat?" Townsend asked.

"He thought I was gorgeous," she said. "He kept nervously brushing this forelock of hair away from his forehead. I kept crossing and un-crossing my legs to keep him off balance and interested and anxious to do anything I wanted."

"Jesus, I wish I could extract information just by moving my legs in a chair. I guess you gave him a good rustle of stocking with each cross and uncross," Townsend surmised.

"I wasn't wearing stockings, but you're picking up on the general idea. The next thing I know, he's reaching into his file, pulling out Sarah's account. He sold her *two* tickets New York to London via United Airlines, Paul. Then she would be in Paris for a week. No hotel. Staying with friends, both places. Then she would be picking up a car and touring Europe. No return flight till September."

Townsend stared at Caryn, his irritation mounting with his confusion. "Then where the hell are we going? Why are we in Connecticut? Who's the second ticket and what are the goddamned dates?"

"Patience. It's not obvious?" she asked.

"No. Not to me. Not yet."

"Sarah's been laying low in the United States since her father died, Paul. She leaves for London *tomorrow*. Evening flight from J.F.K. Does that help?"

He was putting it together, his mind racing, trying to connect the pieces.

Caryn continued. Her approach impressed Townsend. "Who was she always talking about, Paul?" she asked. "From what you told Harry and what you told me, she was divorced. But she had this one anchor.

You told me that yourself. She had this one person who kept her in the East and—"

"Oh, Christ!" Townsend said, wondering how he had missed the point so far. "Right! Of course!"

"After a few minutes, I sent my man Herm off to the water cooler to get me a cup of water," Caryn said. "I picked up her whole file and read it for myself. "Andrew Stuart," Caryn said "The name on the second ticket."

"Her son," Townsend said. "Andy."

"But why would she hang around this long? I wondered," Caryn continued as they passed Stamford on the turnpike. The radio station finished what they claimed had been a forty-minute music marathon. "I figured her son was the most important thing in her life. So the reason she hadn't left the country yet had to be there."

"Good guess," Townsend said. It was.

"Thank you. I checked with his prep school," Caryn said. "Their first summer session ends tomorrow at twelve noon. See? The chronology fits perfectly. I say Sarah Stuart turns up at the school at noon to pick him up."

"You're guessing?" Townsend asked.

No, she wasn't, she said. Not anymore. The school wouldn't confirm who was or wasn't a student, she knew. And a student couldn't be reached directly by telephone. But a message could be left for boy or girl who was enrolled. Caryn called and left a message for Andy, one that would sound like a wrong number or a mistaken identity. But by taking the message, the school, in Wallingford, Connecticut, confirmed by default that Andy was there.

"I assume you know what Andy looks like," Caryn said.

"I've seen pictures," Townsend said. They would have to spot him out of two hundred summer students. But the odds could be narrowed down: Eliminate all girls. Eliminate younger, shorter boys, plus Asians, African-Americans, and Hispanics. That narrowed it down to four to six dozen.

"If we find him, he'll lead us to Sarah," Caryn said. "She'll either be at the school waiting for him or he'll take a train and lead us to her. Agree?" she asked.

"My guess is she'll leave nothing to chance on a day she's trying to make a flight out of the country. She'll be there by car to pick him up. And if we miss her there—"

"I have the United flight number from J.F.K. We can know right where to find her at the airport."

The problem at the airport, they both agreed, was that if Sarah didn't want to talk to them, she could call airport security. Stalling for half an hour could then allow her to get onto her flight. It was imperative that they cut her off first and present her with a situation where she *had* to talk to them. Townsend was already thinking of ways to turn the screws.

Townsend thought more about the logistics of it. "Did you, Caryn, by chance . . . ?" he began, delving ever deeper into a morass of nonethics.

"Call the airline?" Caryn snapped with mock indignation. "Did I pretend I was her and reconfirm the flight time just to ascertain that she was still booked?"

"Well, yes," he asked, pleased that they continued to think along the same lines.

"Of course, I did," she said. "Think I'm dumb?"

He looked at her and shook his head. Then they both laughed. She turned the volume back up on the radio. It was Hot Punk or New Funk again and this time it didn't sound so awful. If his mood was right, he told himself, he might almost learn to like it.

"Nicely done," he said, relaxing back in his seat as the Connecticut Turnpike led through Norwalk. "You've displayed the ethics of a snake but you got the job done."

She laughed again. "Exactly what you would have done, in other words."

"If I'd thought of it, yes."

New Funk was what her music was called, actually. And Townsend could hear it again, an hour and a half later, when they were booked into a motel in Wallingford. He and Caryn took separate rooms. But his was right next to hers and he could hear her music, plus her singing along to it, through the wall.

Yes, indeed, Harry, he thought to himself as he sat in his own room. *Whatever you had, I've fully caught it by now.*

Lord was home in Texas, gleefully anticipating the two major political conventions which would follow in July and August.

"An exercise in self-destruction," is what Jerry Huddleston, Lord's media honcho, called the convocations of the two major parties. And conventional wisdom, for what it was worth, was on Huddleston's side. Lord continued to run well in the national polls. Frighteningly well, to those who equated the first coming of John Lord to the second coming of Huey Long. In a three-way contest, Lord was polling more than 40 percent across the south from Texas to North Carolina. The situation was so severe that the Democrats were thinking of writing off the South.

The Republicans were hysterical. They badly needed the South plus the West to retain the White House. With Lord in the picture, they weren't going to get either.

But the Democrats weren't in any better shape. They bravely made noises about Lord's three-way strategy backfiring on him. With two conservatives in the race, they argued, they, the Democrats, would inherit the liberal vote—which, petrified of Lord, would turn out in numbers. Thus they would have a shot at getting the middle ground of the electorate as well.

But this was also where their theory came apart at the seams. Lord was encroaching daily on this middle ground. As the credibility of his candidacy strengthened, more voters who called themselves moderates said they found him "attractive," "articulate," and "intelligent." They said he "talked plain sense" and they "planned to vote for him." In short, they found him, "Presidential."

Ohio and Pennsylvania, for example, were hardly centers of extremism. Yet Lord was flirting with 36 percent solid in those states, too. That was enough to win in November with the other candidates in the high twenties. The remainder was undecided.

"Can't anyone step forward to stop him?" was a familiar refrain of Lord-bashers. Did the country not have an elder statesman who could come forward to excite the public? Was there no one qualified who was willing to be President?

The answer to all these questions seemed to be, No. Someone in California made a lot of money fast when he started marketing some trendy red, white, and blue campaign buttons for two bucks a pop:

HE'S TANNED
HE'S RESTED
HE'S READY
*
NIXON IN '96

Some people wore the buttons as a joke, recalling Richard Nixon as the disgraced figure of an earlier turbulent time. Yet others saw the former President as an individual of Bismarckian stature, the man history would ask to take a national leadership role at an advanced age to block the ascendence of a tyrant.

Alas, the former President was eighty-three years old. He was also not exactly a fresh face for the coming millennium. And as Mr. Nixon himself also pointed out—regretfully, some said—he was also ineligible to run, having been elected President twice already in three attempts.

Then again, perhaps it made little difference as only 32 percent of the voting public could identify his name.

All of this underscored the obvious. Twenty years into its third century, the American political system seemed morally bankrupt. The nation was no longer producing Roosevelts, Wilsons, or Lincolns, much less Washingtons or Jeffersons. It was producing Warren Hardings, Spiro Agnews, and Huey Longs. It was a sick, weak system, just begging for a latter-day Manchurian Candidate.

As the July Fourth holiday beckoned, some genuinely gloomy editorials began to appear in liberal and moderate newspapers across the country. That is, many editorialists with a fondness toward high-minded democracy were already conceding the White House to John Lord.

Let us all pray,

wrote Martin Ansglinger in the *Detroit Free Press,*

that we elect a U.S. Congress that will hold a tight leash upon President Lord. Let us all hope to hell that we don't all go goose-stepping into the year 2000.

Some of these same commentators also pronounced the year 1996 as the official end of the American empire, the watershed date when the nation finally took too literally the old belief that "anyone can be elected President."

Edith Winslow, a political columnist for the *Boston Globe,* had a backhanded spin on the subject.

Those of us who have reached our forties have survived Ford, Nixon, and Reagan.

Winslow wrote,

So it is entirely possible that we might survive a political neanderthal like John Lord as well.

There were also more than a few editorials discussing the nation's mood and philosophical bent, both present and future.

As Warren Roberts of the *Oregonian* put it:

Presidents establish a moral tone for our nation. Consider the age of greed under Reagan, the era of idealism under Kennedy, and the period of overt cretinism under Nixon. So what are we to expect from a fundamentalist redneck who's not much more than a George Wallace recycled for the nineties?

If it is true that people get the government they deserve, we are proving that we don't deserve anything very good.

It was a fine time for John Lord. The river was rising for his enemies and they were desperately looking for sandbags. It was also a time when he could enjoy the national holiday, preside over a Methodist barbecue in Texas, and cherish his rise in the national opinion polls. He could control his access to the friendly press by ruminating in public on his potential choice for Vice President. He had in mind a university president from the Northeast, he said one day, but was also considering a military man who had been the hero of the Gulf war, he said the next. The academician, he went on to explain, happened to be Jewish and the war hero happened to be black. This struck further terror into the hearts of the major parties. Now Lord was positioning himself nicely even among the minority groups who should have most fervently opposed him.

In short, Senator Lord didn't really need to start a fight or a controversy at this juncture of his campaign. Thus, given his penchant for the unpredictable, he started one anyway.

He picked a strange punching bag, the leader of the Russian Republic, Ivan Litvinov.

It was on the Fourth of July itself that Lord fired his fusillade. "Ivan Litvinov is a lying Red rat bastard," Lord told a small gathering of reporters. "Our leaders in Washington can't see through him. Litvinov hates America and Americans. Always has, always will. He's not a man we can do business with."

"Sir, would you clarify what you're saying?" asked Gail Haymen of *USA Today*.

"Nothing to clarify, Gail," said Lord. "Just print what I said. That Russian's a lying Red rat bastard, and I can prove it. Our current President should be impeached just for breaking bread with him."

The Laptoppers, the scribblers, and the men and women with hand-held tape recorders took down every word. Then they published and broadcast all of it.

As it happened over a holiday, Lord had much of the news to himself. His statements were the big story of the Independence Day weekend. When he was asked exactly what the Russian leader Litvinov had been "lying" about, he begged off, saying that he would elaborate at a later time. When the Hostiles reminded him that he had stated that he could "prove it," Lord seemed caught off base for the first time in the campaign. So the press prepared to keep after him on this point. His opponents, sensing his awkwardness for a change, studied the development and prepared to counterattack.

But the public didn't seem to mind. It had been *so long* since an American leader had come down on a Russian politician so hard that the attack was almost quaint, practically an exercise in nostalgia.

"A lying Red rat bastard." That was a good one. The man in the street kind of wondered if John Lord could make it stick.

T HERE must have been two hundred cars at Andy's private school, with those picking up summer session students parked at random among faculty and employee vehicles. The parking areas were scattered across ten acres within the central part of the campus—some by classroom buildings, some by an infirmary, some near a chapel, and others near the school's main building and dining hall. Finding a particular vehicle, that belonging to Sarah Stuart, was turning into a more daunting task than Townsend had originally envisioned.

By eleven twenty-five, he had already spent half an hour among the distinctly New England architecture of the school campus, trying to spot Sarah or her car. By five minutes before noon he still had no luck. He knew also that some students took the train from Wallingford to New York. Townsend had already checked the railroad timetables. No train would depart until twelve thirty-six. If he hadn't spotted Sarah by twenty past twelve, he and Caryn would race directly to the train station.

Caryn slowly drove her Miata through the tree-lined town streets that crisscrossed through the campus. From the passenger's side, Townsend studied every young male face and he scanned every car that had a female driver. He stepped out of Caryn's car twice near a white-columned red brick main building and walked through groups of parents and family members. He still couldn't find Sarah Stuart.

In his mind, Paul Townsend tried to focus on her appearance. He tried to tell himself that yes, he accurately remembered how she looked and how she dressed. It was a strange sensation, he told himself, considering he had shared laughs, good times, and a bed with this woman in the months before she had deceived him. At a point in time that remained not too distant, he could easily have fallen in love with her. But that was life, wasn't it? That was how one's plans were frequently derailed.

Several more minutes passed. They drove to an area of cars parked near an athletic field. They parked and stepped out of the blue sports car. With Caryn next to him, Townsend wandered through row after row of vehicles. The area was shaded by several immense oaks. It was there, at about seven minutes after noon, that he saw an attractive woman in a pale pink suit emerge from a rented Ford.

She had a figure that he admired first, then recognized second. She leaned into her car to retrieve a purse. Townsend stopped and watched. He was about ten feet behind the woman. He motioned to Caryn to stop as well.

The woman in pink stepped away from her car and stood up. She held her car keys in her hand. She fumbled with a pair of sunglasses and pushed the driver's side door shut. Townsend spoke before she could spot him.

"Hello, Sarah," he said. "How've you been?"

Sarah Stuart turned. Her eyes widened in disbelief. Townsend let the moment last as long as it could. "Oh, God," she finally fumbled. "Paul! What are—?"

Then, before she could finish the sentence, she realized that the meeting wasn't chance. She began again. "How did you . . . ?"

"Find you?" he asked.

"Yes," she murmured, still in disbelief.

"I have my ways," he said.

Townsend moved closer to her. He stayed at arm's length. Sarah's gaze traveled past him and came to rest on the woman beside him.

"This is my associate, Caryn DiCarlo," Townsend explained, almost as if she were a stranger. "Ms. DiCarlo and I are *both* writers for the *Sun*. And, in case there's any glimmer of doubt in your mind, Sarah, this is not a social call."

"What do you want?" she asked. Townsend could tell. She was

unnerved but rallying. The element of surprise had departed and she was rebuilding her defenses. He reached to her and very firmly removed her car keys from her hand.

"Paul . . . ? What are you—!"

"There's only one thing left for you to give me, Sarah," he said. "I don't want your affection anymore. I could never trust you again as a friend. But I do need some answers. Some explanations."

"I'm sorry, Paul. I'm sorry about taking you to my father. I'm sorry about the story he told you. I'm sorry about the man who was murdered in Brooklyn and —"

"His name was Harry Dubrow," Townsend said sharply. "He was my best friend." He could feel his fury building and sought to temper it.

Sarah trembled a little. "There's really nothing I can tell you," she said.

Townsend sighed. He nodded to Caryn and handed her Sarah's car keys.

"What are you doing?" Sarah demanded.

"Can I see your wrist?" Townsend asked.

"What?"

"Let me see your wrist, Sarah," he said.

Unwillingly, she let him take it. From his jacket pocket he pulled the pair of handcuffs he had borrowed from Anthony Duncan's office. He clicked one of the cuffs onto her wrist. She began to resist.

"Damn it, Paul!" she snapped, her own anger rising now. "How dare you—!"

But he was much stronger than she. He pulled her wrist downward and snapped the other half of the manacle onto the door of her car. Then he tossed the handcuff's key to Caryn.

Sarah Stuart bit off the next sentence. "I am going to scream if you don't release me, Paul!"

"Go ahead," he dared.

She didn't.

"I'm very upset with you, Sarah," he said, now as if he were speaking to a disobedient child. "I'm leaving you here to think things over. I'm taking a walk up to that building over there. I think it's the infirmary. I saw a pond behind it. I'm throwing the keys into the pond. I guess you'll be booking another flight. By the time you get a locksmith to separate you from the car and by the time you get another car, your original flight will have departed. Bye!"

He turned. For effect, he took Caryn's hand and they began to walk toward the pond.

"Paul!" Sarah started to shout. "Paul! Don't do this to me! Paul,
Andy will be here any minute, damn it! How am I supposed to—?"

Townsend turned back toward her. "Then answer some questions
for me," he demanded, still in a very polite tone. "I've come a long way.
I want answers, Sarah, damn it! Answers! I want you to confirm what
I think I already know."

He waited. Sarah drilled him with her eyes. In frustration, she gave
a sharp tug on the cuffs. The metal rattled against the car. Nothing
budged.

"All right," she finally said. "What do you want?"

"Much better," he said softly.

Townsend walked back to her. She waited.

"So that was in fact your father whom you took me to meet," said
Townsend. "You just confirmed that for me. So I'm correct at my
starting point, right?"

"You are."

"Colbert Davies, right? Your father was Colbert Davies."

She nodded, hesitantly at first.

" 'Lyndon's Man,' " he said. "That's what they called him. That's
how he thought of himself. I'm still correct?"

Sarah nodded. There was no reluctance to this answer.

"Did they just call him that? Or was there a much greater reason?"
Townsend asked. "A special assignment for the President, perhaps?
That's what I'm starting to suspect, Sarah. Can you help me on that?"

She shook her head. Her face expressed complete consternation.
Townsend knew he was jumping too far ahead.

"Okay," he said. "We'll go slowly. Let's backtrack. On the night I
met your father," Townsend began, "he lied about who he was. Gave
his name as Wolik. But Len Wolik was probably his good friend. His
protegé, if I'm not stretching the point. But otherwise, aside from lying
about who he was, I suspect your Dear Old Dad told me the truth."

It took her a moment. Then, "That's right," she said softly.

"Your father just told it from a slightly different perspective,"
Townsend persisted. "He told it as Leonard Wolik might have if Wolik
had been alive."

Sarah nodded again.

"Why would he do that, Sarah?" Townsend asked.

"I don't know," she said.

"Oh, you must have a guess. He was your father. You knew him.
You loved him."

Again she held a silence.

"Maybe," Townsend suggested, "he wanted Wolik's obituary to

serve as his own. After all, 'Lyndon's Man' was a secretive sort during most of his lifetime. Didn't really exist officially. So secretive that his name isn't even in the CIA files presented for public consumption. Am I still on the right track?"

"I think you are, Paul," she said.

Students were starting to appear from their final classes. But Townsend and his former lover still spoke out of the earshot of all others, aside from Caryn DiCarlo.

"But if he had such a story to tell, and finally wanted to have it known, why not tell me straight out?" Townsend pondered. "Why not tell me everything he knew and let me run with it? Instead, I suspect he only told me half of what he might have. He posed me a riddle, he did, let me get ambushed with a fake obituary, and then left me hanging. Never told me the answer. Why would your father do that? Only one answer occurs to me. Got a guess what it is?"

She shook her head. "I don't know," she said.

"Try," he suggested.

More exasperation, a shaking of the head. Then, "The way my father thought . . ." Sarah began. "He admired your work. Your writing. Your reports. The way you went after stories." Townsend's eyes were fixed upon her. They made her distinctly more uncomfortable.

"I'm not patronizing you," she said. "I'm not just telling you what you wanted to hear. My father felt that you were the best investigative reporter of your generation, at least the best he'd ever seen. He told you that himself, didn't he?"

"He told me a lot of things," Townsend answered.

"Maybe that's why he wanted to set you up," Sarah offered. "Then you would be furious. Back when we, when you and I were . . ." She retreated and rephrased, seeing Caryn again. "When you and I had something between us, Paul, I . . . I used to tell Dad all about you. How you worked. How you investigated . . . How you would dig and dig and dig until you'd uncovered everything." She raised her eyes to look squarely at him. "I assume that's exactly what's going on now, right? You're digging and digging."

"Right," he said, conceding at the same time that if that had been Davies's intentions, the dying man had gotten what he wanted. "That was my theory, too. If Colbert Davies had told me something outrageous, I might have looked into it and dropped it. But if I had to vindicate myself, as I did after the Wolik obituary, then I was stuck with a story which I would eventually have to prove. Right?"

"Remember, Paul. As far as I know everything he told you was true.

He just told it to you from Len Wolik's perspective. His way of getting back at his employers, I guess."

"Employers?

"CIA," she said. "I'm sure you knew that by now, didn't you?"

"I'd formed a few theories here, too," he said. "Black operations, I'd guess. Deep cover for thirty years. Maybe even a special Presidential assignment in 1964 and 1965. That's the angle I'm working on. Colbert Davies knew Lyndon Johnson personally, didn't he?"

Sarah nodded. But the expression on her face gave him nothing more. For a moment, Townsend watched a girl of about eighteen enter a nearby car with her mother and fling her textbooks into the back seat. Finished for the summer. Townsend remembered the feeling of freedom and envied it. Then, fleetingly and by association, he thought of his own daughter in California.

"The thing is," Townsend said, tuning his concentration back in, "a career man in a secret world often thinks of imminent death as a final victory of sorts. A final silence. Take all the nasty secrets to the grave, William Casey style. But your father didn't do that. Why? What changed his mind? He wanted the air cleared eventually. I think I have the explanation to that, too. And if you confirm it for me, it will be the next part of the trail that I follow."

"I couldn't," she said. "I'd only be guessing. I couldn't prove—"

"We're speaking informally, Sarah," he said. "Just tell me what you might suspect."

She drew a long breath and sighed.

"He was obsessed with Len Wolik's death," she said, confirming what Townsend had hoped. "Len Wolik died suddenly in 1985. It was said to be an accident. Dad was always suspicious. Didn't think it was an accident at all. He was always looking for a way to get back at the people who might have done it. 'Wreak some havoc on the devious deceitful bastards,' he used to say. I guess that's what he had in mind at the end."

Townsend nodded. "Thank you," he said. "That's as I suspected as well." He paused. "Did Wolik have a family? Any close friends you might have known of?" he asked.

"No family," she said. "Friends? I wouldn't know."

Townsend looked her up and down. "I suppose that leads me to the inevitable question," he said.

"You and me, right?" Sarah asked.

"Yes. What *about* us?" Townsend asked. "Did your father put you up to—?"

"No," she said, very definitively. "I never went out to meet you for his purposes. The way we met, you and I, Paul, was just the way we would have. It was only later, when my father first got ill, that I mentioned your name. Then, when his time to die was close, he begged me for an introduction. I said I'd bring you. Then, at the last minute, he told me what he was going to do. He was going to tell a story and tell it under his old friend's name. I begged him not to. But he insisted."

"So in the end," Townsend said, "you knew he was going to set me up."

She was uneasy with his question. "Paul," she said. "It was the only request of a dying man. He insisted on it. Even up until the night we had you there, I didn't realize that he was really going to do it."

"But when you did . . . ?"

"What could I do?" she asked. Again, she said, it was her father and his dying request. And in a strange sort of way, he understood. He nodded.

"Paul?" she finally asked. "Aren't you forgetting something?"

"Like what?"

"You never really asked me the big question," she said.

"What's that?"

"What was his secret? What was it he wanted you to uncover?"

"I don't know yet," he said. "And I figured you don't know, either. Otherwise, someone would have killed you, too. Same as Len Wolik. And same as Harry Dubrow. Harry was killed by someone who was waiting for me. Someone who figured that I knew whatever your father had known."

"What do you think it is?" she asked him after a moment's reflection.

"I don't know yet," he said. "But I have a few theories forming."

"What if—? Oh, God, Paul. Here comes Andy!"

She shook her hand against the steel cuffs and gave a nod toward a handsome young man of eighteen who waved to her from a distance of a hundred feet up a walkway.

Townsend calmly retrieved the key from Caryn. He unlocked the manacles and pocketed them. Apparently Andy hadn't seen them because he gave no indication that he knew anything was amiss. Instead, he greeted Mr. Townsend by name. Andy and Townsend had met on a previous occasion. Sarah's son remembered that his mother's friend wrote for the *New York Sun*. Townsend introduced the boy to Caryn, before whom he suddenly seemed shy.

Everyone was studiously polite. Townsend wished Sarah and Andy a good, safe journey to Europe and back. Then, moments later, he and

Caryn took their leave. No further questions were posed and none were answered.

It was evening. Townsend sat with Caryn DiCarlo at a table for two in the dining room of their motor lodge. The motif was Early American but the ambience was Middle American. They could have been in any of the fifty states.

"So what have we got?" Caryn asked. They had finished dinner. Now they lingered over drinks. "You know who the man was whom you talked to in Westchester. You know he was in the CIA. You know he was angry over his protegé being murdered."

"We *think* that," Townsend said, interrupting. "We haven't proved that one yet. We don't even *know* that Leonard Wolik was murdered. Look," he said, "you can work all sorts of scenarios in a game like this. Maybe Davies was instrumental in Wolik's death. Then years later he feels remorse. He wants to do something. So he 'dies' in Wolik's place and garners Wolik's obituary."

"Farfetched," she said.

"Caryn, honey," he said, a trace of pomposity creeping into his voice. "Watergate was farfetched. The rise of Hitler was farfetched. The collapse of communism in the late 1980s was farfetched. Half the cases I was looking at in these CIA files were farfetched. Know what? Life is farfetched. You can't eliminate any possibility until you've disproved it."

She finished a drink.

"So what's next?" she asked.

"Wolik. How he died. *Why* he died. Who might have been involved." Thoughtfully, he tapped a finger on the table. "If we consider this a long-running story and make Harry the most recent victim, then we might establish Wolik as an earlier victim. Maybe we try to link the two. Maybe we try to see what there is in common."

She nodded slowly.

"Where did Wolik die?" she asked.

"Maryland. Outer fringes of Baltimore," he said. "I say that's my next stop. Or *our* next stop if you're coming with me. Are you ready for a seven-hour drive tomorrow?"

"Would I miss it?" she asked.

He sighed. "I'm sure I can use you," he said. He mused upon it for a moment. "For one thing," he said, "if we both go, I don't have to rent a car when we get there."

"You've got a point," she said. "I'm so glad I'm good for something."

"J-schoolers," he teased. "I finally found the right use for them in the journalist hierarchy. As drivers in the car pool."

Caryn smirked, then laughed.

"We're you in love with her?" Caryn asked out of the blue.

"What?"

"Sarah?" she asked. "Don't be so surprised. You knew I'd ask."

"No, I didn't know you'd ask."

"Well, I did ask."

He thought about it. "No," he said. "I might have fallen if things had worked out differently. But they didn't." He paused. "Funny. I was thinking about it this afternoon when I saw her."

"I thought so," she said.

"What do you mean, you 'thought so'?"

"I could tell. By the way you were looking at her."

"Oh, come on!" he scoffed.

Caryn nodded. "Yes," she insisted.

He shook his head. "Caryn, either you lie like a rug or you're ten times sharper than I ever gave you credit for. But I don't know which it is."

"Hang around long enough," she dared him with a coy smile. "And maybe you'll find out."

He fixed his gaze on her. "Maybe I will," he said. "Maybe I will."

Caryn looked away for a moment, then came back to him. "Did she break up your marriage?" she asked.

"Who?"

"Sarah Stuart?"

"Sarah came after my marriage," he said with remarkable calm.

"Then you're officially divorced?"

"My wife is signing papers any day now," he said through a wall of exhaustion. *"Then* I will be officially a single man. Sarah came and went long after my legal separation."

"Did you mind my asking?"

He thought about it. "No," he said. "We're working together. I don't mind your asking."

At the far end of the nearby bar, an overweight salesman from a hardware company had had too much to drink. He wore a rumpled brown suit and a two-tone tie. He was loudly trying to talk either of two teenage girls into going back to his room with him. The girls wore T-shirts and tight jeans and looked to be local misses out to either tease a middle-aged traveling man or relieve him of some money. Or both. His voice was so loud that it attracted Townsend and DiCarlo's attention simultaneously. They studied the setup.

"Think that fat guy will score?" Caryn asked in a loud, amused whisper and with her usual subtlety.

Townsend studied the setup for only a moment. "No," he guessed. "Unless he shows a huge bankroll and gets them roaring drunk."

He turned back to her. "I've about had it," he said.

"Me, too." They each finished their drinks. Townsend left money on the table and stood. Caryn stood up with him. With a wobble more from exhaustion than anything, he turned toward the door.

Moments later, they were outside. They walked down the same corridor toward their respective rooms. There was silence between them. Townsend almost found the situation awkward.

"What are you thinking about?" she finally asked.

"Baltimore tomorrow," he said, not entirely lying.

"No," she answered, "tell me the truth. Tell me the absolute truth. What are you really thinking about right now?"

He looked at her uneasily. "What do you think I'm thinking about?"

"No fair answering a question with a question," she said. "And I asked you first."

They arrived at her door.

"What are you getting at?" he asked. "Pardon me if I'm wrong, but what we're talking about here is sex, right? We're getting hung up. We've flirted with the subject, right? But we haven't yet tackled it head-on."

She grinned.

"You're trying to figure out if I'm going to ask you? I'm trying to figure out whether you'll be insulted if I do. Or insulted if I don't. Frankly, I still can't figure out whether you've got a man in your life or ten of them. But I also know that doesn't mean that I've got an invitation to—"

"It's no big deal," she said.

"What isn't?"

"Men. Sex."

"Fine."

"And I don't, by the way," she said.

"Don't what?"

"Have ten men in my life."

"I'm so glad."

"I used to have one. His name was Fred. He was an architect and we were together for six years. You know, the husband and wife thing."

"You were married?" He was amazed.

"Call it 'common law.' "

"Oh, come on. It was either a legal hitch or it wasn't. Which was it?"

"We lived together," she said. "First in Boston. Sommerville, actually. Then about thirty miles from here when I worked for the *Hartford Courant*. We split two years ago. I came to New York to work for the *Sun*. Aren't you happy? Now you know."

"Yeah, I'm happy. Finally! A straight answer."

"You're welcome," she said. Her eyes sparkled. "So?" she asked at length.

"So what?"

"I'm curious," she said. "I really am. You claim you can't read me, but sometimes I can't read you. I think you'd like to go to bed with me, but I can't tell."

"I would," he said, almost involuntarily.

"Oh." She thought about it. "Well, now I know *that!*"

"Should I not have told you?" he asked.

"I asked. So I run the risks." After another pause, she asked, "And what do you suppose that would do to our professional relationship? I mean, we're working here, right?"

"At best," he shrugged, "it might improve it. At worst . . ."

She finished the thought for him. "It would wreck it completely."

"That's correct."

He stood at his door and waited.

"As you said, Paul. Now we know. Now we understand each other better." She pulled her key from her pocket and unlocked her door. "Good night." She leaned to him and kissed him on the cheek, as a female friend might.

"Good night," he answered. He watched her step inside and shut her door. The lock clicked into place.

Townsend exhaled a long breath and stepped back. Then he went to his own door, which was the next one on the motel corridor, and unlocked it.

Put it out of your mind, he told himself as he stepped inside his room. *It was probably a bad idea, anyway.* He had been telling himself that all along. He went to the motel room's only chair and sank into it. There he stayed. He didn't move for several minutes.

He thought of turning on the television to watch the news, but didn't have the energy to make the effort. Instead he stared at the empty screen across the room. He wondered what his family—or was it his ex-family by now?—was doing at that moment in California. He stared at the telephone and had the urge to call Nora. Then he decided, no, he would call from Maryland, instead. It had been that type of day—seeing Sarah again and interrogating her. At the end of it, everything required a huge effort.

He heard a low, muffled noise which became louder. Then he realized it was from Caryn's room. She must have had her own antenna because she somehow knew where all of her music stations were no matter where she traveled. Then he heard her singing along with it again. On the stations she listened to, night and day apparently did not exist. They played the same music relentlessly through both. If she had been a stranger next door, he might have threatened to put a fist through the wall and tell her to shut up.

Instead, he propped a chair under the knob of the door to his room, a precaution he always took. Then he went into the bathroom, ran some water, and tried to ignore her. He pulled off his shirt and stared into the mirror. He studied the lines on his face and the shadows under his eyes. He looked the way he was: hot and tired. He ran the water of the shower.

He shaved and took a long shower which refreshed him and eased his muscles. He toweled off and returned to his room. He sat down on the bed. He cocked his head. He could hear nothing more from the next room. Had Caryn gone to bed already? How did these women of her age fall asleep so quickly? How could anyone knock off thirty seconds after her head hit the pillow? He looked again at the telephone. Now he gave the situation two minutes of final, serious thought.

"What the hell," he eventually said aloud. He had long ago learned that when he wanted something, the only way to get it was to pursue it.

He turned off all the room lights except one by his bed. He went to the door of his room and opened it. He left it slightly ajar.

He read the motel's number off the telephone. He dialed it. He heard the voice answer from the front desk.

"I'm trying to reach a Caryn DiCarlo who's registered there," he said to the night clerk. "I wonder if you could connect me?"

A few seconds later, he distantly heard the ring in the next room. She answered on the third one.

"Hello, Paul," she said.

"How did you know it wasn't the front desk calling?" he asked.

"The front desk wouldn't call. And you're the only one who knows where I am."

"My door is open," he said. "I'm leaving it that way for the next five minutes. Then I'm going to kick it shut in agony and go to sleep alone. But until that time . . ."

"Is this proposition?"

"Consider it one."

"And you're letting me make the decision? Very clever."

"Want me to make it for you?"

"No," she said. "But I'm a confused lady. I thought you didn't like us J-schoolers. My late friend Harry used to tell me the nasty things you used to say."

"I've changed my mind," he said boldly. "At least in your case." There was silence on the line. "Of course, maybe it's too late."

"Maybe," she said. "And maybe not. Sweet dreams, Paul. Have a nice night."

She hung up coolly. He turned the remaining lamp off and lay back on the bed. He watched the outline of the exterior light against the door frame.

Maybe. Maybe not. Her words. Invitation and rejection, coiled tightly together. Would he ever learn? Probably not. Two minutes passed. Then three.

Jesus, he said to himself. *What a jerk she's made out of me. I'm going to end up apologizing in the morning even though nothing—*

Then he heard a door gently close nearby. Hers?

A hand appeared in his doorway. The hand pushed the door open.

Then, rearing up out of the past, the old paranoia was suddenly upon him again. Everything was so clear that he was stunned that he'd missed it so far! Sure enough. He had just signed his own death certificate! He could be on his own necrology page in the *Sun* within twenty-four hours!

Where was his notebook? he wondered insanely. *Where was the page where he had started—but never finished—his own death notice?*

Caryn worked for McMorris and the CIA! And for that matter so did Ken Shaw! She was positioned perfectly to watch him, make sure everyone knew how much of the story he was on to, and to lead him to this moment.

He had stripped, turned the light off, and lay in bed under an assumed name at an obscure motel. The door would fly open. She—or whomever she worked with—would step in, raise the pistol in the dark, fire six shots and—

The door opened. Caryn stepped inside. She was wearing a robe. Who knew what she was concealing? A gun? A knife? She had had the perfect opportunity to get something from her room. Her associates would ambush Sarah and Andy Stuart at the airport. Everything was in place!

Caryn would claim he attacked her and—

"I heard you shower. It kind of turned me on. I got all cleaned up, too," she said. She pushed the door shut. He heard her lock it. The room was dark. She drew the window shade. He sat on the bed as his eyes fought to adjust. There was some light. Just a little. Just enough to slowly make out a figure. Hers. A nicely shaped woman in a sheer summer robe.

"I like that just scrubbed all-fresh-and-clean feel," she said.

"Me, too," he said.

But he spoke hesitantly. His heart pounded. It flashed through his mind that this could go either way. She was coming to make love to him. Or she was coming to kill him. One or the other.

She walked over to him. He could now see her better in the dim light as she approached. She stopped in front of him. She reached to her waist. He could see her hands. He looked up and he could see her face.

Yes, indeed. She was extraordinarily pretty like this. But what—

She undid the sash to her robe and she let the robe fall open. Then she let it drop to the floor. He reached out and took her hands. They were empty and she was completely naked.

No, he thought to himself with an overpowering sense of relief, *no death tonight. And his thoughts had been nothing more than the old galloping paranoia.*

He moved his head forward and kissed the taught flesh of her tummy. Then he let his gaze wander up her body until his eyes settled into hers.

"Your pal in the travel agency was right," he said.

"About Sarah?"

"About you," he said. "You said he thought you were gorgeous. He was right."

She smiled. "He was guessing," she said. "You get to arrive at your own conclusions via actual experience."

"I'll take that alternative," he said.

He pulled her down to him and onto his bed. His arms wrapped around her and he brought her down on top of him.

"I told you to have an nice night," she said. "I thought I'd come by to make sure we both had one."

"Damned thoughtful of you," he said.

"Want to know a secret?" she asked.

"Try me."

"I'm starved for some good sex," she said. "How 'bout you?"

Gently, he pulled her forward. Their lips met. She slid her hand onto the firm muscles of his right thigh. A second later, her hand delicately arrived upon his penis and discovered how hard it was.

"Does that answer your question?" he asked.

"Uh huh."

They both laughed. Then their lips met again. And for the first time in several days, there was no need for words, questions, or explanations.

* * *

Sometime between five A.M. and six, he came half awake and felt her body intertwined with his. She was tucked under his right arm, breathing gently and evenly. He nuzzled her. When she responded, they made love again. Then, when they awoke together shortly after eight A.M., he pushed away the sheets that covered them. As daylight flowed into the room, he saw her afresh and, in retrospect, he wondered how he had been able to resist her for as long as he had.

He held his right arm around her waist. "I refuse to release you," he teased.

"Until when?" she asked.

"Maybe not for a long, long time," he said. "Sorry."

"Sounds interesting," she said as she kissed him. "But isn't there *any* way a girl can win a few hours of freedom?"

"Only one way," he answered.

Caryn drove him crazy: the presence of her, the sight of her, the touch. In the light of morning he discovered that she wore a pale pink make-up powder between her breasts. And there was something else that he had missed twice in the dark: a rose—red with a delicate green stem—tattooed to the small of her tummy. "Just below my bikini line," she explained. "A flower for lovers only. Like it?"

He did. And it demanded his attention. He pulled her to him a third time, though this time she played the role of the aggressor, climbing on top and drawing him inside of her.

Not surprisingly, they didn't check out of their motel until after nine thirty. Fortunately, her Miata was exactly where she had left it, untampered with and untouched. She started the car and pointed it toward Maryland.

They split the driving. She took the car across the George Washington Bridge to New Jersey. They stopped on the turnpike and he drove the rest of the way. With a stop in Delaware for lunch, they lost pretty much of the entire day, in terms of work, at least, arriving in Baltimore toward six in the evening.

They explored the waterfront, checked into one of the city's better hotels—maintaining straight faces as they registered as Mr. and Mrs. Kenneth Shaw of New York—and went for dinner at Obrachi's.

It was a marvelous day's respite from the challenge and danger before them. They behaved as if they were newly in love, which in a sense they were. The hotel room was big and comfortable and overlooked the harbor. They returned to it toward ten in the evening, showered together, and climbed into the world's most sensual bed. Or at least it seemed so through the second night of their affair.

It was not until the hours after midnight—when Townsend was finally drifting off to sleep beside the woman who was now in his life—that visions of the late Leonard Wolik began to appear again like a ghostly presence before his mind's eye.

Thereupon, the need again arose to face reality. The next morning, bright and early, he would again pursue the secret that had already laid more individuals than he could have imagined in premature graves.

< < < < **33** > > > >

PAUL *TOWNSEND* sat in the main newspaper morgue of the Baltimore public library. At a microfilm viewing stall, he read fine newspaper type in eleven-year-old publications until his head swam and his eyes ached. Once again, Townsend was prowling into the affairs and secrets of a deceased party, hoping against hope that the dead could somehow talk.

Caryn sat nearby at a separate reading booth, duplicating his efforts, poring over the same reels as Townsend as soon as Townsend had finished. She followed his path in the off chance that he may have missed something.

They worked the month of February 1985. They searched for any item that might have mentioned the name of Leonard Wolik. The dead man's name had not appeared in any subject or necrology index for the *Baltimore Sun* or the *Baltimore Evening Sun*. But Townsend and DiCarlo scanned each paper anyway, in case the name had been missed by—or specifically deleted from—any computer listing. They concentrated on any dates around February 8, which had been the date of the death certificate he had seen in the CIA file. Townsend began to wonder whether the date was as fallacious as the fictitious Dr. Schmidt who had "signed" the document.

After three hours, Townsend leaned back from his viewing machine. "Nothing," he said. "How about you?"

She shook her head. They had scanned every article, no matter how small, on every page for the entire month. They had also done the same for the Washington dailies.

They went out for a sandwich at the noon hour.

"Makes no sense," he said. "A man like Wolik dies. No write-up in any paper. No accident report buried on page thirty, no small obituary. Either he never died, and the accident never happened, or someone went through and purged every accessible account from the official record. Who would do something like that?"

"The same people as would walk you into a reading room with forged background documents," she said. "The CIA."

He nodded. "Of course," he said. In an illogical field, it was the only logical answer. "And that returns us to our original question. *Why?* What are they covering? *The greatest secret of the sixties.* What have they gone to all this trouble to pull a curtain over?"

He tried to tie it back to Angleton, Nosenko, and Golitsin. Or Zarudni in Paris. Or Sarah's father: Lyndon's Man. He had the sense of trying to force square pegs into round holes.

"Goddamn it," he said. "And for this we'll probably end up getting shot at."

This remark, offhand as it was, seemed to arrest her attention. "You're exaggerating a little bit, right?" she asked.

"No," he said. "Not really." The image cast a small pall over lunch. He was sorry he had said anything.

"Ever been shot at?" he asked, trying to make light of it.

"No," she said.

"It's exhilarating," he said, "as long as they miss. Otherwise, it's a problem."

She gave him a sour expression. "What about official police records?" she asked finally, changing the subject. "Are they accessible?"

"If we're lucky," he said. "That's what we look for this afternoon. *If* we finish with the newspapers."

They returned to the reading room before one P.M. Townsend requested microfilm of any suburban dailies or weeklies for the month of February 1985. These hadn't been placed on film yet, so an effeminate bearded librarian named Maurice presented him with a stack of four different publications. One was a counterculture publication which had been founded in the sixties and had teetered through the eighties. The three others were suburban. Townsend and DiCarlo spread out their task on a long rectangular reading table. Shortly after three in the afternoon, Townsend hit gold.

Buried toward the bottom of page eighteen of the *Pikesville Eagle* was a small item without a byline. It recounted a motor vehicle accident on Route 1 north of Baltimore.

"Jesus Fucking Christ," Townsend muttered aloud when his eyes settled upon it. "I got it!" Caryn looked up. Then she came to his side and read over his shoulder.

The article didn't give much. But it gave enough. In the early morning hours of the previous Thursday, there had been a one-car collision in bad weather conditions on Route 1. The tentative identification of the man involved was "Leonard Wallach." The conditions surrounding the death were not dissimilar to what even the CIA file had stated.

Silently, Townsend raised his eyes and thought about what was before him.

Wallach. Townsend allowed for an inaccurate spelling by the night reporter who probably took the account over the telephone. He read further. A Baltimore city detective named A. Lakaitis was following the case further, assisted by another police officer named C. Nevell.

That was all. Townsend counted. Sixty-three words. He reread the article and photocopied it. He ran a computer check and index check on the name "Wallach" just in case it had appeared inaccurately elsewhere. It hadn't. Nor had there ever appeared any follow-up of the story, even in the *Pikesville Eagle.*

Therein, more than a decade after the event itself, the two reporters from the *New York Sun* had the confirmation that they wanted. An "incident" really had occurred, probably involving the State Department officer who had been in Paris in 1964—65. Leaving the city library, Townsend found a map of Baltimore and the surrounding area. He found the precise spot on the map where the accident must have happened.

The article was enough to move Townsend on to the next step. What he needed now was someone who had been at the scene of the accident— or crime—and who could remember in detail exactly what had happened. Townsend thus turned his attention in the most obvious direction.

<<<< **34** >>>>

THE new brick and glass administrative headquarters for Baltimore county's municipal police department was on 33rd Street, two blocks from a sprawling high school and the now abandoned old Memorial Stadium. But it was in a refurbished old factory building—a bizarre edifice with turrets and a clock tower—on 32nd Street, about a block west of the gleaming new main building, that archival records were now kept. Those who ran the police department called the old building the Annex. Those in the department, with good reason, called it the Haunted House. There old log books, files, case reports, budgets, minutes of investigations, and accounting ledgers were sent. These pieces of history went to the Annex not so much to die, but to rest in administrative purgatory until someone thought of some place better for them or some way to put them on a computer. Hence, the name. A place for ghosts. The Haunted House. Or sometimes more colloquially, simply the House.

Caryn dropped Townsend there at four P.M., then returned to the central library to run Wolik's name through any final indexes or suburban newspapers that they had so far missed. She would return for him in an hour.

Townsend used a main floor file to locate the information he wanted. Then he went to the basement of the House where he sought specific records. There he passed through a door that led to a damp, musty-smelling room occupied by a single gray-haired man. A counter separated Townsend from an archival area. The man sat at a desk behind the counter watching a small portable television.

The old man looked up as Townsend entered. He wore the three-striped chevron of a sergeant on his sleeve, and his shirt was that of a Baltimore policeman. But he wore street slacks and no sidearm. Townsend guessed he was a police retiree augmenting a pension. A name tag over a shirt pocket gave his name as Jenkins.

"Help ya?" Jenkins asked, looking up. He spoke in a drawl that sounded more southern than Maryland.

"Yes," Townsend began pleasantly, "I suspect you can."

Again, Townsend didn't lie. He merely enhanced the truth. He told Jenkins he was a writer, working on the life of a man who had died in Baltimore county eleven years earlier. Car wreck, Townsend explained. Problem was, the details of the man's final days were sketchy as he left no kin. Newspaper coverage, he might have added, seemed like something out of the Soviet Union during the glory days of the Stalin Era.

"What I'm wondering," Townsend said, "is whether I could locate the police officers who attended the wreck. Any detail they could provide . . . Well, sometimes when you're writing something, any little thing helps."

Jenkins didn't think the request was odd. Either that, or he had spent so many years in uniform that nothing seemed odd.

"So what do you need?" Jenkins asked. The television continued in the background. The reruns of "Charlie's Angels" were in their fourteenth year.

Townsend produced his map and showed the location of the accident. "Can you tell me what police district that might have been in?"

"Don't have to look that up," the man drawled. "Spent twenty-seven active years on the job here. That's third district."

"Who would have been the district commander in 1985?" Townsend asked.

Jenkins ran his hand through his hair. "That, I'll mosey back and look up," he offered.

Jenkins was not a computer man. He trudged through an aisle of open stacks which stood behind his desk, packed solidly. He laboriously unfolded a pair of glasses and put them on. He consulted a pair of volumes which were hard bound but the size of city telephone directories. Townsend watched Jenkins's movements. The man was seventy years old if he was a day.

Jenkins put the books away and padded back to the front counter. He took his glasses off and folded them into a shirt pocket.

"Captain John Mooney," Jenkins said. "He was district commander as well as chief of detectives."

"Know where I might be able to find him?"

"Yup."

"Where would that be?"

"St. Michael's Cemetery on the Fredericktown Road."

"Captain Mooney's deceased, huh?"

"About two years ago, I'd say." Jenkins paused for a moment. "Good man, Jack Mooney. I knew him."

"Know him well?"

"No. Just knew him."

Townsend pondered his next move. He reached to his file case and browsed through it until he located the one photocopy he had from the *Pikesville Eagle*. He placed it on the counter and presented it to Sergeant Jenkins.

"I wonder about these two police officers," Townsend said. "A. Lakaitis. And C. Nevell."

Jenkins's curiosity was piqued. He read the whole article, then looked up.

"They're both retired," said Jenkins. "I remember them."

"You've got quite a memory, remembering two people out of . . . How many would it have been?"

"The Baltimore force was only about eight hundred back then. I put in a lot of years," Jenkins said. "I tended to know people."

"Guess so," said Townsend, with admiration.

Jenkins added that by rights he should have been off the force completely now, out fishing on the Chesapeake. But the politicians who ran the city had screwed the honest cops out of most of their pensions. So there he was, Jenkins explained. "Fifteen hours a week in the records office at eight lousy dollars," Jenkins said, "an hour."

"Bunch of dickheads, aren't they, the politicians?" Townsend said, sensing where the conversation was leading.

"You can say that again."

"If you want me to, I will." Townsend coaxed a recalcitrant grin out of the old man.

"Ever heard of this Wolik fellow?" Townsend asked.

Jenkins shook his head.

"Would there be anything about him in any records you have here?"

"Nope. He was an accident victim. We got cops and bad guys and people who worked for the department. You'd have to go after hospital records or coroner's records."

"As I thought," Townsend said. "What about these two police officers?"

"What about them?"

"Know them personally?"

"Nope. Different district. Never worked in the Third." Jenkins paused and decided that he liked his first visitor of the week.

"Then how did you know them at all?" Townsend asked.

"They created a little stir, those two. Worked together quite a bit," the records officer said. "Maybe too much."

"Really?" Townsend asked, with all the fraudulent innocence he could muster. "In what way?"

'Well, Lakaitis . . . One of the best men on the force. Good, honest, thorough. Back then he was a big, good-looking guy. Officer C. Nevell. That's Christine Nevell. Female. One of the first girls on the force. Nice looking. Don't know why a nice-looking girl would want to be a cop. See? Man, woman. Bad idea in the workplace, see?"

Townsend said he didn't see.

Jenkins made a semilewd gesture with his hands, joining them together. "Not good as a cop team," Jenkins said.

Townsend blinked once and it set in. "Now I see," Townsend said.

"Being a cop is a man's job. These women. Ah, they're just on the force to find husbands. I don't know why—"

"Do they still live in the area?" Townsend asked, glancing down at the names. He read from his own clipping to get the names right. "Lakaitis and Nevell?"

The clerk pursed his lips and shook his head. Townsend's spirits took a tumble. "Don't think so. Moved out of here. The two of them. Different directions. Good idea for both, particularly the girl." He paused. "You working on something important?"

"Rather," Townsend said.

"Not supposed to give out any information," the clerk said. There followed his longest, most suggestive pause of the encounter. " 'Course, we must have got an address here in this building somewhere. They both draw pension checks."

Jenkins smiled.

"Is that a fact," said Townsend, not as a question.

"Now might be a good time to look around. If I felt like it. There's no one else in this here office."

Jenkins waited for a moment as the subtlety of his message sank in on Townsend. "You conducted business in Baltimore County before?" the clerk inquired.

"No," Townsend said. "But I'm catching on."

The man behind the counter grinned again.

Townsend reached to his wallet and found a twenty-dollar bill. He laid it on the counter.

"I'm most grateful, sir," the clerk said, picking up the money. "I'll buy a savings bond for my kids."

"How old are your kids?" Townsend asked amiably. "In their thirties?"

"Grandchildren is what I mean, sir." He looked at the single twenty-dollar bill, lying on the Formica counter in all its loneliness.

"Series Double-E Savings bonds are a minimum investment of twenty-five dollars these days, sir. Twenty-five dollars for a fifty-dollar bond."

Townsend looked at Jenkins and grudgingly laid out another five dollars.

"I have two grandchildren," said Jenkins, looking to double the ante. "I'd be really pleased if I could buy each of them—"

"Give me a break, Jenkins." Townsend said softly. "I've got a kid of my own and she's still growing.

"Yes, sir," the clerk said, properly chastised. He picked up the twenty and the five. " 'Scuse me, sir. Won't take a minute."

Townsend nodded. There was nothing quite so disarming as flagrant, petty, Mid-Atlantic graft. And when a favor needed to be done, Townsend mused, there was rarely anything as cost effective. Townsend idly wondered where he could sneak the twenty-five dollars into the expense vouchers that he would ultimately hand in to Ken Shaw.

The clerk disappeared into the maze of shelves and volumes behind him. So did the twenty-five dollars. And it didn't take a minute, as Jenkins had promised. It took several, during which Townsend listened to the irritating drone of the portable television. When the clerk returned, it almost came as a surprise.

"Got a pencil and paper?" Jenkins asked.

Townsend opened his notebook.

Jenkins presented Townsend with a piece of paper. On it were two addresses, one for former Baltimore police officer Albert Lakaitis, the other for Christine Nevell. Both now lived outside the state of Maryland.

"These addresses are current as of two weeks ago, sir," said Jenkins softly. "That's when the most recent pension checks went out."

Townsend reached for the sheet of paper. Jenkins drew it back from him.

"Copy it," Jenkins said. "I can't let this go in my own handwriting. And as far as I'm concerned, I never gave it to you."

"Uh huh," Townsend said. He looked at the addresses and began to enter them in his notebook.

"I'm sure," Jenkins said defensively as Townsend wrote in silence, "that you'll put these only to good purposes. Nothing sneaky or sly, you understand. Nothing illegal."

"My motivations," said Townsend as he finished, "are beyond reproach."

"That means they're good, right?"

"That means they're good," Townsend reassured him. The reporter returned his pencil to his pocket.

Jenkins took back the paper. He crumpled it and put it in an ashtray. Then, with a pocket butane lighter, he set fire to it.

"Have a good afternoon and evening, sir," Jenkins said.

Townsend said he would and left the clerk's office. He was back on the street waiting for Caryn with a half hour to spare. And, despite the task at hand, felt a surge of pleasure and excitement when he saw her turn the corner in her blue sports car and arrive to meet him.

"How's our gasoline supply?" he asked, getting into the car.

"I just bought some."

"Good," he said. "We'll need it."

He gave her an address in Delaware. They drove north. By coincidence, they took the same road that Leonard Wolik had traveled during his final trip in a motor vehicle. Townsend studied the point on his map and when they arrived at it they stopped.

They stepped out of the car on the side of the road and, as traffic passed them, they tried to picture a one-car collision on a snowy winter's night. Townsend tried to pull from the location some feeling or some extra sense of what he was about. But he failed. He stepped back into the Miata and they continued.

She had found another one of her New Funk radio stations and it played vibrantly in the car. The beat was infectious. He almost started to like it. Or did he like it, he wondered, because it was something else about her—another aspect, a little detail like a bracelet or the way she would slide in and out of her shoes.

He was quiet in the car. His thoughts alternated between Wolik and Caryn. Occasionally, Harry Dubrow came back to life in his mind's eye, said hello, told a joke, and departed.

Then they were in Delaware, heading toward an address in a town named New Castle and an uncertain reception.

Townsend kept an eye on his watch, and another eye—every so often—on the rearview mirror. But he felt no unseen eyes upon him these days. He trusted his senses on this point. And in an illogical kind of way, he felt safe traveling with Caryn.

The time moved quickly. It was just past six in the evening when the blue Miata rolled to a halt in front of the home of Al Lakaitis, former police officer for the city of Baltimore. Lakaitis's home was a single family ranch house on a neat suburban street. From the architecture and the height of the trees, Townsend calculated that the street had been conceived in the building boom of the early eighties. Most of the properties appeared to be less than twenty years old, but some were already starting to show age.

When they stepped out of Caryn's car, Townsend's eyes rose toward Lakaitis's home. There was a slight flutter of a curtain before a large window on the first floor. Townsend took the area to be the living room. He quickly scanned the other windows. Every shade was drawn.

"You'd be amazed how many times I've seen this before," Townsend said to her. "This guy doesn't like visitors and he knows immediately when he's got some. See how much we know already? And we haven't even spoken to him."

They walked up a front path which led to three stone steps. The steps rose to Lakaitis's front door. Townsend carried a compact tape recorder in his pocket and his reporter's notebook in his left hand.

"Act friendly," Townsend said softly. "Keep your hands visible so he doesn't think we're up to something. I'll do the talking."

"It's your show," she said.

They went to the door. Townsend rang once. Then he rang a second time. He could hear the doorbell sound within the house. When there was no response, Townsend knocked. When there was no response to the knock, he rapped harder and longer a second time.

Several seconds more elapsed.

"What do you suppose he's doing?" Caryn asked.

"Anything from putting his pants on to loading a shotgun," Townsend said. "But Rule Number One: If the individual is home, don't leave of your own free will."

"Thanks for the tip," she said. "You're just kidding about the shotgun, right?"

He gave her a smile. "No," he said. When he saw that she was apprehensive, he sought to calm her.

"Look," he said, "sometimes these things look rough going in. Then they turn into a piece of cake."

" 'Piece of cake,' huh? I'll keep that in mind."

"Try to."

Then there was the sound of latches unclicking on the other side of the door. The door slowly opened. A large glowering man, thick through the arms, shoulders, and midsection, filled the door frame. He held the door at a three-quarters point, concealing his left hand and hip.

Townsend had seen this tactic before as well. He assumed the man was armed. It was impossible to see past him into the dark house.

"Yeah?" the man asked. His thick eyes darted from Townsend to Caryn, then back again. Townsend knew they had been carefully checked out when they came up the front path.

"I'm looking for Al Lakaitis," Townsend said.

"You found him."

"That's you?"

"Yeah."

"My name is Paul Townsend. This is my associate Caryn DiCarlo."

"Hi," she said sweetly.

The presence of a woman did nothing to soften Lakaitis. He continued to glower.

"We're writers for the *New York Sun*. I wonder if we could talk to you for a few minutes."

"About what?"

Townsend knew no way to mask his subject or even ease into it. He knew straight-ahead was the only approach. His witness, Lakaitis, was obviously jumpy enough already. If he smelled a trick, he'd clam up forever.

"An incident that took place on one of your shifts eleven years ago when you worked for Baltimore County," Townsend said. "A one-car motor vehicle accident on Route—"

"I got nothing to tell you," Lakaitis said. He attempted to close the door. Townsend slowed the door with his hand.

"I didn't tell you which incident," Townsend said.

"It don't matter. I got nothing to tell you about anything. Now get out of here."

Lakaitis tried to close the door again. Townsend, in best journalistic fashion, placed his foot in it. When the door failed to close, Lakaitis looked down. His eyes slowly filled with anger.

"You must be pretty stupid. You want me to break your leg?" he asked.

"This would just take a minute or two of your time," Townsend insisted. "It's really very important."

"Read my lips, pal! I got nothing to tell you."

"February 8, 1985," Townsend said. "What is it about that incident, Mr. Lakaitis? We can talk in confidence. I'm not going to quote you."

"Beat it!" Lakaitis said again. "And you got two seconds to move that foot."

"I wouldn't bother you if I didn't have to," Townsend said. "I'd talk to Captain Mooney, but—"

Lakaitis's eyes rose from the foot to Townsend's face. "The Moon's been dead a couple of years," Lakaitis said.

"Exactly," Townsend said calmly. "That's why I came to you." Townsend slowly withdrew his foot. "He was a good captain, I hear."

"Damned good."

"Stuck up for his men," Townsend suggested.

His foot was out of the door frame. Lakaitis eased back slightly. "Yeah. He watched out for our asses."

"Look, I can appreciate that. My dad was a cop," Townsend lied.

"Yeah?" Lakaitis glared him in the eye and sounded as if he didn't believe it.

"I apologize for my foot," Townsend said. "Sometimes I lose control over it. I'm sorry I put it there."

Lakaitis grunted. The door stayed open. Townsend read the body language. *He'd like to talk but knows he shouldn't. He needs a reason.*

"I know there are some things you don't like to talk about," Townsend tried. "I can buy that. But what is it about that crash on Route One? Everyone treats it like poison. Big wreck like that. A man who's a government employee gets killed. No obituary. Virtually no newspaper coverage. What gives, Mr. Lakaitis?"

Lakaitis studied him. "I don't know," the ex-cop said sullenly. "I've forgotten."

Townsend smiled amiably and shook his head. "No. No, you haven't. You were one of the best detectives in the department. You haven't forgotten. You just don't want to talk to me. Why is that? Just tell why you don't want to talk. That will help me understand your position."

Caryn looked at the situation as if it were set to explode, which it was. For a moment, Townsend thought the former policeman was about to give. But he was wrong. Lakaitis's resolve was strong.

Townsend waited until he knew that Lakaitis wasn't going to open up at that time and place. "All right, then," Townsend asked at length. "What about the other officer on the case?" He consulted his notepad. "Christine Nevell?"

At the invocation of her name, Townsend saw something in Lakaitis's eyes that he didn't like. Something blazed. Townsend knew he'd made a mistake.

"What about her?"

"Know anything about her?"

"Got married. Left the force. Moved away. Leave her alone." Lakaitis's face was turning crimson. Very slowly, he reached to a shirt pocket and withdrew a pack of Big Red chewing gum. He yanked out two pieces, pulled away the wrappers and stuffed the gum into his mouth as he listened to Townsend. The air in front of Townsend was redolent of cinnamon.

"Don't have a current address, do you?" Townsend asked.

"For who?"

"Police Officer Christine Nevell."

"Why would I?"

"Just asking. She's next on my list." Townsend looked at his notebook again, then peered up at the former cop. He had the sense of running in mud. He flipped the notebook shut. He glanced up. "Would you tell me if you'd spoken to her lately?"

"You better take off, pal," Lakaitis warned.

"All right. But it seems to me since you don't want to talk to us," Townsend said, "then I'll have to find Christine Nevell. Seems a shame. You had the seniority on the case. I got to track her down out of state. And all I wanted to know is—"

The door flew open. Not for the first time in Townsend's life, a pair of strong hands grabbed him by the shirt. The ex-cop was old and bulky, but somewhere he was still working on his power lifts. He briskly hoisted Townsend as if the reporter were a large doll, raised him easily him off his feet, and flung him violently backward.

Caryn was too startled to do anything but watch, as if it were happening in slow motion before her. Lakaitis hurled Townsend backward down the front steps. The reporter's notebook flew into some shrubbery, as did the tape recorder from Townsend's pocket. He landed hard on the grass in front of Lakaitis's home.

But Lakaitis wasn't finished. He followed Townsend, leaned down, and grabbed him again. Townsend threw a punch to deter him, but Lakaitis blocked it easily. Lakaitis hauled the reporter to his feet as a stream of profanities cascaded out of the former cop's mouth. At the same time Caryn rushed to Townsend's defense. She deflected Lakaitis's arm just enough to lessen a blow to the side of Townsend's head. Then Lakaitis threw her aside like a doll.

"You goddamned fucking—! Get out of here!" Lakaitis raged to both of them, too angry to form sentences. "It's been eleven years. Just stay away!"

There was indeed a service revolver on Lakaitis's left hip. Lakaitis stood above Townsend and glared down at him. Townsend waited for the perfunctory kick in the crotch and prepared to block it. Fortunately, it never came.

"You've made your point," Townsend said from the ground. "We're leaving." He carefully got to his feet. He retrieved his notepad and recorder, never taking his eyes off Lakaitis, waiting for the ex-cop to strike at him again.

"This is one case that don't need no press nosing around, you hear me?" Lakaitis said. "You turn up here again and I'll break your head on sight."

"Have a good day," Townsend said. He retreated toward Caryn's car. Caryn walked with him, watching Lakaitis the entire way. Slowly, the retired cop made a retreat of his own, back up his front steps and toward his house. But he didn't enter it. He stood on the front landing and waited.

Townsend and DiCarlo climbed into Caryn's car. She started the engine. " 'Piece of cake,' " she said. "Right?"

"Sometimes I'm wrong. I admit it." The right side of his head started to throb. It occurred to Townsend that the deflected punch had landed pretty solidly after all. Townsend was grateful that it hadn't been in the nose or teeth.

"Let's get off this block," Townsend said, "before he comes after the car."

She didn't need to be talked into it. She threw the car deftly into gear and pulled away from Lakaitis's home.

"So what do we have now?" Caryn asked after several minutes of thought. "Another dead end?"

"No. Just another obstacle," he said. "Damn!" he snapped bitterly. "This guy knows a lot and he's not telling us. See how defensive he got when I brought up his former partner's name?"

"I couldn't quite miss it."

"It was all over his face even before he decided to work me over," Townsend said. "Goddamn it. I've been doing this for too many years. I know it when I see it." He flipped his notebook open again, found the most recent pages, and began to read.

"Captain Mooney is dead. The official record of Wolik's death has been purged. One of the two cops involved won't talk. That leaves us with the last known whereabouts of the other cop." He glanced at Caryn. "How do you feel about dropping me off at the Baltimore airport?" he asked.

"Not good. Where are you going without me?"

He flipped the pages in his notebook again, this time to the most recent ones he had filled in the town clerk's office.

"To visit Christine Nevell," Townsend said. " 'Quit the force. Married. Moved away,' " he added, mocking Lakaitis. "Seems a little abrupt, doesn't it?" Townsend asked. "Most young female cops don't fly off like that, do they?"

"I wouldn't know," Caryn said.

"I would," Townsend assured her. Then he read to her the most recent address for Lakaitis's former partner.

Christine Nevell had married a Florida man named Hubbell and had bought a home with him in Fort Myers. She had dropped the nickname of Chris and had replaced it with Tina, which is what her new husband preferred to call her.

Townsend had an address for her that was as current as her most recent check.

"That's my next stop, Caryn," Townsend said. "It's also our only fresh lead. You're going to have to go back to New York, keep Ken Shaw happy, and file some sort of story that's vague but enticing about an ongoing investigation."

She started to argue. She insisted that a drive to Florida from there—the both of them, in other words—wouldn't be unreasonable.

But, "It's out of the question," Townsend answered. "And while you're in New York, stop off at Saint Patrick's and light a candle for this project. If I don't get lucky in Florida, well, then we *might* be at a dead end."

<<<< **35** >>>>

*F*OLLOWING the murder in Fort Myers, the assassin drove a rented car north to Tampa where he went directly to the airport. He scanned the departures board and found a flight to New York which would leave in an hour.

He approached a ticket counter for an airline upon which he liked to fly. There was a pretty red-haired girl named Kathy behind the counter. The killer told her that he was supposed to meet a friend at this terminal and may or not be flying accompanied. Would spaces be available if he waited another twenty minutes?

She checked her computer. "The flight to New York is wide open, sir," she said. "There are plenty of seats available."

He thanked her. For half an hour he then sat in the airport lounge, studying faces. He had little fear of authority since in some ways—as the employee of a government, for example—he represented authority, himself. Local police could be a problem, however, as could state police if the proper preventive measures were not taken. So watching his back was always a noble precaution. He was soon convinced, however, that no one was trailing him.

He turned his attention back to Kathy. Following a murder, Mr. Chalmers liked to have sex with a woman he had never seen before and would never see again. It was part of his ritual—both a way of cleansing himself and celebrating. Young Kathy, who looked to be about twenty-two and wholesome, might fill the bill nicely. *But how?* he mused. He did have another assignment coming up. He decided to pass her by.

At twenty minutes before flight time, he bought a ticket to New York. He paid in cash, flirting with the pretty girl behind the counter as he did so. Kathy asked him for identification and he produced some impressive stuff in a leather I.D. case. She entered the name he gave, Mr. Robert Chalmers, which bore no resemblance to the one he had been born with, into the airline's computer. Thereupon, she issued a ticket.

"Thank you, Kathy," he said as he took it.

He winked at her and didn't move for a moment, still toying with his secret plans for her. Then he gave up and walked toward the departures gate.

For a moment she watched him. There was something about the man that unsettled her. Kathy dealt with thousands of passengers a year and rarely had a similar impression. Today, however, she did. She couldn't kick it but she certainly felt it. For a moment she considered the idea of alerting airport security. But then again, he hadn't really done anything. There was just this aura of quiet menace about him—the eyes, the powerful shoulders, the thickly muscled upper arms. . . .

Then another passenger was in front of her, a younger man, nice looking and closer to her own age. So she forgot about the previous creep.

The killer arrived at Kennedy International Airport in New York at 6:18 in the evening. He took a taxi to a Manhattan hotel and registered. An advance reservation had been placed in his behalf.

Again, he used cash and his fictitious identification as Robert Chalmers. He was treated well by the hotel staff and booked into a modest two-room suite at $420 per night. He said he would stay for two.

"Any messages for me?" he asked at the desk.

There was some checking behind the counter by a well-spoken young man who bore the nameplate Sajit. Sajit found a single envelope. It was manila and five by seven inches. Its contents were thick, covered within by two layers of cardboard. The assassin felt the envelope carefully with his thumb and forefinger. He smiled. The next part of his connection was well in order.

A female porter carried his single bag and guided him to the elevator. The name tag above her left breast announced her name as Brigitte. She had dark hair, very light brown skin, and a trace of a New York Hispanic accent.

Brigitte wore a tight crisp uniform. As the killer followed her into the elevator, down a hallway on the twenty-second floor, and into his room, his thoughts strayed again to services not specifically provided by the hotel. Mr. Chalmers flirted with the idea of engaging her in a friendly conversation with the intent of setting up a seduction for after she went off duty. His instincts told him that she would be easy—even eagerly adventuresome—for a night or two if he flashed a big roll of bills. He had spent enough time in various cities around the country and around the world to make such quick assessments. But then he decided against it. Bad idea right there in the hotel when he still had work to do. Besides, one of the reasons he stayed in this particular hotel was its liberal approach to morality: if a man brought a *presentable* call girl back to the place, and as long as she didn't have a day job in that same hotel, the house detectives in the lobby never batted an eyelash.

Then again, the killer mused, call girls were not as much fun. There was never any conquest, no corruption. So he was quite gracious with Brigitte.

"You've been very helpful," he said. "And you're also very pretty. Here." He gazed upon her appreciatively and handed her a ten-dollar bill.

She was appropriately amazed and flattered. She wasn't quite sure how to react.

"Go ahead," he scoffed. "Take it. Money's nothing to me. I'm just showing my appreciation."

She accepted the extravagant tip with profuse thanks. Then she departed. As soon as she was out of the room, he turned directly to more serious business.

The assassin bolted the door from within and opened the manila envelope. In it, he found a handwritten address on East 3rd Street circled in green ink. He read it and burned it in the bathroom sink, washing the ashes down the drain. There were also two thousand dollars in cash and a metal ring with three keys upon it. He knew that two keys were to an apartment. The other was to a car.

"Good," he said aloud.

He smiled. He turned on the television, perused the room service menu, and ordered a seventy-five-dollar dinner.

Later that evening, shortly before ten P.M., the killer took the Lexington Avenue subway down to Astor Place. He walked to Broadway and turned south. When he came to 3rd Street he found the address that had been written on the paper he had burned. The building was a tenement on a garbage-strewn block. The building had filthy windows and grates on the first two floors. Much of the block comprised of walk-ups in even worse condition.

The assassin surveyed the block, then worked quickly. In front of the building was a green Ford Fiesta. The color of the car matched the circular ink within his instructions. He went to the rear of the car and pulled the key ring from his pocket.

He took a final look around. He saw no one who would bother him. "Good," he said again, to no one other than himself.

The assassin opened the trunk at the rear of the car. In the trunk, wrapped in a brown plastic bag that he immediately tore open, he found a thirty-eight-caliber Colt revolver in a clip-on belt holster. With it was a forged set of identity cards, some with his photograph in the name of Kevin Maguire. There was also a badge that would identify him as a sergeant with the New York State Police, plus two boxes of bullets—thirty-eight and twenty-two caliber. At any given moment, the killer could become Sergeant Maguire. There was also a compact pair of binoculars that the assassin slipped comfortably into his jacket pocket.

Mr. Chalmers, or whoever he was that day, quickly checked the handgun and confirmed that it was loaded, with the exception of the chamber above the hammer. He clipped the gun onto his belt. He pocketed the identification and the bullets.

Bound together with heavy twine were two cartons he had shipped the previous evening from Florida, the cartons containing his weapon. He looked upon them approvingly and picked them up. He held them under his arm as he shut the trunk of the car.

Then he walked to the driver's side of the automobile. He waited as a car passed. Then he unlocked the Fiesta's door and reached in, turning down the sun visors on each side. This would be a signal to his confederate that the car could be removed. The pickup had been made.

He walked back to Astor Place. He found a taxi with an Off Duty sign on. The cab picked him up immediately. He asked to be taken to a movie theater at 92nd Street and Broadway. The driver was pleased with the fare and attempted conversation.

The killer hated conversation with people he considered his social inferiors. He responded to most questions with one or two words until the driver took the hint. The latter took twenty blocks.

The killer arrived at 92nd Street and Broadway at a few minutes after eleven. He tipped the driver and watched the cab disappear. Still carrying his two bound-together packages, he walked against the traffic on Ninety-second Street for half a block, then quickly reversed himself.

Again, no one followed. For the first time, the killer knew his trail was completely clean.

He walked up Broadway. He bought a pack of cigarettes along the way. On West 98th Street he strolled east until he crossed Amsterdam Avenue. He stopped.

There he saw it, the building where Paul Townsend lived. The assassin counted up the floors to the fourth where, those who had briefed him said, Townsend lived. The lights were off in Townsend's apartment now. That was predictable because Townsend, the killer knew, was out of town.

"Well," the gunman said to himself with a laugh. "He won't be out of town forever. And then he *will* be out of town forever."

He laughed again. Some men took considerable enjoyment from their work.

The killer, Mr. Chalmers, Sergeant Maguire, all three of them, then turned and walked back down Broadway. He went to a safe house which his employers had maintained since the old rent control days of New York real estate in the 1960s. The assassin had known this place on previous occasions, but also knew for a fact that it was rarely used.

The safe house was an apartment in the rear of the fifth floor of a building on the north side of West 96th Street. One key on his new key ring allowed him into the building. The other key let him into the apartment.

He stepped in and closed the door. He finally put down his packages. He stood very quietly and heard nothing. "Good," he said again. Sometimes, everything proceeded with consummate ease, just as it had in Fort Myers.

The apartment had a musty smell. No one had been there for a while, at least not for any length of time. The assassin turned on some lights and opened a window in each of the apartment's three rooms.

Then he stood in the bedroom and looked out the window. He withdrew the binoculars from his pocket. He found Paul Townsend's building easily.

Townsend's living-room window, to the naked eye, was just a small speck. But with powerful binoculars, the killer readily saw, movement within the window would be easily discernible. The profile of a man within, or a woman within, would be seen easily.

The killer knew he had his shot. He estimated that it would be six hundred fifty, maybe seven hundred yards. But he had his shot. With a modern sniping weapon, such as the one he had brought with him from Fort Myers, such a proposed hit was hardly out of the question. In fact, the killer was confident. From this range, with this equipment, he could do this job.

He stashed his packages in a closet and left the safe house. He took a taxi downtown to his hotel. This time his driver spoke no English, for which the killer was grateful. In fact, the driver needed directions to the hotel. During the ride downtown, the killer ran through some telephone numbers in New York.

Escort agencies. As any man who traveled a lot knew, some of the most delicious call girls in North America worked the businessmen's hotels of this fair city. Mentally, the killer made his selection as he arrived at the hotel a few minutes after midnight. He would like an Asian girl tonight, he decided, a young pretty one with jet black hair and large breasts.

Then fate conspired to make the evening more interesting. He passed through the lobby to the bank of elevators. The elevator, as it rose, stopped on the sixteenth floor.

Brigette, the woman who had shown him to his room, stepped in. She smiled when she saw him, recalling the ten-dollar tip.

"Hello, Mr. Chalmers," she said very formally. "Good evening."

"You're still working?" he asked, charming and surprised.

"I just finished."

"I'm glad I ran into you," he said, improvising quickly. "Did you lose an earring?"

She checked both ears as the elevator door closed. The elevator continued upward.

"No," she said.

"I found one in my room. I thought it might be yours. I think it's a diamond." He gave her a mischievous smile.

"No," she said. She smiled back. "Not mine."

"Well, come with me for a moment," he said. "Let me give it to you. You can turn it in at the desk or even keep it if you like."

She was apprehensive, but only for a moment. The elevator stopped on Twenty-two. He gently took her by the hand, as an old friend might and led her to his room. He unlocked the door. She left it slightly ajar as she stepped in behind him.

"I can only stay a moment," she warned.

"I know, I know," he said. "I'm sure you have someone waiting for you."

She didn't answer.

He walked into the bedroom. He pulled off his jacket and quickly stashed his pistol in a drawer beside the bed. The bedroom had been made down by the hotel staff. The chamber was softly lit.

He reached to his wallet. He put his hand on several one hundred dollar bills.

"Come in here for a minute," he called out.

Brigette appeared in the bedroom doorway. When she looked in, she saw the man she knew as Mr. Chalmers sitting in an armchair near the bed. On the foot of the bed there were five one hundred dollar bills, laid out visibly and right in a row.

"There's no earring, Brigette, dear," he said. "But there's a very nice offer."

She stared at the money.

"What's that for?" she asked.

"That's if you stay for an hour," he said. "I'm lonely. I'm generous. I won't hurt you. I even promise that you'll find it exciting." He paused. "I'd like to be your lover," he said.

He watched the young woman's face as she tried to make her decision. He loved to corrupt women. Almost as much as the act of sex itself, he enjoyed seeing their scruples fall and disintegrate.

Brigette turned and left the doorway. The killer remained in his chair. Seconds later, he heard the door close between the living room and the hallway.

He smiled appreciatively.

"Good," he said softly, again to himself. He was confident. He could tell, just by the touch of the door closing, whether it had been pushed or pulled.

He settled back and loosened his tie.

Brigette reappeared in the doorway a moment later. Five hundred untaxed dollars was a lot of money to a working girl like this, he knew. And for some naughty fun with an attractive, muscular man . . . ? Well, who could blame a girl if she did something foolish just this once?

She grinned at him sheepishly as she gathered the money.

"Take it. It's yours," he said.

"I've never done anything like this before." she giggled. She folded the money into one of her pockets. "I feel so sinful."

"Don't bother," he said.

They both laughed.

As she began to undress, she asked him his first name. As he watched her, he had to catch himself for a moment. Then, with only the slightest hesitation, he recalled which first name he was currently using.

Immediately, Townsend knew he was too late.

He arrived by car on the street where the Hubbell family lived. He had come directly from the airport. He counted the numbers on the houses, continued, turned a corner, and saw a police cruiser sitting in front of a house.

Townsend had ventured across this scenario many times when he had been working the obituaries on the *Sun*—usually in the case of a murder or a tragedy. The world at large, gawkers, and bothersome reporters in particular, were being kept from the bereaved family of the victim.

Townsend cursed violently to himself. At the same time, his heart pounded more rapidly. He knew he was on the right trail. He knew, because he was sharing it with the opposition.

He pulled the car to a halt across the street. A single cop—a black female—sat inside the police cruiser. She was reading a magazine. The engine of her car was running. Her air-conditioning was on and her windows were rolled up.

She looked up at him as he stepped out, still surveying numbers on houses. He crossed the street toward her.

She pressed a button inside her car. Her window lowered smoothly.

"I'm looking for Twenty-six Stacey Lane," Townsend said.

"What for?" she asked.

"Looking for a friend."

"Yeah?" she asked. Challengingly, she looked him up and down. "That's number twenty-six right there," she said, indicating the Hubbell residence. "But I can't let you go to the door 'less they be expectin' you. They expectin' you?"

"Well, no," Townsend conceded. "Not really." Townsend looked at the house. The shades were drawn. One car was in the driveway but the garage door was down. The yard was tidy. It looked exactly like what it was—a tract suburban home following a death.

"It's Mrs. Hubbell I'm looking for. Would she be around?"

The cop looked at him suspiciously.

"You a little late, I'd say."

"Am I?"

"Yeah." She assessed him very critically. "Where you been?" she asked. "You ain't been 'round here."

"No. I traveled a bit to be here."

"Yeah? From where?"

"New York."

"Whew. You come a long way for nothin', mister."

While never taking her eyes off him, the policewoman reached to a newspaper folded on the seat beside her. It was folded to the appropriate page. She glanced down at it, then looked back at him.

She handed him the previous day's copy of the *Fort Myers News-Press.* The story of the woman murdered on the beach was the lead front-page story. It was not, anyone would agree, the normal sort of thing that happened here.

Townsend stood in the broiling sunshine and read the account word for word. Not only was the murder a local scandal, but it was inexplicable. No one had seen anyone near the woman, but many people had seen her suddenly crumple. Two bullets had hit her—one in the chest and one in the head. Either would have been fatal.

Townsend continued to read.

What baffled police was this: the caliber of the shots was low. Twenty-two caliber, it appeared. But the shots appeared to have traveled some distance as they fragmented on impact, making proper ballistics identification difficult at best. Added to that was the problem of what kind of weapon could propel a live round of that caliber for a long distance, and do it with accuracy. The fact that Mrs. Hubbell had been hit twice suggested that the shots were not random, although there was the usual discrepancy among witnesses as to which way the victim was facing when she was first hit.

There were no leads. There was nothing, the article concluded, in the woman's past or present that would have suggested that she had enemies. She was a local housewife, the account said, and left a husband and two small daughters. Nowhere did it mention that she had once been a city detective way up north in Baltimore, Maryland.

The policewoman's hand came out of the car. Townsend returned the paper.

"Thanks," he said.

She closed her window without a further word.

Townsend went to several newsstands before he could find a copy of the previous day's *News-Press.* But he found one and reread the article. Then he went to the beach where former police officer Christine Nevell had been shot.

He walked the path she must have taken. Townsend kept his eyes up and studied the houses and motels several hundred yards in the distance.

"It must have been from over there that the shot originated," he said aloud to himself. "There's no other angle, no other point of origin." Presumably, he guessed further, the local police had come to the same conclusion and had clumsily obliterated any possible clues in their haste to investigate.

But beyond his cynicism, he cringed. The fact that he was dealing with firepower of that sort confirmed the sophistication of his opponent. And it told him something further about the stakes.

Several minutes later, he found a pay telephone and called Caryn DiCarlo at the *Sun* in New York. She had filed a report in the *Sun* updating the investigation of Harry Dubrow's murder. The article kept Ken Shaw happy and brought *Sun* readers back into the story. The other New York dailies, the wealthy dull gray one and the cocky suburban tabloid, had already dropped the story. So by keeping it alive, they had a mini-scoop that Shaw could break on page two.

"I'm going back to Baltimore," Townsend told her. "And I can use you with me," he said.

"What's going on?" she asked.

He told her. Whoever was on the other side, they had found Christine Nevell first. "She's dead," he told her.

There was a long pause on the other end of the line. "That really sucks," she finally said.

"Tell Ken Shaw that I need you with me," he said. "Do you want to drive or fly?"

"This time I'll fly," she said.

"Then get a plane to Baltimore. I'll meet you at the airport."

She found a flight schedule and they coordinated times. He would be flying back from the other direction.

"What's in Baltimore?" she finally asked.

"We're taking a drive to see our last good witness," he said.

"Who's that?"

"You've already met him," Townsend explained.

"Are you kidding, Paul? Lakaitis will assault you on sight."

"He'll want to. But he won't. This time he'll talk."

" 'Piece of cake,' right?"

"You said it this time. I didn't."

She blew out a long breath in exasperation.

"One other thing," he added.

Caryn waited.

"Remember that spy camera we were fooling with? Tony Duncan lent us one along with the handcuffs."

It was not the type of thing she would have forgotten. "I remember," he said.

"Bring it," he said.

Then he hung up.

<<<< **36** >>>>

*I*T was half past two in the afternoon when Townsend and Caryn DiCarlo pulled their most recently rented car to a stop in front of Al Lakaitis's house. The ground was strangely familiar to Townsend, even though he had left these premises in defeat only two days earlier. At this point, however, he was grateful for anything that didn't present new terrors.

Caryn stepped out of the car at the same time as Townsend. Townsend was not surprised to turn around and watch the drawn shades again move very slightly in the living room of Lakaitis's home. Lakaitis was standing near the curtains, very still, probably with his weapon. Townsend hoped that Caryn's presence—and the sight of a couple coming to his door instead of a single man—would soften his approach.

"Should we lock it?" Caryn asked, speaking of the car.

"Never lock it," he said. "You don't know when you'll be leaving in a hurry. We're already being watched."

Instinctively, her eyes shifted to the window. This time, as they both turned, the curtain moved more perceptibly.

They went to the door together. Townsend, carrying a Florida newspaper under his arm, rang the bell. He rang it two, three, four times and there was no response.

"Mr. Lakaitis?" he called out eventually. He rapped sharply on the door.

"Come on, open up!" Townsend called. "We're not here to cause trouble! We just want to talk!" He paused and listened. He might as well have been rapping on a mausoleum wall.

The entire house remained silent.

"Detective Lakaitis!" Caryn called out. "We're not enemies! Please talk to us!" she asked loudly.

Perhaps she had stumbled across the magic word. Maybe it was a woman's voice that turned the mood. Or whatever. The door flew open and Lakaitis's hulking presence again filled the door frame.

For a moment no word was spoken. The ex-cop wore a dark sports jacket over a soiled T-shirt and jeans. Had he added a necktie, he would have looked like a bouncer at a waterfront beer-and-crab joint.

Townsend grasped for an appropriate greeting. "Sorry to bother you again," he said. "But we really need to speak."

Lakaitis glowered at the two reporters, the focus of his attention dancing angrily from one of them to the other.

"Didn't I tell you I had nothing to say to you?" Lakaitis demanded. "Can't you understand English?"

"Things have changed," Townsend said.

From under his arm he withdrew the copy of the *Fort Myers News-Press.* Townsend presented the newspaper open to the first page where it bore the account of Tina Hubbell's murder. The dead woman's picture was face up under the headline.

"I'm sorry," Townsend said with condolence. "But I think you should see this."

Lakaitis was about to respond in a fury. But his gaze jumped sharply downward to the newspaper and settled upon Tina Hubbell's photograph. Reacting in shock, he slowly took the newspaper from Townsend and began to absorb what his eyes were telling him. Then his angry mouth went open in astonishment.

"No," he said, reading. His tone was low and disbelieving. "No," he said again—long, low, and doleful this time. He was very still as he read.

"I'm very sorry," Townsend said softly. "This isn't of my doing. I'm the same as you: I would have done anything to have been there in time to prevent it."

A stricken look came across Lakaitis's face as he moved through the first paragraphs. Lakaitis's composure didn't melt or fade. Rather, it crashed. He sank his teeth into his lower lip but the flesh of his chin quivered. His gaze fell toward his shoes. But he fought with his emotions. In the presence of strangers, he was a man ill suited to loss of control.

Lakaitis's left hand passed across his mouth, then upward to his eyes, which were wet. Then the hands continued across his brow to his hair. Several additional moments passed, uncomfortable for all present.

"So they got her, did they?" Lakaitis finally asked. "I'll bet they're goddamned pleased with themselves, murdering a woman like that. The filthy fucking bastards!"

"Who got her?" Townsend asked.

Lakaitis looked his visitor in the eye. *"They* did," he said belligerently. "Goddamn it. I don't have names! Never had names. And do you think I'd give them if I did?"

"The Florida newspapers spent a lot of time on this," Townsend said. "So have the local police. They don't seem to understand it. No one does. But *we* might. The three of us."

Lakaitis gave an angry shrug.

"Goddamn you, Mr. Townsend," Lakaitis finally said. "What the devil do you want?"

"A few minutes of your time," he said. "I'm after the people who did this to Christine. You can help me. Possibly *only* you can help me. Could we talk? Please . . . ?"

Lakaitis made a decision. He stepped away from the door, backing into his home. He gestured with his hand as if nothing at all mattered now. So Townsend and Caryn DiCarlo could follow.

Townsend watched him very carefully. It was not his imagination that before closing the door, Lakaitis scanned for any shadows that lurked even in the afternoon sun.

"All right," Lakaitis said. "I'll talk a little."

Moments later, they sat together in the living room. Lakaitis had taken a chair near a curtained window which allowed him a view of both the street and the room. Townsend sat on a sofa across from him. Caryn sat on a chair to one side. Lakaitis found a pack of cigarettes and smoked the first of several.

Townsend knew that he would progress here or never. And as he read the situation, he would have to gently push.

"I understand your pain, Mr. Lakaitis," Townsend said, casually taking a notebook from a jacket pocket and laying it on the sofa beside him. "I understand your grief. But now, while both are fresh, might be the best time for us to talk."

Lakaitis's right arm stayed motionless against his hip. Townsend had no idea what he would do if Lakaitis lost control and went for his weapon. Meanwhile, Lakaitis's gaze swam moodily around the room, then settled angrily into Townsend's eyes. The former cop seemed wound so tightly that he was set to snap. Townsend kept talking, as soothingly as possible.

"Let's put it this way," Townsend said. "I know you have principles. Standards. You made a vow to yourself never to discuss certain things. In that respect a policeman is very much like a doctor or an attorney or a priest. Or even a reporter."

Here Townsend tried a slight smile. It was not reciprocated.

"Let's be friendly," Townsend said. "May I call you 'Allan'?"

"It's Albert," Lakaitis said grudgingly. "Christine used to call me Allan. Less ethnic. I liked the way she said it, so I let her call me that." He raised his sad eyes. "You call me anything you want," he said. "It don't make no difference."

"Thank you," Townsend said graciously. He glanced to his left and saw skepticism upon Caryn DiCarlo's face.

"What I'd like to do is put a thesis to you, Albert," Townsend continued. "I have some theories. Maybe you could just listen and guide me along."

The cop's eyes were red and strained. Townsend sensed a softening, but didn't know if it was wishful thinking.

"May I begin?" Townsend asked very professionally.

It *had* been wishful thinking. Lakaitis still stared at him, the hand not more than a dozen inches from the gun.

"Thank you," said Townsend, in the absence of a response. Quickly, he began.

"Your involvement in this began eleven years ago," Townsend said. "You were on duty in Baltimore. Late evening, I think it—No," he said, interrupting himself. Townsend referred to the notepad beside him. "Very early in the morning. Let's keep it as precise as we can, shall we? I'd put the time at about two A.M. on February eighth, 1985."

Lakaitis was listening, still maintaining a silence now borne by bereavement and shock.

"You were doing your job," said Townsend. "You were on patrol on the overnight shift. You responded to a call of an accident on Route—"

"What did the fucking bastards do?" Lakaitis asked with controlled fury. "Just walk into her home and shoot her?"

"Excuse me?" Townsend asked.

"Christine," he demanded. "Did they shoot her in front of her family?"

"She was murdered from ambush as she walked on the beach," Townsend said.

"Dear God," Lakaitis muttered. He said nothing more. This time he refused to put his hand to his face. But from across the room, Townsend could see the tears welling. "They just walked up and shot her?" he asked.

"A twenty-two-caliber bullet," Townsend explained. "If the initial ballistics report can be believed, the bullet was fired from long range. Maybe several hundred yards."

"Small caliber, long range!" he snarled. "Who the hell travels around with fucking big-time weapons like that?"

Lakaitis knew the answer and so did Townsend.

"No one knows who fired it or where it came from," Townsend said. "The police in Fort Myers are beginning their investigation by checking all locally registered twenty-two's."

Lakaitis made a dispirited scoffing sound. "Jerking themselves off, in other words," he said. "Jerking themselves off while the real killer is long gone!"

Townsend agreed with him and returned to his thesis.

There was something horrible about the way Lakaitis folded his arms to this story. His face grew gray and gloomy. Sweat formed in beads along his hairline. This combined with the retired policeman's sense of suspicion and duty. Lakaitis's eyes were as intractable as his spirit. Once again, Townsend would have to run a deft obstacle course between fact and hypothesis to get the information he needed.

"You were doing your job," Townsend began again. "You were on patrol in the early morning of February 8, 1985. The weather was bad. Sleet. Ice. You—"

"You've got it haywire already," said Lakaitis, interrupting softly. A nervous tick: every minute or so he glanced out the window and scanned his property. "You're saying I was on patrol," Lakaitis corrected. "I wasn't. I had finished my shift. I was on my way home and I saw the incident myself."

"You *saw* it happen?" Townsend said.

"With these same eyes," said Lakaitis, indicating the ones that were still set firmly in his head. "And it wasn't any 'accident.' That's what you called it."

"No. It wasn't, was it?"

"Keep talking."

"You witnessed the incident then, didn't you?" Townsend asked, groping slightly. "You went to the scene of the car wreck. And there was a man at the wheel of an overturned car. Correct?"

Lakaitis nodded very slightly.

"You and another man were afraid that the vehicle might explode. So you pulled the body from the car."

"That's right. We did."

"But the man in the car was very badly injured," said Townsend. "Plenty of blood, I'd guess."

"Plenty of blood," Lakaitis said, keying on this detail.

Townsend was at a crucial juncture already. He proceeded as cautiously as a man walking a child across a busy street.

"I'd guess the victim was already dead," said Townsend.

Lakaitis nodded. "That's the way I saw it, too. But I'm not a medical man."

"Who pronounced him dead?" Townsend said.

"Paramedics. From the ambulance."

"No doctor?" Townsend asked.

"Not till the body went to the M.E.'s office."

"Then who examined him?" Townsend asked.

Lakaitis stared off into the middle distance, then returned with a name. "Bauerman," he said. "I think it was a Dr. Michael Bauerman. I remember it 'cause no one liked him."

Townsend nodded and wrote the name in his notebook in large block letters. B-A-U-E-R-M-A-N.

"So it wasn't a Dr. Schmidt?" Townsend asked.

"Who's Schmidt?"

"Schmidt's the name on the bottom of the only existing death certificate," Townsend said.

Lakaitis thought about it and his face turned into a pensive frown. "Makes no sense to me," he said.

"Me, neither," Townsend said, again finding ground for agreement. "But what about these paramedics? Did they examine the victim carefully?"

Lakaitis practically spit out the words. "Of course not! Do they ever, if they can't find a heartbeat? They get paid by the county. They do what they're told to, and that's if you're lucky. Then they go home and forget it."

"But *you* didn't forget it, did you?" Townsend asked. "For many reasons."

This assertion was met by a glare and a noncommittal shrug. Townsend knew he had to show more of his cards. He kept talking.

"I'm sure the injuries probably looked like they would have been reasonably consistent with an auto accident." He paused and timed his gambit. "My guess would be head injuries."

Townsend waited.

"Your guess would be good," Lakaitis said, with almost a flicker of an upturned frown.

"But the injuries didn't happen in the car, did they?" Townsend asked. "I'm probably following the same line of reason today as you did eleven years ago. Someone killed him. Then someone stuck him in the seat of a car and sent him down Route One in the direction of Garland Boulevard. That's the first part of my thesis. It's also the easy part: the man was dead before he got into the car. How am I doing so far?"

"Real good," said Lakaitis.

"Thank you," said Townsend. "Now. Part Two: How does a dead man drive a car so fast?" he asked. "And who would have realized that the injuries happened *outside* the car and *before* the impact? After all, we both *think* it was a murder. But we don't *know.* "

"What's your guess?" Lakaitis asked.

"I don't have one," Townsend said. "Help me here. Will you?"

Lakaitis's gaze settled to the floor again. Townsend sensed an impending failure. Then, "Stones," the retired cop said.

"What?"

"Stones," said Lakaitis. "That's how they did it."

"Killed him, you mean?"

"No. That's how they made the car go."

Caryn DiCarlo hung on every word spoken before her, though she remained in the background.

"What do you mean?" Townsend asked.

"See, they fixed up a series of stones to the accelerator," Lakaitis said. "They wedged them in. Very unnatural. Against the side boards. Wouldn't have aroused suspicion had they jarred loose."

"I'm not following you," Townsend said.

"Poor Christine," Lakaitis said, gazing out the window for a second. "Poor girl." He looked back to Townsend.

There is a moment in every difficult interview when either the interview fails or a final wall crumbles. Here it was for Paul Townsend and Albert Lakaitis. The ex-cop found his voice and began to talk.

So, suddenly it was snowing again on the early morning of February 8, 1985. Lakaitis told how the runaway vehicle had nearly killed him as he attempted to access Route 1. He told how he saw the car leave the road and flip. He recalled how he was there within a minute, pulling the driver out. A fire truck was there within another few minutes, hosing down the chassis. That's why it hadn't burst into flame, both Townsend and Lakaitis agreed, analyzing it together now. And flames were what those who had contrived this ugly scene had intended.

"Otherwise, I never would have seen the stones. Or the blood. And I wouldn't have heard no engine."

"Sorry," said Townsend. "You're losing me again."

"Ever been to a car wreck?" the cop asked.

"A few," Townsend said.

"After you've seen a few of them," Lakaitis said, "they look alike. So you remember what's particularly ugly. Or unusual." Lakaitis's eyes visited his front lawn again, then returned.

"Once I went to this accident on Route Ninety-five south of Baltimore," Lakaitis said. "Head-on collision in the middle of the interstate. A pickup truck jumped the meridian, came up in the wrong lane, and took out this family from Jersey. Truck driver was drunk. Four people died."

Townsend waited.

"The vehicles weren't burning," Lakaitis explained. "There was just smoke and steam rising, 'cause the engines had been smashed together on both vehicles. There's this woman sitting in the one car with her nose sawed off by a piece of windshield. She's still alive. What's weird is this: When the nose is missing from someone's face, you're looking right down that person's throat. This was the first time I'd looked right down someone's throat."

Caryn grimaced. It didn't work on Townsend, however. "Yeah?" Townsend asked. "So?"

"This same accident," Lakaitis said, "the man sitting next to her, his head was gone. Chopped off by the hood of the truck. But he was still wearing a jacket and a tie. That's how I knew it was a man. And he still had his seat belt on. So he was strapped into the car, but his head had flown out. We found it the next morning two hundred and fifty feet down the highway at the foot of this big green and white sign that says, SEAT BELTS SAVE LIVES."

Townsend wondered how this would circle back to Christine.

"The ugly and the unusual. That's what you remember," Lakaitis said. "And, see, in this incident you want to know about there wasn't anything that was really ugly. But it *was* unusual. See, the car was overturned, but the motor was still racing. See? That's wrong!"

"For the motor to race," Townsend said, "you need a foot on the accelerator. Or a drive train malfunction."

"You don't get either of those in accidents. The car was going fast enough to have turned over, but the wheels were still spinning. First thing I did was look to see why."

That's when he saw the stones, Lakaitis remembered, lodged—or more accurately *wedged*—against the side of the accelerator in such a way as to keep it pressed down. And that was further what made Lakaitis take a second look at the whole scene.

"It was the blood that convinced me," he said. "It didn't pay much attention to the laws of gravity."

"How do you mean?"

"The body should have flown around that car to pick up its injuries," Lakaitis said. "That would have splattered the blood all over. But the injuries were to the back of the head. And the blood had run straight down the deceased individual's back and onto the car seat. See what I mean? The bloodstains flowed *downward* on the car seat. But the car was upside down. The blood should have flowed upside down, too."

"And you voiced your suspicions?" Townsend asked.

"They weren't suspicions. I told Captain Mooney that we were looking at a homicide."

"And what did he say?"

"He gave it to me to investigate."

"Did you?"

"Of course I did!" He paused. "For about forty-eight hours. Me and—This is where it gets complicated, you see," Lakaitis said defensively. "See, this is how Chris and me . . . You know . . . How we sort of got involved with each other," he said. His eyes were misting, conscious again of her death. "The bastards!" he said bitterly, leaping back to the present. "Why don't they come for me, instead? I'm ready for them. Why did they go after her?"

"I think you know. That's part of my thesis. But we're jumping ahead."

"Are we? Frig it! Who cares?"

"I do," Townsend said. "And you do, too. Two things happened at this point," Townsend theorized. "If you were on to a murder case, there must have been a reason that you didn't see it through. You were a detective and it fell into your lap."

"That's right. Captain Mooney gave it to me."

"But soon after he gave it to you, the case vanished," Townsend recalled. "It never appeared again in any newspaper. Not in Baltimore or in any neighboring county. Seems strange, doesn't it? My guess would be that someone took the case away from you. And that the someone was not from this department. The someone was from Washington."

Townsend's guess, Lakaitis said again, was smack-dead on the money. He described in detail how a "Suit," as he disparagingly called it, had turned up three days later.

"So you *saw* the man?" asked Townsend, momentarily amazed. "The man who came from Washington."

"Sure did. It was a Sunday morning. He sat this far away from me." He indicated the distance between himself and Caryn. "I got a damned good look at him, Mr. Townsend."

"Do you think you would remember him?"

"You got him somewhere?" Lakaitis asked with a vengeance.

"Maybe."

"I'll take a look whenever you want." He paused, anger creeping back up. "Particularly *now*," he said. Townsend took that as a reference to Christine.

Lakaitis blew out a long breath. He turned away and rubbed at his eyes. This was clearly the most painful part.

"See," Lakaitis said, "this case changed everything. Christine and me, we were told to forget about it. I saw the Suit in Captain Mooney's office and I'd been around long enough to know when to lay off. You know: men understand their limits sometimes. But Chris wasn't like that. She's like a lot of women. No offense," he said, remembering Caryn's presence in the room, and looking toward her. "But she never knew when to drop something. Principles, she kept saying. A man had been *killed*. We couldn't just sit on that. She sure didn't know when to drop this. 'Mr. Carman.' That's what we called it between the two of us. 'Mr. Carman.' That was our little code name for it, see, so that we could talk about it with no one overhearing."

"Did you talk about it a lot?"

"Yeah. A real lot," Lakaitis admitted. "It really bothered her. We started to meet for a few drinks after work. We'd talk about it. Talk about Mooney. Talk about Mr. Carman. What it must have involved. She wanted to take it higher up in the department than Mooney. She didn't want to be part of someone's cover-up."

"How did you feel about it?"

"The cover-up?"

"Yes."

"Didn't like it at all," Lakaitis proclaimed. "Same way I don't like captains and inspectors taking payoffs to keep dice games going. But I couldn't do nothing about that, either." He paused. "Then eventually, we started talking about other things as well. Her and me. You know. Romantic stuff."

Townsend asked the next question consolingly. "Were you in love with her?" he asked.

The question, and the suddenness with which Townsend asked it, devastated Lakaitis. The ex-cop opened his mouth to answer, but no words came out. Instead, there was a tremor of a lower lip and a gagging as he tried to talk. His composure collapsed again and he nodded. Yes, he had been. "Very much," he managed to say.

"We, uh, we got involved together about a month after the Mr. Carman incident," he said, wiping at his eye, then gathering himself again. "I can . . . I can tell you honestly. I had never met a woman like her. She was smart. She was sexy. She was tough. She knew," he concluded, "she knew how to be a woman. Know what I'm talking about?"

Townsend said he knew.

"How long did your affair go on?" Townsend asked gently.

"About two years," Lakaitis said. There was a very long pause. "I wanted to marry her."

"She didn't want to?" Townsend asked.

"She turned me down," he said. "And it was because of this case."

From the corner of his eye, Townsend saw how focused Caryn was upon their subject. Her eyes were set like a pointer's.

"Christ, I loved her," Lakaitis said, letting go with a deep breath. "We tried not to let anyone else know we were carrying on. You know, two cops together. People talk. It didn't look good. Some of our friends knew but they kept quiet." For the time being at least, the torment was leaving Lakaitis's voice little by little. He spoke with greater ease. So Townsend waited.

"We'd do things on our days off," Lakaitis said. "Go to the ocean. Go to the eastern shore. Maryland, you know? We'd stop off in rooming houses, go to bed, sleep, make love late the next morning, then go back to sleep." He paused. "I loved everything about her. Know that? I loved the way she pulled her stockings back on after we'd been in bed together. I loved the way she looked lying next to me with her clothes off."

His face stormed over. His eyes found Townsend's. "Where did the bullets hit, Mr. Townsend?" The question was very cold.

"I don't know, Albert." Townsend considered himself an excellent liar when he needed to be.

"Yes, you do," the cop said, seeing through him immediately.

"She died instantly," Townsend said.

Lakaitis looked down and ran a hand across his face again. Then he disappeared into a happy memory again and for a moment his smile fought with his tears. Then the clouds rolled in anew.

"But, see?" Lakaitis continued. "Always there was this *thing* between us. *Mr. Carman.* Mr. Carman this. Mr. Carman that. Chris wanted me to talk to the police commissioner. She'd done some snooping around. Asked a lot more questions than she should have."

Lakaitis gave it a long, long pause, combined with plenty of thought. Then his gaze fell upon Townsend's. "It was a CIA job, wasn't it?" he asked.

Townsend nodded. "I think so. But I can't prove it yet."

Lakaitis shook his head. "Goddamn it. I warned her. I warned her *so damned many* times, Mr. Townsend. I told her this particular case, *this one above all,* don't touch it. For your own sake, Chris, drop this one." He was still shaking his head and his voice rose. "A beautiful, stubborn woman. Wouldn't listen. That's what ended our relationship," Lakaitis said.

"Mr. Carman? The death of Leonard Wolik?"

Lakaitis nodded. "She wanted to take the story to the newspapers," he said. "To the television stations. To the police commissioner. To the courts. The more important she thought the story was, the more she wanted to talk about it. Even had this one delusion about writing a book."

Townsend rolled his eyes.

"No, she was real serious about it," Lakaitis said. "Doing all this research, making all these notes. *She had theories, Mr. Townsend. Same as you.* And she was one smart lady, but none of us male assholes would listen to her."

"Regrettably," Townsend said.

"She wanted me to do it all with her," he said. "But I drew the line. I warned her. I said it would do no good. She got real mad at me. 'We're partners in this from the beginning,' she'd say to me. 'You drew me into this case.' It wrecked our relationship. She said I wasn't standing by her. I didn't have any balls, she told me. I retired from the force. We saw each other less. I went off on a vacation to think things over. Thought maybe, just maybe, I would see it through to the end with her. Instead, no. She met the hardware man while I was away."

"Her future husband?" Townsend asked. "Jim Hubbell?"

"That's him," Lakaitis said bravely. "Got my woman, he did. Made off with the only female I ever loved." He paused. "Couldn't protect her, either," Lakaitis said bitterly. "Did he? When the bad guys were after her head, did he stop them? No!"

"In fairness," Townsend said, "he probably didn't even know she was in danger."

"Would it have mattered?" It was a rhetorical question. Lakaitis sank back in his chair. "Once they've drawn a bead on you, there's not much you can do. Hide, maybe. Go live somewhere else and keep your mouth shut. That's what I told her to do."

A long and terrible silence gripped the room, as if there were nothing else to say, much less do. Lakaitis steadied himself and sat up a bit. "Must be one hell of a secret," he concluded.

" 'The biggest secret of the sixties,' " Townsend said, almost involuntarily. "That's how someone described it to me."

"Yeah? So what is it?"

"I don't know yet."

"Who's guarding it?"

Townsend shrugged again.

"Why's it so damned important that people are dying a generation later? What's it worth, pal? You're the man with the theories. Got a good one for that?"

"That's what I'm working on," said Townsend. "All I can tell you right now is that I'm sorry. And that Christine will get her wish."

"What's that?"

"Give me enough time and it will be all over the newspapers," Townsend said. "I can promise that."

"That's good," Lakaitis said pensively. "That's real good." He pondered it for a moment. "What about those heavy-handed FBI fuckers?" Lakaitis asked, switching gears slightly. "Where do they fit in this?"

"Excuse me?" Townsend asked.

"That's what made me write to Christine again," Lakaitis explained. "That's when I knew this was heating up again. They came to see me."

"*Who* did?"

"A couple of Suits, 1990s style," said Lakaitis. "You know what these federal pricks are like."

"In person? They were here?"

Lakaitis nodded. "One of them sat right where you did."

"You wouldn't have a specific date of the visit, would you?"

Lakaitis stopped and figured the numbers backward. He arrived at a date in May four days after Leonard Wolik's obituary had appeared in the *Sun.*

"Remember much about them?" Townsend asked.

"One of them was a big, tall bastard," Lakaitis recalled with some effort. "Close cut, clean, mean face. Looked like a marine drill instructor or something. The other one looked like his gorilla. Shorter. Squatter. Immense arms between the shoulder and elbow. Strong-looking fucker."

"They asked about Christine?" Townsend asked.

"Damned right," Lakaitis said. "I told them she was the one with the crazy theories about Mr. Carman. I told them *she* needed protection. I didn't know anything and I said I'd blow the head off any fucker who came by to hassle me. They knew I meant it."

Townsend knew he meant it, too. He listened to the rest of this with a sick chill. "Names?" Townsend finally asked. "Flynn and Grodine, maybe?"

Lakaitis scrunched up his brow. The identities they had given hadn't made a tenth of the impression that their appearance had, for Lakaitis couldn't easily pull the official handles out of his memory. "I can't recall," he said at first.

"Then please try harder," Townsend urged.

A moment passed. Lakaitis put some effort into it.

"You know what?" Lakaitis finally said. "Yes. That was them. Flynn and Grodine? Was that a lucky guess, Mr. Townsend? Or are you and they traveling the same routes?"

"I don't know," Townsend said. "But now that you mention it, maybe. Maybe we are."

*T*HE article in the *New York Sun* appeared on page three, which was as important a news page as was found in that publication. The bylines belonged to Paul Townsend and Caryn DiCarlo.

Informed sources have indicated to the *Sun,*

they wrote,

that the death of Leonard Wolik, an official of the United States Department of State, actually took place on a highway outside of Baltimore, Maryland, during an ice storm on February 8, 1985. The man misidentified in these pages earlier this year as Mr. Wolik has now been confirmed as Mr. Colbert Davies, also a State Department official. Mr. Davies was close to Mr. Wolik, dating from a time in 1965 when they were mutually assigned to the United States Embassy in Paris. What remains unclear—but which also remains under investigation by this newspaper—is how the confusion over their identity may be linked to the murder of *Sun* sports editor

Harry Dubrow in Brooklyn this past June. Both Mr. Wolik and Mr. Davies may have had significant links to the Central Intelligence Agency. Mr. Dubrow did not.

The article—a full half page, plus a six-inch, one-column overlap onto page fifty-four—went on to recap the two reporters' findings following their inquiries in Washington, Maryland, and Connecticut. They identified no sources and spelled out the many inconsistencies in their investigation as they saw them, using the unanswered questions in the case as a hook to lure reader interest. Then, in that same day's edition, obituaries appeared for both Colbert Davies and Leonard Wolik. Caryn DiCarlo wrote the former. Townsend wrote the latter.

The story appeared in an edition in mid-July. Townsend read it the next morning and was pleased with it. Shortly after nine, his phone began to ring with inquiries from other news agencies. The *Sun* had little credibility among the established news media. But Townsend—the ersatz Wolik obituary of several weeks earlier notwithstanding—had considerable credibility among other professionals who knew him. He talked at length to each caller, but revealed nothing further than what his own publication had set in print that morning.

Then, by eleven o'clock, he was ready to make a call of his own. He dialed a number at the police precinct on West 95th Street. He waited. After five rings, a gruff, busy voice came on the line.

"Detective Duncan," Anthony Duncan said.

"Hey, Tony. It's your old nuisance maker."

Duncan recognized his friend's voice. His tone changed to a friendlier one. "Hey! Are you still alive?" Duncan teased.

"Yes. But through no fault of my own."

"I would have thought some sorehead would have finished you off by now."

"Don't get impatient. I got another favor to ask before someone does finish me off."

"Shoot," said the cop.

"A couple of FBI agents," Townsend said. "They work out of the bureau's Washington headquarters. If I give you a pair of last names, what can you find out about them?"

"I can send them through normal inquiry channels. What do you need to know?"

"Whose office they report to, for starters. Any background. Any profile. Other cases . . ."

"A fishing trip, huh? You want to know anything I can find."

"Pretty much."

"Consider it done," he said. "Well, almost done. How about two days from now? Should have something by then. How's that sound?"

Townsend said it sounded fine. He hung up. Then he disappeared downstairs to the computer room. There he ran all the new names he had encountered—Christine Nevell, Albert Lakaitis, and the permuted "Wallach" spelling of Wolik—through Big Wally, the computer. Big Wally had nothing to add on any of the subjects.

While Townsend was at work, Lou DiCarlo wandered into the room and looked at him. Lou wore no nose jewelry today. Only an earring.

"Hello, Lou, my friend," Townsend said amiably.

DiCarlo regarded him strangely and quietly, then strolled out of the room. Townsend took that to mean that DiCarlo knew he was having an affair with Lou's sister.

"Okay," Townsend said while he studied the computer screen and while Lou was still within earshot. "Don't speak."

Still no response.

After lunch, back upstairs, Townsend's telephone jangled anew. This time it was another recognizable voice. It was not a friendly one, but one which Townsend had expected within a day of the Wolik write-up.

"Townsend?"

"Yes."

"Bruce McMorris," announced the annoyed voice on the other end. "What the hell are you trying to prove? You said we had an agreement, goddamn you!"

"We had an agreement," Townsend answered. "But you violated it."

"*I* did? You cocksucker! You're the one who's printing material that we agreed would remain classified." McMorris's mood resembled that of a bear who'd missed breakfast.

"I didn't violate anything," Townsend said. "Everything I printed I obtained from other sources. Further, your own files were riddled with falsehoods."

"Not true," said McMorris."

"I know what I can prove," Townsend said. "And it contradicts what I found in those files under Wolik."

There was a long sigh on the other end of the line.

"Townsend," said McMorris, "before you get yourself into anything you're sorry about, I suggest you get your ass down here again. I'll clear up any questions or misconceptions you have."

"Same as you did last time?" asked Townsend sarcastically.

"If there's something in the files that you found inaccurate, I'll try to clear it up for you," McMorris said. "You just have to tell me."

"Want a list?"

"Sure. Bring it."

"I would if I were coming."

"It would be a good idea if you came," McMorris said. Townsend couldn't tell whether McMorris's voice conveyed a threat or a friendly warning.

"I'm not walking into your building again," said Townsend. "It will have to be in a public place."

"The bar of the Four Seasons," McMorris suggested.

"Not a chance. It's got to be outdoors this time."

"Townsend . . ."

"We don't have to meet at all."

"You're an ornery prick," McMorris said. "Christ knows, I'm trying to help you and you give me a hard time."

"There's a bench on the northwest corner of Dupont Circle," Townsend said. "How does three o'clock tomorrow afternoon sound?"

"That's one of the busiest corners in the city," McMorris said. "Any particular reason?"

"That's kind of the point."

"Oh, don't be so damned melodramatic!" McMorris blew out a sigh of exasperation. "I'll be there if you will," he said.

"It's a date."

"Townsend?" McMorris asked. "Please don't do anything cute. For both of our sakes?"

"Wouldn't think of it, Bruce," Townsend said.

Townsend hung up. He stared at the telephone for a moment after he had set it down. He rose from his desk and walked to Caryn DiCarlo's office next door.

"We're traveling again," he said.

"Where are we going?"

He told her. Then, "Do you remember that camera we borrowed from Tony Duncan?"

"The little spy job?" she asked.

"That's the one. Figure out how it works and get some film for it."

"I already have," she said.

He grinned. "Figures," he said. He returned to his own office.

For the rest of the afternoon, Caryn finished several pieces of paperwork that had lingered in her office since the previous trip. Townsend oversaw the operation of the obituary page and helped construct two

death write-ups when the afternoon deadline closed in on the two reporters working the page.

Then he assembled many of his own notes on the story he was
piecing together himself. In the process, in his notebook, he came across
the proposed obituary he had begun to write on himself. He toyed with
it for several minutes, then went on to what he believed to be more
pressing work.

Townsend and DiCarlo stayed at the *Sun* until half past seven. They
went out with a couple of other writers—one from sports, one from city
politics—after work and listened to several mean-spirited profane bits
of office gossip surrounding Ken Shaw and Max Kohlheimer. Then they
took leave of their friends and went to dinner.

Afterward, they went to Caryn's apartment. She packed a bag for
the next two overnights, then accompanied Townsend back to his building. In the lobby, as Townsend retrieved his mail, they encountered Jim
and Barbara, the lovebirds who billed and cooed—and much, much
more—on the other side of Townsend's bedroom wall. Townsend
greeted them and said hello, without introducing Caryn.

"Who are they?" she asked after Jim and Barbara had gone upstairs
ahead of them.

"You'll find out in about an hour," he said.

"What?"

"You'll see," he promised. But his attention was already diverted.
Within the bills and junk mail was a communication from his wife. He
could tell by the writing as well as the return address and California
postmark. He tucked it away unopened before Caryn could spot it and
ask about it. Townsend supposed it was his final divorce document—
signed, sealed, official and delivered—and he was not in the mood for
it.

So he took Caryn's hand and they went upstairs.

The assassin looked through the sight of his weapon and could
barely believe his eyes. Townsend had come into his apartment with a
woman. The assassin, dressed in slacks and a single T-shirt within which
the muscles of his chest and arms bulged, turned off all of the lights in
his own apartment. He sat down at the scope of his rifle, watched and
waited in ambush.

Lately, his vigil had been marked with frustration. Townsend had
been so rarely in his apartment that the killer gave long thought to
trying to hit him somewhere else. That, of course, would need permission from those above him. And he hadn't asked for it yet.

He set down the can of beer that had been in his hand. He waited.

Waiting for just the right moment to make a kill was a frustrating task. One could wait weeks, sometimes even months, for just the second. Then one would have to recognize the moment and seize it.

The lights were on in some of the windows of Townsend's apartment. The killer's weapon was focused into the bedroom, however. It was there that he would have a clear shot of Townsend as he lay in bed or sat at his desk.

The killer waited. He sipped his third can of beer. Townsend was in the habit of leaving the shades up, which made the assassin's task possible.

The assassin watched with fascination. . . .

In Townsend's apartment, Townsend lounged onto a chair in his living room. He glanced at the rest of his mail. Caryn went to the kitchen, found some beer and soft drinks, and poured some refreshment for both of them.

About half an hour later, a light flashed on in the bedroom. The assassin was poised and ready to fire. If only his target, Townsend, would sit down or lie down for two seconds, he would have his shot. This task was infinitely more difficult than the shot in Fort Myers.

He watched. He waited. . . .

It was not Townsend who appeared in the bedroom, however. It was Caryn. This night the assassin was on the receiving end of more than he bargained for. Or deserved. He sipped more beer and watched.

Caryn pulled off her blouse and skirt. A moment later, moving quickly in Townsend's bedroom, she was completely undressed. The assassin watched intently through the telescopic sight on his rifle. He felt a surge of jealousy and anger at the reporter. To have a woman as fine looking like this naked in his bedroom was more than a middle-aged newsman could merit.

The killer's anger was translated into a mad desire to get a shot off and see that the job was done. He would make his hit before the couple could make love. He had the bed within his sight. He would get them as they lay down together. This, he told himself, would be some shot!

In Townsend's apartment, Caryn stepped into the shower. The warm spray felt good on her. She washed herself completely and stepped out. She jumped slightly when the arm of a man slid around her waist.

"I didn't expect you!" she said.

Townsend stood near her. "Well, the door was unlocked. So why wait outside?" He was still dressed. But he pulled Caryn to him and kissed her.

"Can't a woman have any peace while she's showering?" she pouted.

"Not if she's as pretty as you, is completely undressed, and is in a man's bathroom," he said. He leaned forward and kissed her again.

As Caryn toweled off, Townsend stepped into the shower, blasting himself with the warm water. As he shaved, she borrowed one of his robes and dried off. She went into the bedroom and sat down on his bed. From several hundred meters away, a weapon's sight was upon the right side of her temple.

The assassin peered through the sight. His finger slowly went to the trigger. What the hell, he thought. He'd kill the woman, too. Two quick shots and—

Caryn sat up for a moment. She removed her robe and tossed it to a nearby chair. She sat naked on the side of the bed, thumbing through a magazine.

"Good," the killer thought. "Perfect. I'll get them both. Why not?" He lowered his sight. He had her heart targeted. The weapon's honing system was on the ribs near her left breast.

A second later, Townsend appeared in his bedroom, a towel around his waist.

"Took my robe, huh?" he said to her.

"It looks better on me than you," she said.

"I like you just the way you are," he said. "Without it."

The killer's hand was upon the stock of his weapon now. His finger tightened on the trigger. With his other hand, just for a moment, he adjusted the weapon's scope.

"If I don't have clothes," Caryn asked her lover. "Why do you?"

She reached to him and pulled his towel away. She flung it in the direction of the robe. She pulled him down to her, but she hardly needed to. He followed her onto the white sheets of the bed.

The killer checked his radar mechanism. It was working perfectly. It was locked on his target. He put his eye back to the sight. His hand slowly moved back to the trigger. He had the man now. He would get the man first and when he tumbled away he would shoot the woman in her bare lower abdomen. The double kill would just take a few seconds now. Maybe ten.

Then eight . . .

Then seven . . .

Caryn sprung up from the bed.

"Where are you going?" Townsend asked.

The assassin saw her perfectly as she walked toward the window.

"I can't make love with a window shade up," she said. She strode purposefully toward the room's only shade. The assassin felt his own urges come to life as he looked at Caryn completely nude as she walked toward him.

"Women!" Townsend said.

The killer adjusted his sight. *Yes! He would shoot over her shoulder! He still had a shot at the man! Straight toward Townsend's chest and heart!*

His eye was back on the sight. His finger tightened on the trigger. Caryn was at the window reaching upward.

Two seconds . . .

First the man. Then the woman . . .

"Here," Paul Townsend said. "I'll knock off the light, instead." He reached to the bedside lamp and turned off the only light in the room.

One second . . .

Caryn yanked down the window shade. She turned and looked at her lover, waiting for her in the dark, his penis erect. She giggled and felt like running over and jumping on him. So she did, taking a girlish leap and slowly coming down astride him.

No seconds. No shot, either . . . !

As Caryn and Paul made love, they remained blissfully unaware that in shutting out the light, she had shut out the death angel as well. The window shade worked as a screen. It had jammed the sensors of the weapon trained upon them from many hundred yards away.

The next morning, they rose early. Caryn went for her car. While she was out of the apartment, Townsend opened the letter from his wife.

It was not a completed divorce document. It was a heartfelt message and one that took him by surprise.

Nora was willing, she said, to attempt a reconciliation if he wanted one. She said she accepted what he did for a living. In a funny kind of way, she missed some of the excitement. And, needless to say, his daughter missed him horribly. Worst of all, or best, depending on one's perspective, Nora said she still loved him. She realized that after his last stay.

Townsend stared at the letter for several seconds after he finished reading it. Then he went back and read through it again, slowly this time.

Good God, he thought to himself. *Do the surprises in life ever end?* Actually, he knew the answer. No, they never did. He folded the letter away, not even sure of his own reaction to it.

Then he walked downstairs. Caryn smiled and waved to him from the Miata as she came around the corner of West 98th Street and rolled to a halt.

Townsend switched seats with her. He took the wheel and they departed for Washington.

<<<< **38** >>>>

"*TOWNSEND,*" McMorris said. "I never gave you any guarantee that every little detail in our files is accurate. *Never* did I say that. I was generous enough to give you access, however. From that, you transposed that I've set you up with a pack of lies."

The two men sat on a bench at the edge of Dupont Circle. Traffic moved by, as did pedestrians. Townsend tried to figure out whether he was under surveillance. He didn't see any, though McMorris had a beige Ford sedan waiting for him in a No Parking zone. A driver, presumably a company man like McMorris, waited in the car.

"I don't think I saw anything that would cause you or your agency any discomfort," Townsend charged. "That's my problem. I think there's more information somewhere. And your agency is sitting on it."

McMorris opened his hands in disgust.

"My feeling is that I've been more than fair with you, I've done things I didn't have to. I've given you access where you didn't deserve any. From that, you sense a conspiracy. I don't know what further I could do."

"You could level with me for a change."

"About what?" McMorris snapped angrily. "I don't have everything memorized in our files. If I did, we wouldn't have computers. Or a reading room."

"What about this Colbert Davies?" Townsend asked. " 'Lyndon's-Man'? Was he one of your people. Or was he working for Lyndon Johnson?"

"You met him," McMorris shot back sarcastically. "You should have asked him yourself."

"My guess is he was actually doing something for L.B.J.," Townsend said. "But what? He sure got Ambassador Merriman moving around in a hurry."

"Don't try to bring BRONTOSAURUS into it," McMorris said with disdain. "That old theory, that old canard, died out with Jim Angleton. Or didn't you know?"

For a moment Townsend couldn't follow McMorris's line of thought. Then he realized the confusion.

"I said *Merriman*," Townsend corrected. "Ambassador Kenneth Merriman. Not Averell *Harriman* who was the subject of the BRONTOSAURUS inquiry."

"Oh," said McMorris. It was a funny sort of coincidence, Townsend noted immediately, and he wondered why McMorris had jumped to make the confusion. Somewhere in the back of his mind, Townsend put the incident on hold. "Sorry," said McMorris. "Foolish of me."

Townsend was still staring at him. *Merriman. Harriman.* What was it about the confusion between the two ambassadors that riveted his subconscious attention?

"And while we're at it," McMorris said, "Why don't you leave poor old Lyndon Johnson out of your muckraking? The man's been dead for twenty-four years. Can't you let anyone rest?"

"You know how it is with us retired obituary writers," Townsend said. "Just can't leave a man alone just because he's slipped into the next dimension."

"Very funny."

"It wasn't meant to be. Nor is the fact that we're wasting each other's time. Got anything substantive to tell me?"

McMorris shook his head. Townsend stood to leave. Then he felt a hand on his wrist.

"Hold it, Townsend," McMorris said. "Sit down. We're not finished."

"I am."

"I'm not," McMorris answered.

Townsend slowly sat.

"All right," the CIA man said with a sense of import. "You've pushed this thing to its limit. You've minced around in the quicksand for as far as anyone can tolerate. To my mind, I've been tolerant. Reasonable. Now I'm giving you a warning."

"I'm waiting."

"Drop this."

"Drop what?"

"What you're investigating. Wolik. Colbert Davies. BRON-TOSAURUS. Just can it, if you know what's good for you."

Townsend looked at him long and hard.

"So there *is* more to it, isn't there? A lot more!"

"I'm not in a position to comment. I'm only warning you. And that's why I brought you here. Let it drop. If you care for your safety. If you care for the safety of the woman you're working with. If you care for the security of your family out on the West Coast."

"You son of a bitch," said Townsend slowly. He felt like striking McMorris, but held off. "So it's threats now, huh? You and you're people aren't much different from the lowlife hoodlums I used to write up in Philadelphia and New York."

"Don't be a moron!" McMorris said. *"I'm* not threatening you. I've got nothing to do with this. I'm just a keeper of the records. Some stories just shouldn't be out to the public. It would do no one any good. This is one of them. Okay?" Now it was McMorris who was finished. With a short gesture of his left hand, he signaled to his waiting driver.

"Do you know what it is?" Townsend pressed. "The complete story?"

"No comment."

"But it goes back to the mid-sixties, right? Kennedy–Johnson administration. Vis-à-vis what was then the Soviet Union, right?"

"No comment."

"Come on, McMorris!"

"I'm not saying anything more. I called you to warn you, not put you through college."

"Goddamn you!" Townsend snapped, his temper rising." It's why Harry was killed, right? It's why my car blew sky high. It's why that policewoman was murdered in—"

"We've talked enough, Townsend. If you choose to be foolhardy after this, that's a decision you've made. But I guarantee you, no good will come to you from it. Understand me? If it doesn't kill you, you'll wish it had."

McMorris's car rolled to a halt at the curb.

"I don't scare easily, McMorris," Townsend said.

McMorris stood. "No. Apparently you don't." He paused and looked at Townsend as if to suggest it might be the final time. "Pity. I guess some men never learn. So long, Townsend. Don't bother me again."

McMorris turned and walked to the car. The driver kept his eyes intent on Townsend and vice versa. Moments later, Bruce McMorris and his bodyguard disappeared into a sea of other nondescript cars within the flurry of traffic around Dupont Circle.

Townsend reached next to him to a newspaper. He picked it up for a moment and nervously pretended to read. He made a great target just sitting there.

Five minutes passed and finally Caryn's Miata rolled to the curb. Townsend folded the newspaper under his arm and joined her in the car.

"Get it?" he asked anxiously as he closed the door.

"Could I miss?" She motioned to the spy camera on her lap. "Twenty-two shots I took of him as he was talking to you. I must have something good. You can supply the subtitles and show them to your grandchildren."

"I should live so long," he said. When he realized how bad that sounded, he accompanied it with a grin. "Come on," he said. "Let's get them developed."

Developed. Townsend's contact in Washington was his own newspaper's capital bureau, an elaborate suite of offices on Connecticut Avenue about seven minutes from the White House. The *Sun'*s national bureau contributed to all the Kohlheimer papers, meaning there was plenty of money to keep the setup well oiled and efficient.

A photo technician named Isaac Schoer was the main honcho of the photo department. Townsend had dealt with him before, twice in person but more frequently over the telephone. Schoer was a New Yorker whose newspaper background reached all the way back to the teetering history of the *World-Journal-Tribune* in the early 1960s, the collective last gasp of nine once solid dailies. Schoer was also a fan of Townsend's old-style punch-in-the-nose method of reporting. He didn't owe Townsend favors, but he owed admiration.

It took Schoer less than thirty minutes to develop Caryn's photos. She had done an excellent job. She had likenesses of Bruce McMorris that glistened with clarity. Townsend put his arm around her and hugged her shoulders when he saw them.

"None of that here," Schoer said of the display of affection. "Save it for the darkroom."

But there was little to laugh at that afternoon. Townsend picked out the best shot and put it onto a Photo-Fax transmitter to Det. Anthony Duncan's precinct in New York. Duncan was primed to wait for it. When he received it, which was moments after transmission, he set it into his own computers for photo veneration. Townsend sought to turn back the clock eleven years on Bruce McMorris.

Townsend and DiCarlo waited. It took an hour for the response from New York. The hour seemed like three. Then Schoer's Photo-Fax terminal came to life with a gentle electronic transmission tone. And into its plastic basket dropped Duncan's computer imaging of Bruce McMorris, plus an assortment of five others—five more expired felons from Duncan's trash collection—which Townsend had requested as well.

There was also text attached. Duncan asked that Townsend call him immediately. "We need to speak," read the note.

"May I?" Townsend asked, looking up and indicating the telephone. Schoer nodded.

Townsend picked up the telephone and dialed Tony Duncan in New York. The line was busy. He set down the receiver and next called a number in Baltimore. Following two rings, Al Lakaitis picked up in his home.

"Albert," Townsend said. "This is Paul Townsend on the *Sun.*"

After two seconds, "Yes, Paul?" The tone was neither friendly nor hostile. It was flat, with a suggestion of wariness.

"What are you doing in about two hours?" Townsend asked.

"Firing bullets at whoever comes to my door," said Lakaitis. "Why? What's on your mind?"

"I thought I'd stop in and say hello."

"Got something to show me?" Lakaitis asked.

Townsend stared at the photo lying on the desk in front of him. "Might be a waste of time," Townsend said. "But I'm willing to make the trip if you're willing to take a look."

"I'm willing," Lakaitis said. He set a time.

Townsend tried Anthony Duncan again in New York. Again the line was busy. He hung up and placed all of the photographs in a large white envelope.

Caryn and Paul Townsend went to the Miata. Caryn flipped her car keys to him, meaning he could maneuver through the rush-hour traffic leaving the District. He did. Within half an hour, they found themselves on the beltway heading north. She offered to take over the driving, but he declined. His own adrenaline was rushing now. He felt he had something. When he hit some open road on Route 95, his foot gained weight. They sailed past Baltimore, which brought back a world of thoughts of Wolik, Christine, and even Lakaitis himself. Then they were on to Delaware. They arrived at Lakaitis's home past seven in the evening.

He came to his door to meet them, almost regarding them as allies now, compatriots against a common enemy—the force that had struck down the woman he loved. He greeted them with a handshake for the first time and took his usual scan of the surrounding lawn behind them. Then he locked the door.

The former detective led them further into his home now. It was a modern house completely devoid of any input by a woman. The furnishings were masculine and without character. Two days' worth of coffee cups sat near a television. A stack of tabloid newspapers was on a floor by a worn sofa.

Lakaitis led the two reporters to a room with a television and bookcases in the rear of the house. There were venetian blinds on the windows. They were drawn. Lakaitis sat down on a chair near one of the windows.

"Okay," he said finally. "Let's have it."

"Tell me if you recognize anyone," Townsend said. He handed Lakaitis the white envelope that contained six photographs.

Lakaitis reached to the envelope and opened it. He flipped through the half-dozen color pictures. He stopped at the fourth and pulled it out.

He held the picture in his hands and stared at it.

"Never thought I'd see that ugly kisser again," Lakaitis said. He gave it a few more seconds of somber thought, then turned it back to Townsend. Caryn studied his selection. He had pulled from the field the photograph of Bruce McMorris.

"I'm pretty sure I know the answer, Albert," Townsend said. "But make it official, will you? When did you see him before?"

"Morning of February 11, 1985," Lakaitis said. "Baltimore, Maryland. Chief Mooney's office."

It had been McMorris, Lakaitis said, eleven years earlier, who had shown up three days after the death of Leonard Wolik to guide the police inquest to a harmless conclusion. It had been McMorris who had plucked the case from Detectives Nevell and Lakaitis.

"Who is he?" Lakaitis asked.

"Pretty much what you thought."

"A real Suit," Lakaitis said, with all the derision the word could contain.

"A real Suit," Townsend confirmed. And for a moment the three of them looked at each other. They had linked together so much after so long.

"Can I use your phone?" Townsend finally asked.

"You sure you want to?" Lakaitis asked. The paranoia was rampant, but the point was well taken. Townsend found a pay booth down the road in New Castle half an hour later.

He pushed the numbers for Anthony Duncan in New York. He hoped Duncan was working late, as he often did. Duncan was.

Townsend thanked him for the photographs. But Duncan had more serious matters on his mind. "Better take care of yourself," Duncan warned.

"Why? Specifically?"

"I don't know what kind of dangerous fuckers you're dealing with this time," Duncan said. "I can only imagine."

It took a moment for it to register. "My FBI guys?" Townsend asked.

"Yeah. Your FBI guys. You got a problem here, Paul."

Townsend felt a surge of true fear.

"What is it?" he asked.

"You *met* these guys, right? Flynn and Grodine, was it?"

"Right."

"You *saw* the names? And the shields?"

"Right," Townsend agreed again.

"And they *looked* legitimate?"

"As pure as gold," said Townsend.

"Then watch your ass, man. You're dealing with some dangerous fuckheads."

"Give it to me," Townsend said.

"There's no one on the FBI rolls who matches what you gave me," Duncan said. "And there's no one on special assignment or undercover, either. Your guys are frauds. Bogus. No good, man. FBI's never heard of them. Chances are, eventually you'll wish you hadn't, either."

Townsend rang off. He slowly set down the phone. Then he stood very still. He felt his shirt go wet with sweat and a tremor of deep fear rippled through him. It was like the old days, all right, back when he was a marked man walking around the city as if there were a target painted on the back of his head. When *would* the shot finally come that would finish him? Or when would he ever learn to lay off when it was in his own interests.

A hand landed on his shoulder. He gasped and jumped.

The hand pulled away and there was Caryn—not Flynn or Grodine. And by the look on his face she knew that something was very wrong.

"Sorry," he said. "I'm jumpy."

"You're also lying. Be honest with me," she said. "I'm a big girl. I came into this case knowing exactly what I was getting into. So what is it?"

He paused several seconds, then he told her.

"And the worst part of it is," he said as she tried to maintain her own composure, "that they're out there somewhere looking for us."

* * *

In 1996, the Democrats held their convention in New York City. For twenty years the party had been able to win any election in the United States except for the one for the White House. This year—again—they did everything possible to keep their losing streak alive.

The party nominated their front-running candidate, the black man who had won more primary delegates than any other registered Democrat. This gave the party bosses, and the veteran party insiders, a bad case of migraine, made worse by the fact that they couldn't admit that they already knew they were well on the path of defeat once again.

The nominee himself was as qualified to be President as anyone, though that had little to do anymore with actually being able to win the office. What the game was about was fund-raising, media image, and whether or not the candidate could evoke enough enthusiasm to win a national election.

This particular candidate had been excellent at getting his own constituency to the polls, which was enough to capture the nomination. He was lousy at the other aspects of winning the White House. Some insiders sourly suggested "letting him have" the nomination so that he'd lose and go away, rather than making a nuisance out of himself for the Democratic party every four years.

After his nomination, there began the even more mortifying task of finding a running mate. No one with any national ambitions or stature wanted any part of the ticket. This left the party in its most humiliating public position since the McGovern debacle of 1972 when Sargent Shriver, the Kennedy-in-law, was the candidate's twelfth choice for Vice President. That ticket carried Massachusetts and the District of Columbia. Then again, some historians pointed out, the Republican ticket that year carried forty-nine states and both "winners" were out of office within another two years.

Finally, the nominee pulled a Vice Presidential candidate out of the hat. A former governor of Minnesota, who was still moderately popular with farmers and labor in his state, was willing to run. The man had served as governor for eight years and had spent the last few years teaching at the University of Minnesota, who were known as the Gophers. But the governor had worn out his welcome on campus. One of the best-kept secrets of his eight popular years in the state house was that his public image as a liberal and humanitarian masked one of the foulest personalities in the politics of the northern Midwest. That was also why he had worn out his welcome in academia. Now he was running for Vice President as a favor to a few of the friends he had in the national party. In return for running and losing on the national ticket, his friends would fix him up with a job in the party hierarchy after the inevitable defeat in November. As he wasn't doing anything else at the time, he agreed. He and the Presidential candidate had always found each other personally obnoxious and overly ambitious. It made a curious scene, to those who knew both, to see them on the podium on the concluding evening of the convention, holding each other's arms aloft and flashing transparently fake "V" for victory signs.

It struck the public as curious, too. Even given the upward "bump" that a convention often gives a candidate, the Democrats were in solid with 21 percent of the electorate as of the day after their convention.

They even had an excellent chance to carry Massachusetts and were looking good in the District of Columbia, too. So, all things considered, they could do no worse than McGovern did in 1972 when he went down to the worst defeat in modern Presidential history. In American politics, there was always an optimistic way of looking at anything.

<<<< **39** >>>>

A *MONTH*—a very grim gray month—had passed since his wife had been murdered. Now Jim Hubbell sat quietly in a corner of his living room and attempted to shed some light—any light—upon the death of his wife. A reporter had reached him on the telephone and then had flown down from New York just to talk to him. But for the time, Jim Hubbell couldn't find any light.

"I, uh, don't know what I can tell you that I haven't told the local police, Mr. Townsend," the widower said. "I've gone through everything I think is relevant." He opened his hands and closed them again. "What can I say? Tina's gone. I don't know who killed her."

Townsend looked at the bereaved man across from him. Hubbell was a pudgy man with thick black-framed glasses. He was about forty and chunky with a shaggy mustache. From a few minutes of initial conversation, Townsend also sensed that Hubbell was a decent individual whose vision of life had rarely extended beyond the successful ledger sheets of his hammer-and-nail enterprises. His sister was staying with him since the loss of his wife.

"What sort of angles are the police following?" Townsend asked.

Hubbell shrugged. "What sort do they have? They're following their noses, I guess," he said.

"Please tell me anything you can. It could only help," Townsend asked. There was a certain sympathy in the way Townsend spoke. He'd approached widowed spouses so many times in their worst anguish, that he had developed a keen instinct for it. It served him here, for Jim Hubbell wanted badly to cooperate.

Hubbell explained further. The Fort Myers police were checking local weapons. They were interviewing anyone who might live within walking distance and own a gun. They had questioned everyone in the area who was a known small-caliber hunter or small-caliber crook. But so far, no breaks. And since most weapons in Florida were not registered, this avenue proved almost worthless. The cops were also going door to door in the area where Tina had been shot. Someone had to have seen *something,* the local gendarmes theorized. Yet the few people who had actually witnessed her death claimed she had just dropped cold.

No sound, no fury. No visible assassin.

"Are they digging into her background at all?" Townsend asked.

"What do you mean by that?" Hubbell asked, almost defensively.

"Well," Townsend began, "I don't mean this with any disrespect. But often a husband doesn't know everyone with whom his wife may have been previously involved." Townsend could see Hubbell bristle slightly, taking sexual innuendo from the question.

Townsend deftly moved along to a more professional level. "For example," he said, "she was a police officer in Maryland for several years. She made arrests. She put felons in jail. There could have been a residual grudge somewhere . . ."

Hubbell shook his head. "I know the local police checked that. They said she didn't have any felony arrests."

Townsend blinked. "Then your local people didn't pursue that very carefully," he said. "I checked that, too," he said. "I found several arrests."

"You did?"

Townsend nodded. His own inquest in Baltimore had brought to the surface scores of good collars and a half-dozen cases in which a convicted criminal might have borne a special hostility to a persistent policewoman then named Christine Nevell. But in two of those cases, the perpetrators were now dead. In three, they remained in prison. In the final case, the man was on work-release parole in Washington, D.C., and had been at his job at the time of the murder.

"You checked all that yourself?" Hubbell asked.

Townsend nodded.

"Why's this so interesting to you?" Hubbell asked. "You work for a New York paper. Don't you have enough murders up there?"

"More than enough. Close to three thousand a year if an honest count were kept."

"Well then . . . ?" Hubbell seemed nonplussed.

"I'm approaching this case from a different angle," Townsend said. "Do you want to know what it is? It may upset you."

"Mr. Townsend. My wife was taken from me. I'm upset already."

"I can't prove it yet and I don't know all the specifics," Townsend said. "But I think there's a tie to some sort of espionage operation."

A silence followed. It was so thick that Townsend felt he could cut it with a knife.

"Spies?" Hubbell finally asked. His brow contorted with the question.

"Call it that if you like," Townsend answered.

"What sort of spies?"

"I don't know. Russian? American?" He shrugged as if there were something routine about it. "I wish I could tell you, Jim. If I find out, I will."

Hubbell exhaled slowly. A perplexed expression crept across his face and stayed there.

"Like James Bond? That sort of stuff?" Hubbell inquired.

"Not quite. More rooted in reality."

"*Whose* reality?"

"The politics of the 1960s maybe. I don't know, Jim. I'm still guessing. Same as you." Townsend paused. "That might be one hint for the *way* she was killed. "I think the shot was fired from several hundred meters away. Who uses weapons like that? Who *has* weapons like that?" Townsend returned Hubbell's sense of wonder.

"But why my Tina? What did she do?"

"Again, I don't know, Jim. But I want to know. That's why I'm here."

For what seemed like a long time another silence held the room. Then a rueful smile tiptoed across the widower's face. He removed his glasses and cleaned them with a paper napkin as he spoke. His eyes were red and moist.

"Christine was a fan of that sort of Ian Flemming and Tom Clancy stuff," he said. "She'd of been fascinated if it hadn't been her who'd been killed." He thought about it for a moment again. "I never read any of it myself. I'm not much of a reader. She was, though. College girl, you know."

"University of Maryland. Bachelor of Science in criminology," Townsend said.

"How did you know that?" Hubbell looked at his visitor with suspicion.

"I looked at her file in the Baltimore Police Department," Townsend said. "I'm good at knowing and understanding people who are deceased."

"Jeez. You sure are. You done more research than the police here."

"I don't doubt that." Then, when Hubbell gave him a strange look, Townsend softened the remark. "That's often the case," he added. "The police are very busy."

"Too busy for a murder?"

"No, but reporters also approach things differently."

Hubbell thought about it. "Guess so," he finally said. Hubbell stood. "Come on in here. I want to show you something, Mr. Townsend."

Townsend stood and followed his host. They walked through a dining room into what was apparently a small library carved out of a corner of a sitting room on the first floor of the Hubbell home. Hubbell led Townsend to a series of bookshelves on one wall of the room.

"These belong to Tina," he said, still talking of his wife in the present tense. Hubbell surveyed the books. "I don't know whether you're able to get a grip on a person's personality by looking at their things after they're gone. Ever do that?"

"Many times on my current newspaper," Townsend said. "I used to write obituaries."

"Ah. I see. Well then," Hubbell said thoughtfully. "Maybe this will tell you something. I don't think there's a book here that she didn't read." Hubbell shook his head. "Great reader, that girl."

Townsend studied the selection. There were mysteries and historical novels. Spy stories and political thrillers. Everything was arranged by author. Then the fiction gave way to the nonfiction. Tina had had a taste for political intrigue that boiled over from the imagination of underpaid novelists and into real life. Maybe too much so.

"Fascinating," murmured Townsend. He was waiting for his thoughts to take shape.

In nonfiction, there were two entire shelves on Presidential deaths—the ultimate in newsworthy obituaries. The section began with Lincoln, continued through Garfield and McKinley, then leaped across sixty-odd years to John F. Kennedy.

Not just Presidential deaths, Townsend noted with a slight tremor. *But Presidential assassinations.* For a moment, Townsend felt his analysis buckle when he saw a book on President Harding. But then he pulled it from the shelf. *The Strange Death of President Harding* was its title. The book was hardcover in black cloth and had no dust jacket. It had been published in 1928 by a long-caput Boston firm named Bower & Stepford. And it suggested—by stating its case outright in the first paragraph—that Warren G. Harding, the twenty-ninth President of the United States, had been murdered.

Townsend ran his hand along the late woman's library, trying to sense what it was telling him.

"She was fascinated by all this stuff," the hardware man said. "Read all this stuff in college, then wanted to become a policewoman. Then got disgusted with it and quit the force. Quit suddenly. We met shortly thereafter. Got married."

"When were you married?" Townsend asked.

"October 14, 1987," he said.

"Why did she leave the force so suddenly?"

"She never really explained fully," he said. "And I never asked. She spent a lot of her own time thinking and reading. Tried to do some writing, too," he said. "Don't know whatever happened to it."

"No?" Townsend looked at him.

"Guess she threw it away," her husband said. "I never found it. Whatever it was. I've looked."

"No one took it, did they?" Townsend asked.

"Why do you ask that? Who'd take it?"

"Who'd kill her?" Townsend answered. On this point, he had Hubbell.

Hubbell pursed his lips and looked back to Tina's collection.

"Did the Fort Myers police ever look at all these books?" Townsend asked.

"No. Why would they?"

"As I suspected," Townsend said. He removed his hand from a book on President Lincoln's last day alive. Next to it were thirteen books taking issue with the Warren Commission's findings. Then his hand drifted to the most worn book on the shelf—a hardcover condensation of the Warren Commission's report. Tina—or someone—had been through it hundreds of times, Townsend guessed. Why?

"I guess the police would have no reason to browse through a library," Townsend said. He was about to put the Warren report away when his eyes alighted on the Presidential signature at the end of the preface. Lyndon Johnson. The geometry of some investigations never ceased to amaze him.

"Want my opinion?" Hubbell asked.

"Sure, Jim," said Townsend, hoping for something bearing on Tina's death.

"I think education for a woman is like pouring honey into a fine watch. Didn't do Tina any good. Only made her unhappy." He shrugged again. "Who knows. Maybe it even . . ."

"Got her killed?"

"Yes."

"Who knows, Jim? We're guessing, aren't we? Sometimes that's not a very wise thing to do."

Hubbell nodded sadly. He agreed that yes, they were guessing.

"If anything further occurs to you, if you find anything, if anything comes to you as out of the ordinary," Townsend asked, "please call me." Townsend handed him a business card, then placed a consoling hand on his shoulder. "Call me collect if you want. Or, even if there's nothing specific. Anytime you want to exchange thoughts. Okay?"

Hubbell thanked the reporter and said it was okay.

"And do me one favor," Townsend added. "If you call, my line is secure. But who knows about yours? Go to a phone booth, even though you'll feel like a jerk when you're doing it."

"A phone booth. Why? You think . . . ?" His voice tailed off as he motioned to his home phone.

"You just never know," Townsend said. "See, my theory is that someone had something very specific against Mrs. Hubbell. She did something. Maybe she knew something. She . . . I don't know. Sometimes operators listen in, you know, Jim. Who wants to be fodder for local gossip, right?"

Jim Hubbell agreed. Local gossip could be dreadful. He thanked the reporter for his time, interest, and sympathy. Townsend was the first person Hubbell had ever met from New York whom he actually liked.

Then Townsend departed and caught the next flight back to Kennedy.

Two days later, Ken Shaw, managing editor of the *New York Sun*, raised his eyes from his desk and looked back and forth at the two reporters who sat before him. Neither Paul Townsend nor Caryn DiCarlo had anything more to say.

"Well?" Shaw asked. "What are you telling me? Dead end?"

Townsend shrugged. "No," he insisted. "I'm not telling you it's a dead end. What I'm saying is our leads are running cold. We have to find some new ones. Come on, Ken. That takes some time. You know that."

"*I* know that. *You* know that," he said, looking them back and forth again. "But does Max Kohlheimer know that?" he asked. "Come on, Townsend. Let's face it. You're churning this story. You know Max. 'The public's got an attention span of ten seconds!' he'd tell you. 'If you can't get something new on this story every two days, the public will drop it.' Thus we drop it."

"Is that what he's telling you on the phone, Ken?" Townsend asked.

"Mr. Kohlheimer and I talked about a lot of things."

"And that's one of them?"

"That's one of them."

"How recently did you talk about it?" Townsend sparred. "What time today, for example?"

Shaw was growing angry. The vein on the left side of his neck bulged. "Look, Paul," said the editor. "Try to put this in perspective. What you have is a hodgepodge of events. You're putting this newspaper's credulity on the line because you think—I repeat, you *think*—that you can tie everything together eventually in a neat bundle." He paused. "What if you can't?"

"I will."

"You're working on a case that by your own admission dates back thirty years," Shaw said. *"Thirty years.* People who had jobs like ours when this began are in nursing homes now. Unless you can come up with something big on this, *who the fuck cares?"*

"Ken . . . ?"

"No, really! *Who the fuck cares!"*

"Ken. That's going to cost you twenty bucks. Language purification, remember?"

"Screw it!" Shaw said. He was inordinately angry.

"It has to tie together somehow," Townsend said. "Ken, look, trust me for another couple of weeks. I'll *make it* tie together. Okay? How's that?"

"Not good enough, I'm afraid."

"What are you telling me?"

"Here's what I'm telling you," Shaw said. "I only reflect what Mr. Kohlheimer tells me. And—"

"We know that, Ken. We know you're the personal mouthpiece for management." Caryn DiCarlo studied her shoes as Townsend battled. "Now skip ahead to something new."

"I've had the two of you on this case for almost seven weeks," Shaw persisted. "An employee of this august journal costs approximately two thousand five hundred dollars per week in salary, pension, health insurance, expense, toilet paper, rubber bands, and so on. So we've made an investment, I calculate, of more than thirty-five thousand dollars already, plus I'd say another five to eight grand in travel, telephone, and so on."

"Ken. Owning this paper is like a license to print money. We're millions of bucks in the black. What's the problem? Get to it, damn it. Would you, Ken?"

"We make millions of dollars because we run a tight ship and we don't let hard-earned dollars hemorrhage out the bilge pumps. How's that?" Shaw glared. "This story simply isn't earning out," he said. "Occasionally we get some page three or page ten stuff. But I can't have a pair of our better people—that's you two, I admit—on a story that's not productive."

"May I remind you, Ken? Other reporters have been calling us trying to pick up the story. It must be interesting to someone."

"Other reporters are trying to pick up the story and they're not even able to substantiate what you've printed," Shaw answered. "Know what some of them are whispering? That Paul Townsend has been divorced by his wife and his brains at the same time."

"So what are you saying, Ken?" Caryn asked, stepping in quickly. "What are you going to do with us?"

Shaw ignored her. Townsend was his target.

"Come on, Paul," Shaw continued. "You know how the system works. Max wants stories that grab the public by the balls each day—pardon my lapse, Caryn—or he doesn't want the stories at all. And, damn it, I'm the managing editor here and I agree with him. The public is tuning out on this one. I can feel it. I can show it to you. You've got a few pieces of what you say is a puzzle. Cute. Maybe even interesting in an obtuse way. But nothing's coming together. Your story isn't even bullshit. It's a gigantic yawn."

"Ken!" Townsend shot back, almost coming to his feet. "Harry's probably bored, too, lying in that grave in Brooklyn where he can't tell jokes about you or worry about the Yankees or his diet. Have you forgotten? One of our people was killed, remember?"

"And who's to say why? Really? Have you linked it to anything? Have you *really* tied it to the rest of your case?"

"It's related!"

"Who says? Not the NYPD. They don't say anything. All they say is that Harry followed you to a bunch of storage lockers in the Brooklyn jungle at midnight. You were supposed to meet some woman who was supposed to explain why you made an ass of yourself and printed a bum obituary. And dumb old Harry got himself killed for his troubles."

Shaw sensed Townsend's anger flirting with the explosion point. He eased off slightly.

"Paul," he concluded, "I liked Harry Dubrow, too. He was a friend of mine. I hope the cops catch his killers and fry their balls—pardon me again, Caryn—in peanut oil. But until you come up with something hot—something fresh, something new—it's almost a dead issue. Am I making myself clear?"

Townsend blew out a breath in boundless disgust.

"Too clear, Ken," Townsend said. "So clear that I can see right through you. What's Kohlheimer want? Us to drop the investigation?"

"He wants me to reassign both of you to something more productive." Shaw patted a pair of files at his elbow. "We've got some stories around with some sex appeal." The displeasure of his reporters was thick enough to hack with a meat cleaver. Even a man of Shaw's keen instincts couldn't miss it.

"Look," Shaw proclaimed buoyantly. "It's not all bad. You'll find yourselves back right on the front pages probably."

Townsend and DiCarlo exchanged a look.

"You two like working together?" Shaw's eyes twinkled lasciviously. "Looks like you do. Word reaches me that you do. Fine. You can stay as a team. I don't care. I just want something *current* on the front pages. Something that will—if I may borrow one of Max's pet expressions— reach out and bite people on the ass if they walk by a newsstand."

"Ken," Townsend said evenly, "you're subtle beyond words."

"Am I?" he answered very seriously. "I'm not trying to be." He glanced back and forth again.

"Can we have a week?" Townsend asked. "To wrap things up. To see if anything new comes by."

Shaw moaned as if he'd been poisoned.

"Come on, Ken," Caryn said. "Listen. I have an idea. After seven days we'll give you everything we have. We'll put it together as a special investigative report. We'll make the whole thing hang together like an unsolved murder case. Let the readers ask the questions. Let them mail in solutions."

"We're going to turn it into a contest?" Shaw asked sourly.

"No, but Caryn's got a point," Townsend said. "There's something that won't be in any other paper or on any broadcast station, either. It'll be a *Sun* exclusive."

"Seven days?" Shaw asked. "Then that's it. Unless you get a breakthrough."

Townsend nodded grudgingly. Caryn followed Townsend's lead.

"All right then," Shaw agreed. "Now. There's something else I need to take up with you as well," he added.

"What's that?"

He looked at Caryn.

"This publication will be making an endorsement early in the Presidential campaign," Shaw said. "I don't think I need to tell you where Mr. Kohlheimer's sympathies lie."

"With the crypto-Nazi senator from Texas," said Townsend. "You don't mean we're actually planning to endorse him?"

"Those are Mr. Kohlheimer's wishes," said Shaw. He eyed the new wave of disgust on the faces of his two reporters. "On most of Max's papers that would present no problem. The *Sun*'s a little different situation, this being a big city and all. What I want to know is whether it's going to be a problem here."

"Problem how?"

"With the reporting staff. Or with labor?"

"To answer your last question first, Ken," Townsend said. "This paper busted the printers' union pretty thoroughly when it started up. So your labor problems are minimal. As for the reporting staff—"

"Folks like you and Caryn," Shaw interrupted. "I'm not going to see any blood in the corridors, am I? We won't have an insurrection of liberal reporters that's going to serve as an embarrassment, will we?"

Townsend tapped a finger on the side of his chair. "You want an honest opinion or a polite opinion?" he asked.

"Maybe you could politely give me an honest one."

"Most of the people who are employed by this rag joined the work force during the Reagan years. I doubt if you got five people in this place, other than the two sitting in front of you, who have any scruples, much less who care who's President."

"Good," said Shaw. Then retreating a bit, he added, "By 'good,' I mean, that there'll be no trouble."

"Ken, I'm not guaranteeing it, I'm just giving you my guess."

"That's fine. That leads us to one final point."

"What's that?"

"*Before* the *Sun* endorses Senator Lord for President, we want to do an in-depth profile. A nice shining series which is going to run for a full week. Something that allows Senator Lord to address the issues of the day and shows the candidate in a positive light."

"A seven-day puff piece, in other words."

"Jesus Christ, Townsend!" Shaw finally snapped. "I have never seen a man who so habitually nips at the hand that feeds him!" He angrily looked back and forth from Townsend to DiCarlo. Caryn was almost laughing. "I'm offering you something here—either one of you: the opportunity to interview the next President. And you're mocking it."

"You want one of us to do the interview? Is that it?" DiCarlo asked.

"I'm *offering* it," Shaw said.

Townsend kept silent. Caryn stared at him.

"Any takers?" Shaw asked.

Townsend folded his arms and studied the floor. "Until I hear differently I already have an assignment," he said.

"I do, too," Caryn added.

"Fine," Shaw said huffily. "Don't say I never offered you an easy slot on the front page for a week running."

"Ken," Townsend said with a perfectly straight expression, "I'd never say something nasty like that about you."

"Ingrates!" Shaw barked. "Both of you. I pay you good money and you bite my hand. I don't know why I keep you on. Against the entreaties of some of my closest advisers, I might add."

They laughed.

"All right," Shaw concluded. "That's it. Out of here."

<<<< **40** >>>>

A T their convention in Miami Beach, the Republicans did not do what political analysts reckoned they would. They placed in nomination the name of the incumbent Vice President. Then a congressman from Arizona took the floor by surprise and nominated John Lord as well. This set off some of the first truly spontaneous events at a national political convention since the "We Want Wilkie" convention in Philadelphia in 1940.

On the morning of the balloting there was a boom—call it a boomlet, actually—for drafting John Lord. There was a good deal of sympathy for Lord and his politics on the convention floor. Now, since his name had made its way into nomination, why not skunk the Democrats completely? Why fight Lord? Why not go with him? The current Veep was seen as a loser. So a few influential U.S. senators urged making an eleventh-hour approach to Lord, impressing upon him that if the party "drafted" him, he would have the resources of the party at his disposal. Money, workers, and so on. The strategy thus was to stymie the current Vice President that evening in his quest for a first ballot nomination. Then, with a deadlocked convention, they could dramatically wheel in a "new, moderate, mainstream" John Lord.

This strategy looked fabulous on paper and, with the first ballot just hours away, an impromptu committee within the party set about to secretly pull it off.

But then the incumbent President, taking a rare stand on principle, stuck behind his number-two man with a public statement that he was the only Republican candidate for whom he would campaign. Then Lord set up a trap play for the Republican emissaries.

Privately, Lord let it be known that he would listen to a proposed deal. But then when the Republican "Draft Lord" committee, which included two well-known senators and three congressmen, flew to Dallas that morning, Lord went marlin fishing on the Gulf of Mexico.

Jerry Huddleston, Lord's media guru, called the press and told them to check Dallas-Fort Worth Airport. There a team of reporters found the Republicans, discovered what they were doing there, and took plenty of pictures.

Lord had no comment, laughed and said he didn't personally know about any draft.

"But I sure wouldn't accept one from the Elephant party," he said. "Those are the folks who've been running the country into the ground for twenty-four of the last twenty-eight years. Why would I want to talk to them?"

Why, indeed? The Draft Lord committee turned around at the airport, caught a flight back to Miami, and was running a second gauntlet of reporters within two hours. That evening on the news the baffled Republicans were seen skulking angrily through two airports while their dream candidate was seen tanned and fit, stepping off a sport fishing boat with a two-hundred-pound swordfish. Then later that night, to some visible gloom, the Vice President was nominated. The next day, the party chose a female mayor from a western state for Vice President.

All in all, though they had been made fools of by Lord, it wasn't the worst of all possible worlds for the Republicans. Compared with the

Democrats, it only seemed like the second worst. Then again, the party had been in that situation for years.

On the concluding morning of the convention, and one day before he stood to be reassigned to other stories at the *Sun,* Townsend picked up his telephone when it rang on his desk. He recognized a familiar but unexpected voice.

"Mr. Townsend?"

"Yes."

Praise God. It was Jim Hubbell, Tina's widower, calling from Florida.

"Yes, Jim?" Townsend said, expecting very little. He eased back in his chair. His eyes focused on a picture of his daughter on the edge of his desk. "How are things down there on the hot, muggy peninsula?"

"Well, things are fine in Florida, sir," Hubbell said. "But, uh, that's not why I'm calling."

"Why are you calling, Jim?"

"I been doing some thinking about some of the stuff you told me about," Hubbell said. "Then I did some looking around. You got kind of a point."

Townsend slowly eased forward. "What are you talking about, Jim?" he asked.

"Can't really tell you too much on the phone," Hubbell said. "But my Tina had all these sophisticated theories, you know. Like we talked about, you and I. You know, she read all this stuff I was showing you. Heck, I thought she was just playing around with the theories. Guess not," he said.

"Jim, where are you?" Townsend asked with growing interest. "Do you remember what we talked about? About security? With telephones?"

"Yes, sir. I remember," he said. "I remember real well."

He remembered so well, and Townsend's warning had come home to roost so dramatically, that the widower had taken a few extra precautions. He had sent his daughters to stay with his sister in Alabama. He had taken up residence with an old army buddy in Bradenton. And he'd taken to driving to work each day with a loaded shotgun in the car with him, a weapon he also kept in his office when he worked. It was the perfect metaphor, Townsend thought idly, for business in the mid-1990s: a loaded shotgun ready at all times. But then again, this wasn't ordinary business.

He had also taken the initial precaution that Townsend had recommended. He was in a phone booth. And though he was jittery about talking anywhere he could say a little.

"I got some stuff I might like to show you, Mr. Townsend," Hubbell said. "That's if, uh, you could fly down again."

"I can fly down, Jim," Townsend said, "if it's worth my while. I've got all day, but you're going to have to convince me over the phone that it's worth my time. Is it?"

"I certainly think it might be, Mr. Townsend. My Tina, I think she was fussing around with something kind of scary." He paused. "Do you know a bit about some of this spy and assassination stuff, yourself?"

"I know some, Jim. What specifically?"

Hubbell cleared his throat and then asked the question that hit Townsend between the eyes.

"Ever heard of something called 'Project BRONTOSAURUS'?" Hubbell asked.

Townsend said he had. And he also said that he was ready to travel immediately.

This time, the assassin figured he couldn't miss. He sat in his dark apartment sipping the end of his sixth beer in the last hour. And he glared through the alcoholic haze at the light that had gone on in Townsend's building.

The killer loaded his weapon and set his sight. He still rankled from the previous time that he had his target lined up, the night that the naked woman had bounced up from the bed and pulled down the shade.

This time, the killer thought to himself, he would fire quickly. To delay with a shot like this was to look for another postponement of weeks. The killer was tired of being holed up in that New York apartment. How much beer could a man drink? How much television could he watch?

He put his eye to the sight. He had focused on the target. It was late in the evening. He had a man and a woman in his scope again. They had come home late. The man was taking off his shirt. Then he disappeared from the window again.

"Come on, Townsend," the killer said. "Get in there. Get in my cross-hairs. Give me a target quickly and I won't even shoot your girl."

The killer moved his elbow slightly and knocked over the warm beer that remained in his most recent can. The beer flowed onto his table and dripped onto the assassin's knee. But he didn't budge. This was business time. The target had sat down on his bed and removed his white shirt.

The killer had his shot. He set the honing mechanism. The woman sat down next to the man on the bed. But she sat on the other side of him.

"Why don't you start screwing, the two of you?" the killer asked bitterly. "Give me a big bare back to put a bullet through."

The sighting mechanism was set. The target was locked in—same as Christine Nevell had been.

There was light in the room across the way. The target sat still and glanced at his mail. His lady friend talked to him. There was no window shade. The glass of the victim's window might alter the flight of the bullet slightly, but it would also accelerate its tumble.

The killer's finger tightened on the trigger.

The moment was perfect!

The assassin pulled the trigger. He quickly fired twice. He heard the *ppfffftt* sound of the bullets leaving and he felt the kick of his weapon.

One one thousand. Two one thousand. He counted the travel time of his shots in the air.

Then he saw what he wanted!

The victim moved slightly as if starting to stand. Then the target spun suddenly and gripped his left side. An instant later, he clutched an area up below his neck. The woman next to him seemed to panic. She held her man but he was much larger than she. Despite her help, he fell. The assassin, through binoculars, could see a mass of blood on the victim's bare chest. The woman was struggling with him, trying to stop the bleeding with a sheet. She seemed to be screaming. Then she lunged for a telephone.

The killer pulled down his own shade. His job in New York was done. As he walked through his room assembling his possessions and the tools of his craft, his hip brushed the table again, hitting it hard.

Six beers. Probably not a good idea, the killer thought. But who knew Townsend was going to turn up that evening? Anyway, the job was done. He hoped the meddlesome reporter died. It was time to get out of town and celebrate with a woman and some more alcohol.

The assassin finished packing. He went down to the street. As he was looking for a taxi that would take him to the Amtrak station at Seventh Avenue and 33rd Street, he began to hear multiple police sirens.

"Good!" he said aloud. He happily assumed the sirens were in response to his latest kill.

<<<< **41** >>>>

*J*IM HUBBELL looked like a frightened man. He wore dark glasses when he met Townsend's flight at Tampa Airport. He drove a pickup truck and he hadn't been kidding about the shotgun. He kept it up front with him below the dashboard. Hubbell's worldview seemed to be expanding by the hour.

"I would never have believed it," Hubbell said. "If you'd come here, even if you were an old pal of mine, and told me all this, I'da told you to get out. I'da never have believed it about Tina."

"Life surprises you, doesn't it, Jim?" Townsend said philosophically.

"The things you find out about people after you marry them. Jeez."

"You always find things out after people die, as well," Townsend said. "I spent two years writing obituaries on the *Sun.* It never ceased to fascinate me."

"Guess so."

Townsend flipped down the sunshade above his portion of the windshield. The day was overcast, but Townsend wanted the vanity mirror. It didn't take him long to spot a compact blue Chevrolet station wagon, three cars back, taking the same route from the airport toward Fort Myers.

"I hope that's a friend of yours following us," Townsend said. "Otherwise, we'll be needing that shotgun pretty soon."

"You notice things quickly, huh, don't you?" Hubbell said. "That, uh, come from living in New York?"

"It's from being a reporter," Townsend said. "You get paid to notice things. Who's in the wagon back there?"

"Buddy of mine from work," said Hubbell. "Name's Frankie. One of my store managers. He's my buddy but I'm kind of his boss."

"You're that alarmed, are you?" Townsend watched their escort through the mirror. Frankie was a big, moon-faced man with a beard and a red Florida Marlins baseball cap.

"Two shotguns are better than one," said Hubbell, who excelled at such math.

"You're not setting me up, are you, Jim?" Townsend asked. "Or helping someone else do it? I'll be pretty disappointed if you are. Disappointed and angry."

Hubbell looked at him with affront. Townsend knew he'd overstepped himself.

"Just kidding, pal," Townsend said, who hadn't been. He placed a hand on the widower's shoulder. "Is Frankie reliable?"

"Better be. I pay his salary."

"Then sometime give him a tip for the future. If he knows where we're going, he should pull ahead now and then. Otherwise, if you get a real tail some day, someone playing hard ball, he'll make your pal and hit him right before he blows you away. Okay?"

"Okay."

"And if you're really worried about being followed," he continued, "you should hit your brakes and pull to the side of the highway for five minutes. Then see who cuts theirs to try not to lose you. Sometimes it's almost amusing."

Hubbell took his eyes off the road and gazed at Townsend long enough to make his passenger nervous. Then Hubbell grinned slightly. "Sure," he finally said. "I'll tell Frankie. We'll start doing that. Thanks."

Still, Townsend wished he had been able to bring along his own pistol on the airplane. Damn those federal regulations that made travelling so unsafe. Yet, he tried to be positive. "Where are we going, anyway?" Townsend asked.

"To our house," Hubbell said. "That's where I got stuff to show you."

Townsend nodded. He might have known.

The Hubbell house had a dark and condemned air to it when they arrived, as if much of its life had vanished with Tina. The air conditioning had been off and the house was an inferno when Jim unlocked it. Hubbell opened all the doors and two of the downstairs windows. Outside, Frankie sat in his truck halfway down the block, his shotgun presumably across his lap.

Townsend waved to him once. The man raised a single hand to acknowledge Townsend's greeting.

Hubbell's story grew short and succinct. Among his late wife's possessions, he discovered as he gradually went through them, was a pistol. Firearms were nothing new in the Hubbell domicile. But the mister and missus of the house had had a standing agreement. No weapon was ever unaccounted for, acquired secretly, or left without a lock when the children were about. Tina had violated that code. Jim had found the loaded pistol that she carried under the seat of her car.

He had agonized over it for days. Why had she had it? Who had she been afraid of? He was brooding upon that in the kitchen one night, getting up the nerve to call Mr. Townsend in New York and shoot the breeze about it, when Laurie came into the room.

"Daddy?" she had asked. "What are you doing with Mommy's gun?"

"I couldn't believe it, Mr. Townsend," Jim Hubbell related. "I didn't know my wife had an extra pistol. But my eight-year-old daughter knew. It made me wonder. What else didn't I know?"

"How did your daughter know about it?" Townsend asked.

"That's the first thing I asked her," Hubbell said. He led Townsend out the back door of his house toward a garden. "Laurie told me how she watched my wife get up from sleeping one night and walked out here." Hubbell indicated a spot in a flower bed just ahead of them. " 'Mommy dug up the gun,' Laurie said. She showed me the spot." Hubbell walked Townsend to the exact location. "It was right there," he said. "My wife kept a gun hidden down there in a box in the ground. So after a while, I sent Laurie away. I wondered whether Tina had anything else down there."

He glanced at the spot and dug a toe at it. The soil moved easily, like the fresh dirt from a tiny grave. "My wife kept her secrets well buried," Hubbell said. "Some irony, huh? Now she's buried herself, but her secrets are up here with the rest of us."

"Some irony," Townsend agreed. "I assume you dug the spot up," he said. "It looks like you did."

"Yes, sir," said Hubbell.

"What did you find?"

"That's why you're here, sir," said Hubbell. "I just wanted you to understand where this came from. Now I'll show you what I got."

They walked back indoors. Hubbell went to the front window to see if his sentry was still in place. He waved to the man in the truck. Frankie returned the wave, holding his red baseball cap in his hand. That was the "All Okay" signal. Then Hubbell led Townsend back to where all of Tina's books were shelved.

"I thought it was only right that I kept this here, seeing as how she wrote it. And it's sort of on the same subject matter."

Hubbell removed two handfuls of books and reached behind them. He withdrew a brown folder and gave it to Townsend.

"This isn't the original. This is a set of photocopies. I got the originals elsewheres."

Townsend nodded. "Hidden?"

"Hidden real good."

"Smart idea," Townsend said. "May I?" He indicated a chair.

"Please do." Hubbell invited him to sit and read.

What Townsend saw was the copy of a notebook Christine Nevell had started to keep some eleven years earlier and had maintained until her death. Theories. Questions. Isolated facts. Everything that had come into her stubborn, inquiring mind on a subject close to her.

It took Townsend several minutes to begin to read her small, spidery handwriting with any ease. But when he conquered her unorthodox penmanship, her words served as a revelation.

Christine Nevell had been a little girl when President Kennedy had been murdered. Later, as a teenager she'd read some American history. Then as a young adult she had simultaneously developed an exceptional student's feel for history and a police officer's insight into the criminal mind. Applying everything else she knew to the Kennedy assassination, she had been transfixed by the event. She had been so fascinated by it, judging from the notes she kept, that she had not only studied the murder of the thirty-fifth American President, but the murders of Lincoln, Garfield, and McKinley as well. Yet it was the Kennedy slaying that had been the most recent in history. And thus it was the most vivid in Christine's mind.

"Project BRONTOSAURUS," Christine had written as a heading in the initial pages of the notebook and probably eleven years earlier. "Project BRONTOSAURUS was close to the mark. But off the mark. It ties to JFK slaying. AM is wrong."

Brontosaurus? Townsend thought. *How the hell does she know about Brontosaurus? And "AM"? Who is A.M.?*

He scanned dozens of notes. He flipped pages as Hubbell kept a jittery vigil. Townsend couldn't believe what was before him. There were several entries beginning, "Lenny says . . ."

Lenny says. Lenny says. Lenny says.

"Lenny says Zarudni was the key," Tina had written. "Zarudni knew and was going to tell."

Townsend's attention turned manic.

How has a Baltimore policewoman ever heard of Zarudni?

And Lenny. Who the hell's Lenny? Lenny Bernstein. Lenny Bruce.
Lenny Dykstra . . . Lenny Leonard . . . Benny Leonard . . . His thoughts
flew in every direction.

Christ! he suddenly realized. *Leonard Wolik! But how could Wolik*
have said anything to her? How could Wolik have talked about Zarudni to
her? Christine only encountered him after he died.

Christ! he thought again. *Or had she known him earlier? But how*
could—?

His thoughts raced farther afield. Other entries began, "Detal thinks
. . ." Or, "Detal says . . ."

Detal. Detal was constantly in the present tense. Townsend found
dates to some of the entries. Detal did a lot of thinking in the years when
Christine Nevell was a police officer in Baltimore. She had done most of
the thinking since.

Detal. Baltimore. Townsend nailed this one immediately. And with
it he could work part of the puzzle backward.

Det meant Detective in police shorthand. A-L were initials. They
stood for Albert Lakaitis.

The damned liar! Townsend thought. *No wonder he sits by the window*
with a pistol.

"Does any of this mean anything to you?" Jim Hubbell asked.

Townsend looked up. "Yes," he said graciously. "I think with a little
collaboration from a few experts I know, we might be able to come up
with something. This was Tina's journal, I assume. This is what you said
she'd been working on."

Hubbell nodded.

"A secret of sorts. She kept it buried when she wasn't writing?"
Townsend asked.

Hubbell nodded again.

"I can keep this copy?" Townsend asked.

"It's for you. I, uh, haven't mentioned it to the local cops."

"Don't," said Townsend, standing. "It wouldn't accomplish anything."

Townsend grasped Hubbell's hand and shook it. "You take care of
yourself. Keep a low profile. Maybe we can get this thing solved. But
until it is, stay on guard."

Hubbell said he would. Townsend asked to be taken back to the
airport. Already, of course, he was trying to put the missing piece in its
proper slot.

"AM is wrong . . . AM is wrong . . ." If Detal was Al Lakaitis and Wolik spoke to Christine, who in God's name was A.M.?

The answer would not be found in New Castle, Delaware. But other answers would. Townsend took a flight to Philadelphia and rented a car. Just hours after leaving Florida, he turned up at the door of Al Lakaitis's home. This time, without warning.

Lakaitis allowed him in. In the heat of the summer evening in Delaware, they sat in Lakaitis's living room with all the doors and windows of the house closed.

"I didn't lie to you," Lakaitis said, a touch of indignation creeping into his voice, when Townsend broached the subject of the detective's deceased lover. "I told you the truth as I remembered it."

"Yes, you did," Townsend said. "But you didn't tell me the *complete* truth, did you? Shame on you, Al."

"I don't know what you're talking about."

"It wasn't just Christine who had theories, Albert," Townsend said. "I have a copy of the journal she used to keep. She had a collaborator. Or at least someone who knew her theories. You."

Lakaitis began again. "I said it before and I'll say it again. I don't know what you're—!"

Townsend stopped him with an upraised hand. "Save the disclaimer," he said. "I'm not interested in it. I don't want to hear it. Fact is, I read Tina's journal in its entirety on an airplane on my way here. I think I have this piece of the puzzle pretty well straightened out."

"You do, huh?" Lakaitis stared at him dead-on. "For God's sake, Townsend. Why can't you just drop it?"

"The death of a President or the death of sports editor. If it's murder, it's of interest. I report, Albert. I inform the public, most of whom don't give a damn, anyway. But I want the whole story and the names of the guilty. Maybe in fifty years someone will read it and be impressed." Townsend paused. "As for you, Albert, no need to worry. You're just a source. Sources are confidential. Hot pincers won't get sources out of me." He paused a second time. "But if you won't cooperate as a source, I'll name you as a possible material witness in the Brooklyn homicide. Then we can pull you into court to ask you the same questions I want to ask here. This time I want the *complete* story."

Lakaitis looked at him in disbelief. He uttered a long, low string of profanities, which Townsend ignored.

"Correct me where I'm wrong," Townsend requested. "You and Christine worked together several times in Baltimore," Townsend said. "You liked each other. You had a romance. You shared a lot of things.

Either you were a conspiracy buff to start with, or your better educated lady friend made one out of you. Which was it?"

Lakaitis stared at him. His resolve started to fade. He leaned back in his chair. "She made one out of me," he said. "She was always talking about it. The Kennedy case. Oswald. Ruby. The Russians. CIA. The inconsistencies of the Warren Commission."

"Where did you meet Leonard Wolik first?" Townsend asked.

"How the devil did you figure this out?" Hubbell asked.

"Christine's journal. If she conversed with Leonard Wolik, then she knew him before he was murdered."

Lakaitis drew a breath. "I think it was the year before they killed him," Lakaitis said. "June of that year—1984. Christine and me, we used to go to these conventions. You know. Conspiracy junkies would all get together once a year. Like people going to a boat show. Or a *Star Trek* meeting. We'd go and talk over the latest ideas with other people who had our interests. There were always a lot of J.F.K. assassination freaks at these things. Leonard Wolik turned up at one of them. Unassuming little guy. Nice man. Smart as a whip. We struck up a friendship, him and Christine and me. He liked us 'cause we were solid working people instead of the intellectual fairies he normally met. 'Good cops,' he called us. 'Good people.' "

"Where did he live?"

"Up in New Jersey. Far Hills, I think it was. He was retired from the State Department. Retired in disgust that same year, then started going to our meetings. Wanted to get something off his mind. He wondered if he was crazy for thinking what he thought."

"He told you quite a bit. He probably told you much that Colbert Davies told me. And Wolik, the real Wolik, was driving down to see you the night he was killed," Townsend said.

"How'd you know that?"

"Partly it's a guess. But partly because you wanted to investigate the case. And partly because, where else would he be so intent on going at two A.M. in an ice storm? I'm guessing Wolik felt threatened because he'd been talking too much at some of these conspiracy conventions. Maybe he wanted your protection. And maybe he wanted to talk to a couple of true believers before it was too late."

"He was obsessed about his Russian," Lakaitis said. "Zarudni. He said Zarudni held the key to understanding the whole thing."

"Zarudni probably did," Townsend said. "But the KGB found out that Zarudni wanted to move west. The Soviet police found out very quickly and they executed him."

"Got a theory on that part?" Lakaitis asked.

"Maybe," Townsend said. "I'm working on it. But right here, right now, there are other pieces I want to tie together."

Lakaitis looked at him expectantly. "Like what?"

"Why you're alive. And Christine is dead."

"You accusing me of something?"

"Depending how you want to look at it: You lied to save your life. Or, you were smarter in a street sense than she was."

Lakaitis was distinctly uneasy. "What are you saying?"

"Tina was the one who, following Wolik's death, pursued her theories. You told me that yourself. She wanted to take the case as far as it would ride. Courts. Prosecutors. She was a conspiracy buff and here was the biggest one of them all right in her lap. And she had new information. Right?"

After a painful pause, Lakaitis nodded. "Right," he said.

"But you wouldn't join her. You knew better. You knew if the cover-up was so big, eventually anyone who knew too much would be in serious jeopardy. So, at this point at least, you became her silent collaborator. She went and asked the questions. She told you what she was finding. You knew she was onto something. But that was where you parted ways. You didn't want to know any more. She did. And when people like Flynn and Grodine came around, even to this day, they felt you didn't know anything for which you would have to be silenced. But Christine did."

Townsend paused. He could see how painfully Lakaitis reacted to this stretch of the story. "When they came by a few weeks ago, for example," Townsend said, "they left here thinking you were clean. But you, in fact, sent them on to Christine. In doing so . . ."

"All right," the retired cop said. "You got it right." His face was ready to collapse. "Don't you think I won't be living with it for the rest of my life?"

"I'm sure you will, Albert. I'm sure you will. I just want one final question answered.

Lakaitis' eyes were red. "What's that?" he asked.

" 'A.M. was wrong.' What's that mean? How's it tie into Project BRONTOSAURUS? Who's A.M., Albert?"

"I don't know an A.M.," Lakaitis said.

"Come on, Albert. Help me."

"I don't know an A.M.," he repeated. "For God's sake's, man! Don't you think I'd tell you now if I knew? I don't know an A.M. Never did. And I go to church every Sunday praying that I never do."

Townsend nodded. "Thank you, Albert," he said. He stood to leave. "Take care of yourself. Have a nice life."

* * *

Townsend drove to Philadelphia and stayed there overnight. Late the same evening, he telephoned Caryn in New York.

"You missed all the excitement," she said. "At your building. Or maybe, more accurately, the excitement missed you."

"What do you mean?"

"Your neighbor. The young guy who lives next to you. Jim Shields," she said.

"That's him," Townsend said. "What happened?"

"He was sitting on the bed in his apartment," Caryn said. "When a pair of twenty-two-caliber bullets came in the window."

Townsend froze when her words registered. "God Almighty!" he murmured.

"Paul. He was hit in the room next to your apartment. The shots were fired from a long, long range. Heavy tumbling effect." She paused. "I guess that makes *two* people shot in your place."

Townsend didn't have to answer.

"Was he killed?" Townsend asked.

"Critical condition. But he'll live. He was hit in the shoulder and the collarbone. A couple of inches either way and he makes his appearance on your old page at the *Sun.*"

Townsend thought about the shooting for several seconds, trying to envision from what distant sniper's nest the shots could have originated. All of a sudden, Townsend realized how badly he had miscalculated. There were no windows facing his apartment within two hundred yards. But beyond that? With the type of weapon that was obviously in service now? Anything was possible.

"Do something tomorrow morning," he said. "Call Tony Duncan. See if he can get a copy of the ballistics report on the 96th Street shooting. Then tell him about the one in Fort Myers. Maybe he can get a copy of that one and compare West 96th Street with Fort Myers."

She took Detective Duncan's number.

"One other thing," Townsend said.

She waited.

"Do we know anyone named A.M.?" he asked. "Initials. Nickname. Anyone in this case who might be called that?"

"I can't think of anyone."

"Me, neither," he said. "I'll explain it when I get back," he said.

"Now I've got one more piece of bad tidings for you," she said.

"I don't need any more for today, but what is it?"

"Ken Shaw has officially reassigned me," she said. "I'm back on sports starting Monday. The interim editor wasn't working out. So he put me there."

Townsend moaned. "I'll talk to him," he said. "About everything."

"Thanks. I don't think it'll do any good. But thanks anyway." She paused. "It's a promotion, you know. I'm the first female sports editor of a New York daily. I suppose I should be pleased, but . . ."

"Be pleased. Take it. Do what you can."

"On my own time I'll do everything I can to help you," she said.

"Just do one thing for me," he said.

"What's that?"

"Keep your guard up," he said. "We're walking targets, you and I. I worry more about you than about myself."

"Typical," she said, teasing him. But she said she would be careful. Then Caryn hung up.

Townsend put down the phone as well. For several minutes he sat in silence in his hotel room, wondering how often the long-range weapon that had killed Christine Nevell had been trained on him. And when it would be next.

< < < < **42** > > > >

VERY obviously, Ken Shaw had something major on his mind. His eyes rose from his desk as Paul Townsend, whom he had summoned, appeared at his door. "Come in, Paul," he said. "Sit down."

Townsend did. Shaw was pure business today. No opening banter, no token attempt at friendly small talk. "We have a problem," Shaw said, "and I expect you to do what you can to help this newspaper."

It was a war party, just the two of them. Townsend was ready for it. "What sort of problem?" he asked.

Shaw leaned back in his chair. "The third-party convention convenes tonight in Dallas. The USA party. Formality, of course. They'll nominate John Lord for President."

"I'm aware of it," Townsend said.

"If you'll recall, not so long ago I mentioned to you the probability of the *Sun* doing a six-part feature on Senator Lord."

"You mentioned it more in terms of a certainty than a probability, Ken."

"Well, the time has come, as the Walrus said. It's six parts on the senator and his missus. John and Eugenia Lord."

"I think of them as the Sonny and Cher of the nineties, Ken."

"Oh, shut up," he scolded. "This is to be a positive series of articles and Max Kohlheimer will be submitting many of the questions for our writer to pose. Now, I have to assign someone."

"Go ahead. Assign someone. Just don't assign me."

A familiar exasperated look came across Shaw's face. "You *are* assigned. Officially," Shaw said.

"Ken, I don't want it! Can't you understand that?"

"And I'm the editor here, Goddamn it!" Ken Shaw suddenly thundered. "The damned joke is over, Townsend! You don't reject stories at this paper any more than you decide editorial or personnel policies. I'm sick and tired of your insubordination! Is that clear? I allowed you time to work on the Dubrow case and this is the cooperation I get! You've run off in all directions except one that would get us a good day-to-day story!"

"Just get off my back!" Townsend furiously shot back at him. "I can break the Dubrow case and a much bigger one if you don't undercut me."

"Is that a fact?" snorted Shaw, who obviously didn't think it was. Whatever was eating him today was pretty painful. The vein on his neck was already pulsating.

"Know what happened thirty-six hours ago?" Townsend asked. "A fellow who lives next to me got hit with a twenty-two bullet that may have come from the same weapon that shot a woman in Florida. The woman in Florida knew something that touches back into the Wolik case and maybe much, much more. Coincidence, Ken? Or am I getting closer?"

"I haven't any idea what you're talking about. Where does Harry Dubrow fit into that?"

Townsend hesitated. "I don't know yet."

"Five dozen people a day get hit with twenty-two-caliber bullets in our fair burg." Shaw said, calming slightly. "Probably ten dozen on days when the welfare checks arrive. Do you have a definite link yet?"

"I'm checking into—"

"Yes or no?"

"No! It just happened. So, no. Not yet."

Shaw looked disgusted.

"The first thing I want," Townsend continued, "is my collaborator back. Caryn. I need her. Keep her off sports a little while longer. Come on, Ken. Be a mensch for once. Please?"

Shaw, who had worked on papers in New York and Miami, had heard the term often, but still wasn't sure what a mensch was. So he avoided the word. "We had an agreement, didn't we? Seven days? Did I hallucinate? Or did you and Caryn sit before me and agree to that in blood? I speak metaphorically, of course."

"We agreed."

"And is an agreement not an agreement not an agreement?" Shaw asked contemptuously, fingering the gnarled end of his favorite briar pipe.

As Shaw butchered Gertrude Stein, Townsend's eyes involuntarily found the managing editor's pristine squash racket, still in the corner where it had taken root.

"I swear this to you, Ken," Townsend said. "This is the most important story anyone on this paper is working on. Whether you know it or not."

"Know it?" he retorted, his indignation intensifying again. "I'll tell you what I know about stories. I'm the editor here and I can spike any story I damned well choose." He grinned and leaned back in his chair. "So humbug, Paul! Take a good look at me. I'm your new Uncle Scrooge."

"I want my collaborator back," Townsend repeated.

Now Shaw focused on the request. "I'm not assigning her back to you," he said. "That's final." He shot Townsend a condescending look. "How much help is she really being, Paul?" he asked. "Don't you think I hear a smidgen of gossip in my travels? What's your real concern here? Dipping your pen," he suggested, "in the company inkwell? Do it on your own time."

"Ken," Townsend answered, "I don't know whether you're obnoxious or just stupid. Or whether someone somewhere is pulling strings to get you to get me to lay off this case. What's Max Kohlheimer saying to you? Is he trying to ease me off?"

"Mr. Kohlheimer and I discuss a lot of things."

"Am I among them?"

"Sometimes. Not always. Look. I'll be very clear about this. Overtures have been made to the Lord camp by Mr. Kohlheimer. Senator

Lord is an intelligent man. He doesn't want a third-string city news writer. He wants this paper's best writer. He requested you by name."

"What?"

"Senator Lord asked specifically for one Paul C. Townsend to conduct the interview. That's you, I believe." Shaw paused. "Do I need to repeat or did you get the message that time?"

"How does he know who I am?"

"How the hell do I know? Maybe you put a friend of his in jail. Paul Townsend's reputation doth precede him. Flattered?"

"No. Just suspicious."

"This is your assignment. That's all, Paul. Stop giving me grief."

"The country's got one foot in the jackboot already," Townsend said. "And you want me to help slip the other ankle in, right?"

"Christ!" Shaw said in disgust. Here Shaw raised a finger and pointed. "Let me tell you something, Townsend. You and your smug, discredited, New York–northeastern attitudes have had their day. I like Lord. I think he's a good man. I'm willing to overlook some of the questions about his past. The two major parties have run the republic into the ground." Shaw's cheeks reddened characteristically when he barked like this. Townsend found it more irritating and embarrassing than threatening.

"Ken—"

"Let me finish!" Shaw was at his fulsome and avuncular worst. "What are the Republicrats giving us this time, other than a black face, that we haven't seen ten times before? It's the rightful hour for some new thinking in Washington. Time to put an end to the old politics that burns tax money on government that doesn't work. I'm going to vote for John Lord myself. Folks like you are going to wake up the day after the election and find yourself mighty left out."

"I don't doubt it," Townsend said.

But Shaw wouldn't stop. "Half the country's being mugged, another third is hopped up all the time," he declared. "No one does any work. No one prays. No one salutes the flag. I'm sick of it. A lot of Americans are. You'll see."

"What I see is the new fascism," Townsend said, "all candy coated for a new century. And no one recognizes it for what it is."

"That's all," Shaw said. "I can't do anything with you. I assume you're taking this assignment. Mr. Kohlheimer is going to fax the questions upon which he'd like Senator Lord to put forth his views. I should have them by—"

Shaw stopped in midsentence when Townsend stood.

"I'm resigning, Ken," Townsend said. "I can't work at this newspaper anymore. Not under these conditions."

Shaw's mouth was still half open, his sentence still unfinished, when Townsend disappeared out the office door. He went down the elevator, past the fourth floor where his office was located, and into the lobby. Then he walked out of the *Sun* Building completely.

Two nights later, Townsend watched at home on television as Senator John Lord, standing against a backdrop of a forty-by-sixty-foot American flag was hailed as the prophet of America's future.

The convention, which more closely resembled a religious revival and a coronation than a political event, took place at Texas Stadium in Irving. As he had in most other states in the country, John Lord received standing ovations from the true believers and those who wished to climb aboard the bandwagon.

Lord knew no bounds of modesty. His message was mesmerizing on television as well as in person. He railed with an evangelist's fire against "a veritable Sodom and Gomorrah in Washington, D.C." And, holding a Bible aloft for the first time in his long campaign, he compared his own travails as a third-party candidate to the crossing of the Red Sea. "There is a desperate need for revival in this nation so that we may turn back to Him."

Among those present, there seemed none unconvinced or unconverted. Lord attacked "public profanity and indecency," "loose morals," and Ivan Litvinov. His campaign, he said, would "be a nationwide revival to return the love of God to each soul." He was really moving by that time. "We need a whole lot more of Jesus," he said, ripping off lines from an old bluegrass ballad. "And a lot less rock and roll." All this with those penetrating blue eyes hypnotizing the television cameras. All this with the gorgeous voice that could wrap pseudo-Christian respectability around the most disreputable of opinions.

What Lord's words had to do with addressing the national afflictions of inflation, urban decay, arms control, unemployment, drug abuse, immigration questions, and crime was anyone's guess. But Lord wasn't the first candidate to vie for high office in America with no real solutions. And the act played nicely to the studio audience and to the audience of millions watching at home.

It was still playing well in the national polls, as well. That gave Lord's upstart candidacy a better than fifty-fifty chance of going all the way to the White House if Lord didn't do something to self-destruct and if voters didn't return to their traditional parties. Those, of course, loomed as the biggest *ifs* in modern American history.

On the second night of Lord's two-day extravaganza in Dallas he named his Vice Presidential choice. As always, Lord pulled a stunner out of the hat.

He named a thirty-three-year-old woman from California as his running mate. She was a graduate of Wellesley and the Harvard Business School. She had been the chief executive officer of a computer software company until two years earlier when she was elected mayor of a midsize suburb in Orange County. She was smart as a whip, young, pretty, articulate, and—in an ingratiating and intensely charming way— as much of a political neanderthal as Lord. But as usual, Lord had his reasons for the choice.

She was middle class and presentable. She made him look respectable. She softened up his image when they appeared together. They looked *familyish* in the official USA party photographs. But most important of all, if she could bring to the ticket just one or two percent of the young or female electorate in certain states, she could just possibly nudge John Lord over the top in a close election.

But that wasn't what riveted Paul Townsend's attention in the closing moments of the USA party's first national convention. What transfixed him was a two-minute interview with the candidate's wife, Eugenia Lord, which was broadcast in the closing moments over CBS.

Eugenia Merriman Lord, a commentator informed the American public, had been in or near politics and government all her life. Her father, Kenneth Merriman, had been an advisor to several Democratic Presidents, most notably to Kennedy and Johnson. At the end of his career, Eugenia's father had even served as the United States ambassador to France in the mid 1960s. And it was in fact while Merriman was ambassador that his daughter married the then remote but ambitious young Texan, John Lord.

Townsend stared at his television in a state that easily could have been mistaken for catatonic shock. He barely breathed. He didn't twitch a muscle.

Everything was starting to come home to him.

BRONTOSAURUS.

What was it Christine Nevell had written? *AM is wrong.*

Harriman.

Merriman.

That was it! There was the confusion! That was what had never fit together. AM meant *Ambassador Merriman.* That was what she hadn't wanted to put in writing. But that was what she had realized. Project BRONTOSAURUS was on the right path, Leonard Wolik had postulated to her. But the ambassador under investigation was the wrong one.

What was it Harry Dubrow had said many weeks ago?

The greatest secret of the sixties? Who killed Kennedy and why?

Thank you, Harry, Townsend thought. *To use a metaphor from the sports desk, you had it all the way. May you rest in peace, my dear friend.*

Townsend turned off the sound on his television. He crossed his living room and picked up his telephone. He dialed Ken Shaw's home number in New Jersey. Shaw's wife answered. She was a loyal, kindly little woman named Lillian. After some searching, she found her husband.

The voice came on the line. "Shaw here."

"Ken. It's Paul Townsend."

There was a pause. "What the hell do you want, you pariah?" Shaw growled. "I'm standing here with my pants off in the privacy of my kitchen trying to enjoy an Olympia Beer and some cold shrimp. And *you interrupt.*"

"I thought I'd let you know. I've changed my mind. I'll do the Lord interview, if the assignment is still open."

"Come crawling back, have you?" Shaw purred. He was enjoying this.

"Call it that if you like."

"Seems to me you walked out on us."

"Yeah. I did."

"Well, then . . . ?"

"Ken . . . There comes a time," Townsend said, working up as much fraudulent humility as possible. "I don't know. I guess I've just been stubborn. I value my job at the *Sun.* And there aren't any other papers that would hire me at this point." He paused as servilely as possible. "I'll do the story and take Max Kohlheimer's questions. What more do I have to say?"

There was a pause. "Paul, I've known you for a while. I've known about you for sometime longer. You're not going to pull a stunt of some sort, are you? Won't do you any good, you know. Won't accomplish a thing."

"No stunts," Townsend lied.

"I would have iced you two days ago," Shaw said. "But the Lord people wanted to see your repulsive face—and yours alone—for some reason."

"I can't imagine why," Townsend said, though he now thought he knew. "But does that mean I got the assignment back?"

"You have it," Shaw said, sounding somewhere between relieved and skeptical. "I have a telephone number at the office for Shaw's media man. His name's Jerry Huddleston. Big burly guy. Nice man. I'll give you his number tomorrow. You can make the arrangements for time and place with Lord's people."

"That's fine."

"See the convention this evening?"

"I saw it."

"Impressed?"

Townsend was silent.

"Well," said Shaw, meditating on it. "I don't suppose I can incite enthusiasm as well into a sourpuss such as yourself. Let me know the arrangements you make. Mr. Kohlheimer wants the series to begin a week from Sunday. That's ten days from now, meaning you'll have to get on the interview immediately. Can do?"

"Can do," Townsend said flatly.

Townsend set down the phone. On the silent television screen, John Lord and Eugenia were standing before their convocation of zealots, their arms aloft in victory. The Vice Presidential candidate and her husband stood with their arms aloft as well.

But as the camera scanned, Townsend's attention was upon Eugenia Lord, Ambassador Merriman's daughter.

In an illogical field, in a corrupt world, a vague, perverted logic and reason had ultimately risen to the surface. Townsend could almost reach out and touch all the answers now. He had a good idea why the Lord people wanted to see him. He knew why he wanted to see them. Now both would have their opportunity.

< < < < **43** > > > >

NOT for the first time, Townsend's stomach was churning.

He sat by himself in a row of three seats on an airliner nearing Dallas. He tried to put the entire case in perspective, from Zarudni many years ago to John Lord today, from Leonard Wolik dead on a Maryland highway to Jim Shields, his neighbor on West 98th Street, shot from a distance for the crime of being in the wrong room at the wrong time.

Townsend had much of the facts in alignment now. He knew how A followed B and caused C. Chronology was not a problem. Nor, in most aspects of this case, was motivation. But translating the mayhem, homicide, and conspiracy into comprehensible human terms caused him problems. Rational decisions, decisive human acts, were all wrapped together in an ambient madness that formed the backdrop of the middle years of the twentieth century. The inexplicable yielded its secret each time first to a logical progression, then to a larger insanity.

Why, for example, should Presidents be murdered? Yet why should the guardians of public office—including Presidents—engage in criminal activity? Why, to take things a step further, was Harry Dubrow murdered?

Oh, he knew the surface reason. Harry showed up and probably recognized the assailants waiting for Townsend. But why, in a larger sense, did men set out on courses that would lead to such acts? Usually they did it in the name of decency. Sometimes they did it in the name of national security. The citizens of a nation, they might argue, sometimes had to be killed in order to be protected.

The airplane was buffeted by a strong crosswind. Townsend's nerves tingled again. He tried to put himself in perspective. In the end, he was still an obit man, flying into Dallas trying to put some lives in order. That included his own life. No subject that he knew was as simple as a man's death. None was as complicated as a man's life.

An impulse was upon him. He riffled through the worn pages of his notebook till he found what he wanted. Then he saw it: the obituary he had been preparing on himself.

PAUL TOWNSEND, 49
WRITER FOR THE *SUN*
SHOT TO DEATH IN NYC

Where in hell to begin? He suddenly wondered. Where to end? How could he begin to explain his own life? How could he make its final summation? He couldn't even place his finger on the most significant event so far. He wondered:

SOLVED FRIEND'S MURDER

or

INQUIRED INTO J.F.K. SLAYING

or

RUINED LORD PRESIDENTIAL BID

Which did he prefer? None of the three? All of them? He played with the concept:

PAUL TOWNSEND, 49
WRITER FOR THE *SUN*
SOLVED FRIEND'S MURDER,
INQUIRED INTO J.F.K. SLAYING,
RUINED LORD PRESIDENTIAL BID.

Very good, he told himself. He's given himself a five-line heading, something he'd never give to anyone else. Then he noticed that of his three accomplishments he had not yet completed any.

His attention lagged as the plane descended on its approach into Dallas-Fort Worth. Out of his window, he watched the hills and prairies of east Texas disappear as the city of Dallas approached.

John Lord, candidate for the most powerful office in the world, approached as well. The copilot came on the aircraft's public-address system and promised that the plane would be "on the blocks in Big D" in a matter of minutes.

So be it," Townsend concluded. He would survive another flight. The question now really, was whether he would survive another interview, another investigation.

Instinct. His instincts had served him well many times before. And he had bad feelings about this case. He kept his notebook in his lap.

He spent the final few minutes on his approach setting down a few facts which might be used in his obituary. He redid the headline.

PAUL TOWNSEND, 49,
NEWSMAN FOR THE *SUN*
AMBUSHED IN DALLAS

Then he realized. He had written a headline more for a news story than a death notice. So be it. He added few pertinent details on his own life and ripped the page out of his notebook. He found an envelope, stamped it, and addressed it to Caryn in New York.

Caryn, honey,

he wrote on an attached note.

This is just in case things go the wrong way. Take care of yourself. I love you.

Paul

He mailed it in the airport. It would serve either as a macabre joke or an epithet. He would soon know which.

<<<< **44** >>>>

*T*HE next afternoon when Paul Townsend arrived, Senator Lord and his wife were sitting comfortably in the living room of their suite at the Dallas Omni. The candidate and his wife rose when Jerry Huddleston showed Townsend into the room. Greetings were perfunctory. Huddleston left. Townsend sat down with the Senator and Mrs. Lord.

"Obviously you know why I'm here," Townsend said at length.

"My old friend Max Kohlheimer is going to rip me apart in all his papers," Lord joked.

"That's hardly his intention," said Townsend.

"I'm sure it's not," Lord said generously. "Max has always treated me very fairly."

"You could say that," Townsend allowed. He assembled his notes and his tape recorder on a sofa six feet across the room from the Lords. As he readied himself, he gazed at the man on the sofa, the man who wished to be leader of the world's strongest democracy.

The face was the same as he'd seen many times. Too handsome for everyone's good. The voice rang out. The eyes held even a veteran reporter's attention. Townsend had a strange sensation. He could sense that Lord had a tremendous magnetism. But he couldn't decide whether beneath that immensely attractive facade, he sensed something very large or very small. Or maybe even elements of both.

"Can we begin?" Lord asked. "We don't have that much time today."

Townsend glanced up. "We have an hour scheduled today, don't we, Senator?"

"Maybe you do, but I don't," Lord said.

Townsend began to sense what was going on. As he looked up, he caught Lord glancing impatiently toward the door. Townsend turned on his tape recorder.

"Turn off that machine, Townsend," the candidate said. "Take your notes the old-fashioned way. By hand."

"I normally use a recorder," Townsend said. "This way there's no dispute over whether a subject has been quoted accurately or not."

"There won't be any dispute."

"I'll use the recorder, anyway."

"I'm not talking to a recorder," Lord said. "Not to you, anyway."

Anger was helping to steady Townsend's nerves. He set the recorder aside and picked up his notebook.

"Much better," said Lord. "You have to remember that you're talking to the next President of the United States. Some respect is essential here. I suppose that's something a prick like you wouldn't understand, though."

"The country still has to vote," Townsend said.

"It will. It will."

"Perhaps not in the way you think," Townsend said.

"And why's that? Why don't we get right to the real reason you're here," Lord said. "How about that?"

Townsend assembled the notes and papers in his file before him. "My publisher sent several pages of questions he'd like posed to you," Townsend said. "The thing is, I have another list of questions I'd like to have answered first."

"I'm sure you do."

"I'm not sure how much time we'll have for the second group after the first."

"Suit yourself," said Lord. "But you might do yourself a lifetime favor by skipping straight to your publisher's set."

Lord glanced at his wife, who managed a smile.

"What I'd like to know," Townsend said, "is the degree of your knowledge about the assassination of President Kennedy."

Lord laughed. "Mr. Townsend. That was thirty-three years ago. I only know what I've read in history books. And you may have read more of them than I have."

"Maybe," said Townsend. "But you had an advantage. Much of your information comes from Ambassador Merriman's daughter. And Mrs. Lord long ago knew exactly what her father was doing in Paris and who his loyalties were to. Right?"

Mrs. Lord demurely stared at the reporter. "I'm not even following you," she said.

"This is pretty remote and pretty outrageous, Mr. Townsend," Lord said. "You want to retract what you're saying? Otherwise, I'll call up Max Kohlheimer right now and see that your ass gets fired."

"I'll do better than retract, Senator," Townsend said. "I'll spell everything out for you. I'll do it exactly in the way I plan to file my story in New York. And I don't care if the *Sun* doesn't run it. Once I put it on the wire, you'll have a thousand reporters tracing it. Everything will be out in the open."

"What exactly is 'everything'?"

"Thirty-three years ago," Townsend said, "Mrs. Lord's father was the ambassador to France. That was one of his roles. But he was also in the employ of the Soviet Union. Why or for how long, I don't know. I can only guess it was for ideological reasons. Heaven knows, the family didn't need the money."

The room had now fallen very quiet.

"Many things happened around this time, Senator," Townsend continued. "You and Mrs. Lord met, for example. The ambassador didn't care much for you. He rushed home from Paris to try to break off the impending marriage. That created a further problem. You see, there were persistent rumors back then that the CIA had been penetrated by a Soviet mole. There were various inquiries. A defector named Golitsin scored many points by convincing James Angleton that Averell Harriman was the mole. Project BRONTOSAURUS. Harriman was clean. Golitsin's problem was that he had the sketch of a traitorous ambassador correct. He even had the sound of the name right. But it was Merriman, not Harriman. That became evident in Paris, though not until it was too late."

Mrs. Lord had reached for a Marlboro and was lighting it. Her husband folded his arms across his chest.

"A man named Colbert Davies was a career CIA man. He was also Lyndon Johnson's friend. Friend, confidant, and troubleshooter. When the case against Harriman grew ridiculous, he was put on Merriman's case. He took the opportunity to go to Paris in Ambassador Merriman's absence. As fortune had it, that's when a Russian named Zarudni chose to defect."

Lord was now leaning back on his sofa, his hands folded against his upper chest, one finger extended to his mouth. He looked as if he were sitting around a Texas saloon, listening to a dazzling good yarn. Mrs. Lord didn't appear quite as appreciative.

"Back in Washington, however, Ambassador Merriman heard

about the defection when it came across the State Department teletype. Here was disaster. Zarudni, by the force of his argument, by the magnitude of what he claimed he had, could only have been bearing one asset. He had the evidence that would prove Golitsin's case within the CIA. He had the evidence that could link the KGB, at least marginally, to the Kennedy assassination."

Lord smiled. "Keep talking," he said.

"Ambassador Merriman flew back to Paris," Townsend said. "He kicked Colbert Davies out of the embassy. Sent him home. At the same time, he blew the information back through Soviet channels that someone wanted to defect, someone carrying something big. By then, Zarudni's arrest and execution by the KGB were a matter of course. It probably took less than forty-eight hours."

"It did," Mrs. Lord said abruptly, confirming Townsend's theory.

"You know what butchers those Russians are," Lord added with a grin. "Always have been. Always will be." He winked at his wife. "At least for another few months until I become President. Then they'll have met their match."

"Then I'm correct so far?" Townsend asked.

"So far," said Lord. "But you see, Mr. Townsend. Eugenia here is a good American. Kind of ashamed what her daddy did. See, through her, I know chapter and verse on what happened in the 1960s. I know it the way fewer than a dozen Americans alive know it. And after I'm elected, we're going to parlay that into a new world order." Lord seemed immensely pleased with himself. "Got a guess how?" he asked.

"I have a few theories," Townsend said. "But I'm tired of talking. Why don't you tell me?"

"Nope. You talk."

"Ivan Litvinov," said Townsend. "The current Russian leader was a relatively young man in the mid-nineteen sixties. Given his background in the Soviet military and Soviet intelligence . . ."

Lord leaned forward. "Let's suppose further," Lord said, picking up the argument. "Or better yet, let's not suppose at all. Instead, let's go with facts. Litvinov was the control agent of Lee Harvey Oswald when Oswald was in the Soviet Union. And remember further that Litvinov did some time in Cuba in the same era. If you remember, Uncle Sam was trying to do away with Castro at the time. We had all sorts of cockeyed plans, of which the Bay of Pigs was only one. There were poison cigars. Bombs from his mistress. Mafia assassins. Nothing worked. But you can't blame old Fidel for getting angry about it . . . And for wanting to take a shot at the American President in return. With some KGB help."

"Which the young Litvinov provided," said Townsend.

"More than 'provided,' " Lord said coldly. "From what Genie tells me, from what her father knew, Litvinov knew his way around a rifle. He was one hell of a marksman."

The monstronsity of this suggestion sank in slowly upon Townsend.

"What are you saying? That Litvinov backed up Oswald in Dallas?"

"Maybe," Lord teased. "Maybe he did even more than back him up. No one ever proved how many shots were fired. And know what? Oswald's fingerprints were on *a* rifle recovered from the assassination scene. But how do we know what gloved hand might have pulled the trigger? Or, for that matter, how many rifles there were?"

"But *you* know," Townsend concluded. "And you're going to use the information as you see fit."

"Of course. That's why I'm setting Ivan up. Calling him a Red liar. A commie bastard. See, my opponents in this campaign will eventually stick up for him. Then, if I need the issue, I come out with the facts. I can prove everything. As a young intelligence officer Litvinov helped murder an American President. If I don't need the issue in the campaign, I'll use it to blackmail Ivan after I'm elected. See, Ivan needs American help to stay in power over there. So we get any kind of concession we want out of him. Just have to squeeze Ivan's balls in the right place at the right time."

Eugenia smiled. Lord laughed. The candidate for President had it all worked out.

"So after forty years of a cold war," said Townsend, "when Russian-American relations have never been better, you're going to use blackmail as a diplomatic instrument? That represents your worldview?"

"That's how things get done," Lord said. He smiled. That gorgeous smile. "I don't imagine the American people would be too happy with Ivan Litvinov if they learned his full background." Lord paused. "See, I can use this. I have a lot of national priorities to reorganize. Shutting down aid to the Jewish state, for example. Cutting nonwhite immigration to zero. Ending social-welfare programs completely in this country. Ending abortion completely. Making literacy in English a requirement for voting. Getting the Panama Canal back. Putting Christian religion back in the schools. I have an agenda. All I need is the popular mandate."

"And my husband will get that on November fifth," Eugenia added. She spoke with a serenity and confidence which was almost more frightening than her husband's bravado.

"And Bruce McMorris over at the CIA?" Townsend asked, testing other sections of his new orthodoxy. "I assume he's one of your people, too?"

Lord laughed again. "I have something of a fan club in Langley," he admitted. "After all, they know a candidate who's going to give them completely free reign in the field again. Bruce and I have known each other for twenty-five years. He keeps files buried when they need to be and gives the right people access when that's a noble purpose as well."

"I assume 'right people' means you," Townsend said.

"Who else could it possibly mean?" Lord asked.

"And Flynn and Grodine," said Townsend. "They're members of your own private gestapo, as well?"

"I object to your terminology," Lord said. "But, yes. I have a few former agency people who now perform, shall we say, 'security' exercises for me."

"Such as killing Harry Dubrow," Townsend said.

"If he's the sportswriter who turned up instead of you, yes. He recognized my people. So we had to—"

"And Wolik himself?" Townsend asked. "The real Leonard Wolik eleven years ago?"

"The man didn't know how to keep his mouth shut, but that was none of my doing."

"A CIA job, in other words?" Townsend asked.

"Well, of course," Lord confirmed. "You can't have a man like that running around shooting his mouth off to strangers." He paused. "I know Bruce made the arrangements," Lord said. "That's all I can tell you. A lot of agency people were busy during the eighties. So who's to know the details?"

Townsend stared at the candidate. "You know," he said, "I've been tracing this down for months. I've had theories. Suspicions. Wild flights of the imagination. You're sitting here calmly confirming the most jaded ones of all," Townsend said. "And I can barely believe it."

"Believe it," said Senator John Lord. "This country's going so far right in the next ten years that people won't recognize it." He grinned. "Excluding yourself, of course. I'd wager that you don't even have ten hours left."

In the next room, Townsend heard doors open. He expected Jerry Huddleston to reappear.

"You'll never pull it off," Townsend said. "I can link several deaths together. Christine Nevell. Harry Dubrow. Leonard Wolik. All murders. All committed so you could guard this secret, so you could use it for your own purposes."

"Uh huh," Lord said, not upset at all. "The smartest man in sight was Colbert Davies," Lord said. "Lyndon's Man. He held the secret all his life. Then when he was ready to kick off of natural causes, he turned it over to a journalist. He wanted the story brought out, but didn't want to go to the trouble himself. Well, sir, Mr. Townsend, I'm afraid your involvement isn't going to win you any Pulitzer prizes. Instead, it's going to cost you."

Townsend was suddenly aware of two additional presences in the chamber. Then, as he felt a hand on his shoulder, he was jolted to recognize the two men he knew as Flynn and Grodine. Flynn, the tall straight one. Grodine, the stocky muscular one, who drank too much beer and couldn't always hit the right target.

"Drive carefully, gentlemen," Lord said. "And no fuck-up this time."

Townsend felt a thud on his left shoulder. He turned in that direction, but Grodine held him firmly in place. Thus it was too late when he felt the needle of a syringe enter the flesh just below his neck on the right side.

He struggled. He tried to kick and punch. But the hands held him firmly and the needle's cargo found his bloodstream.

He felt a rush of warmth within him. He was conscious of Senator and Mrs. Lord watching him. But they seemed to be at a great distance. And suddenly they didn't seem to be so evil anymore.

Townsend was aware of being stood up and told to walk. He did. The two men with FBI credentials took his notebook from him and gave it to Senator Lord. Then they removed him from the candidate's suite. They led him down the hotel's elevator and into the car in which he had arrived. Townsend saw everything happening, but couldn't speak. He could only move his legs to walk.

Flynn put him in the passenger seat of his own car. There was a conversation between Flynn and Grodine. They were to put him on the highway leading out of Dallas, they said, and take him off on isolated Route 36A which led to a whorehouse favored by certain businessmen. Grodine drove Townsend's car. Flynn followed in another.

The two cars left Dallas. They drove for half an hour. Then the two cars pulled to the side of a highway that had a steep embankment and several boulders and trees to its side.

There Grodine and Flynn moved Townsend back to the driver's seat. There was no seat belt.

This is how it ended for Wolik, too, Townsend found himself thinking. He was alone in the car.

"Now fix the ignition," Flynn said to Grodine. They started to fuss with it. But Townsend mustered one final bit of physical coordination. He pushed his own foot to the floor and found the accelerator. The car began to move. Flynn and Grodine, in astonishment, jumped away from the vehicle.

Townsend pressed with his foot. He was incapable of driving. But at least, he reasoned hazily, he could die of his own impulses. The driver's door remained open as the vehicle started down the highway. Townsend got up as much speed as he could. The car weaved all over the asphalt but he was conscious of going faster and faster and faster . . .

The vehicle swerved and left the road. There was the sensation of flying, then hitting tires to the ground as the vehicle careened between trees and boulders. Next, there was impact, then tumbling, then something very bright . . .

He thought of his wife and daughter . . .

He thought of his late parents . . .

He thought of Caryn . . .

He thought of the write-up he would receive on the obit page of the *Sun* . . .

Then—on a day when Senator Lord hit a new high in the national public opinion polls—there was a final convulsive impact, followed by deep, agonizing physical pain for Paul Townsend.

Then blackness.

<<<< **45** >>>>

*T*HE only poll that really counted was held on election day, November 5, 1996. That day yielded some surprises.

Through the fall Presidential campaign, the Democrat attempted to send the message that he was the only moderate candidate in the race. To some degree he was successful. When the numbers were tabulated on election day, a strong get-out-the-vote campaign in the cities of the Northeast gave the Democrats huge pluralities in the cities up and down the East Coast. Senator Lord's party and the Republican party split what remained almost evenly. In a reverse of how Lord had seen the campaign in advance, it was the Democrats who came away with narrow victories in Pennsylvania and New York. They also carried Massachusetts, Minnesota, and the District of Columbia—what some of the gray hairs among the Laptoppers sarcastically referred to as the old "McGovern-Mondale coalition."

To this the Democrats added Connecticut early on election evening. All of these states were decided relatively early. Hopes soared at Democratic party headquarters, particularly when, a little later that same evening, heavy Chicago voting also tossed Illinois into their column.

But their joy ended at about ten o'clock eastern time. Lord took Florida and Georgia, then began a sweep across the old south, picking up easy wins in Louisiana, Alabama, Mississippi, South Carolina, and Arkansas. Texas was easy, too. The Republicans ran best in northern New England—New Hampshire and Vermont—and somehow the Republicans picked off thin victories in Tennessee and Indiana. In the mid-Atlantic region, there was a little cluster of states—Delaware, Maryland, Virginia, and New Jersey—where the voting was very even. These four would remain too close to call for hours.

Then, in the dying hours of November 5, John Lord's candidacy continued its assault on traditional American electoral habits.

On the ABC network, there was a map of the country which was intended to keep viewers current on who had won what. Republican victories were shaded red. Democratic states were designated in blue. Lord's states were green. By eleven o'clock a glance at the map revealed a green tide sweeping across the South through Texas and then boldly north through Oklahoma, Missouri, and Kansas. It also moved west, covering everything in sight until it arrived at California. One wry older commentator on ABC likened the color to dishwashing liquid and called it the Palmolive tide. But to Lord's foes, there was nothing amusing about it.

As the night grew later, and as midnight arrived in the East, the Democrats picked off Michigan and Oregon. For a while the Republicans held a lead of a few thousand votes in Ohio, while California remained too close to call and too big to ignore. Then at midnight, the reality of the situation was apparent. The Democrats and Republicans were forced to root for each other, hoping to deprive Lord of the 270 electoral college votes he needed to win. If Lord could be deprived of an outright victory, the election could be tossed into the House of Representatives. There deals could be hammered out between the major parties.

For a while, that looked like the most likely scenario. Hawaii and Alaska went Democratic. Toward two A.M. eastern time, however, Lord scored his biggest coup. With 35 percent of the vote, he captured California. But that left him with 256 electoral votes. He had more than anyone else, but he also seemed to have nothing more than a stunning near miss. He was stalled, with every state west of the Mississippi decided.

But not every state in the East. The Republicans took Maryland and Virginia. The Democrats took Delaware. Then, at four in the morning, pandemonium broke loose at Lord headquarters in Dallas.

With 99.9 percent of the vote reporting and double-checked by computer, John Lord had a plurality of eighteen hundred votes over the Republican and twelve hundred over the Democrat in New Jersey, where Lord's first big northern rally had been held the previous May. The state—which Lord himself privately referred to as a "snakepit"—was in Lord's column. Its fifteen electoral college votes gave him a total of 271.

The House of Representatives would not be needed. John Lord had been elected President of the United States. And as for the files of material that Lord had on Ivan Litvinov, Lord had never used it in the campaign. He was saving it now for back-alley diplomacy.

<<<< **46** >>>>

THE man in the wheelchair sat on the wooden deck of the one-story California home that he shared with his wife and family. He was immobile, other than his left hand, which remained on the switch built into the armrest of his chair.

He felt the February sunshine of the American Southwest upon his brow. In the distance, living as he did on a hilltop forty miles south of

Los Angeles, he could see the Pacific. It soothed him considerably to see the ocean, just as it soothed his battered body to feel the warmth of the sun through the winter months.

Behind him, he heard a glass door to the deck slide open. "Honey?" his wife said. "She's here."

Paul Townsend slid his fingers onto the switch in his chair. Slowly the wheelchair turned. Nora stood at the glass door and waited until Caryn DiCarlo appeared in the door frame.

"Hello, Caryn," Townsend said from his chair.

Caryn bit her lower lip. It was the first time she had seen him since his car had crashed off a Texas highway many months earlier. But then, she was his first official visitor. He had refused any friends up until this time.

"Hello, Paul," she said softly.

Nora looked at the two of them, trying the measure the past dynamics between her husband and his female caller. "I'll leave you," she said. "Business is business," she said. "Right?"

"Thank you, Mrs. Townsend," Caryn said.

For a moment, the awkwardness of the situation was too much for either of them to bear. Caryn had rehearsed hard for this visit. She had practiced at being brave. Yet she wasn't prepared for the reality of it, for the sight of the man she had loved to have been rendered an apparent quadriplegic those six months ago.

"Oh, God," she said. "They really did it to you, didn't they?" she said.

"No one did anything," he said bravely. "I had an auto accident." He paused for a moment, then added, "I was drinking heavily and I was driving out to a rural whorehouse. Didn't you read the police reports from the local papers?"

"I don't believe that for an instant," she said.

"Believe it," he challenged her.

Caryn fought back the wetness in her eyes.

"Oh, stop bawling and come give me a kiss," he said.

Caryn came over to him. She placed an arm around his inert shoulders and, to the extent that the wheelchair permitted, she gave him a hug. She kissed him. He could move his head and his neck.

"Can I have a second kiss?" he asked. "That's sex for me these days."

She gave him one and started to cry. "How can you even joke about this?" she asked.

"If you cry, Caryn," he said, "you have to leave. Those are the house rules. I don't want people coming around here just to feel sorry for battered old Paul Townsend. It's difficult enough, all right?" He spoke calmly and almost reassuringly, considering how he looked. He managed a smile.

"Sit down and talk to me," he said. "The scenery here is beautiful," he teased gently, "but a great-looking broad only improves it."

There was a wicker chair nearby. Caryn pulled it over. With remarkable precision, Townsend turned his wheelchair and sat looking at her.

"Well," she said bravely. "How are things?"

"Could be worse. I could be dead."

She exhaled nervously.

"I think I learned my lesson, though," Townsend said. "I think I finally learned when to lay off. And who to lay off."

"It wasn't an 'accident' though, was it?" she asked.

He was silent.

"Was it?" she pressed. "You don't drink like that. You don't drive recklessly. And I *know* you wouldn't have been on your way to a—"

"Sure I would have. Men are men," he said.

"Come on, Paul."

"It was an accident, Caryn," he said politely. "Just like the newspaper reports said. My own dumb fault."

"Bullshit!"

"Why do you want to know, Caryn? Do you want to take a trip off a highway in the same way?" He scolded her with his eyes. Then he waited for a moment. She was speechless.

"Bad news about Jim Hubbell, wasn't it?" he asked with an ominous edge to his voice. "Last October, I think. Blew his head off with that shotgun. Suicide, the police said. No note, but everyone said he'd been despondent since the loss of his wife."

Caryn said nothing.

"And what about Al Lakaitis?" he asked next. "He walks into a liquor store just one day after the November election and a pair of hold-up men come in five seconds later. Kill him and the clerk, then only take half the money from the cash register. Strange crime. What bad luck," he concluded, "that Al happened to be in that place at that time."

"Terrible," she agreed coldly.

"It's curious you should drop by today," he said. "I'm really just starting to get things together again. Know what I mean? Sometimes things finally fall into place mentally."

She didn't know what he meant. Not yet.

"How much older was I than you?" he asked.

"Almost nineteen years," she said.

"Know what? I still am. Who was the first Presidential candidate you voted for?" he asked.

"Dukakis," she answered. "What about you?"

It had been a long time since he had thought about it. "Well, Johnson was afraid to run," he said. "So it was Hubert Humphrey."

They both laughed.

"How are things on the sports desk?" he finally inquired.

"They're okay."

"Sports writing can be the best writing or the worst writing in a newspaper," he said. "It's up to you to make sure that the *Sun* has the former. And I'm going to be getting copies sent to me. So I'll be checking up on you. Understand?"

She understood. She nodded and glanced around.

"Listen, Paul," she said. "There are two reasons I stopped by. One, I'm on assignment in Los Angeles. I allowed some extra time. I wanted to see you no matter what."

"Well, you've been successful with that," he said. "Here I am."

"And two, as you know, Ken Shaw was wondering . . . I know he wrote to you about this but you never answered. He—"

"The political column?" Townsend laughed. "Ken wants to turn me into an Op Ed voice, huh? He flacks the hell out of President Lord in the main columns. Then he wants me to provide a dissenting voice for what remains of New York's liberal constituency on the opposite page. That's the idea, isn't it?"

"Pretty much."

"Ken always knew how to hedge his bets," said Townsend with no admiration whatsoever. "That's a nice way of saying it. The not-so-nice—but equally accurate—way would be to term Ken a duplicit two-faced bastard."

She lowered her eyes and smiled. "Is that your answer?" she asked.

"Tell Ken to stuff it. Those are my words. Tell him to stuff it." Townsend smiled. "Nothing personal. I just happen to think Ken's a high-end jackass. Plus, the further reason is I don't write *anything* anymore. *Nothing. Nada. Zilch.*"

"Really?" she asked.

"No," he confirmed. "I rather enjoy my life without deadlines and threats. I'm physically immobile, but life is finally very peaceful."

"All right," she said. There was evident sadness again in her voice.

"Smile," he said. "I'm nowhere nearly as miserable as you think."

"Sometimes I really can't understand you," Caryn said. "You could be so ornery, yet now you're being so positive."

"What choice do I have?" he asked. "I got an insurance settlement on my injury. I got a generous benefit from Max Kohlheimer, of all people. He seems to like his employees maimed more than he likes them ambulatory."

Caryn managed a weak smile.

"My medical expenses have been picked up by the *Sun,* also," Townsend explained.

For a moment he watched a bird descend from a nearby tree and swoop into a feeder.

"As for pain, I'm paralyzed, so there isn't any. And Nora took me back, as you can see. Sold the house in Pasadena and bought this one. Everything's flat. Nice deck. Perfect for a husband in a wheelchair, don't you think?"

Caryn nodded.

"That was quite a commitment for a woman to make," Townsend said. "So those divorce papers never did get signed. Nora gets me out. We have a special car. I get around. Most important: no one bothers me anymore." He thought for a moment again. "In the bargain, I get to see my daughter grow up, too. That's something that might never have happened otherwise."

"Uh huh," she said.

" 'Course," he said, "it's always best to be positive, Caryn. That's a rule you should follow in life. Never know who's listening in the John Lord Era. So you don't want to give the wrong impression."

His gaze traveled around the base of his house and through the open glass door. Her eyes followed his and suddenly—with a flash of danger that she could feel within her—she began to understand what he was telling her.

"Little electronic ears," he whispered like a madman, his eyes wide. "Could be anywhere. Like mice. Or spooks. Can't see them. But we know they're there."

She nodded. "You're talking nonsense," Caryn said.

"That's right. You must be right. That's what Nora tells me, too. Women. So much smarter and more practical than men. Come along. Let me show you what my wife bought for me."

His fingers found the switches on the arm of his wheelchair again. But this time, they fumbled.

"Want me to help you?" she asked.

"No. Damn it. Sometimes I can't even move my fingers. Got to learn how to do it myself, though. Got to," he said loudly.

The chair came to life. It moved smoothly over the boards of the deck, through the open glass doors and into the rear room of the house.

Caryn followed him, a hand on his shoulder. They were in a room that was set up like a study.

"Slide the door shut," he said. "And draw the curtain completely. Afternoon sunshine can get to be too much."

He led her to a word processor which sat on an open workstation. His chair pulled up to it.

"A computer?" Caryn laughed. *"You?* Paul Townsend now owns a computer?"

"Pick up a disk," he said, nodding toward a neat stack of them. "Nora copied a lot of these new computer games for me. They're for kids, I guess. But they're one thing I enjoy these days. Right on my wavelength. My head got banged up a bit, you know. Don't have all the marbles that I used to. Least that's what they tell me. These doctors, they know."

He indicated a joystick specially adapted for the handicapped. "If you move the control to beneath my palm, I can play them," he said.

She started to do exactly that.

"No, no," he said. "On second thought, access it yourself. You'll see what I mean."

For a moment she thought she had the wrong disk. Or that she had misunderstood. A table of contents came on the computer screen, not a game. The table of contents listed chapters. Someone was writing a book.

"Hit A, then three, then three," he said. "That fires a rocket at the little green man you see there. The point is to keep him moving around outer space without him touching any stars or devoured by Red Aliens." He thought for a second. "Red Aliens. That's a good one, huh? Sounds McCarthy Era."

She pressed A, 3, and 3, as he'd asked. But she had no idea what he was talking about.

The screen was blank for a moment. Then the first page of a sample chapter came on the screen. She bit her lip again when she saw it. It appeared to be a manuscript based on fact. She recognized many of the names.

Wolik. Lakaitis. Davies. Hubbell. It went on. It followed actual events as she recalled them. She was dumbstruck, but rallied quickly.

"See what I mean?" he said.

"Yes. I do."

He let her read for half a minute.

"I'm feeling tired," he finally said. "I don't feel like games. I sleep a lot these days. The doctors say it's the medicine. I guess you'd better go."

"I think I'd better," she agreed.

"Can I have a final kiss?" he asked. She turned toward him. Then she jumped. He raised both of his hands to gently hold her, touching her cheeks and hair. His hands were almost as strong as she remembered them. He kissed her firmly on the lips, as though no injury had ever happened.

For a moment after a long kiss, Caryn DiCarlo of the *New York Sun* stood there in shock.

"I'm damned tired," he said. "And I don't want you to catch anything that I've got."

"No. Me neither," she said hastily. "But if there's anything I can ever do for you, Paul. In the future, maybe?"

"Sure. In the future. I'm sure there will be something." He paused for several seconds. "Got a new boyfriend?" he asked.

She was uneasy with the question. She shrugged.

"Maybe ten," he said, answering for her. "Maybe none. Right? None of my—"

"Yeah," Caryn answered.

They both laughed.

"Good," he said. "Come back anytime."

"Bye," she said.

He watched her turn and leave. She was every bit as pretty as he'd remembered. She was every bit as wonderful as when a short love affair had taken place between them. How grateful he was that he hadn't gotten her killed.

Paul Townsend heard Nora in a pleasant conversation with Caryn. He sat in his wheelchair and waited. A few minutes later, he heard the front door close. His hearing was more acute than it had ever been. He knew when her car started and when it pulled away.

Nora appeared at the door to his study.

"She seems nice," she said.

"She is."

"She's the one who called here last year sometime, isn't she?"

"That's her."

"You always had good taste in women," his wife said.

For some reason, the remark made him think of Sarah Stuart, now out of his life forever. "Sometimes," he said. "Not always."

"Hungry?" Nora asked.

"Ravenous."

"I'll fix some lunch. Half an hour?"

"Thanks," he said. "That's fine. I'm going to play with one of the computer games. Caryn left a disk in."

Nora disappeared toward the kitchen. Townsend fumbled with the button of his wheelchair again. The chair turned. He double-checked the curtain that shielded the glass doors to the deck. The curtain was drawn, just as Caryn had left it.

He guided his wheelchair to a locked closet. He moved his arm. From a compartment within the frame of his chair, he withdrew a key. He unlocked the closet.

He muscled himself to his feet. He reached into the closet and pulled out a pair of sturdy canes. He grabbed them, one in each hand, then braced himself to walk.

Goddamn anyone who thought he could put Paul Townsend down for the count, he thought to himself. *They underestimate me mentally, they underestimate me physically. I'll show them. They'll learn.*

He moved across the room with the help of the canes. Things were improving every day. He had worked on physical therapy relentlessly. He might never walk again perfectly, but—in strictest privacy—his doctor had assured him that he would walk without canes as soon as the legs mended completely.

He arrived at the workstation. He reached to a chair and pulled it into position. He sat down, leaving the canes beside him.

He didn't move about like this in front of his daughter. Only Nora accurately knew of his physical condition. And now Caryn had an inkling. *So much the better,* he thought.

Already the opposition to President Lord was building within the country. The students were angry. Organized labor was angry. So were women and minority group members. People in business finally realized that Lord knew nothing about running an economy.

Lord, in his first thirty days in office, was already putting together a marvelous coalition united against him. But what was needed was a good scandal to get the sparks flying. Something to make sure that Lord was either impeached or, at the very worst, a one-term President.

Townsend knew just how to do that. How dare Lord's people be so careless as to leave him alive! Why, in another few months, he'd teach them an object lesson in attacking an investigative reporter!

Townsend took strength from the historical precedent: In November 1972, Richard Nixon had won the Presidency with an eighteen million-vote plurality and victories in forty-nine of fifty states. By August 9, 1974, he had resigned. Lord had brought his disreputable presence to 1600 Pennsylvania Avenue without even such popular support.

August 9, 1974. That reminded Townsend. Harry used to say that what the nation needed more than anything was a holiday in August. Harry had always suggested August 9. "Nixon Day," Harry had explained. "So who'd argue with that? Americans could have one day off a year to be reminded of the abuses of Presidential power."

The computer screen came alive again. Townsend flicked back to one of the first pages in his manuscript. The dedication page. *For Harry Dubrow,* he wrote.

Then Townsend returned to the body of the work. His notes were mental now but his mind was sound. His fingers went easily to the keyboard of his computer. There was much pain in his soul, but little in his hands.

He drew a deep breath and began his writing for the day, recalling thirty-three years' worth of truth as ferociously and as accurately as he possibly could.

He thought of the motley assortment of crooks, politicos, frauds, and charlatans whom he'd whacked in print in the past. But this would be different. This was the challenge of a reporter's lifetime. This time, by God, he would bring down the whole damned government.